Love Happens

Also by Sarah O'Brien

Hot Property
Gazumped!

SARAH O'BRIEN

Love Happens

HODDER

First published in Ireland in 2005 by Hodder Headline Ireland,
8 Castlecourt, Castleknock, Dublin 15, a division of Hodder Headline
First published in Great Britain in 2005 by Hodder & Stoughton,
338 Euston Road, London NW1 3BH, a division of Hodder Headline

A Hodder Headline Ireland/Hodder paperback

1 3 5 7 9 10 8 6 4 2

A CIP catalogue record for this title is available
from the British Library

ISBN 0 340 83779 9
Ireland ISBN (Including Northern Ireland) 0 340 83775 6

Typeset in Plantin Light by
Palimpsest Book Production Limited, Polmont, Stirlingshire
Printed and bound in Great Britain by
Clays Ltd, St Ives plc

Hodder & Stoughton & Hodder Headline Ireland
Divisions of Hodder Headline
338 Euston Road
London NW1 3BH

NOTE ON THE AUTHOR

Sarah O'Brien has a dual personality – she is both Helena Close and Trisha Rainsford, two best friends since childhood. Keen writers, they have collaborated on everything from teenage romance to weddings, babies and career paths. It was only a matter of time before they began writing together.

In the past Helena has worked in public relations and journalism and Trisha taught Classical Studies. Now they both write full-time. As well as the Sarah O'Brien novels they have co-written a TV comedy drama which is in the early stages of development. In addition, Helena's book, *Pinhead Duffy* and Trisha's book, *The Knack of Life* have both been published this year. Both live in Limerick, Ireland, with an assortment of children, husbands, cats and dogs. *Love Happens* is their third book together.

ACKNOWLEDGEMENTS

As always we'd like to thank our agent Faith O'Grady, our publisher Ciara Considine and all at HHI. We'd also like to thank Hazel Orme. Very importantly we'd like to thank Carolyn Mays and Alex Bonham for the chocolates – keep 'em coming. We're also indebted to Gerry Carew-Hynes for giving us Limerick Junction and John Ryan our crime consultant (yes he is a crook). Finally let's have a word for our sustainers – the coffee growers of the world, Rowntree's Fruit Pastilles and Willie Chang's Singapore Noodles.

This book is dedicated to 'all the lads', the Munster Rugby Team, Fernando Morientes, Zinédine Zidane, George Clooney, Frances McDormand, her husband and brother-in-law and Charlie Kaufmann.

I

The taxi pulled up behind a mud-splashed green Land Rover, parked in front of a long, beige mobile home. The curtains were closed but music was coming faintly from inside. Emerson was probably asleep.

'I'll be back in a second for the bags,' I said, as I unbuckled Paddy's seatbelt. He jumped out of the car and his hat fell on to the hot, gravelled road. It was his special hat – his dad had brought it for him from America, a tatty black baseball cap with ridiculous Mickey Mouse ears. I hated it but it accompanied Paddy everywhere he went, from bed to bath to playschool.

I took his hand and we climbed the steps to the caravan door and knocked. I peered in at a window. The silver photo frame with a picture of Paddy I'd sent to Gibraltar just the week before stood on the draining-board.

I'd go inside, leave Paddy with Emerson, fetch the bags and pay the cab driver. I pulled open the unlocked door and went in. The only sign of life was a couple of empty glasses and the remains of some pasta on the table. Emerson was asleep – it was siesta time.

To the left of the tiny living area was a door that I figured must lead to the bedroom. I pulled it open quietly – already planning the great sex we would have that night. Emerson had been working on the movie in Gibraltar for nearly three months and I felt like I'd been in jail. I was sure too little sex warped the personality.

The bedroom curtains were closed and it took me a few seconds to register what I saw. If it wasn't for Paddy I'd have thought I was in the wrong place, apologised and left.

'Daddy?' Paddy said.

Emerson sprang into the air and turned to us. His face was almost funny, he looked so shocked. All I could see of the woman he'd been straddling was a mass of long dark curly hair spread on the pillows and two huge brown eyes. I studied the top of Paddy's head. At the way his blond hair curled at the edges of the Mickey Mouse hat.

'Paddy?' Emerson said. 'What're you doing here?' Then he looked at me. 'Ruth,' he said.

Pulling Paddy, I walked out of the stuffy caravan, down the steps and into the cab. 'There's been a change of plan. Could you take us back to the airport, please?'

We drove off the film set and I never looked back – not once. I knew Emerson had followed us because Paddy waved out of the back window as we left.

2

The journey to the airport seemed three times as long as it had on the way out. I trundled Paddy and the baggage trolley into Departures and convinced a cross Spanish woman with streaked blonde hair to let us on to a flight to Shannon.

'You are very lucky,' she said, in heavily accented English. 'These are the only seats left on this flight and your ticket she is all wrong. You are a very lucky woman.'

I handed her my credit card. Yeah, sure, I was the luckiest woman in the world. Maybe I should buy a Lotto ticket when I got home.

The flight didn't leave until six. I checked my watch. A quarter to four. Exactly one hour and ten minutes since I'd seen my husband in bed with some woman who had long dark curly hair. My eyes filled with tears and I sniffed as I signed the credit-card receipt. Fuck her, anyway. Fuck him. Fuck the lot of them.

Paddy was sitting on the counter beside me. I kissed his plump, smooth cheek and wished we were at home. 'Happy birthday, Baby,' I said, as we walked away from the cranky Spanish woman. 'I can't believe you're three already.'

'When are we going back to Daddy's work?' Paddy asked.

I looked at his innocent little face. This couldn't be happening. It couldn't be true that on my baby's birthday – which coincidentally was my wedding anniversary – I'd found my husband in bed with another woman. This wasn't the way I'd imagined my surprise visit to Gibraltar.

I knelt down in front of him and did my best to smile. 'We have to go back home.'

'Why?'

'Because . . . well . . . we just have to.'

I could see that Paddy was trying to figure out what he'd seen. That made two of us.

'Is it because there's no room for us to stay at Daddy's house?' he said.

My eyes filled with tears again and I blinked hard. 'Exactly. You'll see Daddy soon. Come on, let's get some chips.'

At the mention of chips Paddy cheered up immediately. I got him some food and juice in the airport restaurant, bought some cigarettes and sat beside him drinking coffee and chain-smoking, trying to think only about the flight home. I hadn't smoked in almost five years, but I couldn't get pissed in charge of a minor and had to do something or I'd crack up.

The cigarettes made me feel lousy but I didn't care. We could check in soon, then maybe find another restaurant in the departure area. They'd want us to board at about five thirty and we were due to take off at six. I could manage all of that as long as I stayed focused.

I'd just lit my third cigarette when the Paddy-alarm went off.

'Daddy!'

I followed his pointing finger. Emerson was walking across the restaurant towards us. Paddy climbed down from his chair and ran as fast as he could on his short legs to his father. Emerson bent forward and scooped him up.

I watched them make their way towards me. Paddy was so like his dad. Not that I hadn't known it all along – he had always been a miniature Emerson. Same blond hair, same big blue eyes, same grin, even. The thing was that, up to a few hours ago, I was happy that my son and husband looked so alike. Now I wasn't sure.

'We're going home on the plane,' Paddy said to Emerson. 'Your work is too full.'

Emerson looked at me. I flicked ash into a saucer.

'Can we talk?' Emerson said.

I shrugged. 'Too late.' I ground out my cigarette and immediately lit a new one.

He sat down across from me with Paddy on his knee. 'Please, Ruth. I wouldn't hurt you for anything.'

I laughed and inhaled hard on my cigarette, which made my head floaty. I sat back in my chair, my face fixed as if I was interviewing him for a job. Emerson seemed uncomfortable – like a man with piles. I was delighted.

But he was so handsome, all tanned, glowing skin, clear blue eyes and sun-bleached hair curling round his ears. Ratfink bastards are usually handsome, aren't they? Otherwise they'd never find some little bitch to shag.

'I wish you'd stay so that we could talk,' he said. I shook my head.

'Ruth, really – nobody planned it. Selma . . . It just happened.'

'Oh, look,' I said, 'it's checking-in time. Paddy, give Daddy a kiss. We have to go.'

'I can stay until you have to leave,' Emerson said.

'Go.'

'No, really, Ruth – I can help. Push the trolley. Take care of Paddy.'

'Just go, please,' I stood up and held out my arms to Paddy. He snuggled into Emerson.

Emerson kissed the top of the Mickey Mouse hat. 'Go with Mummy,' he said. 'I'll see you later.'

I sat Paddy on top of the baggage trolley and made my way out of the restaurant between the tables, legs and suitcases. Selma. I knew that name.

As Paddy and I found the check-in queue I remembered. That little bitch in bed with my husband was Selma Rodriguez, the set designer on the movie. Isn't life ironic? We were so excited when he had raised the money to make the film about Ahmed Ferushi, the Tunisian cabaret idol. Nobody except Emerson knew or cared about Ferushi so it was a miracle that he'd convinced anybody to fund it, but he had. And I had been thrilled for him,

almost as excited as he was, when they set off for
Gibraltar to begin shooting. Little had I known
that Gibraltar would be the rock on which my
marriage perished.

I should have guessed Emerson was having an affair
with Selma Rodriguez – he was always talking about
her. She was *so* clever and *such* a good artist and had
loads and loads of *really*, *really* good ideas. That part
was true anyway, if you counted shagging someone
else's husband as a good idea.

I checked in the suitcase, made the right noises to
the bored-looking girl at the desk, and soon we were
in another restaurant with more chips and more juice.
Few things made Paddy happier than a plateful of
chips smothered with ketchup.

I restricted myself to my new diet of fags and
coffee and watched my baby squishing food and
singing to himself. I wished that his life could always
be as uncomplicated. After what felt like an age, he
and I boarded the plane and strapped ourselves into
our seats beside a smiling Asian nun.

After more faffing around with emergency exits
and seatbelts the plane took off. I gave Paddy some
sweets in the hope that chewing might keep his ears
clear. And it must have worked because before the
plane had reached cruising altitude his eyelids were
drooping.

I leaned close to him and shut my eyes too. Maybe
I'd fall asleep and get some relief from the horror
of what I'd seen. But I couldn't. I flicked through
the in-flight magazine and bought myself the most

expensive makeup compact I'd ever seen. It was the least I deserved.

The flight went without a hitch, my bags arrived and I even got a cab as soon as I walked out the airport doors. Pity my luck wasn't always as good. Had it been only that morning that I'd walked through these doors with my bags and my baby, full of excitement? It felt like a year. A fucking horrible year.

3

The next morning I woke with a start, disoriented. I sat up in bed trying to remember what was wrong. I could see the outline of a suitcase in the corner of the dim bedroom. For a split second I thought that yesterday had never happened, that I'd dreamed the whole bloody thing and that Paddy and I were going to Gibraltar today.

Paddy's body was glued to mine, his head hidden under the quilt. I pulled it off his face and watched him as he slept. It was true – he looked so like Emerson and I fought back tears as bits of yesterday merged together like a jigsaw puzzle. Selma Rodriguez, my bastard of a husband, the trailer with the smell of sex in the air. I'd have to tell Kathleen. I got up quietly and went down to the kitchen to make coffee. I opened the wooden blinds and weak morning sunlight flooded the room. The calendar on the fridge door had yesterday's date outlined with thick black marker. Like a death notice, I thought, as I filled the coffee machine. I sat at the kitchen table and idly checked my mobile phone for messages.

There was a string of texts from Emerson. I read

one – *You'll always be my friend*. That was enough.
I deleted the others. Emerson Burke, prize-winning
film-maker and prize bastard. I'd never be his friend.
And I didn't want that Spanish bitch within an ass's
roar of my son.

Paddy came into the kitchen as I poured the
coffee. He stood in front of me in his Spiderman
pyjamas, hair tousled, eyes bleary.

'When are we going back to Daddy's work?' he
said, and stuck a thumb into his mouth.

I scooped him into my arms and buried my face
in his hair. 'Daddy will come and see you soon,
Pumpkin,' I said, not knowing if it was true.

I spent the day cleaning and rearranging the
house. I took the phone off the hook and switched
off my mobile. My main objective was to remove
from my life the visible traces of Emerson. I started
in our bedroom and dumped his clothes, books and
other personal items into a suitcase. I wouldn't let
myself examine any of it, just scooped it all up in
big jumbles and dumped it in any old way. It wasn't
hard now that I was doing it. Marriages broke up
every day of the week, and sure I hadn't planned
for mine to break up, but so what? I wasn't going
to let that bastard get to me. If he didn't want me,
that was fine.

I went through the house, collecting photographs
and trying not to look at them – but it proved impossible. There was one black-and-white picture of
Emerson on the set of his last film, which had
appeared in all the newspapers at the time. He stood

in the foreground, a camera behind him. I stared at the photo now as if he was a stranger. I could see how women might find him attractive but, hell, I found loads of men attractive and didn't go off riding them in trailers in Spain.

And now he had Selma. A pain broke in my chest but I shook my head clear and turned the photograph face down in the box. I kept one of Emerson and Paddy – a close-up of father and son smiling. I went into Paddy's room and put the picture on his dresser. My son comes from a broken home, I thought, as the reality of the situation hit me. I'll be a frustrated divorcee and Paddy will grow up into a psychopath and Emerson will have a charmed life of movies and glamorous women and endless champagne. I laughed at this stereotypical picture of misery, the laughter rising and rising until tears streamed down my face. I leaned against the dresser and wiped my eyes, still laughing and crying at the same time.

'Can I have some crackers, Mum?' Paddy said behind me, as he came into the room and picked up his favourite teddy bear from the floor.

'No problem, Pad,' I said, wiping away the tears with my hand. 'I think there's chocolate spread in the press to go with them and guess what? After that we'll go to the park and get an ice-cream. What do you think?'

Paddy cheered and threw his teddy into the air. I took a deep breath. I can do this, I thought. I don't need Emerson. I don't need anybody. Paddy was my only concern and Emerson Burke could take a hike if he didn't want us.

But it's never as simple as that. After my cleaning frenzy I'd left the phones turned off. Later, when Paddy was asleep, I opened a bottle of wine and sat in the living room, drinking and smoking, glad of the time to sort out my head.

I wrote a list as I sipped my wine and tried to decide who to tell first.

Ellen.

She was my best friend but had moved to Australia the year before. Then again, she was on the other side of the world and I didn't want her to be worried. Maybe I'd just text her. *My marriage broke up yesterday on my son's third birthday and our wedding anniversary, but don't worry, I'm fine. I just cleared the cheating bastard out of my life and it's OK. Love, Ruth.*

No. A text like that would have Ellen on the first flight home. I'd ring her.

India.

That was a little more complicated: as well as being one of my best friends, India was Emerson's sister. I lit another cigarette and poured a second glass of wine. I'd tell her tomorrow too.

Tracy and Derek.

My next-door neighbours, who were good friends.

Kathleen Brennan.

She was a clairvoyant I'd met a couple of years ago, but the important thing about her was that she was my birth-mother. Once I'd got over her propensity to slip into a trance at the drop of a hat, we had become friends. She adored Paddy and Emerson, and I knew she'd take the news pretty badly.

I lit another fag and turned the phones back on – with my luck someone'd die in the middle of the night. Cigarettes were a great friend, I thought, as I lay back on the couch and enjoyed my smoke. Tomorrow would be hard. I poured more wine, praying that the alcohol would make me sleep.

The wine did its job. I woke the next morning to a barrage of noise. The doorbell was ringing and every phone in the house was bleating. When Paddy woke he joined in the fanfare by playing his plastic keyboard. I struggled out of bed and into my dressing-gown. I decided to let the phones ring and went to the front door, knowing who'd be standing there.

'You should have called me,' Kathleen said, as she marched into the hallway. 'I rang Emerson to see if you'd arrived safely.'

She put her turquoise beaded handbag on to the worktop and kissed Paddy. 'That hat needs a wash,' she said, tapping the brim with her nail. I began to make coffee while she asked him about the plane.

'So he told you,' I said, as I rinsed cups under the tap.

'Oh, Ruth.'

'That's life.'

She came over, put an arm round me, and hugged me to her. A well of tears caught in my throat and I struggled to control myself.

'Let it out,' she said, as she stroked my hair.

'Fuck him,' I said, pulled away from her and poured coffee clumsily into the cups.

'Fuck,' said Paddy, grinning up at us as he played with a truck on the kitchen floor. My heart sank. For all that Paddy looked like a cherub he had a tongue like a soldier. The baby books all talked about children 'exploding' into language but omitted the chapter on exploding into bad language. I couldn't deal with it now. I'd tackle the bad language some other time. My own as well as Paddy's.

'So what did he say? Did he tell you everything?' I asked, as I sipped my coffee.

'He's worried about you.'

'Big of him. He wasn't too worried when he was fucking his girlfriend – did he tell you that bit? Bastard.'

'Paddy can hear you.'

I glanced at him, but he hadn't picked up my latest string of curses. 'Maybe,' I said, 'but what he saw yesterday in that caravan beats the hell out of that.'

Kathleen looked puzzled.

'I'm sure Emerson left out that part when he was telling you how *worried* he was about us.'

I could see that Kathleen still wasn't getting it. Paddy was under the table with two trucks.

'*In flagrante delicto*,' I said.

Kathleen's mouth dropped open. 'Oh, my God!'

'Look, Kathleen, I'm grand, really I am. It happened. It's over, end of story.'

'Oh, love. It's hard to believe.'

I put my cup down firmly on the table. 'I know what I saw, Kathleen. Trust me. I'm not stupid.'

'I meant it's hard to believe he'd do such a thing, the lying bastard.'

I laughed. 'The cursing is catching.'

'The cheating snake in the grass – and on your anniversary. *And* Paddy's birthday. How could he?' Kathleen said, running a hand through her hair.

'I'm fine, Kathleen.'

'No, you're not – nobody could be fine after what you've been through.'

'That bastard won't ruin my life.'

'Of course not.'

'I don't need him – or anybody else.'

'I agree, but it's OK to be upset, love – it's only natural.'

I laughed, but it sounded hollow and hard. 'I'm not upset. I'm fine.'

I could see the concern and sympathy in Kathleen's eyes and felt like crying. I forced back the tears.

'Why don't I get Paddy dressed and take him out for a few hours? We can go to the park – the weather's really nice,' she said.

'Are you sure?' I asked.

'I'd love to. I'll bring back a takeaway for dinner. How's that?'

'Haven't you . . . um . . . consultations . . . maybe a couple of seances to do?' I said, smiling shakily at her.

She laughed. 'You're a terror, Ruth, do you know

that? I don't have any work today, just a couple of birth charts I can do tonight.' She called Paddy. 'Let's get you ready, Buster. We're going to the playground.'

Kathleen and Paddy went upstairs and I began to clean the kitchen. My mobile bleated – Emerson again. I scrubbed the sink until it shone. Kathleen came back with Paddy washed and dressed.

'OK, Nana,' Paddy shouted gleefully, as I opened the front door. 'Race me.'

Kathleen laughed. 'I'm too old but I'll try.'

Suddenly Paddy's face was serious. 'Ready. Steady. *Goooo!*' He ran down the garden path with Kathleen in pursuit. As I watched them I wondered how it was possible for ordinary things still to be going on when my life as I'd known it had gone.

4

By that afternoon I'd broken the news to India. One of her clients was in the high court in Dublin so she'd be stuck up there for at least a week. I gave her a brief outline of what had happened and I knew she was shocked but I was glad of the distance between us. I was much better off dealing with this by myself.

Next on my list was Ellen. I checked my watch and tried to work out what time it was in Australia, gave up and took a chance. Ellen's phone rang and her voicemail answered. Tears pricked my eyes when I heard her voice. I left a meaningless message and went for a bath.

I was applying my expensive new makeup when the doorbell rang. I knew it couldn't be Kathleen, it was too early, and everybody else thought I was in Spain with my loving husband. It rang again. I tried to make out the shape of the person through the stained glass. Tracy. I debated ignoring her but I'd have to tell her some time. When I opened the door I could see that she already knew.

'Oh, Ruth,' she said, brown eyes full of concern. 'Don't tell me I've got a clairvoyant friend as well as mother now,' I said, and walked back to the kitchen. I lit a cigarette and offered one to a surprised Tracy. She was half Chinese, dainty and fine-boned, but when she opened her mouth, she had the strongest Limerick accent I'd ever heard and an attitude to match.

She accepted a cigarette. 'I met Kathleen in town. I nearly died when I saw Paddy with her – I mean, he should have been in Spain with you. She told me a bit and said to call in. Fuck's sake, Ruth.'

'Did she tell you about Selma?'

'Don't mind that bitch. Those Spanish women are all the same. Bad form out of Emerson, though. There's fucking no way Derek will be giving him tickets for the Munster matches this season,' she said.

I burst out laughing. Tracy's husband, Derek, was a cab driver and a mad rugby fan. He'd spent the last year indoctrinating Emerson.

'Tell me what happened,' she said, and sat down at the kitchen table, eyes round with curiosity.

I gave her a quick recap of the story and Tracy interjected with relevant name-calling and curses. Her mobile rang, interrupting our rant.

When she'd finished she put it into her bag. 'It's Derek. He has to go into work, which means I have to mind the brood. I'll try to call round later. How's that?'

'There's no need, Trace, I'm fine,' I said.

Tracy looked at me. 'Fuck off, Ruth. This is Tracy you're talking to. I'm supposed to do a party in Castleconnell but I'll try to get out of it.'

'No way. You can't cancel it. With a bit of luck those Castleconnell women'll buy loads,' I said. She was a party organiser for Mary Winters, the sex-aids company.

'I know. I can't wait to show them our new range of vibrators – wait until you see the Randy Rabbit. I swear, Ruth, it's massive!'

'I might be buying one of those yet,' I said, and we giggled.

'Ohmygodohmygod – I forgot to tell you, Ruth, we got a new neighbour. Wait until you see him!' said Tracy, grabbing my arm.

'Jesus, stop! Who is it? Good or bad?'

'Fucking fit, Ruth. I saw him moving in yesterday and I swear I thought he was a little skater boy. You know, combats, beanie hat, tight denim jacket . . .'

'So, our new neighbour's a teenager?'

'Shut up and let me finish. I was hanging out the washing this morning and there he was in his garden. He's got the face of an angel.'

'At least it's not another gang of students,' I said.

Tracy stood up. 'It'll be OK, Ruth. You'll see.'

Another huge lump was forming in my throat.

She came over and hugged me. 'Fuck him,' she said into my ear, picked up her mock Gucci handbag and left.

Kathleen got back at six with an exhausted Paddy and a huge Chinese takeaway. We ate without mentioning Emerson and I was glad of that: there was nothing left to say. When Kathleen had gone I bathed Paddy and put him into bed. Tracy had rung to say she couldn't get out of her party but I didn't mind. Everybody seemed to think this was the end of the world and that I should be wailing at the prospect of life without Emerson. I was damned if I'd do that.

I opened another bottle of wine and thanked God for the cheap Spanish cigarettes. I lit one and swore to myself that by the weekend I'd be a non-smoker again. I sipped my wine and stared, unseeing, at the television screen. When the phone rang beside me I jumped. I checked call display – it was Ellen.

'Hi, Ruth, how's it going?'

'Fine.'

'I just got your message – we were in Sydney for a few days. Tony wanted to look at property so I went along for . . . Ruth?'

I was crying.

'Ruthie, what's up? Please tell me! Is it Paddy?'

My body convulsed now as all the unshed tears came out in a huge avalanche.

'Ruth, listen to me! What's going on?'

So I told her, in dribs and drabs, punctuated by crying and swearing. We talked for a full hour and by the time I hung up I felt exhausted. It had been good to hear her voice. Ellen was the one person to whom I could tell everything, no holds barred. She always saw through my bravado, which was a relief. She knew my heart was broken, no matter how I tried to hide it. If I was honest with myself that was the simple truth. My heart *was* broken.

5

The symptoms of a broken heart are hard to recognise. It's not immediately apparent that the paralysis that takes hold of you as soon as you open your eyes is the first sign. In the days after Gibraltar – once my initial anger had subsided – I slipped deep into a dark place I'd never known existed. The simple act of getting out of bed was like climbing Mount Everest and became harder as each day passed.

Sure I went through the motions – I washed and dressed, cooked and cleaned. I used what little energy I had in reassuring Kathleen and Tracy that I was fine. I even tried to prove it to them and myself by carrying on with my life as though nothing had changed. But then I'd find myself standing in a supermarket aisle trying to remember what I needed to buy. Or staring out of the kitchen window regardless of Paddy's chatter. Sometimes I wondered how long he'd been calling me. That's the second sign of a broken heart – living in a parallel universe.

But maybe the most obvious sign is that you find yourself bursting into tears any time, anywhere. I cried into the frozen-food cabinet in Tesco, standing and watching as the tears made little tracks along the icy surface of a chicken. I cried in the pet shop when I brought Paddy to buy a goldfish. The owner was distraught as he tried to calm me down and re-assure me that every single one of those poor, poor caged puppies would be in a loving home by the weekend.

I cried as though I was never going to stop when I lost my wedding ring. It was a lovely sunny spring day and I was trying to energise myself by spring cleaning. It was even working a little bit. I tore out the contents of all the presses in the kitchen while Paddy was at playschool. I took down every curtain in the house and washed them, then polished the windows until they shone. I was just hanging out the last line of curtains when I heard a noise like a football rattle. I peered over the clothes-line and saw a big fat magpie at my open kitchen window with something shiny in his beak.

'Shoo!' I shouted, and ran towards the house. I screamed when I realised he had my wedding ring. He eyed me cheekily as he watched my approach, then flew into the air. I watched his black-and-white shape retreat over a rooftop. Was the whole world conspiring against me?

Sobs racked me and I fell to my knees on the paving outside the back door. I bent in two, wrapped my arms round my stomach and cried and sobbed and wailed.

'Ruth! What is it? Are you hurt?'

I struggled to focus through the tears and shook my head.

'He isn't worth it, love. No man's worth that,' Tracy said, putting her arms round me.

I tried to speak but no words came out.

'You were due a proper bawl,' Tracy said, stroking my hair. 'You'll feel much better after it.'

The sobs subsided and I took a deep breath. 'It's not that,' I said. 'I was hanging the curtains on the line . . . The kitchen window was open . . . A magpie stole my wedding ring.'

Tracy pulled away and looked into my face. 'What?'

'A magpie stole my wedding ring. He flew over that house with it in his beak.'

Tracy's eyes widened and a huge grin formed on her lips.

'It's not funny,' I said, a bubble of laughter bursting in my throat.

'I know,' she said, as a guffaw escaped through the hand she'd clamped over her mouth.

And then I laughed too. We held on to each other as we laughed and laughed and laughed. My stomach hurt and I knew my heart was aching and my life was smashed to shit, but at least I had a friend like Tracy. 'Thanks, Trace.'

'No problem – it's good to hear you laugh again.'

'I can't believe a magpie stole my wedding ring.' I got up and put out a hand to pull her to her feet. 'It'd only happen to me. Maybe it's a good omen. Now I can start with a clean sheet.'

'Not with clean curtains, though.' Tracy pointed at the crumpled heap on the ground at the foot of the clothes-line.

'Shit,' I said.

'Ah, fuck it,' Tracy said. 'That's your third piece of bad luck – you're due a run of good now.'

'Do you promise?' I said, leading the way into the kitchen.

'I promise,' Tracy said.

But she was wrong.

The next morning I woke up with the familiar paralysis. It was a wet windy morning. I listened to the rain pelting against the window and wanted to turn over and go straight back to sleep, but Paddy was up. The sound of cartoons drifted up the stairs. I looked at the clock. It was eight thirty and he had to be at playschool in an hour.

I dragged myself upright and headed for the shower in the hope that that'd make me feel better. No such luck. I grabbed the clothes I'd discarded the night before and put them back on. I caught a glimpse of my pale zombie face in the mirror. I looked as bad as I felt. So what?

Paddy had already helped himself to Rice Krispies so I cleaned up the collateral damage in the kitchen and made myself some tea. I lit my first cigarette and sat at the kitchen table to watch the rivulets of grey rain racing down the windowpane. I thought of toast but the idea of food was nauseating. Just as I was trying to summon the energy to drive Paddy to playschool, the doorbell rang. It was Tracy.

'Will I drop Paddy?' she said, as soon as I opened

the door. 'I'm bringing Chloe down anyway and there's no point in both of us going.'

I waved at Chloe, who was standing on the back seat of Tracy's car. 'You're a star – I'll pick them up.'

Paddy was pulling on his raincoat behind me. A quick kiss and a hug and I was alone. I wandered into the kitchen and looked at the clock. Nine twenty. I didn't need to pick the kids up until one. The morning stretched ahead of me like a year. I was going back to bed. No contest. The doorbell rang and I went back to the hallway, wondering what Paddy could have forgotten.

'What did you . . .' The words died on my lips.

Emerson was standing in the porch, his shoulders hunched against the driving rain. I went to slam the door.

He put up his hand. 'Please, Ruth. Don't. We need to talk. I just got off the plane and I have to fly back this evening – there isn't much time.'

I stared at him for a few seconds, then turned and walked back into the kitchen. I leaned against the draining-board, gazing out of the window, and lit a cigarette. I heard the front door close.

'Are you OK?' Emerson said.

I laughed. 'Never better.' I listened to the muted sound of the TV in the sitting room. Paddy hadn't turned it off.

'Is Pad at school?' he said, in a quiet, strained voice.

I nodded.

'Look, Ruth. This is difficult for both of us—'

I whipped round to face my lying, cheating bastard of a husband. 'Well, my heart pumps piss for you. I know it's difficult to be an unfaithful scumbag but if you're looking for sympathy you've come to the wrong place.'

Emerson looked at the floor. 'I'm sorry I hurt you.'

Then the thought that had haunted me since Gibraltar came to mind and I heard myself ask, 'How long?'

He didn't answer.

'How long?' I said again, because now it seemed like the most important piece of information on the planet.

'About six weeks.'

The words hung in the air between us. Where had I been six weeks ago? Looking after Paddy. Planning our surprise visit to Gibraltar. Thinking about summer holidays for our family. Six weeks before – hell, even four weeks before – if I'd been asked to fill in a questionnaire about my marriage I'd have checked all the boxes that said we were happy together. But it was all a big fat lie.

'Look – maybe if I explain—'

'So, while you were telling me on the phone that you loved me and missed me you were screwing that woman all the time?'

'It's not like that, Ruth.'

'Fuck you, Emerson – that's exactly what it's like. Did you tell her your wife doesn't understand you? Did you tell her you loved her as well?'

Emerson's face was creased in pain. 'You don't know what a film set's like – it's another world entirely.'

'I don't care,' I said.

But he didn't seem to hear me. 'When you and Paddy walked in it was like my two worlds colliding.'

I lit another cigarette with shaking hands.

He took a deep breath. 'The thing with Selma . . . It's hard to explain but it was like a cannonball – nobody planned it. But I can't bear the thought of losing you and Paddy.'

'What are you saying, Emerson? That you want it all? That you want the nice cosy family and the bit on the side too?'

'That's not fair.'

'And in this new plan of yours, does it work both ways? Can I have a bit on the side as well?'

Emerson took a step towards me. 'Now, calm down, Ruth. We need to be adult about this if we're to sort things out.'

'Get out of my house, Emerson – I never want to see you again.'

'We have to think of Paddy in this.'

'Pity you didn't think of him on his birthday. Lovely present that, watching his daddy screwing his Spanish whore.'

'Ruth—'

I picked up a mug from the draining-board and threw it at him. He jumped to one side and it smashed on the wall behind him.

'Ruth!'

My eyes alighted on a blue glass vase. I threw it

and it bounced off his shoulder and broke on the floor. I followed it with my cigarette packet, my lighter, a heavy crystal ashtray, Paddy's Rice Krispies bowl and finally a square wooden chopping board. Emerson ducked the missiles like a target in a shooting gallery.

As I searched for more ammunition he backed towards the door. 'This is obviously not a good time to talk,' he said.

I grabbed an African violet.

'I'll give you a buzz later.'

I threw the plant with all my strength and it hit him right on the head. Compost, purple flowers and furry green leaves cascaded to the floor. Emerson left, and a yellow plate sailed into the hallway after him.

The front door slammed and I stood in the centre of the kitchen, panting, sweating, almost blind with rage. Slowly, though, as the rage subsided, a new – much worse – emotion took its place. The raw, screaming agony of rejection.

6

At first the pain was physical. A stomach-ache that tied my innards in knots. It rose in an escalating crescendo until I threw up over the black-and-white tiles Emerson and I had chosen together when we'd moved into the house. Pieces of china, glass and busted pot plant mingled on the floor with vomit.

My legs shook as if they couldn't hold me up and I wobbled to the sink where I threw up again. Sweat broke out on my forehead as I gripped the stainless steel and puked and puked and puked. Eventually it stopped and I sank on to the floor. I leaned back against the kitchen presses, wrapped my arms round my legs, pulled my knees to my chest and began to cry. It was like being inside a kaleidoscope of emotion and memory.

Pictures flashed through my mind. Emerson's face when Paddy was born. The way he always spoke in his sleep. Paddy and Emerson playing in the garden. The sound of their laughter. His kiss on my lips. That warm feeling of certainty and security when you believe somebody loves you – it had been the basis of our marriage. I'd loved him. I'd trusted him.

It had never entered my head that Emerson would

look at another woman, let alone have sex with one. I believed it because that was what he had always told me. He used to say I was the only woman he'd ever really loved. The only woman for him. The best and cleverest and prettiest and funniest. He'd said all of those things. And I'd believed him.

The doorbell rang. I thought it was Emerson again and ignored it. It rang again. And again. The sound echoing in the hallway felt like something scratching my skin. Then I heard my name. It was Tracy. I jumped to my feet and looked at the kitchen clock. The kids! It was twenty to two! Oh, my God! Twenty to two! Paddy and Chloe finished playschool at one and I'd forgotten to collect them. My heart thumped as I ran towards Tracy's voice.

I threw open the front door and Tracy gasped. 'Oh, my God – what the fuck happened?'

I rubbed my face with the palm of my hand. Paddy and Chloe were playing with a balloon in the garden behind her.

'Are you all right?' she said, touching my arm.

'I forgot the kids. I'm sorry. Emerson was here and – and . . .'

'Look, it's no problem. Mary at the playschool rang me – I knew something must have come up.' Tracy glanced over her shoulder at the children. 'Will I hold on to Paddy for the afternoon? You look green in the face – are you sick?'

I nodded.

'Will I take him, so?'

I nodded again.

'Do you need me to come back?'

I shook my head.

'OK. I'll just be next door,' she said. 'Call me if you want anything.' She searched my face with her eyes. 'Promise?'

'I promise,' I whispered. 'Thanks.'

I closed the door then, afraid that Paddy might notice the same thing that had so shocked Tracy. I dragged myself back into the kitchen and cleaned the filthy floor. I couldn't have Paddy come home to that. By the time I'd finished I felt more exhausted than I'd ever felt in my whole life. I went straight upstairs and fell into my bed, which started me off on another crying jag as I remembered all the sex and snuggling and Sunday breakfasts together as we read the papers and swapped the best bits. Eventually, though, even that bout of tears dried up and I fell into a hot, dreamless sleep.

When I woke it was dark and I could hear the TV downstairs and wondered if Paddy had come home or if he was still at Tracy's. I knew I should have got up and checked to see where my three-year-old was but before I could convince myself to move I fell asleep again. Next thing I knew Kathleen was sitting on my bed and the lamp was switched on.

'Tea,' she said. 'Look, right there on the bedside locker. And a couple of slices of toast.'

I struggled to open my eyes. 'I'm not hungry.'

She smiled. 'Sit up and have a mouthful of tea. It'll make you feel better.'

I did as she told me but I didn't feel any better, just more awake, which made me feel worse. 'Paddy?'

'He's fast asleep in bed.'

'Is he OK?'

'Never better,' she said, with a smile. 'Drink your tea.'

I lay back against my pillow. Without warning, tears leaked out of my eyes and down the sides of my face.

'I'm going to stay the night,' she said, ignoring the tears.

'OK,' I said, as if we were having a normal conversation. 'Thanks.'

'No problem,' Kathleen said, and stood up. She bent over me and kissed my forehead. 'Sleep well.'

I tried a smile, but my face couldn't manage it. She closed the door behind her and I switched off the lamp. Within seconds I was fast asleep again. The next time I woke the clock told me it was four a.m. This time I was as wide awake as if someone had emptied a bucket of water over me.

I closed my eyes and tried for sleep but I was out of luck. Within seconds the pictures from the mobile home in Gibraltar had started up in my head. I leaped out of bed and scrabbled for my slippers, found an old cardigan and went downstairs. I'd make myself some tea – not that I felt like tea but it'd be something to do. Then I'd watch TV, maybe, or read a magazine – anything to block my thoughts.

In the kitchen in the dark I listened to the hum of the fridge and the noisy, rolling sound of water boiling in the kettle and couldn't help but wonder where Emerson was. He'd said he was going straight back, so that meant that he was probably in Gibraltar by now. Probably in bed with that woman. The kettle clicked as it boiled and I began to cry. I didn't want tea. I didn't want anything – that was a lie: I wanted my life back.

I reached to the top of a cupboard, pulled down a bottle of brandy and poured myself half a mugful. I drank it all in one go. It burned its way to my stomach but it felt good so I filled the mug to the top and took it to the sitting room. I curled up on the sofa and switched on the TV, but I couldn't make any sense of anything. The images flickered and jumped as emotion rushed through me.

Why didn't Emerson love me any more? What was wrong with me? Was I fat after having Paddy? I didn't think so but maybe he thought I was. Maybe I hadn't taken enough interest in his work. That was probably true, all right. If I'd known more about making movies – cared more – things might have been different. I didn't mind if Emerson made hubcaps as long as he was happy doing it. But maybe I should have cared more.

I took a long drink of brandy and slowly the edges of the world softened. Selma Rodriguez was beautiful. I hated to admit it but it was true. I'd met her once, briefly, and heard lots about her. I'd even read about her in a magazine at the hairdresser's once when she was nominated for an Oscar for her set design on some Spanish movie. Bitch. I slugged back more brandy.

I should have known. They had so much in common, didn't they? They moved in the same circles, spoke the same language. I spoke the language of babies and ordinary things while they were all wrapped up in some cool world of their own. Emerson had said as much. Before I'd started pegging the contents of the kitchen at him he'd said it: a film set is a world of its own.

Maybe Paddy and I should have been in Gibraltar with him. He'd asked me to go but it had been January and Paddy had just started at the Montessori playschool so I hadn't thought it was a good idea. And I hadn't been too keen on living in a mobile home. If I'd gone with him perhaps none of this would be happening now. I finished my mug of brandy and padded to the kitchen to find the bottle and my cigarettes. This time I brought everything back to the sitting room.

I wrapped myself in a plum velvet throw, refilled my mug and lit a cigarette. There was an opera on TV and some woman was singing her heart out but her voice made me want to cry again. I tried to smoke but the breath I needed for the tears made it impossible. Eventually I gave up and threw the cigarette into the grate. I took another long drink of brandy, then put the mug on to the floor, lay down and let the tears come properly. Eventually, I drifted into a drunken sleep.

When I awoke it was dawn and I could hear birds singing in the willow tree in my front garden. I sat up and tried groggily to make out the time on my watch. Six thirty. OK. That wasn't too bad. I picked up the mug, finished off the contents, then returned the brandy bottle to the kitchen cupboard. My head swam and everything looked as if it'd lost definition. I was pretty glad of that: I wasn't too fond of the shape of the world right then.

I fell into bed, wrapped myself in my duvet and was asleep before I could begin to think. As I slept I dreamed I was being chased by lions and woke myself with my screams. Kathleen appeared at one point with more tea and toast. I didn't even pretend this time, just lay on my side as she talked to me and tidied my bed.

She told me Tracy had brought Paddy to school and that everything was all right. I nodded but didn't speak. I knew Kathleen would make sure Paddy was OK and that was all I cared about. I fell back to sleep almost immediately, and the next time I woke Paddy was in bed with me, showing me a drawing he'd made of elephants dancing. I tried to do the mum thing and made some noises I hoped might sound encouraging, but eventually he got tired of me and took off.

Kathleen brought up a tray of food but I couldn't even look at it. Just agreed to drink the glass of orange juice. My mouth felt as if it was full of ashes. She was so pleased I was taking some nourishment that I felt guilty and almost told her about the half-bottle of brandy I'd downed. But I couldn't be bothered.

She brought me up a bottle of fizzy water with a glass, and I finished that off sitting up in bed chain-smoking. It was evening again and I'd slept through the entire day. I was glad. Being awake was shite. I felt hollow and brittle and hurting inside. After four or five cigarettes I lay down and was soon asleep again. It was beginning to feel like a disease, sleeping. It was all I wanted to do because it was the only way I could escape going over and over what had happened. Well, that and the brandy.

I got up again in the small hours when Kathleen and Paddy were asleep and repeated my perform-ance of the night before. Smoking and drinking and crying and trying to watch TV. It felt like being trapped in something like a well-shaft that had sharp bamboo poles sticking out of the sides to wound me whenever I moved. I wished my mum and dad were still alive, with more longing than I'd felt even in the aftermath of their deaths. It didn't matter that they had been my adoptive parents: they had still been my parents and they had loved me.

I imagined that they were still alive and saw Dad warning Emerson to stay away from me, then standing in the middle of the sitting room with his hands shoved deep into the pockets of his corduroy pants telling me not to mind him. And then I saw my mum and her soft face, the way her eyes went hard and glittery if somebody hurt me. She'd have looked at Emerson like that, then looked back at me and her eyes would have been soft again and she'd have put her arms round me and held me while I cried. I wanted them so badly I didn't think I could stand the pain. I drank myself senseless and went back upstairs to bed.

The next day was a repeat of the day before but this time Tracy came to visit and tried to cheer me up with stories about her kids. I made a tiny effort to respond but my head hurt so badly I couldn't lift it. Mostly I longed for her to go away so I could go back to sleep. Which eventually happened. I think Paddy played in my room for a while but I can't be certain. I remember kissing him and hugging him to me. He wriggled and protested and told me I smelt funny. I told myself he meant I needed a shower.

Like clockwork, I was wide awake once more at three a.m. This time I felt a bit hungry. I still hadn't managed more than a few mouthfuls of any of the food Kathleen had carried upstairs to me. In the kitchen I made myself two slices of toast and tried to pretend I wasn't drinking all that much even as I hid the empty brandy bottle and opened some vodka. I ate half a slice of the toast, then brought the vodka and my cigarettes to my nightly perch on the sofa.

I'd given up trying to watch TV. The inside of my head was screaming so loudly that I couldn't drown it with pictures and dialogue. *Emerson doesn't love me. Emerson doesn't love me. Emerson doesn't love me*, the voices in my head sang, and I knew they were right and that it was probably my own fault.

The taste of snot and brandy, tears and cigarette smoke mingled as I sat there and struggled. Eventually I toppled over, fell asleep and dreamed I was sailing a boat with my dad.

'Will I get ready?' a voice was asking me, as I stood on the deck and salt spray washed my face.

'OK,' I said. 'Get ready.'

'Do you want Cheerios?' the voice said.

I opened my eyes. Paddy was standing by the sofa, his blond hair sticking up and his fat baby belly protruding over the waist of his pyjamas.

'Will I get you Cheerios too, Mum?'

I struggled to sit up. 'No, darling, I'm fine,' I slurred.

He smiled. 'Are you bringing me to school today? Can Chloe come with us?'

I shook my head. It felt as if it had been smashed to pieces. 'No, love. Tracy will bring you and Chloe again today – that's good, isn't it? You like Tracy and Chloe.'

Paddy's eyebrows met in a frown and he glared at me. He folded his arms across his chest and pursed his lips. I reached out a hand and put it on his arm. He jerked away. 'Paddy . . .'

'When will you be my mum again?' he said petulantly. 'I want you to be my mum.'

Then he ran out of the room. I sat upright, awake and sober. Paddy clattered dishes in the kitchen as he helped himself to cereal. Oh, my God, what was I doing? This wasn't just about me, it was about Paddy too. If Emerson and I were split up, Paddy would suffer some of the consequences and all I'd been doing was wallowing in self-pity. I put my feet on the floor. My head protested but I stood up. In the kitchen Paddy was standing at the table pouring milk into a bowl overflowing with cereal. His Mickey Mouse hat was perched sideways on his head. I watched him for a few seconds before I spoke.

'Pad,' I said eventually.

He didn't look at me.

'I'll bring you guys to school.'

He flashed me a grin. 'Can I bring my talking Spiderman to show the teacher?'

I nodded my broken head.

'And Eagle-Eye Action Man?'

'Anything you like.'

He climbed on to a chair and began to demolish his cereal.

'I'm going up to have a shower and get dressed,' I said. 'Don't get up to anything. I won't be long.'

Paddy nodded, and rubbed at a trickle of milk running from the corner of his mouth to his chin. I went upstairs, stripped off my smelly clothes and stepped into the shower. I stood under the scalding water and, for the first time in a while, my head was almost quiet. Now that I'd turned my focus away from myself I could think about other things. Like Paddy. The smell of brandy seemed to ooze out of my pores but I covered it with apricot shower gel.

By the time I was washed, dressed and downstairs, Kathleen was up. She was in front of the kitchen window, sipping a cup of herbal tea. She turned when I entered the room.

'Morning,' I said, and filled the kettle.

'Good morning,' she said brightly. 'How are you feeling?'

'Not too bad,' I said, plopping a teabag into a mug. 'I'll take the kids to playschool. It isn't fair on Tracy to have to do all the driving.'

Kathleen nodded, never taking her eyes from my face.

'Life goes on,' I said, as the kettle boiled and I poured water on to my teabag.

'That's true.'

'Especially Paddy's life.'

'Well, Ruth, yours too.'

I squeezed the teabag and tossed it into the bin. 'Whatever. Anyway, thanks for everything, Kathleen. I really appreciate it.'

She smiled and her eyes filled with tears, but I wasn't robust enough to deal with her crying on me.

'I'd better give Tracy a buzz,' I said, and hurried off to find the phone.

Chloe answered. 'Are you better, Ruth?' she said.

'Much better, Chloe, thanks. Is your mum there?'

'OK,' she said, dropping the phone on to something hard. I heard the morning sounds of voices, doors and feet on the stairs as I waited for Tracy.

'Ruth?' Tracy's voice said eventually. 'Everything all right?'

'Fine. I'll drop Chloe and Paddy and pick them up today as well – if that's all right with you. Give you a break. You've been doing all the work recently.'

'I don't mind.' There was a short pause. 'How are you feeling?'

'I'm fine. Better, thanks.'

Another pause. 'He's not worth it, Ruth.'

'I know. But it's OK now anyway, Trace. I'm OK, I swear.'

'You're too good for him. I always said that to Derek – Ruth is too good for that fella of the Burkes.'

I laughed at that. 'No, you didn't, you liar.'

Tracy laughed too. 'All right, I didn't actually say it but it's true.'

'I'll see you in half an hour or so,' I said.

'Grand.'

I hung up and returned to the kitchen. Kathleen and Paddy were having a chat in the sitting room and *Sponge Bob Square Pants* was on TV. I took two paracetamol for my splitting headache. It was another horrible, dark, rainy day. A magpie flew past and I wondered if it was the bastard who'd stolen my wedding ring.

My husband was gone, my ring was gone, my life as I'd known it was gone. All I could do was to make a new life for me and Paddy. I was scared at the prospect and felt as wobbly as a newborn calf, but a tiny part of me was hopeful, and I supposed that was a start.

7

The following morning I woke up strangely renewed. As I lay in bed beneath a cobweb on the ceiling I felt clear for the first time since Gibraltar. Scared, not sure of the future, but sure that I'd do everything in my power to make sure Paddy didn't suffer. I had to make a plan.

I rolled on to my side and rummaged through the bedside locker until I found a pen and a notebook. I propped myself up on the pillows and flicked through the notebook. I almost lost my resolve when I found the list I'd made before we went to Gibraltar.

Me	Paddy
Knickers (some sexy)	T-shirts
Bras (all sexy)	Shorts
New skirt	Underwear
Sandals (blue, thong and espadrilles)	Sandals
Camera	

I tore out the page, rolled it into a ball and threw it across the room. To hell with that. I needed a new list.

To Do

(1)   *Get job.*

(2)   *Open bank account in own name.*

(3)   *Change all utility bills to my name.*

(4)   *Paint hallway (I always hated that colour).*

(5)   *Take Emerson's name off my car insurance.*

(6)   *Find my father.*

I dropped my pen and reread what I'd written. *Find my father.* I couldn't believe my eyes. There it was, large as life, and now that I saw it written down I knew it was true. I did want to find him. It'd be a good thing to do for Paddy's sake. I was tired of not being able to tell doctors his full medical history.

Then I remembered: a couple of years ago, not long after Kathleen and I had first met, she'd given me a folder with some information in it about my father. I jumped out of bed, opened the bottom drawer of my oak bureau and, underneath a bundle of never-worn nighties, found a manila folder. I pulled it out and brought it back to bed. Inside was a photograph of two teenagers, arms round each other, laughing. They were standing on O'Connell Bridge in Dublin. On the back was scrawled *Me and Junior, 28 March 1976.*

I turned it over, studied the laughing faces and wondered if I had been conceived when it was taken. They looked so young that I couldn't imagine them having sex, let alone babies. But they'd had both: I was the living proof. I unfolded the single sheet of paper that was also in the folder. This wasn't the first time I'd looked at the photograph or read Kathleen's sparse recollection of my father but maybe I'd see something now that I hadn't noticed before.

According to the typed notes, his name was Junior Kennedy. But Junior wasn't a real name, was it? I'd have to ask Kathleen about that. He was eighteen, a Libra. He loved rugby, Pink Floyd and Steve Heighway crisps. And that was it. It wasn't a lot to go on. My heart sank. How was I supposed to find my father with so little information? Unless my mother used her psychic powers I was up shit creek without a paddle.

I lay back, closed my eyes and thought about my to-do list. The best place to start was at the beginning. *Get job.* That was my priority. I'd focus all my attention on finding work. And that was exactly what I did.

Twenty-one days later I had a job. It wasn't my first career choice but I was desperate. In my pursuit of a real job I'd emailed my revamped CV to anyone and everyone, but I'd known it would take time. Meanwhile I was willing to accept anything that was going.

When I wasn't looking for a job I was spending my time avoiding the Burkes, all nine of them – now that *was* a job of work – but so far so good. Emerson's parents, Ann and Joe, lived on an organic farm in Ogonnolloe, and I'd ducked them since my return from Gibraltar. They were the original flower-power–hippie parents, with a huge clatter of children, all of whom had extraordinary names. The children tended to be either arty/bonkers like their mum and dad or the complete opposite. India fell into the latter category. The court case in Dublin had kept her out of town but I knew I was due a visit over the weekend. I just hoped the Burkes didn't arrive *en masse*. I really wouldn't be able for that.

I wanted part-time work because Paddy needed me now more than ever. Kathleen had offered to help out with the babysitting. She had been one of England's foremost clairvoyants for almost twenty years but now that she was back in Ireland she restricted her practice to a small, select clientele.

In my job quest I'd rung the hotel where I'd worked as a receptionist before I married and although they had nothing at the moment they had agreed to keep me on file. I had to get a job: I was damned if I'd let Emerson pay maintenance for me as well as Paddy.

When Tracy suggested I try being a party organiser with Mary Winters I had laughed, then decided to go for it. The money was good and the hours suited me. The job scared the life out of me, though. How could I stand in front of a group of women and demonstrate all the sex-aid goodies Mary Winters had to offer when I hadn't seen any action for months? I said as much to Tracy when she brought down my party kit. It was Saturday morning – twenty-one days after Gibraltar.

'I'll give you a quick demo. How's that?' she said, as she sat down at the kitchen table, cigarette in one hand and a strangely shaped green vibrator in the other.

'Jesus Christ,' I said, as she switched it on. She held it up as if it was an Olympic torch.

'Humpasaurus, for the woman who likes a bumpy ride,' she said, and grinned. She picked up a huge silver yoke. 'Robocock2—'

'Stop! They all have names?'

Tracy took a drag on her cigarette. 'Yep, and if they don't, make them up! You have to do a party next week and you need to put on a show. That's how you sell your products. Here, catch!'

She threw a huge lipstick-pink one at me. I caught it and switched it on by accident. 'It sounds like a chainsaw,' I said.

'Our best-seller and that's the new model – the Randy Rabbit. Now, Ruth, hold it to the tip of your nose. That's how you let the women test it.'

I did as I was told and felt glad that Paddy had gone to the park with Kathleen.

Tracy picked up another vibrator. 'This boyo is the Dark Invader, and this one here is Pocket Pleasure. It fits in your handbag.'

'Why would you be carrying a vibrator around in your handbag, Tracy? I mean, you're hardly going to be in the checkout queue in Dunnes and suddenly feel the urge to shag a piece of plastic, are you?'

'Your job is to sell, not to ask questions. This one is the Pink Panther – feel it. Soft, isn't it?'

'Excuse me for asking, Trace, but it isn't soft we

should be looking for in one of these, it should be the opposite.'

Tracy giggled. 'There's no accounting for taste. Now, are you OK on the vibrators?'

I nodded. I didn't know a Dark Invader from a Humpasaurus but I'd study the catalogue. Tracy emptied a bag of what looked like underwear and black bin-bags on to the table. She stood up, then held a coral-coloured basque, matching suspender-belt and thong against her, batting her eyelashes at me. 'Our Indulgence collection. Derek's current favourite,' she said, and picked up the black plastic.

'Bondage gear. A great seller.' She tossed me a plastic bra.

'You must be joking!' I said.

Tracy scooped it back into the bag and lit another cigarette. 'Did you talk to him?'

I examined my nails. I'd scrubbed the bathroom this morning and ruined my French manicure. You can't have nice nails and a clean house.

I reached for one of Tracy's cigarettes.

'Well?'

I lit it.

'What's the story? Did ye sort anything out – money, access, stuff like that?'

'A bit. Emerson says there'll be no problem with money or maintenance.'

'Do you believe him, Ruth? Because I guarantee you that bitch'll start complaining soon about money. Mark my words. You should get a solicitor and take Emerson to the cleaners,' said Tracy.

'I don't want his money. He can pay maintenance for Paddy but I'll support myself.'

Tracy's eyes widened in disbelief. 'You're a fool, Ruth Burke, a big, innocent fool. You should make him pay. I bet he's loaded. All those movie fellas are.'

I laughed. 'What's this?' I asked, pointing at what might have been a nurse's uniform.

'The costumes, you eejit. There's the nurse, the French maid, the wench and all the crotchless gear. Now, my advice is leave all the raunchy stuff until the party is well on its way. Get the women to model those for you. It'll be more fun and you'll sell more too. Oh, I almost forgot. Don't drink. I never do – it's a bad idea.'

I had a feeling my new career wasn't going to last long. Tracy must have seen my anxiety. 'You'll be grand. The first party's the hardest. After that it's plain sailing all the way – you'll have a laugh, Ruth, *and* it'll get you out of this house.'

'That's what Kathleen said when I told her. Except I said I was selling Tupperware.' Tracy and I collapsed laughing.

'It's still hardware – well, kind of,' said Tracy, and broke into another fit of mirth. She put my brand new kit into a company briefcase and handed it to me.

'Do you want some coffee?' I asked.

'Have I ever said no?' She filled the coffee machine. It was an expensive Gaggia that Emerson had bought me last Christmas. Bastard. I didn't want to think about him. I didn't want to think about any of it.

'I've something to tell you, Ruth,' said Tracy, and sat down in front of me. I knew from her face that it was serious. Her Oriental eyes were clouded and she reached for another cigarette. We'd need breathing apparatus in the room soon. I took a cigarette, too, as my heart did a little dance in my chest. Tracy was a dear friend and mother to four young children. She couldn't be sick – I bloody well wouldn't allow it. And I knew her marriage was good. Although I'd thought mine was great until twenty-one days ago. I braced myself for bad news.

'I . . . I've been thinking about something for a long time and . . . well . . . I've made a decision . . .' She stood up and poured the coffee.

'Jesus, Tracy, will you tell me? I've you dead and buried and the children orphaned.'

Tracy smiled. 'It's nothing like that. I'm having a boob job. What do you think?'

'Fuck off!'

'I'm dead serious.'

I knew she was. 'You can't.'

'What?'

'You can't. For fuck's sake, Tracy, a boob job? What did Derek say?'

'He doesn't know. I'm not going to tell him until it's done and now I'm sorry I opened my mouth to you.' She tapped her cigarette on the ashtray.

'Look, Tracy, all I meant was that you're a beautiful woman with a fabulous figure. Why would you want to stuff your breasts full of silicone? It's dangerous and—'

'And it's easy for you to say that, with your double Ds. Do you know what it's like to be flat-chested?'

She had me on that one. I had a large bosom that I'd cursed as a teenager but loved as I got older.

'Look at you. You're like Kylie Minogue with tits. I'm like a half-Chinese Kylie aged nine.'

I laughed. 'Know what I think? You get the right tits for your shape. You've got a tiny frame and if your chest is bigger you'll have all sorts of problems.'

'Fuck it, Ruth, I want cleavage, I want to be able to wear clothes and not look like a kid playing dress-up. I'm sick and tired of it.'

'What about a Wonderbra? Ellen swears by them. And I wear one myself if I really want the wow factor.'

'Wonderbras are grand if you've got something to put into them.'

'Chicken fillets!'

'What?'

'Silicone breast enhancers – I saw them in a magazine. Wait, I'll find it!' I ran upstairs to my bedroom and rooted through the magazines on my bedside locker until I found the one I was looking for. I ran downstairs, delighted that I might have a chance of talking Tracy out of a boob job.

'See?' I said, as I opened the magazine, 'Two hundred euros for the really good ones – how much is a boob job?'

Tracy studied the magazine. 'Three thousand per boob.'

'My God! That much?'

'Yeah. I've saved half and I'm getting a loan of the rest from the Credit Union. I told them it was for architect's plans for an extension.'

'Try the chicken fillets first, Trace. Please?'

'I've a consultation in a couple of weeks, but if it keeps you happy I might give these a go. They do look the business, don't they?'

I nodded vigorously.

'They probably airbrushed boobs on to the models but, shit, it's only a couple of hundred euros and I can get them straight away.' She stood up and put the magazine under her arm. 'Gotta go. Derek's working soon and I've a party later.'

''Bye, Trace, and thanks for everything,' I said, and opened the front door for her.

Tracy stopped suddenly. 'Did you meet him yet?'

'Who?'

'You know – New Neighbour?'

'Skater Boy? Nope. Haven't seen sight nor sound of him. Maybe you imagined him.'

'No, I didn't. Not even I could conjure up an angel's face like that.'

8

By that night I felt as if I'd known the angel face all my life. The weather was fine and in the afternoon I sat in the back garden while Paddy played in his sandpit. He talked to himself while he moved the same pile of sand endlessly around in a bright red truck. I dozed on the reclining chair, enjoying the early-summer sun and trying to remember the names of the vibrators in the Mary Winters catalogue.

I wouldn't allow myself to think about Emerson. Or Emerson with Selma. When thoughts of them together crept into my mind I sang Abba's 'Waterloo' and forced myself to think of something else.

Sitting in the garden with my gorgeous son was about as good as it got. I didn't need Emerson. I didn't need any man. Although I had to admit that the lack of sex was getting to me. I was beginning to fancy the postman, who looked about thirteen. But no matter how desperate I was I couldn't bring myself to fancy a piece of plastic called Randy Rabbit.

'Mum, the cat's flying off the tree – look!' said Paddy.

'Is that right, love?' I said, as I settled down for another doze.

'Pssh, pssh, pssh,' Paddy called, to his new friend the cat, and ran down the garden. 'Can I come up too?'

'No climbing, Pad,' I said, sitting up and shading my eyes from the sun. There on the garden wall was the most beautiful tabby cat I'd ever seen. He looked totally uninterested in his new fan.

'No climbing,' I said again, and went back to dozing. I might get Paddy a kitten. I'd ask Tracy – her mother kept cats.

'Who are you?' said Paddy, at the bottom of the garden.

'The Claw is mine!'

That wasn't Paddy's voice. I jumped up and my heart almost stopped. Paddy was standing near the shed, head tilted back, finger pointing. The shed had a slanted roof and the gorgeous cat now sat on the apex. Half-way up the roof slope, a small boy in blue dungarees was scrambling up towards the cat.

I made myself stay calm and surveyed the situation. A mature cherry tree in the garden next door hung over my wall. The child must have climbed it, then crawled along the wall until he could pull himself on to the shed roof. I walked towards him, afraid to call out in case I startled him. I knew I'd be able to climb the wall and reach him but I knew also that, in the blink of an eye, he could fall.

A wide concrete footpath circled the shed – he might hurt himself badly if he slipped. Where were his parents? I reached the shed and Paddy clapped his hands and screeched. The little boy stopped climbing, looked down at Paddy and slid precariously. My legs went weak.

'What's your name?' I said, trying to conceal my fear.

'Mikey Regan.'

'And what's your cat's name?'

'The Claw.' He slid another foot and my heart somersaulted.

'Mikey, hold on and don't move. I'm coming up,' I said, and began to scale the wall, glad of the footholds the old stone provided.

'Mum – wait for me,' Paddy shouted, scrabbling at the bottom of the wall.

'Stay there, Paddy.'

'I want to come up on the wall.'

'Paddy!' I shouted. 'If you climb up here there'll be no TV for a week. I mean it!'

Paddy glared, folded his arms and walked away in a sulk. I turned back to Mikey. I stood on top of the wall and walked along it until I reached the shed. Then I pulled myself on to the roof, using its light guttering as support. I could hear it tearing under my weight, but I pulled myself across it anyway. The child saw me below him on the sloped roof and started to climb, as if this was a new, dangerous, version of tag.

I scrambled up as quickly as I could and finally had him round the waist. He protested but I held on. 'Sorry about this, Mikey, but it's for your own good.'

Mikey flailed as I edged myself round to face the

garden. The cat sauntered down the roof, leaped on to the wall, then down into my garden. Paddy ran after him.

There was only one problem now. How was I going to get us down safely? I'd never manage to carry Mikey with me. I searched the other gardens, looking for neighbours or Batman.

'He's *my* cat,' Mikey said, and pointed at the Claw. Paddy was playing with him.

'What will we do now, Mikey?' I said. 'What do you think of the view? Look you can see St John's Cathedral.'

Mikey regarded me as if I was an idiot, but he'd stopped struggling.

'I have an idea, Mikey. How loud can you shout?' I said.

He didn't answer and I wasn't sure how much longer I could hold on to him. I'd have to go for it myself. 'Help!' I shouted, at the top of my lungs.

Mikey stared at me in amazement, and Paddy ran back to the wall. 'Come on, Pad,' I yelled, 'you too. Shout, "Help," at the top of your voices, boys, both of you.'

The three of us let rip.

My plan worked almost instantly. The back door of my new neighbour's house swung open and Skater Boy dashed down the garden. 'Mikey, where are you?' he bellowed.

'Up here,' I said.

'Jesus Christ,' he said. He had climbed over the garden wall and on to the shed roof in a matter of seconds. He sat down next to me, took Mikey in his arms and kissed the top of his blond head.

'Jesus Christ,' Skater Boy said again. He wore a beanie hat – and Tracy was right: he had the face of an angel. His eyes were pale blue, his cheekbones high and angular, almost girlish, his lips full and red. His skin was lightly tanned and he hadn't shaved that day. He looked like a thirty-year-old Viennese choirboy.

'I presume he's yours?' I said, as I eased myself down the roof.

'Thanks so much. He's always climbing something, aren't you, Mikey?'

I propelled myself gingerly on to the wall and got down. Paddy hugged my legs.

'Hand him to me,' I said to Skater Boy.

He slid down the roof on his bum, with Mikey locked between his legs, then held him out to me. I put Mikey on the ground and watched as his father climbed down. He wore dark green army combats and a sleeveless grey vest. He was slight and not very tall, five eight or nine.

He held out his hand. 'I'm so bloody grateful to you. I'm Kevin Regan – I just moved in next door.'

He had a nice firm grip. 'I'm Ruth Burke and this is Paddy.'

'Look, I don't usually – I'm never that careless with Mikey. That's what they all say, isn't it? I was writing this piece and the editor rang and we had a screaming match on the phone . . .'

He smiled apologetically and shrugged his shoulders. 'Lucky you saw him. Thanks again.'

'Paddy saw him first. Mikey followed the cat on to the roof.'

'That bloody cat,' he said.

'The Claw? Is he called after the rugby player?'

'Damn right. He's a nuisance – always causing trouble – but he doesn't bite ears unlike his namesake.' Kevin Regan smiled. Then he glanced at the shed and shuddered. 'Christ, it could have been really nasty – I mean, if he fell . . .'

Paddy and Mikey had run off towards the garden swings and were chattering away to each other. Kevin smiled boyishly at me. I smiled back.

'Look, what are you and your partner doing later? Can't you both call in for a drink and a bite to eat? I want to thank you properly.'

'I don't have a partner,' I said. 'I did have a husband until recently and now I don't.'

I cursed myself for saying anything so personal – this man was a total stranger.

'Me too,' he said.

'What? No husband?'

He grinned broadly. 'No wife. Orla and I are having a trial separation. I think she likes it.'

'Do you?' I asked, wondering how the conversation had moved so swiftly on to this level.

He shrugged again. He seemed to be a nice guy, although I no longer believed that nice guys existed.

'Come over later with Paddy. The least I can do to repay you is cook. About seven?'

9

Kevin turned out to be an excellent cook and we dined on Thai green curry and glass noodles. He'd made pizza for the boys, which they ate with enthusiasm. The curry was delicious and so was the wine. Kevin's company wasn't bad either. We chatted away like old friends and I even half told him my Gibraltar story, matter-of-factly, without faltering. I was proud that I didn't break down. He sipped his wine, rubbing his shaved head as he digested my tale.

'What happened with you?' I asked, hoping I didn't sound nosy. I was dying for a fag but couldn't see an ashtray.

When Kevin smiled his eyes crinkled at the corners. 'Smoker?' he asked.

'Not really. Giving them up on Monday. I'd love a fag, though,' I said, deciding that the craving for nicotine was way stronger than the desire to be virtuous.

Kevin stood up, took a packet of cigarettes off a shelf and offered me one. We lit up. He opened the back door and stood there to smoke. I joined him.

'No one else was involved, not at the start anyway. Just Orla's job – she's a doctor – more demanding than any lover,' he said. The sun had set, leaving the sky orange-streaked. I could hear Mikey and Paddy singing along to *Bob the Builder* in the living room.

'How often do you get to see Mikey?'

He dragged deeply on his cigarette. 'I have full custody.'

'What?'

'I know it's probably hard to believe after today but, yeah, he lives with me. Orla's hours are all over the place and we just thought it was the best thing for Mikey.'

'And what about yours? How do you manage to work?'

'I'm a journalist, freelance, so I can work around Mikey. It's grand most of the time, except when he gets it into his head that he's a super-hero.'

We both laughed.

'What about you? Do you work?'

I considered telling him about my new career in sex aids but decided against it. 'I'm looking for a job at the moment, part-time. Kathleen – my birth-mother – will babysit. She's a clairvoyant.'

Kevin burst out laughing.

'It's true!'

Kevin laughed even more and wiped his eyes. 'It's the way you said it – like she was a hairdresser! So, you're adopted?'

I nodded. 'My parents died a long time ago. Kathleen made contact with me a couple of years ago.'

'Using her powers?'

'Nope. An agency.'

Kevin laughed again. 'You're a gas, woman.'

A shriek from the living room made us jump and we ran to see what was up. Mikey had decided to climb the curtains and had got half-way up when he lost his nerve. Paddy was watching him, astonishment all over his face.

Kevin lifted his son off the curtain. There was a track of pizza-coloured handprints on the cream linen. 'Mikey's really a monkey, not a boy,' said Kevin to Paddy. 'Will we put him in the zoo?'

Paddy and Mikey shrieked with delight. We settled them back in front of the TV, then returned to the kitchen and took up where we'd left off.

Kevin poured us more wine and we chatted like old friends. At one point, while he was in the loo, I had a wander round his kitchen and found a cork noticeboard wallpapered with newspaper clippings and printed articles from websites. They all dealt with the link between industrial pollution and birth defects. Kevin came back as I was reading an article about asbestos pollution.

'Scary stuff, isn't it?' he said.

'Are you working on this?'

'A group of residents from Ballymoran in North Limerick came to me about six months ago. They'd just lost a case against a company they're convinced is dumping asbestos in their area.'

'Doesn't it cause cancer?'

'That's right. The residents believe it's the cause of the rise in birth defects and cancers in that area since 1989.'

'And they took the company to court?'

Kevin grimaced. 'Last year, but they lost and now they're fundraising to pay the costs.'

'Where do you come in?'

'I'm their last chance and I've always been interested in that whole big industry versus Joe Soap stuff.'

'Like Erin Brockovich?'

'Exactly, but without the boobs.'

'What do the residents want you to do?'

'Keep the subject live. One of the residents, Joe Taylor, firmly believes that the environmental-impact reports used in court were falsified.'

'Wow! That's serious.'

'What's more serious is that he's probably right, but I can't find any evidence. I've just finished a big article – it'll be in the *Sunday Tribune* in a fortnight – and that's about it. Unless something new turns up we're snookered.'

'You never know.'

Kevin moved close to the noticeboard and touched a picture of a bald teenage girl. 'That's Joe's daughter, Michelle. She's thirteen and she's one of four from her school who have leukaemia.'

'Jesus, you're joking! Poor kids. Poor parents.'

'I know,' Kevin said. 'Hopefully they'll recover – the prognosis is good for kids with leukaemia. But there's definitely a cancer cluster, and there are other health issues. The problem is proof.'

I gazed at Michelle's smiling face and my heart ached for her. I hoped Kevin was right and that she'd live to be a grandmother. My problems seemed minuscule in comparison. At that point Mikey and Paddy raced each other into Kevin's kitchen, demanding more ice-cream, and we returned to lighter subjects.

I didn't leave Kevin's house until midnight, with a sleeping Paddy in my arms. Kevin and I had watched *Zoolander* on TV and the two boys crashed out on the sofa.

When I got home I checked my messages. There were ten, all from various Burkes. It was as if they were having a family get-together on my answer-machine. There was one from India, saying she'd call in the morning if that was OK. Another from Ann, Emerson's mum, saying she had vegetables and a nut roast for me. There was one each from Emerson's brothers, Lake and Palmer, both of whom lived abroad.

Finally there was a message from Emerson. The sound of his voice made my heart thump. Bastard. He wanted to know if it was OK to send Paddy regular videos of himself while he was away on location. Trust Emerson to be the perfect screen dad.

India arrived at lunchtime the next day, accompanied by her little daughter Alyssa. Paddy loved his cousin and dragged her straight into the living room to watch *Finding Nemo*. India didn't say a word at first: she just came over and hugged me tightly. I blinked away tears.

'I'll make some coffee,' I said. She was wearing a white linen trouser suit, her hair was a dark shimmering bob of perfection and her makeup was flawless. How did she always manage to look so perfect?

I was pretty good at scrubbing up and quite enjoyed it, but I could never maintain it to India's standard. She was the complete opposite to her parents and, indeed, to Emerson, who was casual about appearance. But he was a perfectionist where his work was concerned so maybe there was a family resemblance.

'It must be really hard, Ruth,' India said, as she sat down at the kitchen table, eyes round with concern. 'How do you feel?'

'I'm all right. Would you like something to eat? A sandwich? Pizza?'

'No, thanks. I'm going to Mum's for lunch.' She made a face. 'Nut roast,' we chorused, and laughed.

India stirred her coffee and I reached for a fag.

'Smoking?' she asked.

'Looks like it,' I said, and lit up. 'Giving them up tomorrow.'

'We're all really upset over the whole thing.'

I shrugged.

'Mum is so cut up, she can't even bring herself to talk to Emerson on the phone.'

I shrugged again.

'And all the others are stunned. That's the word we're using.'

I examined my nails.

'It's a bit difficult for me, Ruth. He's ringing me and . . . well . . . I'm kind of piggy in the middle . . .'

'A bit difficult for *you*, is it?' Suddenly I was angry.

'All I meant was that I'm his sister *and* one of your closest friends. That's all.'

'Your mother doesn't find it difficult. She has no qualms about letting Emerson know what she thinks.'

'It's not as simple as that, Ruth. Eventually she'll have to talk to him. I don't indulge him, if that's what you think.'

The doorbell rang. I got up and opened the door to Kathleen. She was dressed in navy linen with high, strappy sandals – sophisticated, in a Joanna Lumley way.

'Hi, Ruth. I didn't bother phoning, just thought I'd surprise you with an invite to lunch.'

'Come in,' I said, and walked back towards the kitchen, glancing first into the living room to make sure the children were all right. Mikey's antics the previous day had put me on my guard.

'I see you've visitors. I really don't want to be interrupting.'

'No, it's fine. It's only India,' I said, as we went into the kitchen.

India rose and they shook hands.

'How are you, Kathleen?' said India.

'Great. You?'

'Good.'

'Tim? Alyssa?'

'Great.'

There was an awkward silence.

'Actually, I need to get going, Ruth. I'm in Dublin for another couple of weeks but I'll ring you,' India said.

'That'll be grand.'

She picked up her white handbag. 'Goodbye, Kathleen, nice to see you,' she said, and headed towards the living room to get Alyssa.

I walked them to the door, then kissed mother and daughter goodbye. Paddy, in true three-year-old fashion, didn't bother with social niceties, particularly with *Finding Nemo* on TV. I closed the door and went back to the kitchen.

'What had she to say?' asked Kathleen.

'About what?'

'About her snake of a brother. What else?'

Blood really was thicker than water.

'Did you do something new? Hair, eyebrows? There's something different about you,' I said, as I cleaned off the worktop.

Kathleen patted her streaked blonde hair. 'Nothing like that. But there's something I want to you to know. I was going to tell you ages ago but with all the Gibraltar stuff . . .'

'What is it? Good or bad? I don't want to hear anything bad, Kathleen. It's got to be good or nothing.'

'It's good, really good, I promise.'

I wondered what her news could be and then I thought of Tracy's last week. 'Oh, please! Not you too? You're not having a boob job, are you?'

'What do you mean?'

'Nothing – tell me your news, especially if it's good.'

'The best, Ruth. Get Paddy ready. We're going

to the Waterfront for Sunday lunch. I'll tell you there.'

We waved at Kevin and Mikey, who were returning from the shop as we pulled away from my house in Kathleen's silver Punto. She had a permanent baby seat in the rear for Paddy, which saved all the lugging when she babysat.

'Who's that?' she asked, as we pulled out of our avenue.

'My new neighbour, Kevin, and his son, Mikey.'

Kathleen stared at me. 'He has a son?'

'Watch the road, Kathleen. Yeah, he's not as young as he looks.'

'So he's sixteen and not twelve?'

I giggled. 'He's at least my age.'

'I wonder what moisturiser he uses.'

We pulled up outside the posh Waterfront restaurant. It was a warm sunny day so we sat on the terrace, overlooking the Shannon. Paddy pushed his police car along the table, making siren noises. We ordered our food and Kathleen went to the loo. While she was gone I wondered what her news was. Maybe she'd bought a new house, a holiday home in Lahinch – she'd been talking about that for a while. It'd be great for Paddy and me in the summer. When she sat down again, she held Paddy's hand, then reached out and took mine.

'We'll be having group hugs in a minute, Kathleen. Come on, spit it out,' I said.

'I'm pregnant,' she told me.

IO

I laughed and Paddy joined in. Kathleen was still holding my hand. Paddy had pulled his away and was banging the table.

'That's a good one,' I said, 'a conversation stopper if I ever heard one. I'll have to tell Tracy that – she'll love it.'

Kathleen tightened her grip. 'I'm pregnant, Ruth, and I'm over the moon. You're going to have a little brother or sister.'

'Fucking hell.'

'Fucking hell,' echoed Paddy.

'A brother or sister?' I said, incredulously.

At that moment the food and drinks arrived. I couldn't see my plate, let alone eat anything. Paddy tucked into his chips, unaware that he was about to acquire a new aunt or uncle, who, incidentally, would be younger than him.

Kathleen began on her Caesar salad.

I poured myself a large glass of wine. 'And has this baby a father?' I asked, doing my best to be polite.

Kathleen stopped eating. 'Now, Ruth, don't be like that.'

'I think it's a reasonable question under the

circumstances.' I took a large gulp of ice-cold wine. The seafood aroma from my plate was making me feel sick.

'I know it's difficult for you, Ruth, but it was carefully planned and I'm delighted,' she said, and continued to eat.

'You're a bit over the hill for the baby lark, aren't you?' I said, and rooted in my bag for fags. Maybe I could duck out for a smoke. I needed one badly.

'I'm only forty-three, Ruth. Hardly ancient. People wait until they're older now to have babies.' She smiled reassuringly at me.

My mind was a jumble and I felt irrationally angry with her. She'd had me when she was sixteen and given me away just like that. Her recollections of my birth-father were vague at best and she hadn't bothered to look for me for twenty-six years.

I took another gulp of wine and turned away from the table to watch the Shannon wind its way beside the restaurant terrace.

My mother was pregnant. I had a baby and now my mother was having one. I repeated these things in my head to make them more real.

'Congratulations,' I said.

'Thank you.'

'When is the big day?'

She stopped eating and smiled at me. 'The twenty-fifth of December. Christmas Day.'

Great. My clairvoyant mother was probably giving

birth to a Messiah. The second coming or whatever they called it.

'Lovely,' I said.

'I'm thrilled. I'm going for my first appointment next Wednesday.'

'That's nice. By the way, did you get your car serviced?'

Hurt passed swiftly across Kathleen's face. 'Tomorrow.'

My mind was still in turmoil. Did Kathleen expect me to play happy families with her? And where was the father? I mean, she was pregnant so there must have been some cut of a man around for her to achieve that. Or maybe it was a phantom pregnancy in the true sense of the word. Maybe she'd had a visit during the night from a hunky man spirit and couldn't help herself.

'This is delicious,' I said, taking a spoonful of seafood chowder. I couldn't taste a thing. 'The food's always good here. I remember coming last summer with – with Emerson. We sat over there and watched the sunset. And then it started raining . . .' I took another spoonful. Kathleen wiped Paddy's mouth with a linen napkin.

'God, is that the time? I promised Tracy I'd look after the kids for an hour.' I picked up my bag.

'What about dessert? Coffee! You always have coffee.'

'I won't today, thanks.'

★

Next day as Paddy and I were having breakfast, the postman came.

'Postman Pat,' said Paddy, and ran to pick up the letters. He loved this daily ritual.

I rummaged through the pile he brought back and my heart flipped over when I saw Emerson's handwriting on a thick package. I ripped it open and found two videos inside. There was also a note.

> *Dear Ruth*
> *Please show these to Paddy. I want him to know the sound of my voice. I miss him like crazy.*
> *Imagine if it was you.*
> *Love to both of you*
> *Emerson*

A single tear rolled down my cheek and I wiped it away with the back of my hand. Bloody bastard. Why had he done it? Why had he thrown it all away like a piece of clothing he'd outgrown? I'd loved him to bits. I took Paddy and the videos into the living room, then slipped a cassette into the machine.

'Look, Pad, it's Daddy,' I said, as the TV crackled and Emerson's smiling face appeared on the screen. Paddy was transfixed. Then Emerson's voice filled the room and I ran out to the kitchen, tears streaming down my face. I could hear him strumming a guitar and singing, 'Hit the road Jack'. That was Paddy's special song, which Emerson had sung to him every night. I could hear Paddy singing his version of the refrain 'more no, more no, more no'. I laughed and cried, then sat at the kitchen table and put my hands over my ears.

My first Mary Winters party was that night and I was nervous. There was no sign of Tracy – she'd deserted me in my true hour of need – and to top it all Kevin, next door, had asked me to look after Mikey for an hour. This would have been grand, except Mikey was bonkers. Cute, lovable but bonkers. A news story was breaking and Kevin was stuck.

I plonked Paddy and Mikey in front of the TV with instructions to behave and not climb anything. Both children nodded, with innocent eyes. I went to the kitchen and tidied up, listening to my favourite Johnny Cash album. I checked the children a few times, but they were sitting on the couch like two little angels.

By the time Kevin came to collect Mikey I was feeling confident about the party and had everything ready, including my party kit and my outfit. I even had my makeup on and my nails polished.

'You look good,' Kevin said, as he came into the kitchen. 'A hot date?'

'No, it's work actually. Tupperware,' I said.

'My mother used to buy that stuff when I was a kid. The bowls had lids and they were great for keeping maggots fresh.'

'Lovely, Kevin.'

'When did you get the job?' He was leaning against the fridge.

'It's just a temporary thing. The hours suit me and it'll do until something else comes up.'

'What's the story with the barbecue, Ruth?'

'First I heard of it.'

'One of the neighbours called – Tracy. She invited me and Mikey to a barbecue.'

'That's nice,' I said. 'When is it?'

Kevin laughed. 'Twenty-first of August. Does she always plan so far ahead?'

I smirked inwardly. Tracy'd had to dig deep for a reason to call and check out our new neighbour. 'Not usually. I'm sure she'll remind us again when it's closer.'

'She said she was a friend of yours.'

'She is, a really good one, actually. They're sound, Tracy and Derek. Did you meet Derek yet?'

'No, but I heard he's a mad Munster fan so I like him already.'

'She's a fanatic too. God, I'll be surrounded by Munster fans! I'm glad the season's over.'

Kevin winked. 'That's what you think. Tracy told me she's got all last season's matches on video so we're going to have regular Munster nights. Coming?'

I shook my head. 'You must be joking! What was the big story?'

'Nothing much. Some actor guy staying in the Clarion. I had to interview him.'

'What was he like?'

'A wanker – they usually are. Lance Harding.'

'I know him – he's a friend of Emerson's. He's not the worst of them, you know.'

'He was a wanker.'

'He's a bit of a pain, all right.' I picked up my cigarettes and offered one to Kevin.

'No, thanks. I gave up on Monday. I feel like a new man.' He pummelled his chest.

'I'm giving up next Monday. Did I tell you my birth-mother's pregnant?'

'Serious?'

'Yep.'

'That must be weird for you. I mean, she had you and . . . well . . . it must be strange.'

I was surprised at Kevin's reading of the situation. When I'd told Tracy, the only thing that had interested her was the identity of the father.

'Is she happy about it?'

'Delighted – all planned and wanted. There doesn't seem to be any daddy around, though.'

'Well, there must have been at some stage,' Kevin said.

I shrugged.

He glanced up at the ceiling. 'What's that noise?'

'What noise?' I said.

'Listen, it sounds like . . . Shit!' Kevin dashed out of the kitchen and up the stairs. I followed – and nearly cried at the sight that greeted us in the bathroom. My party-kit briefcase lay empty on the bathroom floor. Mikey was stirring whatever was in the toilet with a huge pink vibrator. Paddy was standing in the bath, laughing, and the floor was flooded with water from the overflowing toilet.

'Mikey! What *are* you doing?' asked Kevin.

There was no reply. Mikey shuffled his feet sheepishly.

I peered into the toilet. All of the Mary Winters lingerie was stuffed into it, along with the contents of a bottle of shampoo, the toothpaste tube, and some unidentifiable green goo that might have been hair gel.

'Oh, no,' I said.

Kevin had taken the vibrator from Mikey.

'It's not mine,' I said.

'No. It's the pregnant clairvoyant's, of course,' he said, trying to suppress a smile.

'OK, OK. It's this stuff I'm selling, not bloody Tupperware, and what am I going to do now? I've got a party in less than two hours.'

At that moment the doorbell rang. I knew it was Kathleen.

'I'm really sorry, Ruth.' Kevin was holding the vibrator as if it was a Cornetto.

'That's Kathleen. I don't want her to see this,' I said.

Mikey had climbed into the bath and stood there with his arm round Paddy. They were giggling, evidenty delighted with their day's work.

'Leave it to me, Ruth. You answer the door and I'll bring this stuff into my place. I can wash and dry it there and I'll bring it all back like new.'

'Really?' I said.

'Absolutely. It's the least I can do. Go on, I'll look after it,' he said. He put the vibrator on the wet floor and began to pull the sopping lingerie out of the toilet.

I ran down to answer the door. Kathleen was full of excitement about her appointment at the ante-natal clinic and didn't hear Kevin and Mikey slip out a few minutes later. As I listened to a detailed report of my unborn sibling I prayed Kevin would have my kit back in time for the party. Tracy would kill me if I messed up. She'd organised the whole thing for me and I didn't want to let her down.

I chatted to Kathleen, made Paddy some pasta and tried not to watch the clock. I was due at the party at eight and by seven thirty there was still no sign of Kevin. I ran upstairs to change. As I struggled into my sandals I realised I could hear Kevin talking to Kathleen in the kitchen.

'Here she is now,' said Kathleen, as I came in.

Kevin looked me up and down and said nothing. I felt almost uncomfortable under his gaze. 'Well? Did you manage to sort out the laundry?' I said.

'You look great.'

'Where's Mikey?' I asked, afraid he was demolishing my living room.

Kevin laughed. 'It's all right. Orla came for dinner so he's at home with her. And the laundry is grand. It's in the hallway.'

I said goodbye to Kathleen, kissed Paddy and left them, Kevin following.

I picked up the briefcase. 'Thanks a million for sorting it out,' I said, as I opened the front door.

'No problem. It was my brat who caused the chaos,' said Kevin, and leaped over the garden wall like Nadia Comaneci. 'See ya later. By the way, you

really do look great – wasted in a roomful of women,'
he called, as I climbed into the car.

It was amazing how uplifting a little compliment
could be. I had a feeling this party business was
going to be a doddle.

11

And the party was a doddle – for the first ten minutes. By the time all of the women were sitting sedately, glasses of wine in hand, waiting expectantly for the show to begin, my confidence still hadn't deserted me. I faced them with my bag of tricks beside me. They seemed to be a grand bunch. I handed out Mary Winters catalogues and the all-important order slips Tracy had warned me about. There was no flies on her when it came to business.

She had made sexy nametags for the women and they served as a great ice-breaker. We laughed at the names: Luscious Linda, Bernie Blowjob, things like that. We even put one on the dog – he was Sarah Slut for the night.

Then I launched into my sales patter, using the catalogue as a kind of autocue. The women nodded encouragingly as I described the first items in the catalogue.

'Give us a look, love. You can't judge from the pictures,' said a robust blonde with a pretty face and a nametag that read 'Vicky Vibrator'.

'No problem,' I said, and opened my briefcase of merchandise. I could smell fabric conditioner. Kevin

really had done a good job. I looked for the coral
basque and thong from the Indulgence collection
and held up the set for the women to see.

'Isn't this gorgeous?' I said. They smiled broadly
at me, so I passed it round for them to feel the
quality. 'And this is from our new Daredevil range,'
I said, taking out the next outfit and holding it up.

'I didn't know they did Mary Winters underwear
for Barbie Dolls,' said Vicky Vibrator, as she held the
basque against her.

Then I noticed what the smiles were about. Kevin,
the stupid eejit, had shrunk the lot. The Daredevil
chemise in my hand was about six inches wide. I
dropped it and took out a nurse's uniform that seemed
to have come from the Early Learning Centre.

I picked up a black vibrator and switched it on.
Nothing. Vicky Vibrator laughed. I turned bright red.
The woman who was hosting the party – Horny
Hannah – fidgeted in her seat, then slugged back a
full glass of wine. The vibrator was dripping water
on to the carpet. I wanted to murder Kevin – after
I'd throttled Mikey.

I took a glass of wine from a nearby table, ignoring
Tracy's advice. I needed a fag too.

'It was Mikey's fault, the little shit,' I said then,
deciding honesty was the best policy. 'He and my
young fella Paddy took the party kit and dumped it
down the toilet, added hair gel and stuff and stirred
the lot with the Randy Rabbit. They're three. Then
Mikey's dumb father washed and dried the gear for
me.'

Laughter spread through the room like a Mexican wave. I laughed so hard my mascara ran down my cheeks.

'I take it Mikey isn't yours?' asked Bernie Blowjob.

'No – thanks be to God for small mercies,' I said. 'He's my neighbour's child.'

'Let's open another bottle,' said Horny Hannah. And we did.

After four glasses of wine I decided to ring Derek and ask him to collect me. We ended up singing Westlife songs, using the vibrators as percussion instruments. Vicky Vibrator had squeezed herself into a French maid's outfit and I was in the nurse's, which felt like a strait-jacket. I sold a *huge* amount. The women had given me the sympathy vote. The party was wild by the time Derek arrived.

'Jesus, Ruth, what were they on? Vodka and Red Bull?' he said, as we drove away in his cab. I'd collect my car in the morning.

'Just a few glasses of wine.'

'A couple of kegs I'd say.' Derek was a body-builder: drunk as the women had been, that fact hadn't escaped them – Vicky Vibrator thought someone had ordered a kissogram.

When I got home Kathleen was asleep on the sofa. She had the baby monitor in her hand and I could hear Paddy's deep, regular breathing. I shook her shoulder gently. 'I'm back.'

'Oh. I'm sorry. It's just that I'm so tired. What time is it?'

'Eleven thirty. Look, why don't you sleep here tonight?'

Kathleen sat up and put the monitor on the coffee-table. 'No. I'll go home, Ruth. I'll sleep better in my own bed.' She yawned.

'Are you sure?' She was very pale.

'How was the party? Isn't it amazing that Tupperware came back into fashion? I must order some from you,' she said, as she went into the kitchen to get her things. I followed.

Maybe I should get Kathleen and Tracy together – they could do a double act: free tarot reading with every vibrator. The alcohol was definitely affecting me now. I saw her to the door and collapsed into bed, not even bothering to take off my makeup.

A few weeks later I was an old hand on the party circuit. I wasn't anything as good as Tracy but I was making some money. Emerson had tried to insist on paying maintenance for me as well as Paddy and although we'd agreed on a monthly sum for our son I'd refused anything for myself. We were no longer a family unit and I had to be independent. I didn't have a mortgage and I could manage just fine.

My big problem was the job. Some people are cut out for sales and I knew now that I wasn't. I felt uncomfortable selling overpriced lingerie to people who couldn't afford it. People who became reckless after a few drinks and spent money they didn't have. Tracy scoffed at this. 'They're getting what they want and you have an income – what the hell is wrong with that?' she said.

'Well, I'm not comfortable doing it, that's all. But I'm grateful I have something – don't get me wrong,' I said, and took one of Tracy's fags. I was definitely giving them up after the weekend.

'Know what, Ruth? You think way too much. It's a job. Go and do it. It's like driving a cab or being a doctor,' she said. I could hear the children squealing in the garden and glanced out of the window to check on them. Paddy was sitting on the swing and Tracy's two youngest girls, Lauren and Chloe, were taking turns to push him. He was singing some nonsensical song – probably full of curses if only I could have heard the words.

'Your girls are angels,' I said. They had shiny black bobbed hair and gorgeous almond-shaped dark eyes. 'They're going to be two little heartbreakers.'

'Well, if one of them ever arrives home with Mikey Regan as a boyfriend, I'll disown her,' said Tracy. Mikey was already a legend in our neighbourhood.

'Poor Mikey – he's a mad laugh.'

'He'll be grand. My Jordan and Jade were like that, twin lunatics. I thought I'd go crazy when they were his age. That was why I started doing the parties – I had to get away from them. They're fine now.'

Tracy's eldest two were eight and the sweetest kids you could meet. 'Tell Kevin that – it'll cheer him up,' I said.

'Let him live on the edge for a couple of years.'

We both laughed.

'Did you buy the chicken fillets?' I asked, suddenly remembering Tracy's boob job.

'No. I had my consultation yesterday and Mr Nixon said I was the perfect candidate.'

'He probably says that to all the women. I mean, it's a silicone implant, not a heart transplant, so how can you not be the perfect candidate?'

Tracy shrugged. 'I'm only telling you what he said, Ruth. And I believe him. He's a big shot in the States, so they say.'

'Don't do it, Trace,' I said beseechingly.

'There's a three-month waiting list. It'll be September at the earliest. You'd never believe so many women in Limerick were having cosmetic surgery, would you?'

I was glad about the waiting list: it gave me a little more time to talk her out of it. 'You're perfect the way you are,' I said.

'Any news from Bastard?' said Tracy.

'He rang last night to talk to Paddy.'

'Big of him.'

'He sends videos every week too.'

'Jesus! He's a model father.'

Tracy was one sarcastic bitch but I liked her for it.

'Did I tell you we're having a barbecue for Derek's thirtieth?' she said, as she lit another cigarette.

I checked the kids again. They had put the Claw into a toy wheelbarrow and were pushing him up the garden path. 'Kevin did. When is it?'

'Twenty-first of August. I know it's ages away but

the summer flies when the kids are off school and, anyway, it's going to be a huge affair. It'll be brilliant.'

'Hope it doesn't rain.'

'It won't. It can't rain on my brand new gas barbecue. Ask your mother if she'd like to come.'

'Are you sure?'

'Yeah. She might liven things up with a few readings. I haven't seen her in one of her trances yet.'

I laughed. 'You know something? I haven't either since she got pregnant. Maybe her powers have deserted her.'

'The question is, has the father deserted her? Aren't you mad to know who he is, Ruth?'

'No. Yes. I don't know.'

'That's a yes.'

Just then the doorbell rang.

'There's Kevin now,' I said. 'Are we ready to go?'

'How did I let you talk me into running this bloody lunch?' She asked him, as soon as he walked into my kitchen.

'My animal magnetism and pictures of sick babies,' he said, with a grin.

She pretended annoyance, but as soon as Tracy had heard about Kevin's crusade for PAP – Parents Against Pollution – she was practically running the show. She'd immediately phoned Father Johnny, our parish priest, and persuaded him to give us the sacristy for a deluxe fund-raising lunch and had a list of other ideas.

★

Tracy's lunch was a roaring success. The sacristy was thronged with hungry, enthusiastic parents and children, who had identified with the plight of their peers just a few miles down the road.

Tracy was soon in a corner talking to a group of young mothers – probably persuading them into having a Mary Winters party in the sacristy next week. Kevin and I sat on a pew, drinking coffee.

'Is it this Sunday that the article is in the *Tribune*?' I asked.

He nodded. His head was newly shaven, and he had a tiny scar just on his hairline.

'Any new developments?'

'Nothing. Looks like this is the end of the road for PAP. At least they'll be out of debt, thanks to Tracy.'

'Maybe something will turn up.' I searched the room for the kids: Chloe, Lauren and Paddy were sitting on the floor, playing with what looked like some sheets, and Mikey was standing on a shelving unit with priest's vestments draped over him. He held a silver chalice in one hand and was dropping another down to a little boy in a red T-shirt.

Kevin had his back to this little show but Tracy had spotted it and was holding her sides, helpless with hilarity.

'Kevin, you'd better get Mikey before Father Johnny comes back and has a stroke,' I said.

Kevin turned and ran to his errant son. Mikey, as usual, thought this was part of the game and starting throwing candles, crucifixes and any other object, sacred or not, that he could find on the shelves. Father Johnny came back just as Kevin reached him.

'It's OK, Father, I'll take all the vestments home and wash them. They'll be as good as new,' Kevin told him.

'You must be joking, Kev,' said Tracy, and we fell about yet again.

12

On Saturday afternoon, Kathleen, Paddy and I were in the garden. The Claw had more or less deserted Kevin's house in favour of ours and was on Kathleen's lap. I was just about to open the brand new edition of *Hello!* when the phone rang.

'Hi, Ruth, it's India. How are you?'

'Good. You?'

'Grand. Listen, my Dublin case is finally finished. I was wondering if you'd like to go out for something to eat tomorrow night?'

I'd missed India – even if she was a Burke. 'I'd love to.'

'Brilliant. I'll book it now. I'll try for a table in Luigi's – Tim knows the manager. I'll meet you there, say, around eight? If there's any change I'll ring you back.'

'Excellent.'

'See you then, so.'

''Bye.'

I hung up and looked at Kathleen.

'India?' she said.

'I'm going out with her tomorrow night. To Luigi's, I think. I'll get a babysitter, Kathleen – I feel like I'm taking advantage of you lately.'

'It's a pleasure to mind Paddy and I'm delighted to see you going out.' Kathleen stroked the Claw, who stretched languidly. 'What will you wear? It'll have to be something nice, Luigi's is very glam.'

Mentally I rooted in my wardrobe. I hadn't bought any clothes in ages. 'I'll find something.'

I arrived at Luigi's feeling like a new woman. I'd put heated rollers in my hair and transformed it into a shimmering blonde mane of curls – I'd have got a part in *Dynasty* it was so big. I spotted India as soon as I went through the revolving doors. She was the most punctual person I knew. Sometimes I thought she was adopted, like me, and that her parents had omitted to tell her.

'Ruth, you look absolutely great,' she said, stood up and kissed me.

'I'm a great ad for being dumped,' I said, and sat down. She'd already ordered a bottle of wine and poured me a glass. 'How was Dublin?'

'I'm just delighted the case is over. I missed Alyssa so much. Sometimes I'm tempted to cut back my hours completely.'

'And just do the forty, is it?' I said.

'I'm not like that any more, not since Alyssa came along. By the way, Tim was asking for you.'

The waiter came over to take our order. He wore tight black pants and I wondered what he was doing later. He looked very young, though – he was probably doing homework after he finished at the restaurant. 'What are you having, India?'

'Oh, bruschetta, cannelloni and tiramisu, my favourites.'

'I'll have the same,' I said, and handed the menu to the waiter. I caught him scoping out my cleavage and winked at him. I felt great. Like my old self – before Gibraltar. Before Emerson.

'How's Paddy?'

I drank some wine. 'He's great. Kathleen is babysitting.'

'How's she feeling?'

I'd told India on the phone about Kathleen's joyous tidings. 'She's fine. Still no sign of a father, though. I'm beginning to think it was an immaculate conception.'

India smiled. 'How's the work search going?'

'Not bad. I've applied to all the hotels and something will come up. And the Tupperware's grand for the time being.'

'You know, there's no need for you to do that – I mean no financial need. Emerson said—'

I put my wine glass on the table and folded my arms across my chest. 'Really? There's no need, is there? I'll be the judge of that, India. And, to be quite frank, I couldn't give a fuck what Emerson says about anything.'

India examined her nails as I rooted in my bag for a cigarette, then realised I was indoors and that I'd be arrested if I smoked. I tapped the table with my fingers and gazed round the crowded restaurant. I was glad when our starters arrived.

'I'm only concerned for you, Ruth, you know that,' said India, eventually. 'If anyone knows the pressures of being a working mother I do, and I have Tim to share the job. You're on your own and it's tough.'

I knew she was speaking from the heart but ever since I'd arrived at the restaurant it was as if Emerson was sitting between us, preventing us connecting properly with each other.

'Since that case dragged on in Dublin I'm tempted to quit altogether. I missed Alyssa so much – and I don't care what anyone says, Ruth, small children need their parents.'

I was surprised by this coming from India. She'd always been the most career-driven of my friends. 'Could you work part-time?' I asked.

India shook her head. 'Even then it's a juggling game and I'm tired of living my life like that. I always admired that about you, Ruth – that you didn't give a damn about a career.'

'You have to do the thing that's right for you.'

'Is it right for you to go back to work now?'

'Absolutely. Paddy's at Montessori so I'll work part-time. I have to do it for myself, India. I won't live off Emerson's money.'

'But you're the mother of his child and it's what he wants too – for Paddy to have you twenty-four/seven.'

'It's not what I want. I love Paddy and I'll be a better mother to him if I can hold my head high.' I was dying for a fag.

'Let's get some more wine,' said India, and beckoned the child waiter.

Our main courses arrived and as the wine flowed the atmosphere at our table warmed considerably. India had given up sipping in favour of drinking – if she kept going at that rate I'd have her smoking by the end of the night.

'Let's go to the pub,' India said, as we finished our tiramisu.

I widened my eyes in mock-horror. 'The pub? What's got into you, India? Are you possessed? I hope not, because Kathleen doesn't do exorcisms.'

India hooted. 'Come on. We can go to the one near your place, Moran's – do they still have music on a Sunday night?'

'You're not serious?'

'Totally. I'm off work tomorrow and I feel like some fun. Come on, Ruth, it'll be a laugh.'

This was a big change. Normally I was the one dragging my friends to the pub.

'I'm on,' I said, and signalled Boy Waiter for the bill.

13

We arrived at Moran's in high spirits. An Abba tribute band called ABBAsolutely were thumping out 'Mamma Mia' and the crowd loved it. We stood at the bar and ordered drinks.

'Ruth, is that you?' a voice said behind me.

Kevin was with a gorgeous-looking woman. She was taller than him, with a sheet of blonde hair that reached her bum. She was very slender but with a great cleavage and I wondered if she'd had a boob job. Her makeup was so subtle it was almost invisible and she had huge brown eyes that looked great with her golden hair.

'What brings you here? I should have known you were a secret Abba fan,' he said.

'It's no secret.'

'This is Orla. This is Ruth, my neighbour.'

Orla shook hands, then looked expectantly at India.

'India – Kevin and Orla,' I said.

'I think I know you,' said India.

'I know you too. Do you shop in Dunnes?' said Kevin, smiling at India.

'I know you from the courthouse. You're the guy who's always asleep in the press gallery.'

'That'd be me, all right. You're not a judge, are you? Judges hate me. They take the falling-asleep thing personally.'

India took a huge slug of beer. I'd be rolling her home later. 'No, I'm just a plain old solicitor,' she said.

'I wouldn't say plain,' said Kevin, and India giggled like a teenager.

I could see that Orla was not impressed. 'Let's sit down,' I said gaily. 'There's a grand table over there in the corner.'

We walked across to it and India went to the bar to buy a round. Orla examined me as if I was something in a test tube. 'Kevin tells me you're in sales,' she said.

I threw Kevin a murderous look, but his expression was all wide-eyed innocence.

'That's right,' I said. 'Hardware.'

India arrived with the drinks just as ABBAsolutely launched into 'Dancing Queen'. 'I love this one,' she said, sat down next to Kevin and joined in with the chorus. Orla rolled her eyes.

'So, Orla, what do you do? Oh, Kevin mentioned it – you're a doctor, aren't you?' I said, when India stopped singing.

'A surgeon, actually.'

'That's nice,' I said, smiling sweetly.

Orla shook her blonde mane.

'She's a great one with a knife, aren't you, love?' said Kevin.

'Be careful, Kevin, you might arrive into me some

day for a little operation and God knows what I might slice off by mistake,' she replied.

We all laughed. She touched Kevin's arm lightly and whispered something into his ear. He murmured back and smiled. She didn't let go of his arm. They were the weirdest exes I'd ever seen.

'I want to sing,' declared India.

'You can't – you're not in the band,' I said.

'I'll ask them if they'll allow me. "Fernando", that's my song,' she said.

'They're taking a break now, India. Sit down,' I ordered. A drunken India was a new concept for me and I was wishing we hadn't come to the pub. Orla went to the bar for another round and India went to the loo.

'So, what do you think of her? Gorgeous, isn't she?' said Kevin, and drained his glass.

'Who? India? She's grand but a bit drunk.'

'I meant Orla. But India's cute too.'

'You look like a couple,' I said.

'Yeah, until we have to live with each other. Orla says I'm really difficult to live with and she's probably right.'

'It takes two, you know,' I said.

'She's usually right, though.'

'Do you still love her?' I couldn't believe the cheek of me, asking a question like that.

Kevin grinned at me. 'What's love? I don't know. I love being around her. I hate when she disapproves of me, which seems to be most of the time. Is that love?'

'You're asking the wrong woman, Kevin. I think love is only a word.'

'Is it a word when you say it about your kid?'

He was sharp, this guy.

Just then Orla and India arrived back.

'I met John Dixon at the bar. Do you remember him, Kev, from university?' said Orla, as she placed the tray of drinks on the table. She wore a simple black fitted dress that accentuated her long legs.

'Yeah – how's he doing?' said Kevin.

'He's just been appointed as a consultant at the Regional Hospital.'

'Good for him. Are we going to hear you sing "Fernando", then, India?'

'Don't you go encouraging her,' I said.

India held up her beer bottle. 'My Dutch courage is on the wane. I'll have to drink up.'

'I'm meeting him for dinner on Thursday night. Just to fill him in on the locality and stuff.'

Kevin twirled a beer-mat on the table. 'That's nice,' he said.

'You will be back, Babe, won't you?' she said.

Kevin nodded, but didn't look at her. 'Wednesday night.'

'I'll pick you up at the airport,' she said.

'Whose round is it anyway?' said India.

'Where are you going?' I asked Kevin.

'New York. Just for a couple of days – big story. Hey, will you mind the Claw for me?'

'Of course. Paddy and Kathleen will be delighted.'

'Ruth's mother is a clairvoyant – did I tell you that, Orla?' said Kevin.

'How nice,' said Orla. 'A psychic mum – that's something.'

The band were in full throttle again.

'I'm singing and if they won't let me I'll sue the pants off them,' said India, and got up and walked to the stage.

I stood up to follow her but Kevin caught my hand. 'Leave her. It'll be fine,' he said. I sat down and watched India talking to the members of ABBAsolutely. Then she climbed on-stage and some-body handed her a microphone. She coughed into it, and waved at the audience, coughed, smiled and waved again. Then she cleared her throat and began to sing, tentatively at first but as she approached the chorus she sounded like she was singing for her life. The crowd loved it and when she finished Kevin and I wolf-whistled.

The band asked her to do another number. By this time she had found her stage feet and began to talk to the crowd. 'This second song is for my friend Ruth, whom I love from the bottom of my heart. Ruth, I love you,' she said, and waved at me. I was mortified.

'Ruth, I'm going to sing "Waterloo" and, remember, you can survive anything because you are strong and – good – and strong.' The whole bar was gawping at me now. If she didn't hurry on and sing the bloody song I'd throw something at her.

After the longest rendition ever of 'Waterloo',

India returned, delighted with her performance. She drank a full bottle of beer in one go.

'I've got to head home, Kathleen's babysitting and—' I said.

'We'll have one more for the road. Come on, Kevin, your round. Ruth, did I ever tell you how much I love you?' slurred India.

'I have to go,' I said, and stood up. 'Nice meeting you, Orla, see you, Kevin.'

'We're leaving too – we might as well go together,' said Kevin.

Outside, the night air was still warm and India wanted to conduct a sing-song as we walked up O'Connell Avenue. Orla and Kevin walked ahead, holding hands. What weird kind of separation was that?

Just as we turned the corner into our street Derek pulled up in his cab. I put India into it and gave Derek her address. India rolled down the window, told me again how much she loved me and waved like she was leaving Albert Square for ever as the car pulled away.

I walked with Kevin and Orla to my house and said goodnight to them.

All was quiet and Kathleen was asleep on the sofa. I didn't turn on the light and went straight to the window – my nosy-neighbour impulse was too hard to resist. Orla had her car keys in one hand and the other lay on Kevin's shoulder. They were talking to each other in low voices. She put the keys in the car door. He put both arms round her waist and nuzzled her neck. She turned to him and they started to kiss. I heard the car keys drop on the ground. Kevin picked them up, then caught Orla's hand and pulled her behind him up the garden path. They were giggling.

I stood in my dark living room, feeling suddenly cold and empty. Kevin was such a nice guy and she was using him. I mean, she had a date with some hot-shot consultant on Thursday and now she was having a little bit of her ex as well. Some people wanted it all. Emerson wanted it all, but not with me. Kathleen wanted it all again, but hadn't wanted me. India had it all, but now didn't want some of it. Ellen had it all in Australia, but didn't have her friends. I wished life was simple. I wished I was the Claw.

14

That week my work prospects improved considerably. On Wednesday, the day Kevin was due home from America, I was in the kitchen, having a late breakfast with Paddy and the Claw, when the phone rang.

'Hi, is that you, Ruth? This is Susie from Drury's.'

I used to work in Drury's and Susie and I had been friends.

'Hi, Susie, how are you? How's the bump?' she was pregnant with her first baby.

'That's why I'm ringing you. We'd found someone to fill in for me while I go on maternity leave and she rang this morning to say she's found a permanent position.'

I held my breath. I'd love nothing better than my old job back and it'd mean I could kiss goodbye to Mary Winters.

'I remembered your phone call and I rooted out your CV. Interested?'

'Definitely. Thanks a million for thinking of me,' I said.

'Don't mention it. It's easier for me that you know the ropes already. You'll be starting in a couple of weeks. Monday to Friday – 9 to 1. Will that be OK? You'll have to organise babysitters and things.'

'Perfect. I'm delighted.'

'Great. I'll give you a ring next week with all the details. I'd better go – I need to go to the loo again. Nobody told me about that part of being pregnant. 'Bye, Ruth.'

I hung up, then bent down and picked up Paddy, who was playing on the floor with the Claw, and kissed his cheek. 'Mum's got herself a job,' I said, and twirled round the kitchen with him in my arms.

Paddy's Mickey Mouse hat fell on to the floor. 'Fuck,' he said, and squirmed out of my arms to rescue it.

I bit my tongue – all my child development books said I should ignore bad language. The doorbell rang and we went to answer it.

Kevin was there, grinning, with Mikey in his arms and a thrill raced through me.

'We came for the Claw and an espresso from that magic machine of yours,' he said. Mikey gave me an angelic smile – he knew how to disarm his victims.

'Come in! How was New York?'

'Great,' he said.

'You won't believe this but I just got a job,' I said, as I headed towards the kitchen. 'Let the guys go out on the swings – we'll be able to see them from here.'

I filled the coffee machine while Kevin let the boys out with strict instructions to be good. Then he stroked the Claw, who was asleep on the worktop.

The cat opened his eyes, took one look at Kevin and stalked off into the living room.

'Are you giving up Mary Winters? And there I was, hoping for a private viewing of all your – um – hardware. That's the least you could have done for your male friends.'

I threw a tea-towel at him. 'Cheeky,' I said, and poured coffee into two espresso cups. 'My old job, at Drury's – there's a temporary position and they've offered it to me.'

Kevin sipped the coffee. 'When do you start?'

'A couple of weeks, I think. They'll let me know. How was New York?'

Kevin ran a hand over his shaved head. 'I worked my ass off. I had to interview these millionaire business people for a trade magazine – incredibly boring – then write up the copy in my hotel room.'

I was struck by how cute he looked in his trademark combats and a red T-shirt.

'What are you looking at? Is my face dirty?' he said.

I laughed to hide my embarrassment.

'Anyway, how was India last Monday? Bet she'd a sore head,' he said.

'She's still not recovered and she refuses to believe she sang with the band.'

'Did you tell her she declared her love for you?' said Kevin.

'I spared her the embarrassing details.'

'Good-looking, great with a vibrator *and* considerate to her friends.'

'You're looking for a thump in the head,' I said, and mock-punched his face. He gave me Mikey's angelic smile.

'So, how was your night?' I asked.

'You were there, Ruth. You know how my night was.'

I examined the chipped varnish on my nails. 'Did Orla enjoy herself?' I cursed myself for that one: it sounded like I was asking if she'd had a good ride.

'Apparently so. We . . . She came in for coffee afterwards.'

'That must have been nice.'

Kevin raised an eyebrow. 'It was,' he said.

'I mean, it's good that both of you are at a stage where . . . you know . . . you can have coffee together.'

He smiled at me. 'Sometimes we have sex. It just happens. She's gorgeous and I can't resist. I'm a sucker for a pretty face.'

'She obviously still has feelings for you,' I said.

'Sexual ones, if I know Orla. But it cuts both ways . . .'

The Claw sauntered back into the kitchen and rubbed himself against my legs. Kevin scooped him up into his arms. 'Gotta go – loads of articles to write that should have been in yesterday,' he said, and went to the back door to call Mikey. 'Hey, I got you a present – it's a Johnny Cash T-shirt,' he said, as he, Mikey and the Claw walked to the front door.

'Brilliant,' I said to his back, as they walked down the path. I wondered what he'd brought home for Orla.

15

And then Grandma Burke died. After Gibraltar I'd
kept away from the Burkes – except India – for the
best part of two months. Sure the phone calls kept
coming and the odd dozen free-range eggs appeared
on my doorstep but, by and large, I had little to do
with them. Everything was hunky-dory as long as
they were reassured that Paddy and I were fine –
and, yes, I did know they loved me and Paddy, and
I agreed that we were still family no matter what.

Grandma Burke was a fine woman and I'd always
liked her. India rang to tell me about her death.

'Poor Grandma,' I said, trying to convince
myself that Emerson wouldn't come home for his
grandmother's funeral. 'I'm so sorry.'

'No, it's fine – really. She had a great life,' India
said tearfully.

I was disgusted to find I was thinking about myself
when my friend had lost her beloved granny. So what
if Emerson came home? I didn't care. Well, not
much.

'She died last night?' I said.

'It seems that way. Dad found her – he was on his
way into town this morning with some vegetables for

French's restaurant. When he called and she didn't answer the door he thought she might be ill so he let himself in – he had a key – and Dad found her with Florence, her big tabby, asleep on her lap. She was in her reclining chair – footrest up, TV on, a cup of coffee and her cigarettes on the table beside her. She must have been settling down for a night in front of the telly—' India began to cry.

I didn't interrupt for a while. 'You OK, Ind?' I said eventually.

'I'm sorry, Ruth – crying like a baby when it's the most natural thing in the world for a ninety-year-old woman to die, and there you are dealing with a lot more difficult stuff . . .' Her voice rose as she spoke.

'Look,' I said, 'she was your granny and you loved her and you'll miss her and it's perfectly normal to be upset.'

India blew her nose. 'My brother is an idiot.'

'I could have told you that.'

'No, really – I know I've said it before but, Ruth, we all think he needs a thundering great kick in the arse for what he did. Little fucker.'

Which made me laugh. I'd known India since I was seventeen and I'd never before heard her use two rude words so close together. She blew her nose again. 'No, really, Ruth. I mean it.'

'I know you do, love, and I appreciate it. Anyway, what are the funeral arrangements?'

'Tomorrow night at eight from Crosby's funeral home to the Holy Rosary Church. Will you be able to make it, do you think?'

'Of course,' I said, heart plummeting. Anyway, that selfish bastard was probably still too wrapped up with his movie and his new love life to bother attending his grandmother's funeral.

'I'll call Kathleen and get her to babysit. It'll be lovely to see everyone,' I said, warming to the idea of a Burke family gathering minus Emerson.

India didn't reply and the silence told me everything I didn't want to hear before she opened her mouth. 'Emerson is coming home,' she said.

'Shit.'

'I know – I rang as soon as I heard and sure he's a bastard but I suppose he wants to come home and she was his grandma as well.'

'It's OK, India,' I said, but I didn't mean it. Now what was I going to do? I had to go to that funeral and I didn't want to have to deal with Emerson. All I needed now was to hear that Skinny Arse Rodriguez was coming as well.

'And it gets worse,' India said. 'Selma is coming with him.'

There it was. The nightmare was complete. India was still talking and I was tuning in and out of what she was saying about Emerson and work and staying in the Clarion because, well, really, he couldn't expect to stay with his family when he was bringing that floozy home, could he? That word took my attention. 'Floozy?' I repeated. 'I didn't think anybody used that word any more.'

'Well,' India said, 'that's what Tim called her and I know it's a bit old-fashioned but it seems to fit her.'

'Floozy Rodriguez? It's the perfect name for her.'

'Oh, my God! Every time I see her I'll be thinking about it. How am I going to keep a straight face?'

Laughter bubbled in my chest and I knew I was a hair's breadth from crying, but still I laughed until my stomach hurt. Fuck him, I thought, as I bent double holding the telephone receiver. I don't care who he brings home.

I promised India I'd see her at Grandma's funeral and thanked her for telling me about Emerson, then hung up and tried to think. It would be good for Paddy, I told myself, as I started to clean the kitchen. None of this was his fault but he had to live with the consequences of what had happened. I couldn't ruin his life just because his father was a bollocks. I'd have to be reasonable and Grandma Burke's funeral would be a start. One thing was for sure, Paddy adored his daddy and would be delighted to see him in person, not just on video.

Which was how I told Tracy that Emerson was coming home twenty minutes later when she popped in for coffee.

'What?' she said.

'No, really, Tracy. It'll be good for Paddy – he hasn't seen Emerson properly in months and this is a golden opportunity.'

'He's bringing that bitch here?' Tracy said, ignoring my mature attitude.

'Tracy, look—'

'Ruth, answer my question.'

'Yes.'

'The nerve of him. His poor grandmother must be turning in her grave. God rest her soul.'

'Grandma Burke won't be in her grave until the day after tomorrow. That's the problem.'

'Oh, very smart! He has no respect, that fella – neither for the living nor the dead. Are you still smoking? I left my cigarettes at home.'

'No, I'm off them,' I said. 'Mind you, I'm sorry now I quit – I didn't see this coming.'

'Two minutes,' Tracy said. 'Stick on the coffee machine and I'll run in home for the fags.'

I filled it and noticed the manila folder that contained the meagre information I had on my father. I'd brought it downstairs that morning. Now that I had a job and my life was some way back on track my next project was to look for him. It'd beat the hell out of thinking of Emerson and our destroyed marriage. Just as the coffee brewed, Tracy arrived back with her cigarettes. We lit up.

'What's that?' she asked, taking a deep drag from her cigarette and pointing at the folder.

'That, my dear, is the complete and entire dossier on the man who fathered me.'

Tracy picked up the photograph. 'Is that Kathleen? God, she was lovely – but very young-looking. She doesn't look a lot older than my twins. Is that boy your father?'

'Yeah, he is. Though how I'll ever find him when all I have is a thirty-year-old photograph and the name Junior Kennedy . . .'

'Can Kathleen help?'

'She did. This is it.'

'Can't she use her psychic powers?'

I sighed. 'I don't know – maybe they've dried up since she got pregnant, you know, like oestrogen.'

Tracy put the photo on the table. 'I've a feeling you'll find him.'

'Maybe you're getting Kathleen's powers.'

'Anyway, forget that for a minute – I'm going to the funeral with you.'

'No.'

Tracy held up her hand. 'Don't start with me. I'm going. When is it?'

'Tomorrow, eight, from Crosby's to the Holy Rosary. But, Trace—'

'I'm going and that's all about it. Derek'll just have to take a couple of hours off if he's working. You can't go to that funeral by yourself.'

'India'll be there and all the Burkes and – except for Emerson – they all love me.'

'It makes no difference. India won't be able to look after you – she'll be too upset with her granny dead. Jesus, when my granny died I cried for a fortnight.'

'I'll be fine, really, Tracy.'

She sat back in her seat. 'Don't bother arguing with me. I'm going and you can't stop me. Get used to the idea.'

We smoked and drank coffee in silence for a few seconds. I was touched by Tracy's offer – even if I was a bit worried about what she might do at the funeral. 'Don't say anything to Emerson,' I said.

She blinked. 'What kind of person do you think I am?'

'I know exactly what kind of person you are, Tracy Walsh. Keep your gob shut in the dead-house, I'm warning you.'

She tutted loudly. 'I'd love to tell that cheating bastard what I think of him.'

'Well, write him a letter.'

'Oh, don't worry, I won't say anything at the funeral but I can't believe he's bringing that wagon here.'

I shrugged. 'It's true, I'm afraid. Floozy Rodriguez is coming to Limerick.'

Tracy burst out laughing. 'Sounds like a porn movie.'

'That'd be accurate all right,' I said. She held the cigarette packet towards me and I took one. 'Chain-smoking,' I said, and lit it.

Tracy nodded. 'Nothing like it.'

'I think you only want to come to the funeral because you're dying to get a good look at Floozy Rodriguez.'

'Damn straight,' Tracy said. 'But more important than that, I want her to get a good look at you.'

I wasn't sure what she meant by that until the next morning. She arrived at my door at eleven o'clock with an armful of dresses in dry-cleaner's polythene and three-year-old Chloe welded to her. 'If you don't help me remove this toddler from my leg, I swear to God I'm going to have it amputated.'

Chloe's arms were wrapped round her mother's slender thigh and snot was smeared with Weetabix all over her oval, fairy-like face. Her dark brown hair swung as Tracy tried to walk.

'Hey, Chloe,' I said. Chloe was having none of it. 'What's wrong with her?'

'She was having a shave in the bathroom with Derek's razor – see, she cut her chin – and she's throwing a tantrum cos I took the razor away from her.'

Chloe made a snorting noise and buried her face in Tracy's jeans. At that moment Paddy appeared. 'Hi, Chloe!' he shouted.

Chloe lifted her head.

'Chocolate?' I said.

Paddy whooped, Chloe leaped free of her mother, and they charged ahead of me into the kitchen. I rooted out two KitKats, opened the back door and they took off up the garden.

'Thanks be to the Holy Mother of God,' Tracy said, dumping her dresses on a kitchen chair. 'I was ready to murder that child.'

'What are those?' I asked.

Tracy opened her mouth to answer but the doorbell rang.

'Hold on.' I hurried to answer it.

Kevin and Mikey were on the doorstep.

'I hope you're not busy – Mikey was torturing me to bring him to Paddy's house, so I said we'd just call for a minute,' Kevin said.

'No problem. Come in,' I said, pointing towards the kitchen. 'Tracy's here and I have to find out something important.'

They followed me to the kitchen and I found a KitKat for Mikey, then dispatched him to join Chloe and Paddy.

'Nothing nice left for us – sorry,' I said, pouring Kevin and myself some coffee. Tracy was installed at the table with a mug and a cigarette. I lit another and sat down beside her.

'I thought you'd quit,' Kevin said.

'Shut up, Kevin,' Tracy said. 'She's having a traumatic time.'

Kevin put milk and sugar into his coffee and sat opposite us. 'I know that but she told me she'd quit.'

'Yeah, well, it's even more traumatic at the moment and she unquit – is that all right with you?'

Kevin raised his hands in surrender. 'Stop killing me, Tracy.' Then he fiddled with the manila folder, which fell open. He picked up the photograph and I thought how strange it was that people are so attracted to pictures of strangers.

He looked up at me in surprise. 'Where did you get a photograph of Gary Kennedy when he was young fellow?'

'That's Ruth's natural father,' said Tracy.

'No way!' he said, and turned over the photograph.

'Yeah,' she continued. 'She's trying to trace him, aren't you, Ruth?'

I nodded.

'I'll tell you something,' Kevin said. 'He's the image of Gary Kennedy. Do you know his name?'

'Junior Kennedy.'

'Right surname anyway. Anything else?'

'He was eighteen. A Libra. He loved rugby, Pink Floyd and Steve Heighway crisps,' I said.

'Not a lot to go on.'

I shrugged. 'She was sixteen when they had their bit of a fling – I'd say the information is standard for her age.'

'I can't get over how much he looks like Gary Kennedy.'

'Isn't that the name of a town in Tipperary?' I said.

'Yeah, and the up-and-coming big noise in the People's Party – don't you read the papers?' he said.

'I only read what you write, Kevin,' I said, with mock-sweetness.

'Flirt,' he responded.

'Are you saying that Ruth's father is this politician guy?' Tracy said, eyes wide.

Kevin shrugged. 'I'm not saying anything, except he looks a lot like him. Can I take the photograph?'

'Just don't lose it.'

'See?' Tracy said. 'I told you you'd find him.'

I rolled my eyes. 'Yeah, right – it'll be as easy as that.'

'You never know – you're due a break. Speaking of breaks, wait until you see the dresses I have for you. You'll knock 'em dead at the funeral.'

'Dresses?' I said.

'Funeral?' Kevin said.

Tracy stood up. 'This one will fit you, I think. Sandra's like you – all bloody bust – and see, very nice neck, cut just a bit low so you'd get away with it at a funeral, but still showing off your features to their best advantage. If you know what I mean.'

'I'm not wearing a dress,' I said. 'I was thinking of my black suit. But thanks anyway, Tracy, I appreciate it.'

Tracy didn't look perturbed. 'That suit is fine but this isn't a job interview. It's a funeral.'

'Who the hell died?' Kevin asked.

'I know it's a funeral,' I said, 'which is why I'm not wearing a low-cut dress.'

'Selma the Slapper will be there,' Tracy said, holding up the cutest black dress I'd seen in a while.

'Jesus!' Kevin said. 'Did your husband die?'

Tracy and I guffawed.

'Not yet.' Tracy arched one eyebrow.

'Sorry, Kev,' I said, 'he didn't, but his grandmother did and he's coming home for the funeral and bringing that – that woman with him.'

Kevin drank his entire cup of coffee in one go. 'I'm confused.'

'Me too,' I said.

Tracy cleared her throat. 'If I could have your attention, ladies and gentlemen, in my left hand is the short black dress with the scooped neck and in my right is a slightly longer black dress with a slightly higher neck. Now that I look at them I'm disqualifying the second dress. What do you think, Kev?'

'For Ruth?' Kevin said.

Tracy nodded.

'My vote is for that sexy short one.'

'What a surprise,' I said, stubbing out my cigarette and standing up to look at the children in the
garden. All seemed civilised.

'Try it on, Ruth,' Tracy said.

I shook my head. 'I'm wearing the suit.'

'I know, but put it on to humour me.'

'Go on, Ruth,' Kevin said. 'Brighten up a dirty
old man's morning.'

I grabbed the dress from Tracy's outstretched hand.
At any other time I'd have been dying to wear it.

'Please,' Tracy said, hands joined as if she was
praying.

Kevin grinned and scratched his chin.

'OK,' I said. 'Keep an eye on the kids.'

I ran up the stairs to my bedroom. I'd put it on
and they'd see it really wasn't suitable. Then maybe
they'd get off my case. I threw off my T-shirt and
jeans, then slipped the dress over my head. As soon
as I pulled up the zip I could feel that it fitted
perfectly. When you're small, like me, with a skinny
ass and a double-D bust hardly anything fits you
properly – but that black dress felt as if it had been
made for me. It was made of some soft fabric that
moulded itself to my breasts showing just a hint of
cleavage, then nipped in at my waist, back out at
my hips, slid over my thighs and ended just above
the knee. I felt like Cinderella when I admired myself
in the mirror.

I rooted in the bottom of the wardrobe for my
strappy black stiletto sandals and tottered down the
stairs. As soon as I opened the kitchen door Kevin

gave a long, low whistle. 'You look unbelievable,' he said.

Maybe I wasn't an ugly old hag after all.

Tracy was beaming at me. 'That dress is perfect on you,' she said.

'It's fabulous and I really like it, Trace, but I don't think I should wear it to Grandma Burke's funeral – what would she think?'

'Well, first off, Ruth, she's dead, and second, if she was any kind of a sensible woman she'll be floating around at that funeral laughing at her grandson and thinking what an idiot he was to throw away a woman like you. You're gorgeous.'

Kevin was sitting with his chin in his hands, gazing up at me. 'You have to wear it,' he said.

Why didn't I want to wear this amazing dress? It was a bit over the top – that was true – but so what? I loved it and over-the-top had never stopped me in the past. But something inside me had taken such a beating that I found it hard to believe I wasn't the most repulsive creature on the planet. Yet Tracy was telling me I was gorgeous and Kevin was whistling . . . 'Fuck it. I'll wear it.'

16

I needn't have bothered my head trying to figure out how to look my best for the funeral: Tracy had it all planned. Hairdresser, makeup, babysitter, the works. There was no arguing with the woman so I decided to go with the flow. As she was driving me from the hairdresser to my four o'clock makeover I realised that the tiny woman in the car beside me was as organised and determined as any military commander.

'OK,' she said, pulling into the bus stop outside Brown Thomas. 'Sarah is expecting you at the Mac counter. It should take about an hour and a half. I'll see you here at half five. OK?'

I nodded, glad to be taken in hand. I made my way to the Mac counter and the girls sat me down and began their work, chatting as they cleansed and toned and concealed and rubbed and brushed and blended.

When I was finished I waited outside for Tracy. A laughing Irish couple with a squealing Chinese toddler swinging in the air between them almost knocked me over. 'I'm sorry,' the father said, as his small girl tugged at his hand and shouted for her daddy to pick her up. I assured him there was no harm done and watched as they continued on their way. It was obvious they loved their little girl – and that she was adopted.

I'd always known I was adopted, and when I was young it'd never been a problem. I adored my parents and they adored me. I was their only child. They'd been almost forty when I arrived and I was probably one of the luckiest little girls on the planet because they lavished so much love and care on me as I grew up.

Two months after my twenty-first birthday, Mum discovered that she had stomach cancer. It was quite advanced and she died within six months of diagnosis. Dad and I were distraught. But I thought I'd never recover when he died too, of a heart-attack, a month shy of my twenty-second birthday. It wasn't a great year.

After Mum and Dad died I remembered that the woman who'd given me away was somewhere in the world. But I didn't do anything about it. Just thought about it occasionally and determined that if I ever had kids I'd make sure they had two parents. Great job I'd done so far.

Paddy's birth made me wonder more about my natural parents but I still didn't do anything until I was contacted by the adoption agency and informed that my birth-mother would love to see me. That was a bit of a shock. Paddy was only a few months old and at first I wasn't sure I wanted to meet her.

Up to then I wouldn't have said I was angry with

her. After all, if she hadn't given me up I'd never have known Mum and Dad, which I wouldn't have missed for the world. Still, why did she do it? What was wrong with me that she felt she couldn't keep me?

When I eventually met Kathleen and discovered that she was all alone and only sixteen when I was born I felt a bit better. And I was happy with the relationship she and I were developing. She was never going to take Mum's place in my life but she was a good, warm person and I was glad to have her around. Especially for Paddy.

Mind you, the fact that Paddy was about to have an uncle or aunt who was going to be at least three years younger than him was not sitting well with me. Families were complicated, mothers, fathers, children, grandparents, aunts, uncles, cousins and so on. As I waited for Tracy, afraid that she'd forgotten me, I wondered again about the father of Kathleen's baby. Who the hell was he? She still hadn't volunteered that information and I'd not managed to get up the nerve to ask.

In reality I knew little about Kathleen. She and I had been reunited for less than two years. I knew she'd lived in England for more than twenty-five years and that she'd had some success as a clairvoyant. She'd alluded once or twice to working for the police and doing a bit of TV but I hadn't asked much and she hadn't elaborated.

Now, though, I really wanted to know the identity of the father of her baby – my brother or sister.

I wasn't sure why but I thought it might have something to do with my desire to find my own father.

I thought about Paddy and Emerson and for all that I hated my bastard of a husband I could see how much Paddy loved him. And how much he loved Paddy. A car horn made me jump.

'Wake up, gorgeous!' a man shouted.

Kevin.

'Where's Tracy?' I said, sitting into his battered Volvo.

Kevin pulled out into the rush-hour traffic. 'Derek had to do something so she took Mikey and sent me.'

'Thanks, Kev.'

'Not a problem.'

'So? What do you think?'

Kevin looked sideways at me. 'You look nice. But I think makeup is more to do with women than men because, to be honest, Ruth, you look pretty much the same as you always do.'

'Gee, thanks. A wasted hour and a half.'

'No, you fool – I mean you always look pretty good to me.'

I rubbed the top of Kevin's freshly shaved head – it felt like suede. 'Awwww! You're the best neighbour.'

Kevin grinned. 'On the other hand, the dress you had on this morning . . .'

I punched his arm. 'Lecherous pig.'

'I'm a martyr to my hormones. I have a feature to write for the *Tribune* and I'm planning something on testosterone. What do you think?'

'You couldn't do something normal, like holidays in Mallorca, I suppose?'

'Not my style.' Kevin stopped in front of my house.

'Thanks a million for collecting me,' I said, climbing out of the car. 'Wish me luck.'

'You don't need it, but good luck anyway.'

When I let myself in the house was in silence. Kathleen had Paddy and she'd said she'd probably take him to her place for a while. I nuked myself a frozen chicken curry and ate it at the kitchen table as if it was a real meal. Every mouthful made me feel mildly sick but I was pretty sure that was nerves, not salmonella.

After I'd eaten I watched a cookery programme and the news – checking my watch every two minutes. Eventually it was seven o'clock and I went upstairs to dress. Holy God! I looked terrific! A few minutes later Tracy arrived. 'Shit girl, you look like a million dollars.'

'You're not too shabby yourself, Mata Hari. I see you're wearing chicken fillets,' I said, surveying the sophisticated woman standing in my hallway.

'They're only the cheap ones and you needn't think I've changed my mind about the boob job.'

She was wearing a short fitted black jacket, a white camisole (nicely filled out, courtesy of the chicken fillets) and baggy black trousers. She'd gathered her sleek hair into a bun at the nape of her neck and applied just enough makeup to accentuate her beautiful eyes and perfect features.

'You're pencilled out, as my mother used to say,' I said.

'That's sort of what Derek said as well, but it was a bit ruder and included, "Hurry up and come home from that fucking funeral."'

'What a romantic,' I said, grabbing my coat. 'Will we go?'

We stepped out into the warm June evening.

'Which car?' I said.

'Yours.'

I started the engine and turned in the direction of town and Crosby's funeral home. 'Look at us! We're gorgeous! Pity it's only a funeral.'

My heart was playing a samba in my chest and I wished I was anywhere except on my way to meet my treacherous husband and his lover.

17

Crosby's funeral home was packed with sympathisers when Tracy and I arrived. We joined the long line of people and I wondered why the hell had I come. Surely I could have made some excuse. The flu. A sprained ankle. Chicken-pox. Something. Anything that would have prevented me ending up in a beauty-board panelled funeral parlour with my recently made awkward in-laws, my cheating husband and his mistress.

I'd seek out Emerson's father, Joe, and aunt, Deirdre. Offer my condolences, have a quick prayer for Grandma, then make my escape. At the last leg of the journey – the passing through the double doors into the inner sanctum of the funeral home where the coffin was displayed – Tracy gave my arm a squeeze. 'Just do it,' she whispered, as we were swept in with the crowd.

Grandma Burke was lying in state in an oak coffin with bright brassy handles. It was lined with sumptuous silk and I knew immediately that Auntie Deirdre had picked it out. If poor old Joe had made the choice Grandma would probably have been squashed into an ecologically friendly cardboard box.

I paused in front of the coffin. She looked great. Her white hair was neatly permed and her long fingers were clasped together as if she was smuggling her cigarettes into the hereafter. I felt simultaneously sad and glad – sad that she was dead but glad that she looked serene and well finished with her life.

Where was Joe? Maybe I'd get away with just sympathising with him. Surely that was all anybody could expect of me, under the circumstances. I wished the crowd would move so that I could see him. But then again if it did maybe I'd also see Emerson, and I didn't think I was up to that.

Panic rose in my chest. Why had I come? Oh, my God, I wasn't ready for this – it was only three months since everything had fallen apart. I began to sweat. All of a sudden, over the hum of voices, I heard a high-pitched wail. 'Oh, Mama! Mama!' a woman shrieked. Only one person could have had an accent like that at a funeral in Limerick.

I glanced at Tracy and nodded in answer to the question in her eyes. The sound of loud weeping filled the room. The sympathisers speeded up in their condolences and the crying became louder.

I stayed beside the coffin, trying to figure out what to do. As the crowd thinned I saw Emerson's un-mistakable back and felt a sharp pain in my stomach.

Suddenly, I was wrapped in an embrace. 'Oh, Ruthie! You're here! You're totally great, do you know that? The best friend in the world.'

India's face was pale and tear-stained but she was her usual tall, elegant, beautiful self. Her hair was tied back and she wore a black linen coat and calf-length skirt.

'I can't come to the burial in the morning,' I said. 'I'm starting back at work in Drury's.'

'Don't worry – you were great to come this evening.' India glanced at her grandmother's body and smiled. 'She looks good, doesn't she?' she said.

'Terrific.'

'Peaceful,' India said, and patted a stray strand of Grandma's hair into place.

'Look, Ind—' I began.

'Ruth!'

'Oh, my God! It's Ruth!'

Shit! Saffron and Venus. My twenty-two-year-old sisters-in-law. Before I could do another thing they were hugging and kissing me. They were the least similar twins I'd ever seen. Saffron was tall and dark and looked a lot like India, while Venus was shorter, and blonde like Emerson. Now it dawned on me that Paddy took after his auntie Venus even more than his dad. At least that was something.

Saffron and Venus were physically different but their personalities were alike. They were both studying fashion design in London.

'Oh, my God, Ruth! It's *sooooo* good to see you,' Saffron said.

'Yes, it is,' Venus said. 'Is Paddy here? Oh, I can't wait to see him!'

India stepped away from the coffin to have a word with her husband, and the twins attached themselves to my arms. There was no sign of Tracy.

'We hate her,' Venus whispered, loud enough for Saffron to hear.

'Bitch,' Saffron agreed. 'Did you hear her crying? What was that about, for goodness' sake?'

'Always has to be the centre of attention,' Venus said, and her sister nodded.

I had a sneaky look at Emerson. His head was bent and he was talking. I couldn't see Selma. Oh, why had I come? Selma had stopped wailing. Instead she was making a noise that sounded like a fridge humming.

'You look fabulous,' Venus said.

'Totally,' Saffron agreed. 'Is that dress Armani?'

I hadn't thought to inspect the label but I was saved from having to answer by India, who appeared again with her mother in tow.

Ann Burke was still a beautiful woman, though she had to be sixty: all that *t'ai chi* and organic food was paying off. She hugged me and kissed both of my cheeks. 'You're so good to come,' she said.

'I liked Grandma,' I said.

'Still. How's Paddy?'

'Great.'

'Will you bring him out to see us some day? We just bought two foals – he'd have a great time with them.'

'He'd love that,' I said. 'Listen, Ann, I need to get home to him. Is that OK, do you think?'

She took my hand and led me through the crowd to where her husband was discussing something animatedly with his sister. Deirdre was about the same age as Ann but she was processed and finished to look like a reproduction thirty-year-old. She shook hands with me in her limp way, and Joe gave me a hug. 'It's great to see you! You look bloody great! How's that grandson of mine? Hah?'

'It's great to see you, Joe,' I said, and I meant it. 'I'm so sorry about Grandma.'

'She had a good life,' Joe said, 'and she died with her boots on, so to speak. Coffee, fags, TV and her cat.'

'She died happy,' I said.

Joe's eyes misted. He was well into his sixties but still handsome in that rugged, weathered, Robert Redford way. I'd always hoped that Emerson would wear as well as his father. Now I hoped his hair fell out and he wrinkled like a prune, the sooner the better.

'I just came by to sympathise,' I said, 'but I must get home to Paddy now so I'll head away. I'll call, I promise.'

'Come out to Ogonnolloe soon,' Joe said. 'Any time at all, Ruth – you know you're more than welcome.'

'I know,' I said, and fled. I still couldn't see Tracy but I didn't care any more. I'd hide outside until she emerged.

I made it through the double doors into the corridor and the exit was in my sights when I felt a hand on my shoulder. 'Ruth?'

I turned. 'Hello, Emerson. I'm sorry about Grandma Burke – didn't get a chance to speak with you inside but now I need to get back to Paddy.'

'Thanks for coming,' he said. His face was tired and there was a couple of day's stubble on his chin but he looked pretty much the same as he'd always looked. Like my husband.

'No problem,' I said.

'Can I see Paddy?'

I took a deep breath. 'Sure. Of course. He'll be delighted.'

'The burial is tomorrow and I have to get back first thing the day after. But I was thinking that everything will be finished by two o'clockish, so could I pick him up in the afternoon?'

'What time?'

'Three? I'll have to ring you to confirm – is that all right?'

'Great,' I said, anxious to get away from him as the hurt floated free inside me. 'See you then.'

I walked towards the door.

'One thing, Ruth.'

I looked round.

'Please answer the phone.' Emerson said, but he was smiling and I couldn't help smiling back at him.

Suddenly a loud wail erupted in the inner sanctum and Tracy careered through the open doors. 'Fucking lunatic!' she said, hurrying past Emerson without noticing him. I pointed. She looked. 'Oh, hello,' she said frostily.

'Hi, Tracy,' Emerson said. 'How's Derek?'

'Fine.'

'The kids?'

'Fine.'

'How did Munster do in the Heineken Cup?'

'Not great,' Tracy said, before she could stop herself. There was another loud wail.

'I'd better go,' Emerson said.

'Yeah, you'd better,' Tracy said. 'She'll have her out of the coffin in a minute if someone doesn't calm her down.'

Emerson looked at me for a few seconds, then waved and disappeared back into the funeral home.

'Did you do something?' I said, as we hurried back through the balmy evening to my car.

Tracy shrugged.

'Tracy?' I said.

She tutted. 'I didn't say one word about her being the biggest slapper I ever heard of.'

'So what did you say?'

Tracy blew out her breath. 'OK. I told her I was a clairvoyant and that her mother was there and she was speaking to me and that she was with Grandma Burke helping her into the next life.'

'Jesus,' I muttered, but I couldn't help sniggering. We sat into my car. 'Is that it?' I said.

Tracy strapped herself into her seat. 'Well, most of it. The only other thing I said was that her mother was in the coffin too.'

'You fucking headcase! And she believed you?'

'Obviously. She was over at Grandma poking and pulling and everything. They were trying to stop her, which was what made her start bawling again I'd say.'

'Bitch.'

'Shag off, Ruth – she deserved it. I'll tell you something for nothing – he has his work cut out for him with that one. Now, hurry up and drive me home. I have a hot man waiting for me and I want to get there before he dozes off in front of the snooker.'

18

Grandma Burke's funeral was at eleven and I had work from twelve to four. Susie had asked me to come in so that she could show me the ropes before she headed off on maternity leave. I was nervous about the job – it'd been a while since I'd worked there – but when I compared that to how I felt about having to see Emerson alone, there was no contest. I was hoping that, with a bit of luck, Emerson would have come and gone by the time I got home. I left Paddy with Kathleen and set off for Drury's. Susie was a picture of pregnant serenity behind the big reception desk in the foyer of the hotel. 'Ruthie!' she squealed, when I arrived. 'Oh, my God! It's great to see you. You look incredible,' she said.

'And you're like an ad for pregnancy, Susie.'

'Thanks, love, but I know a lie when I hear one. I can't wait to be on maternity leave. I'm going to take to the sofa and not budge until this little lady arrives.'

'It's a girl?'

Susie nodded. 'How are your little boy and that hunky husband of yours?'

'Well, Paddy's fine – he's three now – but Emerson . . . well, we're not together any more.'

Susie paled and she covered her mouth with her hand. 'I'm so sorry. Oh, my God, Ruth, I didn't know. How awful for you. I'm really, really sorry.'

I gave her my most dazzling smile. 'Don't be – it's for the best. These things happen.'

A single tear travelled down Susie's cheek and she searched my face with her huge blue eyes.

'I promise you, Susie, I've never been better.'

She took my hand and gave it a squeeze. 'You're the bravest person . . .'

I wanted to scream, vault over the reception desk and go home to Paddy but I couldn't face selling sex aids so I had to stick it out. Anyway, it was probably a miracle that something like this hadn't happened sooner. 'So!' I said, ignoring the sympathy on Susie's face. 'Let's get going. You have a lot to show me.'

'Will we start with the new switchboard?'

'Great stuff,' I said, glad to be moving away from Pity Central, 'and don't forget that you have to fill me in on all the gossip before I go home today.'

As I listened to Susie, I couldn't help thinking that Emerson was on his way to my house – our house – to pick up Paddy. Would he have *her* with him? Where would they go? Would he take Paddy to McDonald's? I didn't think that was Emerson's style. But then again where does a dad take a small boy when he's trying to have a visit with him?

The thought of it all made me feel tearful but I wasn't going down that road. Just as I was going on a coffee break Kevin called in unexpectedly. 'That's excellent timing on my part – I'll pay for the coffee if I can have your wonderful company for a while,' he said.

'Throw in a Danish and I'm yours,' I said, and led him to the small hotel coffee shop. We ordered coffee and pastries, and took them into the sunny conservatory.

'How's it going?' Kevin said, settling himself in a wicker chair.

'The work or the funeral?'

'Both.' He examined me over the rim of his cup.

Suddenly I knew then the reason for his surprise visit. 'You found him, didn't you?'

He nodded, then picked up his Danish and bit into its flaky crust.

'And? Tell me! Is it him? That Gary Kennedy guy?'

Kevin nodded again. 'I checked out the photo and found another of him at the same age playing rugby for Blackrock College. Definitely him, Ruth. I'm sorry.'

I stirred my coffee. 'Commiserating with me already? Why? What's wrong with him?'

He rubbed his hand over his head. 'He's a politician – my natural enemy.'

I laughed. 'I'm sorry I looked for him now. Why couldn't he have been a milkman?'

'I can't see Kathleen with a milkman.' Kevin put his hand inside his denim jacket and pulled out a large envelope that had been folded in about ten places. 'I keep threatening to buy a briefcase but they look so poncy.' He handed me the envelope. 'His current address, phone numbers and email. Also some of the press coverage and photos.'

'Thanks, Kev.'

'Are you going to get in touch with him?'

'I dragged my heels about contacting Kathleen – I was afraid.'

'Naturally,' Kevin said.

'But see how well that worked. I owe it to Paddy.'

'You might be a bit of a shock for him – he doesn't know you exist.'

'I prefer to think of myself as a surprise and, anyway, if he doesn't want to know me, well, you can't miss what you never had, can you?'

'Let me know how it goes.'

I nodded. 'I'd better go back to work or I'll be sacked on my first day.' I dusted crumbs from my skirt. 'Thanks – you did good.'

Kevin stood up and rested a hand lightly on my shoulder. 'We'll have to see about that.'

We walked towards the foyer. 'Just one thing,' I said. 'Does he have other children?'

'Nope. Not a one. He had a wife but they're separated,' he said, and waved as he left.

I went back to work but I couldn't concentrate. The bundle of information Kevin had given me was like a magnet.

'Susie?' I said, as she chomped her third éclair of the day.

She raised her eyebrows in reply.

'Would you mind if I typed a personal letter?'

'Off you go,' she said, gesturing towards the back office. 'If you leave it in the out-tray I'll pop it in the post for you.'

'Thanks,' I said, my heart racing now that I'd grasped the nettle. I knew if I put it off I'd never do it, and there was no harm in it, was there? Like I'd told Kevin, you can't miss what you never had.

I sat at the desk and scanned the stuff Kevin had given me. Gary Kennedy. Born 10 July 1958, Erinville Hospital, Cork City. Only surviving child of Eileen and Gary Kennedy. I paused – that explained why he was known as Junior. I read on. Grew up in North Cork outside Charleville. Boarder at Blackrock College, Dublin. Rugby. Rugby. Rugby. That must have been all he did – besides have sex with Kathleen – in his teenage years. University College, Dublin, law degree. Called to the bar in 1984. Elected to Dáil in 1986 – TD since then. Married Alison Smith in 1988. No children. Kevin had also included numerous articles on various political issues that featured him.

I couldn't concentrate well enough to read them but I got the general impression that he was a bit of a tree-hugger. Which was fine with me: I liked the environment too. We had something in common. I looked through the badly printed photographs and saw that Kevin was right – there was no doubt about it: the man in the suit waving his arms at the camera was the one who had been on O'Connell Bridge with Kathleen.

I'd seen enough. It was now or never. I turned to

the computer and typed in my address, phone number and the date. My heart was pounding so hard I thought it might crack a rib.

Dear Mr Kennedy

That sounded dumb. I tried again.

Dear Gary

Too familiar. Fuck. Then I had an idea.

A Chara

That'd do.

> *It has come to my attention that I am your daughter. It appears that you had an encounter with my mother – Kathleen Brennan – in March 1976. Do you remember this? I realise that this letter may come as a bit of a shock as I understand from Kathleen that you know nothing of my existence.*
>
> *I would like to meet you. My contact details are above.*
>
> *Mise le Meas,*
> *Ruth Burke*

I printed it off immediately and stuffed it into an envelope. Then I scribbled the name and address on the front and tossed it into Susie's out-tray. The die was cast.

I went back out to Reception and was immediately put to work by my pregnant trainer. The last hour flew and took up my head space. Before I knew it, it was four o'clock and I set off for home.

As soon as I pulled into my cul-de-sac I saw a red Ford Focus parked outside my gate. Damn! It was so obviously a hired car that I knew it had to be Emerson. I considered driving away but to do that I'd have to go down to the end of the cul-de-sac and turn. He'd definitely see me. Anyway, I couldn't hide for ever.

I parked and got out. I could see Selma in the passenger seat of the Focus. If I was small, then she was tiny. She was all voluminous black hair and big dark eyes. She stared at me as I walked towards her and I was pleased I looked sharp in my good suit and wasn't in track pants putting out the bins as was usually the case. Selma stared and I swaggered. Fuck her. I didn't care.

As I approached the house, Emerson was emerging from the garden. He seemed anxious. 'Jesus, Ruth. I'm delighted to see you. I've been knocking on the door for ages and there's no answer.'

'But Kathleen and Paddy should be there,' I said, forgetting the Spanish harlot in the red car. I let myself in home, heart pounding. *Countdown* was on the TV when I threw open the sitting-room door and Kathleen was fast asleep on the sofa. There was no sign of Paddy. 'Kathleen! Where's Paddy?'

Kathleen opened her eyes and sat up. 'Here with me. He was asleep. I sat down beside him and I must have dozed off.'

I ran out, calling his name. No Paddy in the kitchen. No Paddy in the garden. Oh, my God, what was I going to do? I followed Kathleen up the stairs and opened my bedroom door. My heart jumped with relief: he was sitting on the floor by the bed and a thick smell of eucalyptus hung in the air. Little devil! I ran to him and scooped him up.

'Ruth, I'm so sorry,' a pasty-faced Kathleen said. 'I only dozed off for a few minutes.'

'Don't worry about it,' I said. 'He's done it to me loads of times. He's impossible to watch.'

'Daddy!' Paddy shouted.

Emerson was standing in the doorway. I felt the blood drain into my feet and thought I was going to faint. Who the hell did he think he was? He had no right to be in the house, let alone in the bedroom. Yet how many times had I seen him standing there? How many ordinary nights had we passed here? Ordinary but good. Happy and steady. Until Gibraltar.

I stood Paddy on the floor and he ran to his daddy. Emerson's face lit up as he swept his boy into his arms. 'I was afraid he'd forget me,' he said, smiling. Then the smile disappeared. 'I'll go so,' he said.

I couldn't speak.

Kathleen took over. 'Isn't he a little terror? Up here all the time. Where are you off to, Emerson?'

'Maybe into town, and then I'll bring him out to Ogonnolloe for a while. My family are dying to see him.'

'That'll be lovely,' Kathleen said, ushering him through the doorway and down the stairs. I sank on to the bed. All the strength had left me. I listened as Kathleen got rid of Emerson and then the house was quiet.

My head was so full of confusion I couldn't separate out one thought from another. I was so preoccupied that I didn't hear Kathleen coming back and it wasn't until she put her arm round my shoulders that I knew she was there. She persuaded me to go downstairs with her and have some coffee. I was too destroyed to object.

Kathleen did her best to keep me distracted while Paddy was out with Emerson. I tried to talk to her but I couldn't. I drank cup after cup of coffee and chain-smoked for the entire four hours and ten minutes that he was away. Kathleen tried to convince me to eat but I couldn't. I watched TV but it made no sense, and every ten minutes I found myself at the front window peering up the street for any sign of them.

When Emerson returned Paddy – at about nine fifteen – I bolted for the kitchen and Kathleen answered the door. I chewed my fingernails and smoked as I listened to their voices. I worked out that Paddy was asleep because Kathleen and Emerson went directly upstairs. He'd probably nodded off in the car – he always did that.

Eventually the front door closed softly and Kathleen came back into the kitchen.

'He's gone. Paddy's in bed,' she said smiling.

I tried to speak but only a moan came out. Kathleen held me close to her and I began to cry. She didn't say anything, just kissed the side of my head and held me.

When the crying stopped she suggested I go to bed and said that she'd stay the night. I couldn't refuse. I made my way upstairs and peeped in at

Paddy, fast asleep in his bed, then fell, fully clothed, into mine.

Seeing Emerson in our house – our bedroom – had been the final twist of the knife. Now I knew in a way I hadn't known before that my marriage was over. My hard-woman persona was out of town for the day and I was just a quivering emotional splatter. Tears came then, pouring out of me like lava, as I mourned all that I'd lost until exhaustion took over and I fell asleep.

19

The following morning I woke with a start at seven o'clock and went straight to Paddy's room. The sight of him, all red-cheeked and tousled, bum in the air, made me smile. I kissed him and he wriggled in his sleep. I crept out and opened the door of the spare bedroom. Kathleen was fast asleep too.

I wondered how I'd have coped with everything that'd been going on if she hadn't come back into my life. I closed the door and went downstairs. I needed coffee and – no matter what Kevin was going to say – I would have a cigarette.

It was a beautiful summer's morning. The sky was high and blue with wispy white clouds and the birds were singing their little hearts out in the trees in my back garden. I made the coffee, grabbed my cigarettes and let myself into the garden through the french windows in the living room. The air was so crisp and clean it felt like a dip in a river.

Everything looked new somehow, and though my heart felt bruised I no longer felt the desperation of the night before. The french windows opened and Kathleen appeared. Her face was white and she had lips to match. 'Good morning,' she said cheerfully.

'You look wretched,' I said.

'Thanks. It'll pass. How are you this morning?'

'Not bad – and thanks. I don't know what I'd have done without you.'

Kathleen's face lit up. 'I'm delighted to have been able to help.'

I drained my coffee. Then I remembered. 'Um . . . I have something to tell you.'

Kathleen looked at me.

'Um . . . you see . . . Kevin has found out who my natural father is and he appears to be this politician – Gary Kennedy. Kevin gave me photos and stuff yesterday. Here, I'll get them for you.'

I ran into the kitchen and grabbed my handbag. It struck me that I'd ignored Kathleen's feelings in all of this. I was sorry I hadn't waited before sending the letter. I handed her Kevin's bumph and watched her as she leafed through it. 'Do you recognise him?' I asked.

'It's him all right,' she said eventually. 'Is he well known? After 25 years out of Ireland I wouldn't know one politician from the other . . . What are you going to do?'

I grimaced. 'I already wrote to him. And it's been posted.'

Kathleen said nothing, but I could see she was a little hurt.

'I know I took ages to contact you,' I said, 'but it worked out so well I thought I'd jump in at the deep end this time.'

I'd wanted to put it better than that – but it didn't

matter: Kathleen got the message and beamed at me.

'Would you like anything?' I said to her, pointing towards the kitchen.

'Maybe a cup of hot water.'

'Sounds delicious.'

I went to the kitchen, filled the kettle and switched it on. As I waited for it to boil I began to tidy off the worktop. It was then that I saw the small purple jar of Joy Gel. I picked it up and sniffed. The distinctive eucalyptus fragrance brought to mind Paddy and the smell in my bedroom. Where the hell had it come from? I was sure I'd given back everything in the Mary Winters kit.

The kettle boiled and I poured hot water into a mug for Kathleen, put it and the empty Joy Gel jar on to a tray and returned to her. Faint colour had appeared in her cheeks. 'You look a bit better,' I said, and handed her the mug.

She smiled her thanks, sat back and closed her eyes. I pulled a chair over and sat down beside her. 'Kathleen?'

'Yes?'

'Where did this purple jar come from?'

Kathleen opened her eyes. 'Emerson brought it back when he came with Paddy.'

'What?'

'He said Paddy had it in his pocket and that it must be yours.'

I propped my elbows on the table and covered my face with my hands. 'I don't believe it.'

Kathleen put down her mug. 'What's wrong?'

My stomach tightened as I imagined Selma and Emerson examining the Joy Gel. Oh, God, no!

'Ruth? What's wrong?'

'Did you read the jar?' I said.

'No.'

I reached out a hand and patted Kathleen's arm. 'I'm delighted you stayed, by the way. Thanks for that. But have a look at this.' I pushed the livid purple jar across the table. She picked it up. 'Smells like Vapour Rub,' she said. 'I'd really need my glasses to read it.'

'No, you wouldn't. Turn it round.'

Kathleen swivelled the jar in her hands until the ornate gold lettering was facing her. 'Joy Gel?'

'It's from the Mary Winters kit – I thought it had gone back.'

'The Mary Winters kit?'

'Do you remember when you babysat for me so that I could do a Tupperware party?'

'But you felt you weren't cut out for selling plastic bowls.'

'That part wasn't true. I was too embarrassed to tell you I was selling Mary Winters products.'

Kathleen looked puzzled.

'Mary Winters? The sex-aid company?' I said.

'Oh, right – I've heard of them, I think. And the Joy Gel came from Mary Winters?'

'It must have rolled under the bed the day Mikey and Paddy raided the kit.'

'They raided the kit?'

'It's a long story.'

'What's it for?'

I raised an eyebrow.

'Oh,' Kathleen said, 'sorry. How does it work?'

'No idea.'

'It seems more like something you'd use if you had the flu rather than if you wanted . . . you know . . .' A grin was spreading across her face.

I groaned. 'I can't believe I let my child go with his father and that – that wagon with a jar of Joy Gel.'

'Maybe they didn't read it.'

'Unless they're blind they couldn't have missed it. Oh, God, what the hell must they be thinking now? Lonely deserted wife locked in her bedroom with a jar of Joy Gel to keep her warm!'

Kathleen's face was contorted with suppressed amusement.

'It's not funny,' I said, but I couldn't help laughing. Her eyes were dancing and she joined in. Eventually, as we quietened, Paddy came out and climbed into my lap for a snuggle. He tried to grab the purple jar. 'Forget that,' I said, moving it away from him. Oh, God, it was *so* embarrassing – humiliating, even. Maybe I could explain to Emerson about the Mary Winters job. No. That'd make it look worse – as if I was protesting too much. I'd just have to learn to live with the fact that he and the Spanish harlot thought I was pathetic. Well, I'd coped with way harder realities.

I was due to start work on Monday and that would

keep my mind occupied. Things were improving: a new phase was beginning in my life. For the first time in ages I felt optimistic. Who could tell what was round the corner? I was due a run of good luck and I was pretty certain it couldn't be too far away. I was liking the world of women – Kathleen, Tracy, India – I had entered. Maybe I'd overestimated men and the effect they could have on your life.

20

Two days later the telephone rang as Paddy and I were coming in the front door laden with groceries. Paddy ran in, grabbed it from the kitchen table and gave it to me. 'Hello?' I half shouted, dropping a bag of potatoes inside the front door.

'Ruth? Ruth Burke?'

'Speaking,' I said, motioning to Paddy to shoo the Claw away from the food bags.

'This is Gary Kennedy.'

I dropped my handbag and car keys. Paddy grabbed the Claw and carried him in the direction of the living room. Gary Kennedy? *The* Gary Kennedy? My father Gary Kennedy? Holy shit. My knees buckled and I steadied myself against the banisters. I searched the contents of my upended handbag for my cigarettes and lighter.

'Hello? Ruth? Are you there?'

'Mmmm.' I lit a cigarette and took a long drag, but it did nothing for me: I was still shaking. 'Yes, yes, I'm here . . . um . . . How are you, Mr . . . um . . . how are you?'

'I'm fine, really good. Look, I know this is awkward and I hope it was OK for me to call like this out of the blue – your number was on the letter and I thought it might be a good idea . . .'

'No, no, that's fine,' I said, between puffs. 'Thank you for calling.'

He didn't answer for a few seconds and I was sure he'd hung up, sorry he'd called in the first place. 'Listen, Ruth, I hope you don't think this is forward of me but I wonder if we could meet? Face to face, so to speak. Perhaps a cup of coffee or a drink. Whatever you like.'

Now that I was faced with meeting my father I was terrified. But I did want to do it, didn't I? I mean, I'd written to him and then he'd called almost straight away and that had to be a good sign – and it was important for me to know exactly who I was, for myself as well as Paddy . . .

I stopped before I spun into total incoherence. 'That'd be great,' I heard myself say. 'Where? When?'

Gary hummed and hawed for a few seconds. 'I know it's short notice but how about tomorrow? I'll be in Limerick for a meeting. I live in North Cork – well, who am I telling? You know that, don't you?' He laughed then and I laughed too, but I was only being polite. 'Okey-dokey – the Clarion bar? Three-ish?' he said.

'That'd be great.' I paused to take a long, ash-creating drag. The Claw strolled past me and stuck his head into a plastic bag full of vegetables. I pushed him away with a toe and a cabbage rolled on to the kitchen floor. 'Look forward to meeting you.'

'Terrific!' Gary said.

As soon as I'd hung up, I set about putting away my shopping. A few weeks ago I hadn't even known who my natural father was – other than that he was some raw young fella called Junior with a fondness for Steve Heighway crisps. And now – well, now we were about to meet.

I called Kathleen. She didn't say anything.

'Well?' I prompted.

'How do *you* feel about it?' She'd turned the question back on me.

'A bit nervous but OK. I mean, as I keep saying, you can't miss what you never had and I hope it goes well but if it doesn't I'll be back where I am now.'

'I suppose. Would you like me to go with you?'

'No – really. Thanks, though. I'd prefer to do it by myself.'

'Will I take Paddy?'

'That'd be great,' I said. I'd been planning to ask Tracy if Paddy could go round and play with Chloe while I was gone, but Kathleen evidently wanted to be part of this meeting in some way. 'I'm to see him at three so any time before half two would be great.'

'No problem,' she said.

I tried not to think too much about my meeting with Gary Kennedy but it was hard. What if he didn't like me? Was he embarrassed to discover that he had an adult daughter? Would he try to get his spin-doctors – or whoever – to hush it up? I couldn't answer any of those questions so instead of thinking about it I had a clothes crisis. To say that I tried on every single stitch I possessed would not be an exaggeration. And still nothing seemed right.

If it wasn't that my arse looked too fat then it was that I looked slutty, too prim, dull, too summery or wintry, too small, too young, too old. I had every look, it appeared, except the one I wanted for meeting my father. And that was the problem. Exactly what kind of 'look' do you want on such an occasion?

I wished that someone would invent a uniform that was obligatory apparel for meeting long-lost relatives – I'd had the same problem finding clothes when I met Kathleen for the first time. Eventually, I decided on my good black suit with the knee-length skirt – the one I'd wanted to wear to Grandma Burke's funeral – and a white blouse. I agonised over shoes and eventually picked high black courts and made myself go to bed.

Next day, I kept myself busy until it was time to meet Gary. My stomach was churning but I maintained a cool exterior. Tracy called in to wish me luck. 'Don't worry about that fucker, now,' she said. 'You're the one with all the cards – he doesn't know how lucky he is to have a daughter like you.'

I told her she was the best friend in the world and set out for the Clarion. The drive there was fine as I could fool myself into treating it as just another trip to town or work. But nothing could quell the million or so butterflies that took up residence in my guts as I pulled into the car-park.

I steeled myself and walked up the wide front

steps, through the foyer past a tired-looking receptionist and into the bright bar, with its white marble floor and low-backed red sofas set round glass coffee-tables.

I saw Gary immediately. He looked exactly like his pictures. Tall, broad, handsome with grey-streaked blond hair and bright blue eyes. He was sitting alone, nursing a glass, his head turned towards the view of the Shannon outside the window. As soon as my heels clacked in his direction he stood up and looked straight at me. 'Ruth?' he asked, when I was close.

I nodded, unable to speak. He stepped forward and put out his hand. We shook and exchanged lovely-to-meet-yous. He invited me to sit down and simultaneously beckoned a waiter. 'What'll you have to drink?' he asked.

I tried to settle myself in the sofa opposite him. 'Coffee would be great – espresso.' I was longing for a blast of alcohol but I had to drive – and I was so nervous that I wasn't sure I'd stop drinking if I started.

The waiter disappeared. Gary and I smiled at each other for a few excruciating seconds. I wished I was at home washing the kitchen floor. Then the waiter arrived with my coffee and another whiskey for Gary. As soon as he'd left, Gary fixed me with his eyes. 'Can I say something?'

I picked up my cup and nodded.

'I didn't know about you until I got your letter,' he said.

'I know.'

'Jesus, we were only children, myself and Kathleen
– I was eighteen, just starting college, and she was
younger, seventeen maybe—'

'Sixteen,' I interrupted. 'She was only sixteen.'

'Sixteen,' he repeated. 'And how did she manage
with a baby when she was so young?'

'She didn't tell anybody she was pregnant, just
went away and had me in a mother-and-baby home.'

'And you were adopted?'

'I had a wonderful childhood – couldn't have
wished for better parents.'

'And how do they feel about you meeting with me?'

'They're dead.'

'I'm sorry.' Gary took a gulp of his drink.

I shrugged, but my eyes filled with tears, which
I hurriedly blinked away.

'How did you meet Kathleen?' he said.

'The adoption agency got in touch and said she
wanted to meet, if I was agreeable.'

'And she told you about me?'

'Well, yes and no. She had a photograph and a
few details, but it was a friend of mine, a journalist.
He did some research and, well, here we are.'

Gary leaned forward. 'A local journalist?'

'Well, he does local and national work – Kevin
Regan.'

'I know Kevin – he did that piece in the *Tribune*
recently about that poor little girl who has cancer.'

'Yes. It's tragic, isn't it? How can people justify
doing damage to children? I mean, for what? Money?'

'It's a disgrace,' Gary concurred. 'I'm chairperson

of the Environmental Commission, you know, and it's shocking how cavalier we can be about the environment.'

'Are you really?' I said, delighted to have found something to talk about. 'I've been helping to raise funds for PAP – the parents' group trying to find the source of the cancers in Ballymoran. Do you know they have to pay costs for the court case they lost against Boru Buildings a couple of months ago? I think it's terrible.'

Gary looked thoughtful. 'I remember that – we commissioned the report. They were sure that this company – what are they called again?'

'Boru Buildings.'

'That's right. The parents felt because this crowd are involved in removing asbestos from buildings that it was somehow associated with the cancers in the area.' Gary paused.

'And it isn't?'

'Asbestos has to be very carefully disposed of – did you know all ours goes to Finland?'

'No.'

'Well, it does. Anyway, there's no evidence of asbestos anywhere near Ballymoran.'

'Well, something's making those children ill,' I said.

'True – but it's not asbestos.'

'It's outrageous that they have to pay costs – can't your commission do anything about that?' I asked.

Gary finished his whiskey. 'Afraid not – it's our judicial system.'

We sat in silence for a while. Gary motioned to

the waiter and ordered more drinks. 'Great view from here,' he said, pointing towards the river.

I nodded. We were quiet again.

'Tell me about yourself, Ruth,' Gary said, all of a sudden, and when I turned my head he was leaning forward in his seat, looking at me as if I was the most interesting person he'd ever met. Part of me knew that he was a politician and that his speciality was making people feel as if they were the centre of the universe but another part of me just liked the undivided attention.

I started by telling him about Paddy, then about my childhood and my parents. I didn't say too much about Emerson – just the bare facts, married and separated, that kind of thing. Gary seemed to sense that it was better not to press the issue and let me skim on to talk about work in Drury's. And all the time I spoke his attention never wavered. He nodded and listened and asked pertinent questions, but really and truly looked as if he was interested in what I had to say.

Before I realised it we'd been together for over an hour and although I was starting to relax I thought that might be enough for a first meeting.

'Thank you very much for coming,' I said, glancing at my watch. 'I don't want to delay you any longer.'

'I want to thank *you*, Ruth. I still can't quite believe it,' he said.

'A bit of a shock, all right, to discover that you have not only a daughter but also a grandson.' I stood up with him.

He wrapped my hand in both of his and squeezed. 'I'll call you.'

'Great.'

'I'm getting used to the idea of being a dad and grandad,' he said, and my heart ached because my real dad had never seen Paddy. He'd have loved him. I could just imagine them together. My eyes misted and Gary gave me a hug – he must have thought I was overcome with emotion at meeting with him. And maybe he was right.

We said goodbye and I walked as fast as I could to the door of the hotel. It was raining when I went outside and I had to run the short distance to the car-park, but even so I was drenched.

Traffic was heavy in town as people struggled through the unexpected summer downpour, and as I drove I digested my meeting with Gary Kennedy. He seemed nice, but it was hard to tell much at such an early stage. So far so good, was all I could conclude.

As soon as I came in the door Paddy launched himself at me and gave me a jammy kiss. Kathleen was doing her best not to look curious. I made tea and offered her some but she refused, saying she had a seance booked for six thirty and needed to go home to purify the room.

'He was nice,' I said, as I poured my tea.

She didn't answer, just buttoned up a mauve raincoat. I noticed her bump was becoming obvious.

'He asked about you,' I continued.

She still didn't answer. She was pale and had dark circles round her eyes.

'You OK?' I asked.

She sighed. 'I'm fine – I'd better get going.'

We walked to the door. I could see in her eyes that there was something she wasn't saying, but I was so tired after the emotional exertions of the day that I hadn't the energy to ask.

'See you tomorrow,' she said, and headed off. I closed the door and went back to Paddy but the forlorn picture of Kathleen stayed with me as I cooked our dinner. It was traumatic for her as well as for me.

All I wanted to do now was curl up with my boy and watch TV or read a book. Forget about the world, mothers and fathers, husbands and lovers. Forget that everything was up in a heap and pretend that everything was all right. Maybe if I tried hard enough it might prove to be true.

21

'He's a brickie,' Tracy said.

'I don't care if he's Colin Farrell.'

Tracy tipped back in her garden chair and stared at me through a haze of smoke. We were on my patio drinking a glass of wine. It was a beautiful late June day, all blue skies and fluffy clouds. 'You're going. It'll be good for you. Joe Lynam is a nice guy and you need to get back on the bike.'

'No.'

'It's that or speed-dating.'

'Absolutely no way.'

'Emerson will hear about it. Wouldn't that be cool?'

'How will he hear about it?'

She smiled. 'I have my ways.'

I smiled back, and had to admit the idea was growing on me. I would dearly have loved to make that bastard feel even a fraction of the pain he'd inflicted on me.

'He's very nice. I met him last year at Julie Hogan's wedding,' Tracy went on.

'Is he good-looking?' I said.

'Not bad at all. Big – good body. Derek told him all about you.'

'Jesus, Tracy, it's way too soon.'

'Think of Emerson's face when he finds out.'

'That's tempting me, all right. Maybe I'll think about it.'

Tracy picked up her cigarette pack and scrutinised the back.

'What?' I said. 'What are you not telling me?'

'*Weeeell* . . . it seemed like a good idea at the time. Joe's been in the States and he doesn't know many people here any more. One date won't kill you.'

I narrowed my eyes. 'I don't like the sound of this. Date?'

'Just dinner next Friday, sure that'll save you cooking. I'll mind Paddy. He can sleep in my place – just in case you get lucky.'

'Holy Mary Mother of God! Tracy Walsh, I'm going to kill you.'

But of course I didn't kill her and I even ended up thinking that this would be good for me. I needed to get on with my life and this was the next step. It would be hard but do-able. I bought a strappy white sundress that was the perfect combination of sexy and demure – dating was a minefield and I was out of practice.

There had been a time when I was a girl about town, proudly sashaying in short skirts and high heels. But I was no longer that girl. The problem was I was also no longer the happily married woman I'd imagined myself to be. So, who was I now? I had no idea but I hoped that this date might help me work some of it out.

Tracy had arranged for us to meet in the bar of a new restaurant called the Yellow Pepper right in the city centre. I arrived five minutes late and searched the dark interior for Joe Lynam. I saw a large man standing at the bar, furtively examining every customer who came through the doors, and knew straight away that this was my date. I took a deep breath and walked over to him, forcing myself to smile despite my nervousness.

'Hi, I'm Ruth Burke. You must be Joe,' I said, sounding tinny and rushed. He had fair hair and blue eyes, and weatherbeaten skin like Clint Eastwood. Maybe this would be all right, after all.

'Ruth! I'm delighted to meet you at long last. I've heard loads about you – all good.' He took my hand. 'What would you like to drink?'

'A gin and tonic would be great, thanks.'

He ordered it and I sat on a high bar stool, pulling my dress down over my knees.

'So, Joe, you're just back from America?' I said, as I sipped my drink. I would have loved a fag to steady my nerves. Maybe the alcohol would work instead.

'Yeah, I'm back for the last six months. I love being home but I feel like an intruder sometimes. I mean, all my friends are married now, with young families, and I'm . . . well . . . not married.'

Emerson's face popped into my mind, and I couldn't make it go away. It was as if he'd invited himself along on the date too. I slugged back my drink. I wouldn't let him live rent-free in my head.

I was going to do this and do it well. Ruth the party girl needed to resurrect herself. 'Would you like another drink?' I asked, beckoning the bartender.

'No, thanks. I'm fine,' he said.

I paid for mine, beamed at Joe and took a huge gulp. I didn't know what to say next and in my head Emerson was smiling at me. Just then a waiter came to fetch us. Table for two. No Emerson.

We were seated right in the corner of the restaurant. Soft romantic music played in the background and Joe's handsome face smiled across at me. He and I oohed and aahed for ages over the menu, glad of the distraction. The starters and wine arrived and then we talked about them. I tried desperately to think of something to say that didn't sound stilted. But my mind refused to get into small-talk, chit-chat, dating mode. Hell, I'd thought those days were over. I drank two glasses of wine before I'd finished my warm chicken salad. I felt light-headed and surreal, as if I'd landed the starring role in somebody else's dream.

'So, Ruth, tell me about yourself,' said Joe, as our main courses arrived.

I looked at my baked cod, then into Joe's kind, clear eyes. Lovely blue eyes, but not Emerson's. 'There's nothing much to tell. I'm just an ordinary girl,' I said, because I couldn't think of anything else to say. God, I sounded like someone who could only talk in clichés. I should have tried the speed-dating. Wham, bam, thank you, ma'am.

'Tracy told me . . . that you'd been through a rough time lately.'

I dropped my knife and fork and signalled to the waiter. 'Gin and tonic, please,' I said, before he'd reached me.

'I'm sorry, maybe I shouldn't have said that, but sometimes it's better to say things straight out.'

Emerson was back and I was having a debate with him in my head about how he should fuck off out of my subconscious because he was distracting me. If he'd only go away I could do this. I knew I could.

'How are you finding being back at home?' I said. 'Did I ask you that already?'

He smiled. 'It's good.'

I struggled for something else to say and poured myself a glass of wine. 'The wine is lovely,' I said, after five minutes' thinking.

He nodded.

I drained my gin and searched for the waiter. My head was floaty and it felt delicious. Emerson's features were melting into Joe's.

'What age is your little boy?' asked Joe, as our dessert arrived. Mine was crème brûlée, but I couldn't remember ordering it.

'He was three on the twenty-second of April. We went to Spain for his birthday but . . . but we only stayed an hour.'

A tear escaped from my eye and rolled down my cheek. It plopped on to the crème brûlée. Joe pretended not to notice and fiddled with his dessert, swooshing cream round his plate. More tears joined the first and then the floodgates opened.

'What's wrong, Ruth? Did I say something?' said Joe, as he offered me his napkin to dry my eyes.

I wanted to go home. 'No . . . not you . . .' I was sobbing now and a knot of waiters had gathered at the bar to watch us. Emerson, the coward, had retreated from my head. Typical! Does the hurting bit and bolts.

'I'm sorry . . . I . . . It's just that . . . I need to go to the loo,' I mumbled. I stood up unsteadily, fumbled for my bag and shawl, then went to the back of the restaurant and the ladies'. I locked myself into a cubicle, sat on the toilet seat and cried like the rain. Fuck this! I was tired of crying. I blew my nose noisily, using half a roll of toilet paper, then went out to repair my ravaged face. My blonde up-style was unravelling so I shoved as many hanks of hair back into the clips as I could, weaving a little as I leaned towards the mirror.

Luckily I was alone in the toilets. I looked like Alice Cooper, all blotches and panda eyes. I rooted in my bag for my makeup and patched myself up. I thought I looked grand but I was a bit drunk. Still, the evening was young – there was time for damage limitation. I launched myself back into the restaurant. But then I saw Joe across the room, twirling his napkin between his fingers. And almost simultaneously I saw the front door.

I hit O'Connell Street and took off up the road as fast as my stilettoed feet would carry me. I ran and ran until I found myself standing outside Mullins', a tiny pub in Edward Street where Emerson and I used to go. There was a snug at the rear of the bar and I pushed open the door and headed straight for it, without raising my head. It was empty and I sat down opposite the serving hatch. I needed a drink. Poor Joe. He'd had one balls of a night.

I took a tissue out of my bag and wiped my eyes, got the attention of the barman and ordered a gin and tonic. I sat and nursed my drink, wondering if Joe was still waiting for me to come out of the ladies'. God, what a night. Tracy'd kill me, but at least I wasn't still sitting there with a stranger, trying to force conversation and play the dating game when my head was full of Emerson.

Once I'd met him I'd hung up my party-girl image for ever – I knew that now for sure. I'd found something else, something real and loving and lasting – at least, that was the way it should have been. I sipped my drink and tried, yet again, to work out where my happy-ever-after had gone wrong. All I'd wanted was a normal, happy, secure relationship. Exactly like my adoptive parents had had. And I'd really believed I had it. I'd never doubted Emerson's love. Never even once. How stupid can you get? That big blunder had whipped the confidence mat right from under my feet.

When you've had a loving relationship, it's just too hard to go back to the dating game. Its whole point was to find what I'd had with Emerson – and he'd flung it in my face. I finished my drink, put my glass on the bar, caught the barman's eye and gestured at him for another.

At least the crying had stopped. I never wanted to go back to the hell-hole of depression that had engulfed me straight after Gibraltar – but I felt lonely, sitting by myself in the snug of an uncool pub on a Friday night. If there was one person I'd have loved to see walking through the door at that minute, it was India. I'd lost my husband and I'd lost her too. She was the collateral damage. Tracy was great, but India and I had been friends since childhood. She knew me inside out. But this huge thing had happened in my life and I felt uncomfortable talking to her about it. She had divided loyalties.

I slugged back the second gin. My head felt light and I knew I'd had enough alcohol. I made my way out of the pub and hailed a passing taxi. Paddy was sleeping at Tracy's so at least I didn't have to face her when I got home.

She rang first thing the next morning. 'Did I wake the sprinter?' she asked.

I stopped pouring milk into a bowl of Weetabix. 'How did you hear, Trace? I'm sorry.'

'And you should be. He waited ages for you to come out of the loo.'

'Oh, God, I'm sorry. I don't know what came over me.'

'Derek was out in the taxi and saw you belting up O'Connell Street like the clappers. He tried to follow you but you were gone.'

I said nothing.

'So, what was it, Ruth? His BO? Bad breath? What?'

'He was perfectly fine – nice, actually.'

'So there was nothing wrong with him?'

'Nothing. And everything. Oh, Tracy, I felt like Emerson had come out on the bloody date with us and it all got too much. I mean, trying to talk to a complete stranger, I felt like a forty-year-old sixteen-year-old.' I stopped because Tracy was laughing.

'It wasn't funny,' I said, laughing too, in spite of myself.

'What did you do?'

'Sat in the snug in Mullins' and drank gin.'

'Jesus, that's sad – Mullins'? The place where everybody is over seventy-five and the barman knows what you're drinking before you do?'

I laughed. 'Yeah. How's my son and heir?'

'Brilliant. Derek took the lot of them to Playworld. I'm going to the shopping centre – today's the grocery packing for PAP.'

I'd forgotten that Tracy had organised another fund-raiser for Parents Against Pollution and that I'd volunteered my Saturday for it. My head throbbed. I stood up and searched the press for Solpadeine. 'I'll be there. What time?' I said.

'Come around two. I'm short of people in the afternoon.'

I dissolved the tablets in water and swallowed the contents of the glass. 'That's fine.'

'Just one thing.'

'What?'

'Go to the loo before you come.'

'Why?' I said. 'Aren't there any toilets there?'

'Oh, there are toilets, all right – I just don't want you running off.'

'Ha, ha. Very funny. Are you ever going to let me live that down?'

Tracy sighed. 'Probably not. Derek's calling you the Road Runner.'

'Shit.'

'It's the least you deserve.'

'I know – I feel so bad about poor old Joe, but I just couldn't go back.'

Tracy laughed. 'Ah, well. Speed-dating has a whole new meaning for him now.'

'I really learned my lesson, Trace – I'm finished with men for the foreseeable future.'

'Yeah, right. Famous last words.'

'See you at two,' I said.

'Beep, beep,' Tracy said, in her best Road Runner impersonation.

'Bitch,' I said, but I was laughing as I hung up.

22

India rang on Wednesday evening, just as Paddy and I were finishing our chicken, broccoli and alphabet potato shapes. 'Hi, Ruth, how are things?'

I tucked the phone under my chin and began to clear up the table. Paddy stood a Ninja turtle on top of a pile of broccoli. 'Fine. How are you after the funeral?'

'I'm OK. Listen, Ruth, I wonder if I could call over later on?'

'What's up?'

'Does something have to be wrong for me to call to see my friend and my favourite nephew?'

'Your only nephew. Sure, call over.'

'See you in a little while,' she said, and hung up.

I cleaned up the kitchen, bothered by India's call. She wasn't a spur-of-the-moment girl, and we had arranged to have lunch on Friday. Maybe she just wanted to see Paddy. Anyway, I could tell her more about my meeting with Gary. She knew the gist of it from a quick phone call but maybe she wanted all the details. Still, that could have waited until Friday.

I'd just put Paddy into his pyjamas when she

arrived. She took him into her arms. 'Where's Alyssa?' he asked.

'That's nice, Paddy. Don't mind your auntie India,' she said. 'Can I put you to bed tonight? I'm the best story-reader in the world.'

'Yeah, yeah, yeah! I want *The Owl and the Pussy Cat*.'

'Give your mum a kiss so,' I said. Paddy leaned over, put his arms tightly round my neck and planted a wet one on my cheek. 'Night, Mum.'

India climbed the stairs with a chattering Paddy and I went into the kitchen. I flicked on the TV and half watched an old episode of *Changing Rooms* where Laurence Llewellyn-Bowen had furnished a whole room with MDF, glue and suede remnants.

It was just at the part where all would be revealed that India returned. 'He's such a sweetheart. He went straight off to sleep once his story was finished. Alyssa would never do that.' She sat at the kitchen table.

'Would you like tea, coffee, a glass of wine?'

'Tea'd be great.'

I began to make it. 'So, is something up, Ind? Are things OK?'

'Fine. I'm glad the Gary Kennedy thing went well. I still can't believe he's your father.'

'Neither can he,' I said. I poured tea into two mugs and sat down opposite her. I knew she had something to say to me and was waiting for the right moment. 'Spit it out, Ind.'

'Typical Ruth, get to the point. You should have

been the solicitor, not me.' She stirred her tea and took a sip.

'What's up? Have you fallen madly in love with a criminal client? Are you going to be made a judge? Jesus, India, that'd be great. We'd get some mileage out of that.'

She steepled her fingers and looked at me, eyes serious. 'I had a long chat with Emerson before he went back to Spain.'

I picked at my nail polish. There was a little narrow band of white on my finger where my wedding band used to be.

'I know this is difficult for you but it's hard for him too. He's very cut up, Ruth. He misses Paddy, he's confused . . .'

I stood up, went to the fridge and pulled out a bottle of Riesling. I found the corkscrew and opened it. I rooted in the cupboard for glasses. Then I found an ashtray hidden behind the breadbin with my cigarettes and lighter. I sat down again and poured myself a glass of wine. I lit a fag. 'So, please continue. Tell me all about poor Emerson's sadness and confusion.'

'Ruth, I'm only trying to help.'

I widened my eyes in surprise. 'Was Selma involved in this little chat?' I slugged back my wine and poured another glass. Anger rose and I tried to swallow it. Bastard. He was home for only a couple of days and he'd got the sympathy vote from his sister.

'Of course she wasn't. Emerson is sad, Ruth. He lost something too – and before you say it, I know and he knows that it was all his own fault but that doesn't change the sadness, the sense of loss.'

An image of Paddy, complete with Mickey Mouse hat, looking at his daddy in bed with Selma flashed before my eyes. Anger and tears vied with each other in my chest. The tears won, and flowed down my face. I tried to steady my voice. 'You really have no idea of my hurt, India. None at all.'

'I'm just trying to help,' she said again.

I poured more wine and tears dripped on to the table. I wiped them away with my sleeve.

India put out a hand and covered mine with it. 'You both need to talk about Paddy.'

'I let him see Paddy, didn't I? Others wouldn't have.' I choked back another flood and pulled my hand away from hers.

'I know you did, Ruth. But you need to sit down and talk about the future, Paddy's future. Look, you should try to work these kinds of things out between you. Once you bring the legal eagles in, things can get dirty.'

'What do you mean?'

India wore the solicitor's beady-eyed expression. 'All I'm saying is that if you two don't work it out then some old fart of a judge will decide Paddy's future.'

'I don't believe this,' I said, anger erupting. 'You come here and threaten me with legalities? Is that the advice you're giving Emerson? To go for custody?'

India shook her head furiously. 'Ruth, you have

the wrong end of the stick. I'm just saying there's an easy way and a hard way to approach these—'

'I feel betrayed.'

'I know. He did betray you.'

'No. I feel betrayed by *you*, India.'

'Look, Ruth, I'm only trying—'

'Oh, please! Every single member of your family is on my side except you. And you're supposed to be my friend! Some friend!' I lit another cigarette. My hands were shaking.

'I'm looking at the situation rationally. Whether you like it or not Emerson is Paddy's father and he wants proper visiting rights. I'm saying work it out between you and try to stay away from the courts.'

'*Rationally?* My heart is broken, India. I feel hollow and empty inside. Do you know that feeling?'

India dropped her eyes and didn't answer.

'No, you don't. Solicitors don't take broken hearts into consideration, do they? They like cold, hard facts.' I gulped more wine.

'Drinking won't help, Ruth.'

That was the last straw. I finished the glass and slapped it down on the table. 'It's helping a hell of a lot more than my friends are at the moment.'

India stood up. 'Ruth, look, I just—'

'You just want to help but you're not, so go.'

India picked up her handbag and walked out of the kitchen. When I heard the front door close I sat down at the table and cried until my whole body shook. Then I let myself think about what had just happened. And, deep down, I knew that India was right and I was wrong. I had to face the future, talk properly to Emerson about custody and visits and maintenance. And that once I'd done it, there would be no going back. That my marriage was really over and that I had to deal with the fallout.

23

The following Monday I started work. It was only part-time and Kathleen was ever on hand to help out but for the first few weeks I was run ragged. When I came home, I'd flop on to the sofa in front of the TV and try to work out what I needed to do so that the whole shooting-match wouldn't fall apart. Laundry? Shopping? Ironing? Could the toilet wait to be cleaned until tomorrow night? Had I remembered to pay the telephone bill?

I thought of all the years I'd worked with women who were doing the ultimate juggle of babies and jobs and felt I should write to each one and apologise for how little I'd understood. There I had been, swanning around, my biggest worry whether I should get a manicure while I was having my hair done or if I should wait. And there they had been, like blue-arsed flies, not only doing their jobs but also another full-time job every evening and weekend. Well, now it was my turn.

By the time I started at Drury's Susie had left to have her baby. I worked every weekday from nine until one. The other receptionist was a pretty – though insane – young one called Avril Johnson. She was about twenty-three, tall and athletically built with a huge bust and a mop of thick red hair. She had a gorgeous face – open and friendly as well as pretty – with pale green eyes. All she cared about was having a good time and finding a boyfriend.

Avril was a bit of a ditz but she was easy to get on with, especially as I didn't see much of her. She arrived every day about ten minutes before I went off and worked until eight.

Once I'd got over my nervousness about being back at work I was fine. I soon mastered the new switchboard and the computer system that had been installed since I'd left. Drury's was a busy tourist hotel so I spent most of my time dealing with Yanks – which was fine: they were funny and polite. They all adored Avril, of course, but seemed willing to put up with me as a substitute.

Apart from dealing with customers and phone calls, I had a small amount of typing and filing to do. It was just enough to keep me busy and not so much that I was snowed under. Except at home.

Gradually, though, I found myself developing a routine and rhythm to my life that made me feel I was going to succeed. I was happy to be busy, and at night I fell asleep as soon as I hit the bed.

By the end of my first two weeks' work Kathleen was into her fourth month of pregnancy and looking less like a ghost. She and Paddy were getting along like a house on fire, and while I was still having the odd weep into my pillow at night, I was surviving nicely and that was good enough. OK, in

my man-free world there were a few drawbacks –
sex was non-existent and the DIY jobs were getting
out of hand – but I was adamant: I didn't want
men in my life.

Ferdia Ryan, the hotel's manager, wasn't in
Limerick during my first two weeks and Sheila
Rodgers, the Galway manager, was imported to run
the show. Ferdia was off setting up the new branch
of Drury's in Lahinch, and though I heard his name
during those weeks I was in no way prepared for
the impact he would have on me. He arrived into
my life and Drury's Hotel on a hectic Monday morning. I'd known he was due back but, having fished
a couple of toilet rolls out of the loo at home early
that morning it had slipped my mind.

I ran into the hotel desperately ticking off my daily
checklist in my head. Had I told Kathleen that Kevin
was planning to take Paddy to the park with Mikey?
Or that there was a serviceman coming to fix the
washing-machine? And then there was the car. What
the hell was that noise it had been making as I drove
in to work?

I was so preoccupied that I didn't notice the man
at Reception until I'd almost banged into him. I
stepped aside, apologising, and smiled. My God,
the quality of the guests was improving. Most of the
men who stayed in Drury's were middle-aged with
the dress sense of a golfer. This man was tall and
rangy with beautifully cut brown hair, and dark eyes
that seemed blue-black in the light of the hotel lobby.
His skin was lightly tanned and he was wearing a

black jacket and trousers, with a taupe collarless top underneath calculated to accentuate his fine body. I didn't need Venus and Saffron to tell me that his clothes were worth a small fortune or that he was truly gorgeous.

As I was examining him, I noticed that he was giving me the once-over as well, and a tingly sensation ran down my spine. I blushed.

'You must be Ruth,' he said, in a soft Donegal accent that increased the activity in my central nervous system until I was ready to faint. He held out his hand and I shook it. It felt firm and warm and his fingernails were manicured. Maybe he was a movie star. 'Ferdia Ryan,' he added.

'Oh, hello,' I said. 'How are you? Welcome back to Drury's.'

'Thanks.' He leaned one elbow on the reception desk and I saw that he was holding a sheaf of papers.

'I just need to drop my stuff into the back office,' I said, pointing and trying not to make it obvious that I couldn't take my eyes off him, 'get to work and all that.'

Ferdia nodded and I made my way behind the counter towards the office doorway. I was sure I could feel his eyes on me and every cell in my body was screaming with desire. It had to be the deprivation, I reasoned, because no man had ever before had that effect on me.

Sure in the past I'd met men to whom I was attracted – God knows, there'd been a good few. But this was different. It was so overwhelming it could only be explained by famine. Maybe I should be taking saltpetre or whatever it was they used to give prisoners to reduce their sexual appetite. My hormones had gone insane – that was the only explanation – and everything would be fine once they'd calmed down.

I hung up my coat and stashed my handbag in the empty office. Then, after a quick check in the mirror, I went to my post. I figured Ferdia Ryan would be gone by the time I got back. That'd be good. I'd have time to compose myself before I had to speak with him again.

But I was wrong. As I emerged from the office he was still standing at Reception. As I came out and took my seat behind the computer he watched me all the time. At first I didn't look at him – because I couldn't – and when I finally made eye-contact he seemed embarrassed and shuffled his papers. I switched on the computer but I could hardly see the screen. This man was beautiful, stylish *and* bashful? I could have shagged him on the spot.

'I see we have a bus tour at eleven,' he said.

'English pensioners,' I croaked.

'Excellent,' he said.

There was silence as we stared at each other. I knew I ought not to be doing such a thing but I was powerless to stop.

'I'd better go have a walk around the place – do some work,' he said eventually.

I pretended to type. 'See you later.' The phone rang. 'Good morning, Drury's Hotel, Ruth speaking, how may I help you?'

He waved and walked across the lobby. My eyes were glued to his back until he disappeared into the bar. How was anybody as good-looking as him? He must be married – surely he was thirty or thereabouts. It was inconceivable that such a man could be free. And if there was one thing I knew I was never going to be it was a Selma – no matter how tempting.

The morning was manic – there were busloads of tourists, constant phone calls and a burst pipe on the third floor. By the time all of that was done it was almost one o'clock and the vivacious Avril was arriving. Ferdia greeted her by name – with almost as much warmth as he'd greeted me, I was disappointed to notice. I gave her a few bits of information she needed to continue with our fifty-six arrivals and grabbed my belongings.

I was on my way out of the door, still talking to Avril, when a tall, thin, red-haired man with glasses collided with me. He came off worst and fell forward into the foyer.

'Oh, my God!' Avril screeched.

The man was spreadeagled, face down on the red, flowery carpet. I helped him to his feet. 'I'm so sorry,' he slurred, holding my hand. 'I hope you're not hurt.'

'Not at all,' I said. 'Are you OK? You took a nasty fall.'

He just stared at me. 'How kind you are,' he said eventually, and his eyes filled with tears.

I was anxious now to get going. 'As long as you're all right.'

But he had no intention of letting me go. 'You have a kind face,' he said.

I smiled.

'Have you children?'

I looked into his bloodshot eyes and felt a pang of sympathy – I knew what sad felt like. 'A little boy. Paddy. He's three. Do you have children?'

Tears ran unchecked down his face. 'Two. Emily and Kieran – the best thing that ever happened to me . . . the best . . . the very best.'

'Are you staying here at Drury's?'

He didn't seem to hear me. 'It's all over . . .'

I wondered what the hell had happened and if he'd done something but still felt sorry for him. Why was life so difficult? I patted his shoulder. 'Things are never as bad as they seem.'

He made eye-contact with me. 'Sometimes they're worse.'

'Look, I've been where you are and I know it's rotten but I promise it gets better.'

He shook his head. 'It's over.' He pulled himself upright and tried to smile. 'Thank you for your kindness. I'd better go.'

'Will you be all right?'

'I'm fine. Thanks again.'

I stood for a few seconds and watched his unsteady progress towards the bar. Poor man. Life really was hard.

As I emerged into the car-park not even the magnificent hot July day could quite dispel the aura of sadness that lingered from my encounter with him. I took a deep breath and tried to clear my head.

The sky was blue, the air was still and heat was rising from the Tarmac of the car-park. I made my way slowly to my car, mulling over the events of the morning. Suddenly I heard my name, followed by loud whooping. Kevin, Mikey and Paddy were running towards me.

'Why aren't you at school?' I asked Paddy.

'Mikey and Kevin got me. Chloe was sick. Her mum made her stay home.'

'We have a picnic,' Mikey said.

'That's lovely,' I said, rubbing Paddy's head as he hugged my legs. 'Where are you going?'

'You mean, where are *we* going?' Kevin said, with a wicked grin.

'We?'

He nodded.

I shook my head.

Kevin nodded again. 'We're going to Fanore.'

'I can't go to Fanore – I have to go home and do some washing.'

'The washing can wait.'

'No, it can't,' I said. 'It could be raining tomorrow.'

'Exactly,' Kevin said, folding his arms across his white T-shirt. 'This is Ireland and it most definitely could be raining tomorrow so we have to make hay while the sun shines – or at least go to the beach.'

'And my washing? How do I dry it if it rains?'

Kevin tutted. 'Why do you think God invented tumble-driers?'

'I don't know, Kevin. For you to shrink clothes?'

'Very funny.'

I could feel a sticky patch of perspiration on the back of my blouse. I was tempted. The sea. The breeze. The cool water.

'OK,' I said, 'you win. Let me go home and change, then we're off.'

'No need,' Kevin said, taking my hand and starting to walk. Mikey and Paddy ran behind us. 'I brought your clothes – Kathleen was in your house and she got them for me, with your swimsuit and a towel.'

We stopped beside Kevin's car. I saw that he'd put another child seat in the back.

'Orla left hers behind the other day,' he said, as he caught me looking it. 'Come on! I want to get there before the sun disappears.'

I grabbed Paddy and Kevin grabbed Mikey and we strapped them in.

'My car!' I said, remembering.

'Leave it here until we get back – I'll drop you by and you can collect it.'

'You've thought of everything,' I said, and sat into the Volvo. As Kevin started the car, I had a look in the bag he'd brought. He hadn't done too badly. A T-shirt and a pair of shorts, my sandals, swimsuit and towel, even some sunblock. 'I'm impressed,' I said.

'Kathleen gets the credit,' he said.

'Well, I'm glad to hear *you* weren't rooting around in my drawers.'

'Don't make me answer that.'

The sounds from the back seat told me that the

motion of the car was rocking Paddy and Mikey to sleep and shortly I followed suit.

As I slept I dreamed that Ferdia Ryan and I were dancing in an empty ballroom and that Kevin, Paddy and Mikey were standing on the stage waving. Ferdia kissed me and a jolt of desire coursed through me. I woke with a start.

'What is it?' Kevin said.

I stared at him and tried to work out where I was. In the back seat, Paddy and Mikey were fast asleep. Slowly I remembered. The Atlantic spread out like a blue silk carpet on my left, and grey rock dotted with specks of green and flowers rose dramatically towards the sky on my right. What was Ferdia Ryan doing now?

'You OK?' Kevin asked.

I nodded. 'Kevin, have you had any girlfriends since you and Orla broke up?'

'That's a bit out of the blue.'

'Sorry. I was just thinking about something, that's all. I didn't mean to be nosy.'

'Don't worry,' Kevin said, steering carefully along the narrow, twisting road, 'I don't mind answering. I haven't had any girlfriends since Orla, is the short answer.'

'Except for Orla?'

'Why are you asking? Have *you* met somebody?'

'Yes – well, no – I don't know.'

His face sobered. 'That might be nice.'

'I don't know if I'm ready for a man after all the stuff – you know.'

'Sure I know. You're probably right. Whoever this guy is – and however nice – it's probably a bit too soon. Anyway, here we are!'

Kevin pulled off the main road and drove along a sandy track until we reached a small car-park facing the sea. Mikey and Paddy woke as soon as he turned off the engine and we piled out. It was magnificent. The sea heaved and crashed on to the golden sand and a warm breeze made the temperature perfect. We changed the boys into their swimming togs and they hopped up and down with excitement. Kevin gave them the buckets and spades that he'd obviously just bought, then got out an armful of bags and towels. 'Ready?' he said.

'Let me change. I'm melted in these work clothes.'

He threw me the keys, then he and the boys started off down the ramp to the beach.

Kathleen had packed my favourite swimsuit. It was a red halter-neck with a low back, comfortable but so elegantly glamorous that it always made me feel like a Hollywood starlet. Once I'd got it on, it took just moments to pull on the T-shirt and shorts and shove my feet into my embossed-leather thong sandals. I was ready. I got out of the car and set off to find the boys.

The beach was half full. Islands of colourful towels dotted the long crescent strand. How was I going to find them? I strolled along, smiling at bare-bottomed babies and running children. Paddy spotted me before I saw them and he and Mikey tore up to me.

Kevin had made us our very own towel island

and I saw that he and the lads had already begun to dig a trench towards the sea. He had taken off his T-shirt and his body was as firm and tanned as I suspected Ferdia Ryan's was under his designer clothes. Oh, my God. I had to put that man out of my head.

'Hungry?' Kevin asked, as I flopped down beside him.

'Starving.'

He handed me a ham sandwich and gave Mikey and Paddy a packet of crisps each. I poured tea from the flask and as the four of us sat there eating and drinking beside the ocean I realised I was happy. For the first time in months.

'This was a great idea, Kev,' I said, wiping a mixture of sand and salt off Paddy's hands. 'Beats the hell out of doing the washing.'

Kevin smiled. 'I'm glad you like it. I love the sea.'

'So do I,' I said, and that was it. We sat there in a silence as comfortable as a feather bed. Once Mikey and Paddy had finished their food they were anxious to get back to their digging so Kevin obliged and I lay down on the towels.

The hot sun made me sweat so I sat up and pulled off my T-shirt and shorts, then lay down again. Soon I was drifting off to sleep and the sounds of children laughing and the thud of the waves made a fuzzy backdrop to my dreams.

I have no idea how long I slept but when I opened my eyes Kevin was lying beside me. He was on his side with his head propped on his hand, watching me. I smiled at him and he put out his free hand to touch my face. Then he leaned down and kissed me. I pulled him closer and kissed him back. He tasted of the sea, ham sandwiches and sand.

And then I realised. 'Jesus! Kevin!' I said, sitting upright.

He pulled away and slapped his forehead. 'I'm sorry, Ruth. I don't know . . . I didn't mean . . . not that you're not . . .'

Paddy and Mikey had given up on the trench and were digging a huge hole, chortling as sand flew everywhere. My head swam with confusion and – funnily enough – desire. Hormones again. Kevin was my friend, becoming one of my best friends, and I had no intention of letting a hormonal rush ruin what we had.

He was silhouetted between me and the sun, his face turned towards the sea. I couldn't see him too clearly. That was all right. In fact, that was good. It was mortifying to wake up and find yourself snogging one of your friends. Imagine if it'd been Tracy!

'Look, Ruth . . .' Kevin began, but whatever he wanted to say evaporated.

'It's OK,' I said. 'If you think about it it was as much my fault as yours. Both of us are in the same boat – we've been alone too long. It's bound to have an effect. Jesus, Kevin, the sheer sexual deprivation alone . . .'

Kevin turned to face me. Tiny grains of sand were caught in his hair – what there was of it – and along the side of his arms. 'So you think we're just a bit frustrated and, well, any port in a storm?' he said.

'Exactly,' I said, clapping in delight. 'I'm thrilled you understand. I'd never do anything to jeopardise our friendship.'

'And something like this might?'

'No might about it,' I said. 'It'd ruin everything between us.'

'Do you think so?' Kevin said quietly.

'I know so.'

Kevin didn't say a word. He really was a very handsome man when you looked right at him. What could Orla have been thinking when she got rid of him? I took his hand. He didn't move or say a word. 'I met this guy at work today. I mean, Kev, yesterday I'd have told you I was finished with men – except as friends . . .'

I looked down at his hand, which lay motionless in mine. His fingers were long and slender, and there was a tattered Bugs Bunny Band-aid round his thumb.

'You and I have both been through the mill but now I feel we're starting to come out the other side. We'll be fine. And the kiss is nothing to worry about. Just a symptom of what we're feeling.' I looked up into his face. 'OK?' I said.

'OK,' he said softly.

I jumped up. 'And now, gentlemen, I believe it's time for a refreshing dip.'

I put out my hands to Paddy and Mikey, who took one each, and we ran towards the sea, the boys

screaming with excitement. I was just getting
worried about Kevin when he ran past us into the
waves and splashed water back at us.

'Oh, it's war, is it?' I shouted, and the boys and
I kicked water at him. The fight helped restore us
to our usual selves, and by the time we got home
with our sleepy sandboys in the balm of the evening
the kiss and all awkwardness were forgotten.

I was glad. I loved Kevin and life was too short
of friends to be wasting any you were lucky enough
to acquire. Anyway, the huge sexual surge I'd
had that day was nothing to do with Kevin and
everything to do with Ferdia Ryan.

As I fell asleep that night, my usual worries were
banished and instead my head was full of thoughts
about work the next day. Not for any particular
reason, you understand. You just never knew whom
you might meet.

24

As I got ready for work next morning Paddy was being a bit of a ratbag, flinging his cereal bowl across the kitchen, effing and blinding as I tried to dress him. But I didn't mind. It was another lovely sunny day and I felt good.

Eventually the Cheerios had been scrubbed off the wall and my tired son was dressed and ready for the day. Shortly after eight Kathleen arrived. She'd offered to drop Paddy to playschool. She followed me into the kitchen where she made tea as I put the finishing touches to my makeup. 'You look wonderful,' she said, leaning against the worktop.

'You don't look so bad yourself.'

Kathleen smiled. 'Well, I've stopped being sick.'

'That dress suits you,' I said, through puckered lips as I applied lipstick. She was wearing a loose coral sleeveless dress that showed off her colouring and her burgeoning bump.

'But you look amazing.' She was staring at me. 'Different. Did you have a great day at the beach yesterday?'

'Brilliant. Thanks for picking out the clothes.'

She didn't answer, and I was in the middle of

dealing with my eyeliner so I didn't look at her. Until I heard the moan.

Her eyes were closed and she was white-faced, swaying from side to side. My first instinct was to grab her before she fell to the ground, but that was followed by a learned response: do nothing. Kathleen wasn't having a miscarriage, just a vision.

Suddenly her eyes flew open and she looked, unseeingly, at me. 'He loves you,' she said, in the voice she used for predictions, 'with all his heart. In the cosmos your souls are linked. There are obstacles but nothing that can't be overcome by twin souls destined to be together. For ever.'

Then she stopped, closed her eyes again and swayed some more. I finished my make-up.

'He's already in your life. You must open your eyes and see him,' she said.

I made coffee and tea, took my cup to the table and sat down. I didn't smoke because I was off the cigarettes. A new leaf had been turned.

I sipped my coffee and watched Kathleen. It was ten past eight and I'd have to leave for work shortly so I hoped her trance would end soon. I couldn't leave Paddy in the care of an unconscious pregnant clairvoyant.

Her eyes flew open again. 'You must open your eyes and see him,' she repeated.

I nodded. She closed her eyes again and her face became tranquil. Good. The trance was ebbing. I could go to work.

Kathleen collected her tea from the worktop.

'What about that?' she said, coming to sit opposite me. 'I haven't had a trance in ages – I thought it was the pregnancy. What did I say?'

'Something about somebody who loves me and how there were obstacles but I had to open my eyes to see him.'

'Really? That's interesting and it was an unusual vision, you know. Very clear. You must pay attention to it because I think the spirit who came with the message was your mother.'

I rolled my eyes. I loved Kathleen but the whole clairvoyant thing was daft. Sure she was right some of the time – but so was I when I was guessing what might happen in the future. Paddy came into the kitchen and sat at the table with us. I filled a cup with milk and he drank it thirstily. Kathleen was staring at me as though she expected me to say something.

'You're my mother,' I said, hoping to put her off pursuing the matter.

She smiled. 'Thanks, dear, I know I am but I realise you have another mother, Brigid, and she's the one who came with the message. Have you any idea how special that is?'

I shook my head.

'Bear the message in mind,' Kathleen said.

'I'll do that,' I said, grabbed my handbag and kissed Paddy. 'I'd better get going.'

All the way to work my stomach was churning with excitement. This was ridiculous, I thought, as I drove through the traffic. I knew nothing about this man. He was probably married, and even if he wasn't it was stupid to act like a teenager about someone I'd barely met.

Anyway, maybe I'd been wrong about him staring at me. I was such a heap of pent-up frustration I was probably imagining things. I had almost convinced myself of that when I got to the hotel. But there was something about the way Ferdia's head shot round when he heard my high heels clacking on the tiled foyer floor that made me think – insane though it seemed – that he had been waiting for me to arrive.

'Ruth!' he said, and a smile wreathed his face. He'd changed his dark suit for a pale green linen number teamed with a washed-out blue shirt and navy tie. He had that delicious rumpled look that made me think of him rolling around in bed and sent my hormones into overdrive. I took a deep breath and smiled, because my voice had deserted me, then hurried to the office to put away my stuff.

I forced myself not to think about him and instead tried to remember the words of the National Anthem. But as I emerged, humming to myself, my heart gave a little flip. He was not only still around but this time inside the counter, searching through a stack of letters on my desk.

I sidled past him in the narrow space and flopped awkwardly into my chair. As I sat down the chair spun a bit, which made me feel weird but nothing like as weird as the man standing beside me. I switched on the computer and tried to ignore him. He sat on the desk to read through a file. I collected the email bookings and tried to concentrate on matching requests with availability but my mind was elsewhere. All over the man beside me, in fact. My heart was thumping and my skin ached with the need to be touched. God only knew where I was sending the poor fools who wanted to stay at Drury's.

I couldn't let myself look at him very often because every time I peeped the desire shot off the scale. Funnily enough, every time I did look at him I found that he was already looking at me. Luckily there was a crisis with another leaking pipe and Ferdia had to attend to it. But he came back as soon as he was finished and invited me to have a cup of coffee with him during my break.

I agreed, and at eleven forty I made Gretta Kelly, one of the bar staff, take over Reception while I met him as promised. Please don't let him be married, I begged God, or the Fates or whoever it is deals with these matters. Please, please, please, please, *please*.

Ferdia was already waiting for me when I arrived and he suggested we take our coffee into the garden. We sat at wrought-iron tables on the manicured lawn and sipped in silence for the first few minutes.

'You worked here before,' he said suddenly.

'Yes – until I got married.'

He mopped a coffee spill with a paper napkin, then folded it neatly. 'Oh.'

Jesus, how the hell was I going to get out of that one? There was only one thing for it. 'I'm separated now – it's one of the reasons I came back to work.'

'I'm sorry,' he said, but I could see that he wasn't. 'I've never been married but I'm sure it's hard when it doesn't work out.'

'Mmm,' I said. Not married! Yippee! 'How are you settling in? I presume you've just moved here.'

'I was in London for years but I got tired of it.'

'Limerick will be a bit boring for you after London,' I said.

'I wanted to come back to Ireland. And I have a feeling that whatever else Limerick might be it certainly won't be boring.'

Our legs brushed together.

'Listen, Ruth, I know you don't know me, and I'm not the impulsive type usually, but I wonder if you'd come out to dinner with me some evening?'

My breath caught and I wanted to suggest that we forget dinner some evening, pay Gretta Kelly to work the rest of my shift, then go and shag our brains out in one of the hotel bedrooms. But as I couldn't suggest that I decided I'd try for the dignified, sophisticated stance. I twirled my empty cup and sat back in my chair. 'That'd be lovely,' I said.

'Great. When would be good for you?'

'Well,' I began, 'I'd have to have a chat with my babysitter. I have a three-year-old son, Paddy.' I paused to check for a negative reaction. Ferdia's expression didn't change. 'OK,' I continued, trying to calculate how soon I could meet him without appearing desperate. 'Friday?'

'Friday would be brilliant,' he said. 'If you can check with your babysitter today and let me know

tomorrow I'd say I'll be able to find us a nice
restaurant even at this short notice.'

'Excellent,' I said, pretending to be calm and
serene. 'I'd better get back to work.'

Ferdia walked me back to Reception and we
chatted about his home town – Donegal – the price
of houses, which supermarkets were best and how
bad the traffic in Ireland had become. I was so
outwardly calm that I was surprising myself.
Inwardly, however, I was already choosing lingerie
and planning to bribe, beg or kidnap a babysitter
for Friday night.

At a quarter to one Avril came running in, waving
the *Irish Times*.

'It's him! My God, Ruth! My father was reading
the paper and when I saw the photograph – God
help us! Who could have guessed it would be him?
I heard it on the news but . . .'

She paused for breath, looking at me expectantly.

'Sorry, Avril, but I don't know what you're talking
about.'

She tapped at the folded newspaper with a
fingernail. 'There. Look. The drunk. The guy you
ran into.'

I glanced at the paper and there was a photograph of the red-haired man I'd bumped into. He
was smiling, his hair was brushed to one side and
he was wearing a neat suit, but it was unmistakably
him. I read the headline and short article that
accompanied the picture.

CLARE ENGINEER FALLS FROM TAX
OFFICE ROOF

Clare engineer, Ger O'Donoghue, 49, plunged to his death from the roof of the Limerick Tax Office barely missing a young Limerick woman and her baby.

'He just fell out of the sky,' Gillian Jones, the young mother, said. 'I'd just come out of the tax office after sorting out my emergency tax and he dropped down on the footpath in front of me. Me and Amanda could both have been killed as well.'

Mr O'Donoghue was a well-respected engineer who worked for a Dublin-based company. Mr O'Donoghue is survived by his wife, Helen, and his two young children, Emily and Kieran. His funeral will take place in Ardnascrusha on Thursday morning at 11 a.m.

'Poor man,' Avril said, as I finished reading.

'He was a bit distressed, all right.'

'What goes through someone's head when they do something like that?' Avril said, staring into the middle distance.

'Despair,' I said, grabbing my handbag before she could engage me in an in-depth discussion of this poor man we didn't know. 'See you in the morning, Avril. I have to fly – Paddy and I are going to the park with Gary.'

'Aw, isn't that lovely? Meeting his granddad. Did you bring a camera?' Avril said.

I wondered how I'd ended up working with Patience Strong.

Gary was already by the pond in the park when

Paddy and I arrived. I noticed that he was dressed for the occasion – all trendy-casual politician-on-his-day-off. He kissed me and knelt in front of Paddy. 'Hello, young man. Pleased to meet you.' He held out his hand to Paddy, who went in behind my legs.

'Paddy, this is Gary.'

Gary held out a beautifully wrapped gift, which Paddy took shyly. He looked up at me.

'Go on, love, open it.'

He tore at the wrapping and pulled out a red embossed leather book. He looked at me again, in surprise this time.

'Oh, that's lovely,' I said, hoping my mock-enthusiasm would wear off on Paddy.

Gary stood up. 'It's a limited edition version of the original *Wind in the Willows*.'

Paddy flicked half-heartedly through the sombre-looking pages, then handed it to me. 'Can I feed the ducks?'

I fished the bag of stale bread from my bag and he ran to the pond, to scatter it into the water.

'He's a fine boy,' Gary said.

We stood in silence and watched Paddy, and I struggled to think of something to talk about. It was worse than the date with Joe Lynam. Gary, being a politician, was better at it than I was, though, and soon we were discussing my plans for Paddy's education – how long in Montessori, which school he was to attend and so on. As usual I rose to the bait and we were coming up to the subject of college when a shrill scream and a string of curses rent the air.

'Fucking bastards! Get away! Fuck off! Bastard!' Paddy was standing at the edge of the pond with the bread spilled at his feet and at least ten ducks pecking and squawking as they fought for the crusts. 'Fucking bitch, get away!' he screamed, and kicked wildly.

I ran towards him, whooshing the ducks away, and hefted him into my arms.

'Mum, did you see the bastards? The bag tore and all the bread fell down and they were eating my shoes!'

He started to cry. 'Look, Gary, sorry about this but Pad's had a bit of a fright – I'd better take him home.'

'No problem. Are you all right, young man?' He put a hand on Paddy's shoulder and Paddy jerked away. 'I'll call you soon.'

I waved and hurried back to my car. By the time I had Paddy strapped into his seat he'd calmed down. I looked at his tear-stained face. 'Paddy, where did you learn all those curses?'

'Chloe,' he said.

I sat into my seat and drove off. Between Mikey Regan, Chloe Walsh and his broken home, poor old Paddy was a sure bet for delinquency. I probably should have been worried but then I remembered my date with Ferdia.

By the time I pulled up in front of my house I was so filled with excitement at the prospect that everything else was forgotten. It felt good to have something positive to think about for a change.

25

The week passed like a snail, slow and uneventful, but I was feeling positive. I'd thought it couldn't happen – that I'd never have the hots for another man. And now I'd met Ferdia. Maybe India was right: it was time to move on. I'd been thinking about her since our fight and, though I hated to admit it, a lot of what she'd said was true. Emerson and I needed to be grown-up and sort out the shit in our lives. I felt ready now. But first I had to clear the air with India.

'I'm sorry,' I said, as soon as she answered her phone.

'No, I'm sorry. It was too soon but I was just trying—'

'I know what you were trying to do,' I interrupted, 'and you were right. I have to move on.'

'Everything will work out, Ruth – I know it will.'

'I'm beginning to believe that. Anyway, enough about me. How are things with you?'

'Good and bad. I've been offered a partnership.'

'Oh, my God! That's great.'

'Not really – that's the bad part because it'll mean I end up spending most of my time in Dublin at the High Court.'

'What are you going to do?'

'For once in my life I haven't a clue.'

'Poor you – life's complicated, isn't it? Especially when you have kids.'

'Listen, Ruth, I have to go – they want me in court. Can we have lunch some day next week?'

'Sure. Off you go.'

I felt good after speaking with India. Now that my week was unblighted, all I had to do was sit back and look forward to my date.

Ferdia had booked La Conchiglia – he'd heard about it from a friend who was a restaurant critic with one of the national papers. I said I was delighted but I didn't care where we went. I was a lot more interested in what the hell I was going to wear. Every day after work I stole half an hour to scour the shops for something nice and – of course – some decent lingerie just in case I got lucky.

The Fates were assisting me as my shopping expeditions were painless. Ferdia had asked me out on Tuesday. On Wednesday I raced into town after work and, miraculously, the first shop I went into had a magnificent black dress – almost as nice as the one I'd worn to the funeral. It was sleeveless, with a V-neck, clingy body and an asymmetrical skirt that was shorter at the front than the back. Very sexy.

On Thursday, I went in search of a pair of shoes. Again, the shopping gods were with me. Sitting in a window, not five minutes' walk from where I'd parked, was the perfect pair. Black suede pumps

with a kitten heel and a toe so pointed you could
have speared fish with it. They cost as much as the
dress but I figured one last fling with my married-
days credit card wouldn't compromise my principles.
It seemed like poetic justice.

The only thing I had left to shop for on Friday
was lingerie. I searched through my drawers to see
if I had anything suitable, but everything remotely
sexy reminded me of Emerson and everything else
could have been worn by my grandmother. I stopped
at Moulin Rouge and bought a magnificent black
bra with matching lace Brazilian knickers that were
worthy of Mardi Gras.

As I drove home, my hot purchase smouldering
in a paper bag on the passenger seat, it struck me
that I was going to have to put some serious thought
into my new sex life. In the past I'd had an active
and mostly enjoyable one. Now, however, I had
Paddy to consider. There was no way I was having
my child grow up with a string of 'uncles'. Which
meant I'd have to plan carefully. That was a pity but
if it was a choice between planned sex and no sex
I knew which option I'd go for.

Kathleen had agreed to babysit and offered to stay
overnight in case I was late home. OK. That was good.
Not that I was planning to have sex with him on our
first date, but you never knew what might happen.

My afternoon at home after work was hectic.
Paddy was like a rosy-cheeked Antichrist. Ferdia was
picking me up at eight thirty as we had a reserva-
tion for eight forty-five. At a quarter to eight I was

still lying in Paddy's bed trying to cuddle him into the Land of Nod.

I forced myself to take deep breaths. It was OK. I would have time to get ready. More deep breaths. There was no point in freaking out or Paddy would never drop off. Finally, at eight on the button, Paddy relaxed and was asleep.

I slid out of his bed and crept silently out of the room. It was almost five past eight and I had a feeling Ferdia was the punctual type. Pulling off my clothes as I went, I jumped into and out of the shower. Quick towel, slather of moisturiser, dried my hair, slapped on some makeup and got into my sexy underwear and new dress. I had a quick look in the mirror. Getting there. I squinted at my watch. Eight twenty. Paddy gave a loud cry and I froze in my tracks but then there was silence, so I was pretty sure he'd been dreaming about some caper he and Mikey had been involved in.

I slipped my feet into my beautiful new shoes and admired them for a full thirty seconds. A final glance in the mirror and that was it. If he didn't like the look of me there wasn't a thing I could do about it.

I cantered down the stairs and just as I reached the bottom the bell rang. I opened the front door and a magnificent bunch of white orchids and red roses greeted me. 'Oh, Ferdia!' I was overwhelmed by their beauty and the scent.

He stepped into the hallway and bent to kiss my cheek. My face reddened and my heart thumped. 'Glad you like them. Are you ready to go?'

'I'll just pop these into a vase and say goodnight to Kathleen.'

Ferdia followed me into the kitchen and watched as I jammed his bouquet into a glass vase. Then I grabbed my handbag and pointed towards the door. As we went into the hallway, Kathleen emerged from the sitting room.

'Kathleen Brennan. Ferdia Ryan,' I said, gesturing between them. They shook hands.

'It's lovely to meet you, Kathleen,' Ferdia said.

I was anxious to be gone. All I needed was for Kathleen to slip into a trance and frighten away my one good chance of a roll in the hay. 'See you later, thanks a lot,' I said, and hurried Ferdia out of the door before any such thing could happen.

The restaurant was perfect. It was decorated like a sumptuous nineteenth-century bordello – all red velvet, beaded curtains and cushions, not to mention the extremely low lighting. There wasn't an electric lightbulb in evidence anywhere. All the light – such as it was – came from candles and oil lamps. A solicitous waiter seated us at our table and presented us with menus.

'This is lovely,' I said, as soon as he'd glided away.

Ferdia peered at me over his menu.

'I hope he doesn't break his neck on the way to the kitchen,' I added.

Ferdia looked bewildered.

'You know, the candles and stuff – it's almost dark in here.'

'Oh, right, right. But that's on purpose, Ruth.

Creates an ambience. None of your harsh strip-lighting here.'

'No,' I said, scanning the elaborately handwritten menu. 'It also means you can't see what you're eating, which is no harm, I suppose.'

'I don't think it's that. This restaurant is in the Michelin guide and I believe it got rave reviews in all the nationals.'

I had to stop making lame jokes. Jesus, if I wasn't careful I'd ruin my only chance of getting my iron. 'Of course, of course – only joking. I'm sure the food is first rate.'

Ferdia chuckled a sexy little chuckle. 'That's funny. Anyway, have a look at your menu. Marcus says the bass is out of this world. But decide for yourself – we have all night.' He stared at me, and sweat broke out along my upper lip. I hoped he meant what I thought he'd meant. The waiter returned and we both had the other-worldly bass, tiny potatoes and succulent mange-tout, accompanied by a crisp sauvignon blanc, followed by a delicious petit pot de chocolat, then magnificent coffee.

As we ate we chatted about the hotel, Limerick and London. I told Ferdia about Paddy and, though I didn't go into detail, I also told him about my recent separation and finding my father. He was impressed that my father was Gary Kennedy and even more so that Emerson was a movie-maker. But he soon made up for that.

'Ruth, would you mind if I told you how beautiful you look?'

I smiled. 'Knock yourself out.'

Ferdia took one of my hands in his. 'I have to say I've never met anyone like you.'

'I hope that's a good thing.'

'It might be the best thing that ever happened to me.'

A hot flush spread from my head to my toes as he stroked the back of my hand.

'I really don't want the evening to end,' he said, in his soft accent.

'I've had a lovely time,' I said.

'Would you . . . do you think you . . . No . . . I shouldn't . . .'

Ferdia stopped speaking but the pressure of his hand increased and I felt as if I was about to faint.

'What?' I said, 'You shouldn't what?'

'We only met a handful of days ago but I feel like I've known you all my life,' he said.

Welsh rarebit it might have been, but it worked. 'Me too.'

'It's only eleven and I was hoping that maybe you'd come back to my place for a drink.'

'I'd love to,' I said, trying not to shout in my enthusiasm. 'I have plenty of time. My babysitter's sleeping over.'

'Excellent,' Ferdia said.

I spied the waiter at the other end of the restaurant and tried to send him telepathic messages to hurry over with our bill. It worked and he trotted towards us with his silver platter.

As soon as we sat into Ferdia's car he pulled me close and kissed me. It was a long, slow, delicious kiss and if I hadn't been in a new, dignified stage of my life I might have suggested we go ahead right there in the car-park. It was also a bit of a disincentive that we were parked under a huge lamppost. When we stopped, Ferdia stared deep into my eyes for a full minute before he started the engine. 'It's not far,' he said.

Hooray, I thought, but I said, 'That's nice.'

He drove with the concentration of a man whose mind was elsewhere and within five minutes we were in the underground car-park of his apartment building. I was full of lust. It was almost six months since I'd had sex and that was bad enough, but then this gorgeous man with his perfect body and seductive kisses had appeared in my life.

We stood apart from each other in the lift, and when we arrived at his floor I followed him down a green-carpeted hallway. He opened a door and stood back to let me in. It was a nice apartment in a bland, professional-decorator way but the décor was the last thing on my mind.

I heard the door close behind me and turned. Ferdia grabbed me and soon we were kissing, our hands exploring. We staggered towards the sofa, clothes discarded with exquisite urgency, and fell, together, on to its leather expanse. I moaned and Ferdia kissed me. My body felt as if it might explode. And then his did.

Disappointment surged inside me but I told

myself to hold on. These things happen and the night was still young, wasn't it?

With a cry of ecstasy, he writhed on top of me, then lay still. 'That was incredible,' he said, burying his face in my neck. He sat up and kissed my face. 'Wasn't it amazing?'

I forced a smile.

'That was the best ever for me,' he said. 'Was it the same for you?'

'Mmmm,' I said.

'I'm so glad,' he said, cuddling me close as he dozed off.

Less than a minute later he was fast asleep. I rolled off the sofa, found my clothes and got dressed. I glanced at the man asleep on the leather sofa. He looked like an advertisement for handsomeness. His face was so beautiful and his body almost perfect. I thought back over the evening, how attentive he had been and how everything had been lovely. As my body gradually accepted that it wasn't going to get what it wanted, I felt a wave of tenderness towards him.

I leaned over and kissed his sleeping face. So what if he wasn't the best lover in the world? It was probably just a once-off thing anyway and it'd surely improve. Sex wasn't everything. Emerson had been one of the most exciting lovers I'd ever had and what good had that done me?

Ferdia opened his eyes, pulled me close and we kissed. It was warm and lovely. We chatted for a few minutes, and then he insisted on getting dressed and driving me home. As we sat outside my house in his car he asked if he could take me out again. 'Soon,' he said.

'Soon,' I echoed then got out of the car and went inside.

As I got ready for bed I thought about it all. I hadn't had out of the evening what I'd been hoping for but maybe, in a way, I'd got more. Ferdia thought I was beautiful and clever and desirable, and that felt good after the way Emerson had treated me.

He was more conservative and less adventurous than I was used to but maybe – just maybe – it was time I had a bit of that kind of stability in my life.

26

My relationship with Ferdia developed faster than a Ryanair turnaround. I liked being with him. He was interesting and ambitious – he told me all about his plans to own a chain of hotels. And he was interested in me – he listened to my plans and hopes.

He was endlessly understanding about my need to cater for Paddy's needs first and he didn't baulk when I told him about Kathleen. He was like a text-book romantic, constantly surprising me with flowers and small gifts. He had even begun to give me jewellery. As for the sex, well, it wasn't great, but it was companionable and Ferdia was so sure it was wonderful that I couldn't bring myself to tell him the truth. It seemed like a small price to pay.

About three weeks after I'd started seeing Ferdia the telephone rang in the middle of the night. I groped my way across the bed and picked up the receiver.

'Ruth?'

I sat up. I didn't answer.

'Ruth? Is that you?'

'Yes,' I said eventually.

'Look, I'm sorry if I woke you.'

'It's two o'clock in the morning, Emerson. What do you want?'

He was silent.

'Emerson?'

'I miss you, Ruth.'

I lay down in the bed and closed my eyes. 'You're drunk, Emerson.'

'Well, maybe I am but it's true. I miss you and Paddy.'

'Pity you didn't think about that a few months ago,' I said, and slammed down the receiver.

I wanted to scream. Who the fuck did he think he was? Well, he needn't think I was going to come running back now that he was sorry. Where was the love of his life? Why wasn't he with *her* at two o'clock in the morning?

I flopped on to my stomach and tried to get back to sleep, but Emerson's voice was still inside my head. Damn him anyway. Just as I was getting my life together he barges back in and tries to upend it all over again. Well, that wasn't happening, no matter what.

The next day Tracy laughed when I told her about his call. 'Fucking eejit,' she said. We were on our way into Kevin's to collect Chloe and Paddy.

Kevin opened the door. 'I hope you don't mean me,' he said, leading us into the kitchen.

'No,' Tracy said. 'Emerson – he's sorry.'

Kevin made a face. 'Sorry?'

I nodded. 'Rang me at two in the morning. Pissed as a coot. Told me he missed me.'

Kevin handed me a mug of coffee. 'Good.'

'Thanks,' I said. 'For the coffee and the support.'

'I'd say your one is a nightmare to live with,' Tracy said, with a grin.

'Well,' I said, sipping coffee, 'you know what they say – he's made his bed and now he can lie in it.'

'Anything happening with PAP?' Tracy said. 'I think I've convinced the twins' school to have a cake-sale.'

'They need all the help they can get,' Kevin said. 'I had a weird experience – well, if you could call it that.'

We both looked at him.

'Nothing risqué, I'm afraid. Just this weird message on my phone. The voice was distorted using one of those yokes Cher uses in that awful song.'

'Ooooooo,' Tracy said, melodramatically. 'James Bond.'

'Probably a kid playing a joke,' Kevin said.

'But what was the message?' I asked, jumping with curiosity.

'Just "Ballymoran. Find the report. Don't take no for an answer. Find the report,"' Kevin said, imitating an electronic voice.

'That's weird,' Tracy said, serious now. 'If it's a joke it's sick and if it's real, well, what the hell does it mean?'

Kevin shrugged. 'It's probably just somebody acting out a fantasy about being Deep Throat – like Watergate – but I'll have a bit of a search for that report anyway. It can't do any harm.'

'I suppose,' I said, as the kids ran in screaming for Ice-pops.

'I've been meaning to ask you, can I bring Ferdia to your barbecue, Trace?' I said. 'I think it's about time he got to know my friends.'

'Bring whoever you like – the more the merrier.'

'Thanks,' I said. 'You're coming, aren't you, Kevin?'

'The highlight of my social season.'

'That only says how pathetic you are, Kevin Regan,' Tracy told him.

'I know, I have no life,' he agreed.

'We'll have to get you a girlfriend, Kevin,' I said.

He snorted. 'Well, somebody'd better because I don't seem to have too much luck in that field myself.'

'But I thought you had a date on Wednesday night?' Tracy said.

'Did you?' I said. 'You never told me.'

'I had. It was a disaster. She was so boring I thought I might lose my mind.'

'You told me she was a ride,' Tracy said.

'Well, I don't think those were my exact words, Tracy, but yeah – she's a bit of all right in the looks department. Just boring.'

Tracy laughed. 'You see, that was your mistake, Kevin. If you hadn't bothered with the talking part . . .'

'Sex isn't everything, Tracy,' I said.

'Who says?'

'I think we should find Kevin a really nice girl,

one he can talk to *and* get on with, and the sex will take care of itself.'

'I don't know about that,' Kevin said, laughing now.

'I might have the very girl for you – Avril. She works with me.'

'Ask her to the barbecue, so,' Tracy said. 'What do you think, Kev?'

'I'm on, but what'll she think of Mikey?'

'We'll pretend he's a neighbour's child,' Tracy decided.

'Good idea,' Kevin said. 'What's this Avril like, anyway?'

'She's lovely – very pretty and great fun,' I said.

'Don't spend the whole time talking to her now, Kevin,' Tracy said. 'After all a good ride is better than all the talking in the world and don't bother denying it.'

'I'm with you on that, Trace,' Kevin said, and they both roared with laughter.

The conversation was making me edgy. 'Anyway, thanks for the coffee, Kevin – and for having Paddy. I'd better get going – I've a date at eight.'

Tracy winked at me and I collected a squealing Paddy from the garden and went in home. Why had that conversation unnerved me? It had to be the telephone call from Emerson. It had upset me and I couldn't pretend otherwise.

I stripped Paddy, fought him for his hat and threw him into the bath to wash off the grime he'd accumulated in Mikey's garden. As he poured water through plastic funnels, I thought about that phone call. What the hell was wrong with Emerson?

Obviously there was trouble in Paradise, but even so, why was he calling me in the middle of the night? For no good reason I suddenly remembered the prediction Kathleen had made a few weeks earlier about my soulmate already being in my life. Who was that supposed to be? Ferdia? Emerson? That clairvoyant stuff was rubbish! But I still couldn't help wondering whom she had meant.

27

'Ohmygodohmygodohmygod!' Avril squealed, when I asked her if she'd consider coming to Tracy's barbecue as a date for Kevin. 'Oh, my God! I'd love to! Is he nice? What does he look like? Do you think he'll like me? I'm not so sure about my hair since I cut it . . .'

Avril had had about a quarter of an inch cut off her long red hair the day before.

'He'll love you, Avril,' I said. 'What's not to love?'

'Oh, Ruth, you're so kind! And so good to think of me. When is it? What'll I wear? Will it be warm, do you think? How tall is he? I mean, I don't care but he might mind if I'm towering over him.'

'Pity about him,' I said. 'Wear whatever you like.'

'I will. I won't know anybody there, will I?'

'Well, you know me, and Ferdia's coming.'

'Aw, is he? That's lovely. Oh, my God, what will I wear? I don't know if I have anything suitable.'

'It's a barbecue, Avril. Wear whatever you feel like wearing.'

Avril bit her bottom lip. 'I will. But – sorry to be going on about this now, Ruth, you'll think I'm terrible – how tall is he? Look at me, Ruth, I'm not exactly small.'

Avril was like the best of all the Irish stereotypes and even in her Drury's uniform she was stunningly gorgeous. The pale green linen blouse matched her beautiful eyes and set off her porcelain skin and thick, curly red hair to perfection. She was built like an athlete, with long legs, a perfectly toned body and ample bosom. If Beyoncé had been Irish she might have looked like Avril. If she was lucky. 'Forget about Kevin and suit yourself,' I said. 'He'll be delighted to find himself on a date with you.'

'You're so good, Ruth.'

'I'm a saint,' I said, collecting my handbag. 'Now I'd better get on home to my other job. You OK?'

Avril sat down in the seat I'd just vacated. 'When did you say it was on?'

'Saturday.'

'Oh, my God! Two days! How will I get ready in time?'

I waved at her and headed for the door. Oh, those were the days, I thought, as I drove home in the August afternoon sunshine. Those were definitely the days – when I'd thought two days wasn't long to get ready for an important occasion. Nowadays two hours were a luxury.

Kathleen was babysitting for me now that Paddy was on holiday for the summer. She had an appointment with the doctor at three so she left almost as soon as I arrived home. Paddy was asleep on the sofa so I changed into shorts and a vest, made myself coffee, then took it and my book into the garden.

I opened the book and was about to sink into a welcome escape when I heard my name. I looked up to see Tracy's face just above our adjoining garden wall.

'Did you grow?' I asked.

'Only tits – well, not yet but soon these babies will be doing a bit of growing.'

'You're disgusting. What are you standing on?'

'A ladder. Derek was painting the eaves – give me patience. I doubt Michelangelo whinged as much when he was painting that ceiling wherever it is.'

'Is he finished?' I said, trying to see if the Walshes' eaves looked any different.

'No. Gone to work. Anyway, forget that, I have great news.'

'Good,' I said, closing my book.

'You won't believe this – Derek won four tickets for the Munster match in Paris in October.'

'That's lovely.'

'No, you don't understand – you can't get these tickets for any money. In fact, they're not even out yet – he won the promise of them in a Shannon draw.'

'Congratulations. Why don't you climb over the wall and have a coffee?'

'Can't. The twins are in the kitchen washing the dishes and they keep trying to get away.'

'Anyway, you're going to the big match in Paris.'

Tracy smiled. 'So are you.'

'What?'

'Not my idea – Derek insists.'

'I can't take that ticket,' I said. 'It'd be wrong – especially if they're like gold-dust.'

'You have to. He won't sell it, he wants to give it to you. Come on, Ruth, we'll have a great time in Paris and you'll enjoy the match and we can go shopping as well.'

The patio doors opened and Paddy came into the garden.

'Hey, Buster, you woke up,' I said. He ran down the garden and climbed on to the swing.

'So?' Tracy said. 'You'll come?'

'I don't know what to say.'

'Just say yes. I'm sorting out flights tonight – if we do it early we'll get cheap seats. Will I book you one?'

I looked at her pert face disembodied above the stone wall. A weekend in Paris sounded great. Kathleen'd probably offer to take Paddy, and if she didn't feel up to it, he had a queue of Burkes to spoil him for a couple of days.

'Go on,' I said, with a grin. 'I'll give you the money later.'

'Don't worry about that. I'm going to book the hotel tonight as well – for you too?'

I nodded. 'What will you do with the fourth ticket?'

'That's already spoken for,' Tracy said. 'Derek earmarked it for Kevin the minute he heard he'd won. If there's any Munster fan as dedicated as

Derek it's Kevin – I love that, don't you? When a real fan gets a ticket out of the blue.'

'Which makes me feel guilty.'

'No need. We'll convert you yet. Wait until you get into the stadium and hear "The Fields of Athenry" being belted out by thousands of fans. It'll make the hair on the back of your neck stand up, I promise.'

'Thanks, Trace,' I said, overwhelmed by the kindness of my neighbours, 'and tell Derek thanks as well.'

'Don't mention it.'

'Are you all ready for the barbecue? Can I do anything to help?'

'Not now but by Saturday afternoon I'll probably be cracking up. Will you be around?'

'Definitely – just give me jobs and I'll be glad to help.'

'Thanks. Probably the biggest job you'll have to do is keep me calm. Is your boyfriend coming by the way?'

'He is – and I managed to get a date for Kevin.'

'Excellent. Anyway, I'd better get down. I can see into the kitchen and I think that scut Jade has turned on the TV and is standing in the doorway watching it. Talk to you later.'

'Don't fall,' I shouted, as I settled back into my lounger. Paddy was in his sandbox digging as if his life depended on it. Paris! That'd be nice. And Kevin was going too! We'd have a laugh. I hoped Ferdia wouldn't mind, but he wasn't the jealous type and he knew that Tracy, Derek and Kevin were my friends. He might even be able to get a ticket and come along himself.

The more I thought about it, the more I warmed to the idea. I needed a break from my mad life and I loved Paris. I'd been there a few times before but probably the most memorable was a week that Emerson and I had spent there together.

We'd stayed in a small hotel half-way up a hilly street near Sacré Coeur. Our tiny hotel room looked down over the rooftops of Paris from its wrought-iron balcony and the bustle of the street never stopped. We seemed to spend our days wandering around, stopping at museums, galleries and shops, whenever anything took our fancy. Drinking wine as we looked over the Seine. Eating crêpes that dripped butter and honey as we walked, dining each evening in tiny restaurants where the décor was all nineteen-seventies greasy-spoon but the food was authentic and delicious.

The memory was too much and I jumped up and walked purposefully to the shed. I got out the hedge clippers and savagely attacked a fuchsia that was threatening to invade the back of the house. How could Emerson have been dumb enough to plant it so close to the house? I thought, as I hacked and slashed with mounting enthusiasm. Half-wit. Fool. Bloody eejit.

Paddy came running up to join in the desecration and I chopped and chopped and chopped, until all that was left was a gnarled stump. Good, I thought, as I put away the clippers and went indoors to begin the dinner. That bloody thing had needed to be chopped down for a while. Now all I had to do was find a way to destroy the roots and then I'd plant something else in that spot. Somehow the irony escaped me.

The morning of Tracy's barbecue dawned bright and sunny. I spent most of the day on trips between my house, Kevin's and Tracy's. In the early afternoon, Kevin and I staggered into the garden carrying stacked kitchen chairs. Derek was up a ladder securing a huge green canvas gazebo at the end of the 150-foot garden.

'Hey, birthday boy!' I shouted. Derek looked down at us and grinned. He was wearing a black T-shirt with a huge '30' emblazoned across the front.

'Don't go anywhere, Ruth. Let me hammer this home and I'll be down for my birthday kiss.'

Kevin and I arranged the chairs inside the gazebo as Tracy had instructed. Just as we finished Derek jumped off the ladder and presented me with his newly shaved cheek. 'Plant it,' he said.

I kissed him and he laughed. 'I'd prefer a bit of a snog but that wife of mine thinks she's Lorena Bobbitt so I'd be afraid,' he said, and winked.

It was probably my favourite thing about Derek Walsh: while he was full of big-man talk, he was a devoted family man who'd no more think of snogging me than he'd wear a pair of red patent high heels and a bra.

'Thanks for the ticket, Derek, man,' Kevin said, emerging from the gazebo. 'I can't believe I'm going to that match. How much do I owe you?'

Derek grinned. 'Don't be stupid – you can't repay me. That ticket's priceless. You can stand me a couple of pints in gay Paree, though.'

'I can't thank you enough—' Kevin began, and Derek thumped his arm.

'Shut up, you sound like a girl,' he said. 'If you keep doing that I'll give the bloody ticket to somebody else.'

'Jaysus, don't,' Kevin said, in a mock-baritone. 'Fucksake, man.'

Tracy appeared with a tray.

'Coffee for the workers,' she called, placing it on a long trestle table. 'Come and get it.'

Derek, Kevin and I collected our mugs, then sat on deck-chairs and surveyed the garden. The gazebo was festooned with hundreds of strung-together balloons and a huge paper banner with '*Happy Birthday Derek*' in multicoloured letters. The kids had made it without too many disasters, if you didn't count the fact that Mikey had eaten two crayons and Chloe and Paddy had decorated each other's faces and clothes with poster paint.

A series of trestle tables that Tracy had hired stood along one side of the garden with a stack of white tablecloths on the first. Five borrowed barbecues of different shapes and sizes were ranged along the cobbled patio. The Walshes had a really nice garden and it was ideal for a huge party. The end of the garden was devoted to swings and a wooden playhouse that Derek had built for the kids. Both side walls were covered with climbers, clematis, honeysuckle, ivy, wisteria and rambling roses.

There was only one thing I had reservations about and that was a big new water feature that Derek had been building. It had started out as a Zen stone and water thing, which was Tracy's idea and had sounded great, but Derek added new features whenever he had a chance. At first Tracy had objected but eventually she gave up. Now one corner of the garden was a mass of fountains, pools and a small windmill that spun its fins every time the water cascaded. According to Derek, it still wasn't finished. In spite of that it made soothing babbling noises. 'Anyway you could turn up the sound on that so I can hear it in my garden?' I asked.

'No, but if you're good I might build one for you,' he said.

'Promises, promises.' Tracy drained her mug, then clapped her hands. 'OK! Let's get going, slaves, there's lots to be done.'

Kevin and I worked with her all afternoon. By the time we had finished setting things up it was past six so I ran in home for a quick shower. Kathleen had arrived, resplendent in a plain violet sleeveless maternity dress. As I dressed my stomach was full of butterflies. I knew that the prospect of Ferdia meeting my family and friends was freaking me out.

He was such a sweetie. So handsome and kind, reliable and thoughtful. But he wasn't much of a laugh. He took life seriously – and it wasn't that he didn't have a sense of humour, he just didn't think everything was funny, that was all. And that wasn't the worst fault you could have, was it?

The doorbell rang as I completed my makeup and I heard Avril's high-pitched voice floating up the stairs. I'd suggested she come to my house first and that I introduce her to Kevin at the barbecue. Jesus, this matchmaking lark was a struggle and I was beginning to regret it. I'd warned Kevin to find something half decent to wear.

'But it's a barbecue,' he complained, when I told him not to wear shorts, 'and the weather's really hot.'

'I don't care,' I said. 'You're meeting Avril for the first time – you need to make a good impression.'

'She'll be impressed by my wit and sparkling conversation.'

'Maybe,' I said, 'but why not wear those lovely khaki linen trousers you had on when you went to meet your editor last week?'

Kevin groaned. 'Maybe I should wear a suit.'

'Jesus, Kevin, you have no fashion sense! You can't wear a suit to a barbecue. The linen trousers will be perfect, and don't you have a nice black shirt?'

'It makes me look like Alfie Moon.'

'No, it doesn't, trust me. Just wear those clothes and you'll be irresistible to women.'

'All women?' Kevin said, head to one side.

I nodded.

'Promise?'

I nodded again and wondered what that meant

as Paddy and Mikey ran by with the Claw in a huge saucepan.

By the time I came downstairs Avril was chatting a mile a minute to Kathleen. She looked fabulous. Suddenly I felt protective of Kevin and afraid that she mightn't like him. She was wearing a sunshine yellow T-shirt that clung to her breasts and stopped just short of her pierced belly button, tight-fitting washed-out denim jeans and flat sandals. She ran to me as soon as I came into the room.

'Oh, my God, Ruth! Your son is beautiful! You never told me he was so gorgeous.'

Paddy was sitting on the worktop in the kitchen in a clean blue T-shirt that emphasised the colour of his Emerson-like eyes. He was also wearing a pair of three-quarter-length navy shorts, and Kathleen had washed his face.

'Can I go to Mikey's, Mum?' he said, reaching his arms out to me.

I lifted him off the worktop.

'We're going to Chloe's party,' I said.

The doorbell rang at five to seven.

It was Ferdia, just as I'd known it would be. I'd told him to be at my house at about five to seven and so, being Ferdia, he had taken me at my word. As soon as I opened the door, he handed me a bunch of long-stemmed red roses and kissed my cheek. 'Hello, gorgeous,' he said.

I stood on tiptoe and kissed his lips. Ferdia was a good man. A reliable, nice man. I didn't care what anybody else thought of him.

'That was a nice surprise,' he said.

'I'm just happy to see you,' I said. 'Avril and Kathleen are here and we'd better get going, Tracy is probably on high doh by now.'

'I'm a little nervous myself,' Ferdia said, as he followed me into the kitchen. He looked like an ad for manhood. He'd obviously had his hair cut that afternoon so it was fitted almost perfectly to his head. His skin had a lovely glow of health and vitality. His eyes were clear and bright, his body nothing short of beautiful. He was wearing cream linen pants and a black shirt much like the ones I'd told Kevin to wear, but while Kevin's were hit-and-miss chain-store clothes, Ferdia's were beautifully cut designer versions. And I could see that he was telling me the truth – he was nervous. I wound my arms round his waist. 'Why?' I said.

He smoothed my hair and kissed my forehead. 'I'm not the life and soul of the party – I'm just not great at that stuff.'

I stood on tiptoe and gave him a lingering kiss. 'You're great,' I said. 'They'll love you. Don't worry about a thing.'

28

Unfortunately, Ferdia was right and I was wrong – my friends didn't warm to him immediately. Well, when I say 'friends' I mean Tracy. Kevin didn't really speak with Ferdia: all he seemed interested in was Avril, whom he whisked off mere seconds after I'd introduced them. He'd worn the clothes I'd picked out and looked sexy in a boyish, Jude Law kind of way. Which wasn't lost on Avril, who could hardly take her eyes off him from the moment they met.

Paddy detached himself from me and went, screaming with excitement, down the garden as soon as he spotted his partners in crime. Which left me with Kathleen and Ferdia. First we met the birthday boy: Derek was resplendent in a striped apron and tending three of the five barbecues. He waved his tools at us and promised us 'a chargrill to remember'.

The next person we encountered was Tracy's mother, Rhonda, who was working the other two barbecues. Rhonda was a formidable woman. She had three children – Tracy and her sisters, Angie and Denise – whom she'd raised pretty much single-handed. Her husband was a Limerick man called Ollie Hegarty who'd been killed in a car crash when the three were little girls.

Rhonda belonged to a huge Chinese-Irish family and had supported her daughters by working in her younger brother's chain of restaurants. While her passport said she was a native of Hong Kong, her accent clearly marked her as a Limerick woman. She wiped her hands on a cloth and shook hands with Ferdia and Kathleen.

She had a lovely Oriental face, her skin was clear and unblemished and her still coal-black hair was tied in a neat bun at the back of her neck. Within seconds, she and Kathleen had fallen into conversation about the Chinese zodiac – who was a Rat, who was a Monkey and who was a Dog. I told them I could have figured that out without ever knowing anyone's birthdate. They gave me almost identical indulgent smiles, then carried on talking.

Ferdia and I excused ourselves and I led him down the garden towards one of the trestle tables, which was sporting a healthy booze collection. He was polite and lovely to everyone we met, but I could tell that he was still nervous. Maybe if he had a drink he'd feel better.

I filled two glasses with wine. As I turned to hand him his, Tracy appeared. 'Hi, Tracy!' I said. 'I'd like you to meet Ferdia – this is my good friend and neighbour Tracy Walsh.'

They shook hands.

'Lovely to meet you, Tracy,' he said. 'I've heard

so much about you. The party is great, isn't it? You must be really pleased with it – everything's terrific.'

Tracy gave him a half-smile, then pulled her cigarettes from the pocket of her food-spattered apron. 'Do you want a fag, Ruth?'

I shook my head. Ferdia looked at me in surprise.

'Ferdia?' Tracy said, holding the packet towards him.

He took a small step backwards and held up a hand. 'No, No, thanks, Tracy. I don't smoke.'

Tracy lit her cigarette and shook the packet at me. 'Are you sure, Ruth?'

I narrowed my eyes at her. 'I'm off them – I told you.'

'I've heard that one before,' Tracy said, taking a deep drag. 'Well, back into the kitchen. See you later.' She hurried back up the garden towards the house, unhooking Mikey from the apple-tree he was swinging on as she passed.

'I didn't know you smoked,' Ferdia said, as if I'd been keeping vital information from him.

I took a mouthful of wine. 'I don't.'

'But Tracy—'

'Don't mind Tracy,' I said. 'She's just joking. I used to smoke years ago and I've had the odd one since but I don't smoke now.'

Ferdia kissed my lips.

'Any chance you'd get us some food?' I said, handing him my empty glass. 'I'll find us a couple of chairs – I know where they're stashed.'

'No problem,' Ferdia said, and walked off.

I went down to the gazebo and grabbed a couple of folding deckchairs that I'd seen Derek put under a table earlier and set them up in an empty spot. Ferdia was queuing at the long food table, chatting amicably to Tracy's sister, Denise. Half of the women in the place were admiring him, and he was pretty good eye-candy, there was no doubt about that. It was a shame he wasn't more fun—

I caught my breath. Oh, my God! Poor Ferdia – I was such a bitch! What more did I want from him? 'Well, maybe some decent sex,' a treacherous part of me said.

I looked about to distract myself. The garden was full of chattering adults and children. Music, talk and laughter filled the air, along with smoke and delicious smells from the barbecues. Kathleen and Rhonda were now sitting on a bench and, by the look of things, Kathleen was reading Rhonda's palm.

Tracy appeared at the back door, steering a stocky blonde woman out into the garden. She spotted me, waved and disappeared back inside. I searched for a sight of Paddy, but couldn't see him, with all the people. I was fairly sure he'd been with Chloe on the swing just a few minutes earlier. Ferdia appeared, bearing two paper plates like prizes. He sat down beside me and handed me a pile of barbecued chicken, salad and crusty brown bread. The food was delicious and I realised I was starving – I hadn't eaten since breakfast.

'This is very tasty,' Ferdia said.

'Mmm,' I said.

He patted my hand and I began to relax. They'd
all get to know him, I thought, and then they'd like
him. How could you not?

I was just finishing my salad when there was a
huge commotion up by the barbecues. The twins
were hopping up and down shouting at Derek, who
threw his barbecue fork on to the grass and ran
towards the side gate. I stood up and scanned the
garden for Paddy. No sign. The swings were occupied by a couple of teenage girls in minuscule skirts
and even tinier T-shirts. My stomach squeezed and
I dropped my plate.

'What is it?' Ferdia said.

I didn't stop to answer him, just ran up the garden.
As I reached the gate Kevin was behind me.

'What is it? What's wrong?' he said, as we hurried
out to the front.

I shook my head and kept going. Mikey Regan was
shouting and pointing on the Walshes' front wall. Kevin
ran to him, grabbed him and we all followed his finger.
Derek's red Toyota Avensis, with the taxi sign on top,
was making its way down our hilly cul-de-sac towards
the main street with Derek in pursuit. My heart almost
stopped as I saw Chloe and Paddy waving at everyone through the back windscreen. I screamed, climbed
over the wall and began to run. Kevin flew past me.

Within seconds, the driverless car was almost at
the intersection with the main street and I knew
that neither of the men chasing was going to get to
it before it rolled out into the traffic. I ran as fast I
could but I was even further away.

Please God, I begged. Please let somebody get there and stop the car. I'm sorry for all the things I've done that I shouldn't have done. I'm sorry for all the mean things I said about Selma and Emerson. Sorry for only caring about stupid things like having good sex. All I really care about is Paddy. If Paddy's OK I'll never ask for another thing and I'll really try to be a better person.

Like a slow-motion scene, the red taxi left the cul-de-sac and picked up speed as it shot on to the main road. A yellow car skidded and swerved to avoid it. Kevin had outstripped Derek and was almost at the car.

I ran out of the cul-de-sac and straight on to the street as a bus travelling in the opposite direction almost hit the taxi. The driver yanked the wheel and the taxi floated on. It was now heading straight for a stone wall. Kevin grabbed the handle on the driver's door and threw himself inside.

Then, with a horrible crunch, the car hit the wall.

Two seconds after the impact Derek was there and so was I. He opened the back door. Paddy and Chloe had slid on to the floor and were a bit tossed-looking but none the worse. Derek handed Paddy to me and lifted Chloe out. Tracy was running across the road, screaming. She grabbed Chloe from Derek and hugged her.

'She's fine, love, she's fine – they're both fine,' he said.

Tracy was crying and kissing him. Paddy was perched on my hip, watching, and I was vowing to

God to keep all the promises I'd made. Then I remembered Kevin. I walked to the front of the car and screamed. His face was awash with blood. He opened his eyes and looked at me. 'Paddy? Chloe?'

'They're fine,' I said, searching for the source of the blood.

He tried to sit forward but something must have hurt so he sat back again. 'I couldn't get there in time – just swerved a bit. Braked but not enough.'

'No, Kev, it was – the kids are fine, thanks to you. God knows what would have happened if the car had hit the wall at full speed.'

I touched the side of his face and he closed his eyes.

'Fucking hell!' It was Derek's voice. 'Call an ambulance, someone – quick. Kevin? Kev? You OK, man?'

'Fucking hell, call an ambulance!' Chloe roared.

'Fucking hell, call an ambulance!' Paddy echoed.

Kevin didn't move. My breath caught in my throat and I held Paddy tightly. The reality of everything broke in on top of me and my knees turned to water. Derek moved past me and shook his shoulders. Kevin's eyes opened, then closed immediately. Derek punched digits in his mobile phone. Suddenly Ferdia and Kathleen appeared.

'You OK?' Ferdia said, putting his arms round me.

I pulled away. 'Fine – thanks, Ferdia. Kevin saved the kids . . .' I looked at Kathleen. 'Kevin saved the kids,' I said again. She nodded, and my knees began to feel normal again.

'Hi, could you send an ambulance to O'Connell Avenue?' Derek was saying. 'Yeah, that's right – there's been an accident . . . Derek Walsh . . . Thanks.'

I felt as if I was frozen to the spot.

'He'll be fine,' Derek said. 'When they hit the wall he must have hopped his head off the steering-wheel.'

'It was a brave thing to do,' Ferdia said.

'Yes – yes, it was,' I said, and looked back at Kevin, who was stirring in his seat.

'They hit the wall an awful whack,' Derek continued, 'but only for Kevin it'd have been a lot worse. The small fellas'd have been thrown out through the windscreen with the impact.'

'Probably would have been killed outright,' Ferdia said.

'Jesus, Ferdia! Don't say that,' I said.

'It wasn't in their destiny to be killed,' Kathleen said.

'Holy Mary Mother of God,' Tracy said, behind me.

Kevin opened his eyes. 'Where's Mikey?'

'Mikey's grand,' Tracy told him. 'He's in my house – I'll mind him, don't worry about it.'

Then the ambulance arrived and the pandemonium increased as the medics fought their way through the throng from the barbecue who had collected round the car to catch the show. They lifted Kevin on to a stretcher and Derek decided to go to the hospital with him.

'It's the least I can do,' he said, as he stepped up into the ambulance and waved at us. Chloe and Paddy waved back.

Tracy grabbed my arm. 'Can we go to your house?' she said, eyes bright, face distorted with fear.

We started across the road through the crowd who were now socialising on the street. Kathleen and Rhonda were in the middle of the road each holding the hand of one of the twins, who were almost hysterical. As soon as the girls saw Tracy and Chloe they ran towards them and wrapped themselves round their mother and sister, sobbing wildly.

Behind them stood a stony-faced Lauren. Rhonda beckoned her five-year-old granddaughter. She stepped forward, but kept her eyes on Tracy.

Tracy handed Chloe to Rhonda, and Kathleen took Jordan and Jade aside. Tracy and Lauren locked eyes, like something out of *Gunfight at the OK Corral*, then Tracy opened her arms and Lauren pitched forward. 'I'm sorryMummysorryMummysorryMummy,' she wailed, as Tracy caught her.

Tracy kissed her silky black hair and whispered to her.

'I won't drive Daddy's car any more, I promise,' Lauren wailed.

'Good,' Tracy said.

'We were just playing a game of going to the seaside – me and Chloe and Paddy – and I was standing up to get Daddy's sunglasses and I only stepped on the thing in the middle cos I couldn't reach and the car moved away and I jumped out . . .'

Holy shit! I thought.

Tracy caught my eye over her daughter's head. 'Sorry,' she said.

'No harm done.'

Tracy raised an eyebrow.

'No, really,' I said. 'Well, if you don't count the state of the car and that Kevin's in hospital and that your barbecue is ruined . . .'

At exactly that moment a fat drop of rain splashed on to my head. I looked up at an enormous black cloud. More raindrops. Tracy deposited Lauren on the ground and held her hand.

'Come on,' I said, as thunder rumbled. I put my free arm round Tracy's shoulders and we ran towards my house as the long overdue rain bucketed down on to the street.

Just as we entered the cul-de-sac I saw a police car pull up. Ferdia trotted up to me. 'You OK?' he asked, rubbing rainwater off his face.

'They'll probably want a statement and stuff,' I said, pointing towards the police who were surveying the scene.

Ferdia rubbed his arms. 'I'll deal with them, if you like.'

'Would you?'

'It'd be my pleasure,' he said. 'You take Paddy into the house – I can always get you if you're needed.'

I squeezed his arm and kissed him. 'You're the best, Ferdia.'

He turned me by the shoulders until I was

pointing back into the cul-de-sac and I took off again towards the house. Mind you, I wasn't sure why I was running now. Paddy and I were already soaked to the skin. Maybe I just wanted to go home.

29

Ferdia was great with the aftermath of the crash. He dealt with the police, the tow truck, the assembled barbecue guests, protecting Tracy and me from most of it. Everybody was singing his praises – even Tracy. After all the excitement had died down he offered to stay with me. Everybody had gone home – even Kathleen – and Paddy was fast asleep in his bed.

I kissed him. 'No, it's fine. You go on home. You've done enough for one night.'

Ferdia, whose clothes had dried on him by now, wound his arms round me and kissed my lips. 'I can't ever do enough for you, Ruth, don't you know that?' he said. 'It really is my pleasure to be able to help. Will I stay until Derek gets home?'

I rested my head against his chest and listened to the beat of his kind heart. 'No, really. Tracy rang and he said he'd stay another while with Kevin.'

'Oh, right – how is Kevin?'

'They think he's OK but he had a bad bang on the head and they want to run a few tests.'

'I'd be happy to stay,' Ferdia said.

I looked up at him and wondered fleetingly why I didn't want him to – surely I should. I dismissed the thought and decided I was tired and strung out. 'Go home, love. Have a nice hot shower and a good night's rest. You did a lot of great work this evening – we'd have been lost without you.'

'All right – but you'll call me if you need anything?'

'I promise.'

My house echoed with silence as soon as he had gone and my first thought was of Kevin. Why weren't they back yet? Maybe the hospital had discovered brain damage.

I paced around the house, wishing I hadn't thrown away my last packet of cigarettes. When the door-bell rang I jumped and ran to answer it. Tracy was on the doorstep, swaddled in a huge red fleece and holding a bottle of wine and a plate of food.

'Come in,' I said, dragging her into the kitchen.

'They're all asleep in my house. Derek rang – he and Kevin are on their way home.'

'Kevin's OK?'

Tracy poured wine into the only two clean glasses she could find and handed me one. 'He's grand – had to have a few stitches, OK, but the brain seems to be all right, thank God.' She took a packet of cigarettes out of her pocket.

'Give me one of those,' I said.

'I thought you were off them.'

'Tomorrow. Give me one.'

'What would Ferdia say?'

I grabbed them and lit one hungrily. It made me feel dizzy, but I didn't care.

'Thank God,' I said, exhaling slowly. 'Come into the sitting room. I can't sit on a hard chair.'

Tracy followed me in and we threw ourselves into my two overstuffed armchairs, drank our wine and smoked our cigarettes.

'Looks like the boob job is off the cards,' Tracy said, after a few minutes.

'How can you worry about something like that now?'

'The wall made shit out of the cab – I'll have to use the money to replace it or we'll starve.'

'What about the insurance?'

'Our premium would go through the roof if we tried to claim – we can't afford that.'

I considered what she'd said. 'I can't pretend I'm sorry you're not having the boob job but I know you're disappointed so I'm sorry about that,' I said.

'I couldn't care less.'

'Really?'

'After what nearly happened tonight the size of my boobs is a very small thing.' She paused. 'I can't believe I said that – *a very small thing.*'

We laughed.

'Anyway, you know what I mean,' she continued. 'The way I look at it is that at least I have the money to sort out the cab and Derek will be delighted – he was dead set against me having the boob job.'

We lapsed into silence as we finished our wine.

'I'm really sorry about what happened,' Tracy said, putting her glass on the floor.

'It wasn't your fault.'

'I know, but Lauren is still my child and she's too little to be responsible, so I have to think I am.'

'Jesus, if we were all to take complete responsibility for what our children do I'd probably be arrested,' Kevin's voice said.

Tracy and I shot off our chairs and ran at him.

'You're OK,' I said. I couldn't resist touching the row of sutures on his forehead lightly with my finger.

'I might be better than before,' he said. 'Great drugs in that place.'

I hugged him as relief flooded through me. Everything was all right now.

'Jaysus, if I thought I'd have two women all over me like a rash I'd have crashed the bloody cab myself years ago.' Derek's voice.

I stepped away, suddenly embarrassed by the intensity of what I was feeling. 'How did you two get into my house?' I said.

'You left the front door open,' Kevin said, sitting into the armchair Tracy had vacated.

Tracy and Derek wrapped their arms round each other.

'What did the doctors say? Do you want something to eat or drink?' I was hovering over Kevin.

He grinned up at me. 'Which question would you like me to answer first?'

'What did the doctors say?'

'That I was fine, just a touch of concussion. They said to be careful for a couple of days, go back if I had bad headaches, that kind of thing.'

'Great,' I said. 'And food? Do you want anything?'

'I think I'll just go home to bed. I'm whacked.'

'You should come and stay at our place,' Derek said.

'Yeah,' Tracy added. 'Mikey's already there and you shouldn't be by yourself in case you get sick.'

'No, really, I'll be fine,' Kevin said.

'But you might get sick during the night,' Tracy said. 'I won't sleep if I'm worried about you at home alone, Kevin. Come on.'

'Really, I'll be fine, Trace. You have a house full of people already.'

'You can stay here,' I said, before I thought about it.

Everybody turned to look at me. I blushed. 'In the spare room. Kathleen's gone home.'

'That's a great idea,' Tracy said.

'I don't know,' Kevin said.

'Please, Kev,' Tracy said. 'For me? So that I won't be worrying about you? I know you already saved my child today but if you do this one other little thing for me I swear I won't ask you to do anything else ever.'

Kevin laughed and looked at me. 'If you're sure?'

'Of course I'm sure,' I said. 'You saved my child as well – it's the least I can do.'

'That's settled so,' Derek said. 'I'm off home to my bed, come on, wife.'

I showed them to the door and went back into the sitting room to Kevin. He was as pale as a ghost, his new scar livid along his hairline. 'Are you sure you don't want anything?' I said.

His face was tired and drawn. 'What are you offering?'

I ignored the innuendo. 'Tea, coffee, wine?'

'Tea'd be great.'

While I waited for it to draw I piled some of the left-over barbecue food that Tracy had brought on to plates. Then I poured the tea, I put the lot on to a tray and went back into the sitting room. Kevin was lying on the sofa, his hands behind his head, staring at the ceiling.

'Penny for them,' I said, and put the tray on the coffee-table.

Kevin sat up and reached for his tea. 'I was thinking about Ballymoran.'

'What put that into your head?'

'I had another call yesterday from that weird guy.'

'The Cher impersonator? What did he say this time?'

'He gave me the name of this other company, Safewaste, based in Offaly. He told me to check them out.'

'That was it?'

'Pretty much. He doesn't stay on the phone shooting the shit. Anyway, I spent yesterday having a good nose round and I think this guy's genuine.'

'Why doesn't he just tell all instead of dropping clues?'

Kevin sipped his tea. 'I reckon he doesn't want to be identified as the leak.'

'What did you find?' I picked up a cold chicken wing and bit into it.

'I got on to a guy I know in the Companies Office and discovered that Safewaste was closed down in 1987 for illegally dumping chemical waste. Big environmental scandal at the time.'

'But what has that to do with Ballymoran?'

Kevin put down his cup. 'The Ring brothers owned Safewaste. They own Boru Buildings now.'

'You're kidding.'

'No, I swear. And now that they've reinvented themselves, they're back with a vengeance. Anything dangerous you want to dump, then Boru are the boys to do it. They're flavour of the month in waste disposal.'

'So what next?'

'I'll get back on to the Environmental Commission. I need a copy of that environmental-impact report, have a look again at the pollutant levels and the findings.'

He was yawning now, with his newly stitched forehead and his boyish grin, and I felt a wave admiration for him. He wasn't giving up on his story, despite the failed court case and lack of evidence. 'Do you want to go to bed?' I asked.

'With you?'

I mock-glared at him. 'No! Come on. I'll show you to your room. You're knackered.'

'I could do with a couple of hours' shut-eye.'

'Come on, so,' I said.

Kevin and I climbed the stairs, and the atmosphere grew more and more charged with each step. By the time we were outside the spare bedroom I was almost shaking. 'There you go,' I said, in my best cheery voice. 'You're in luck because I changed the sheets this morning.'

'That's great,' Kevin said, eyes fixed on mine. I stood with him in the doorway and tried to move but somehow those eyes held me. Suddenly Paddy gave a loud unintelligible shout in his sleep and the spell was broken.

'He must be having a great dream,' Kevin said.

'Well, it's thanks to you that he's safe in his own bed. Sleep well.'

I walked away and was reaching out to open my bedroom door when I heard my name.

Kevin was standing in the doorway of the spare bedroom, looking at me intently.

I smiled. 'Yes?'

But he just kept staring at me. A variety of emotions skittered across his face.

'Kev?'

He blinked as if he was waking up, and a vague version of his normal smile appeared.

'Goodnight, Kev,' I said.

He nodded. 'Night, Ruth.'

I stood and waited until he'd gone into the bedroom. He was concussed, after all, not himself. I checked on Paddy, who was sleeping the sleep of the oblivious, and as I bent to kiss his cheek I thought it was probably a good thing that he had no idea of how much danger he'd been in.

Then I had a long shower, luxuriating in the needles of hot water, which beat some of the tension out of me. Jesus, I was so tired. I got into bed, positive I'd be asleep in seconds.

No such luck. My body was so worn out after everything that had happened that it almost moaned with pleasure when I lay down – but my brain had other ideas. The day's events played over and over in my head as residual adrenaline kept me wide awake and alert. I sat up in bed and read my book, but I couldn't concentrate. After about an hour, with not as much as a drooping eyelid, I decided to go downstairs and watch TV.

It was almost four a.m. and the house had that silent but occupied feel. I peeked in at Paddy again. Still sound asleep. Then – after a short debate with myself – I opened the door to the spare room. Kevin was lying on his back in the single bed. His eyes were closed and he was as still as a corpse. I stood and watched but he didn't move and all the horror stories I'd ever heard about head injuries flooded into my mind.

I stepped into the dark room but still couldn't hear or see anything. As my eyes adjusted I saw that he'd taken off his clothes and was lying on the bed in his jocks, the duvet in a heap on the floor beside him. His face was luminously pale and his hands were flung back on either side of his head like a baby's.

I crept over to the bed and listened hard. The sound of gentle breathing reassured me. He was fine. Then he sighed and turned on his side. Inside, I felt a flutter that reminded me of happiness. Kevin was

grand, Paddy was grand, and if I was in luck I'd find
a rerun of some old movie meant for insomniacs.
Briefly I considered opening a bottle of wine, then
decided I didn't need it. If I was honest with myself
I'd have to admit that that was another thing India
had been right about: I was drinking too much and,
worse, since Gibraltar I'd been using booze as a
crutch. I had no intention of adding alcoholism to
my list of problems.

As I closed the door of the bedroom silently
behind me, I thanked God for making everything
all right and vowed to keep the promises I'd made
as I ran down the road after the runaway taxi.

30

For the first week or so after the crash I was euphoric. I was so relieved that everything had turned out OK that nothing ordinary could faze me. Once that wore off, I had a bumpy few days. But whether that was caused by the evaporation of the euphoria or the endless hours of listening to Avril about Kevin's prowess in the sack, I wasn't sure.

I really liked Avril – after all, I had fixed her up with one of my best friends. And although we didn't have a lot in common we always got on well during the short periods of time we spent together. But all that changed when Ferdia decided that the only way Drury's Limerick could move into the big-time was to become part of the corporate-conference circuit.

He spent weeks working on a campaign to attract big business and was ecstatic when the Institute of Alternative Practices decided to have their annual conference at Drury's in mid-September. The woman who made the booking said something about the need to complete their business a certain number of days before the autumn equinox. I didn't disagree. Or tell anybody what she'd said. Money was money and 'corporate' was a word that could be interpreted in a variety of ways.

As part of his new strategy to make Drury's a cutting-edge enterprise, Ferdia decided to employ two more receptionists and have Avril and me work together even before the holistics arrived. At first I was glad – the day could be long and boring without anybody to chat with – but by the end of our first fortnight working together I was thinking of asking Ferdia to transfer me to the night shift.

'Oh, I swear, Ruth,' Avril said, one morning in late September, 'I never before knew the heights my body was capable of reaching.'

I looked up from the bookings I was sorting through on the computer and struggled to think of an appropriate response. 'Oh,' was all I managed.

It didn't stop Avril: 'I know it sounds like something out of a bodice-ripper but, honestly, I don't believe I've ever felt like a real woman before.'

'I'm delighted,' I said.

'Truly. Kevin touches me in—'

'Enough! Kevin is my friend, Avril, and there are things I don't need to know about him.'

Avril smiled. 'I didn't mean my body. I just meant that I so love being with him, Ruth. He's funny and knows things and we talk all the time and it's so interesting, and as well as that he's a hell of a ride.'

'Sewer mouth,' I said, laughing. 'I'm glad things are working out for you. Kevin really is a great guy.'

And I *was* glad, but a bit sensitive about hearing the details. I knew that that was at least in part to do with the non-event that was my sex life with Ferdia. After two weeks of trying to dodge details of Kevin's lovemaking techniques, I decided it was time that I tackled that area of my own life. I'd find a book and an opportunity to discuss our problems. Then everything would be all right.

After a few Googling attempts that mostly yielded pornography, I eventually found a book called, *I Come, You Come – We All Come Together*. According to the blurb, it was by a man called Howard Ferris and it was 'a sensitive account of one man's journey to ecstasy through his partner's fulfilment' – which was all a bit cringy, but I was desperate.

Once the Book, as I now thought of it, arrived in its plain brown wrapper, I no longer had any excuses. I arranged to cook Ferdia's favourite meal – tandoori chicken – at his apartment. Kathleen, the saint, was staying over with Paddy. She really was a godsend, that woman. Stable and all as my relationship with Ferdia seemed, I was still slow to have him sleep at my house.

Anyway, there we were, fragrant Indian spices filling the air as we reclined on huge floor cushions eating the delicious chicken. I pretended to be concentrating on the food when all the time I was concentrating on how I was going to bring up the subject of sex and introduce what I'd hidden in my bag. Ferdia finished his plateful before I was even half-way through mine. 'Delicious,' he pronounced, edging close to me.

'It's easy to cook,' I said.

'No, not just the food – though that was delicious too – you. You look delicious.'

I tried to ignore the sinking feeling in my stomach as he nuzzled my neck and unbuttoned my blouse. Was this a good time? It seemed so but then again . . . and, shit, maybe it wasn't – but there was never going to be a great time to tell somebody he was a bad lover, was there?

'Ferdia?'

His fingers were engaged with a button. 'Yes?'

His eyes were so wide and trusting – he was so sure that I was going to say something nice, not something mean. I hated myself for what I was about to do.

He kissed me lightly. 'Yes, Ruth, darling?'

'Ferdia – look . . . I need something else when, you know . . . I mean, not that it's bad or anything . . . just that there's always room for improvement, isn't there? It's not too good for me . . . not bad, of course, but not as good as it could be. Like I said, there's always room for improvement. For all of us – me too . . .' My voice tapered off as his face creased in puzzlement.

'Sorry?'

I took a deep breath. 'Yoghurt,' I said. 'I want to finish my rice and it's a bit dry. Could you pass me the yoghurt, please?'

Ferdia picked up a tiny silver dish and I poured the contents over my rice. It was the wrong time, I told myself, as I stuffed rice into my mouth. There'd be other times – better times – and, anyway, sure it was important but it didn't matter all that much, did it?

As soon as I finished my rice Ferdia took the plate from me and began to undress me. As I tried to work up some enthusiasm for our lovemaking I knew I'd wimped out. Maybe if I left the Book behind he'd find it and read it and get the hint. That idea cheered me up as he reached ecstatic places I hadn't visited in a while. I'd leave the Book somewhere prominent when I went home and think of a way to bring up the topic casually. And then, like Howard Ferris, we'd all live happily ever after.

I left it on Ferdia's bedside locker. Kathleen and Paddy were fast asleep when I got home but I was a bit wakeful after my long night of sexual and verbal frustration. I wished I hadn't quit smoking the day after the barbecue. That hadn't been one of my promises to God, after all.

I looked at my watch. It was only twelve thirty. Maybe Tracy was still up. I could just nip out the front and have a looksee. If any lights were on I might try knocking at the door. I walked out into the warm night. It had just rained and the air was crisp: it was developing that distinctive autumn smell.

I stared at the Walshes' house but it was in darkness. Shit. I couldn't justify knocking if they were all asleep. I really needed to give up cigarettes anyway. I was resolving to get my will-power in order when Kevin's door opened and Orla appeared. I heard his voice and wondered if I made a break for it would I be back inside my house before she emerged. But it was too late. The door clicked behind her and all I could do was pretend that I was coming home from an exciting night on the tiles.

'Ruth?' Orla said, stopping in her tracks. Her sheet of white-blonde hair almost glowed in the moonlight as she adopted a quizzical expression.

'Orla? Hi! How are you?'

'Great. Out for the evening?'

'Yes, yes, I was,' I said, hoping she wouldn't turn round and see that my front door was wide open. 'You're not still working, are you?'

She laughed. 'I'm a surgeon, Ruth, I don't make housecalls – at least not professional ones.'

'How's Kevin?' I asked, to change the subject as the purpose of her visit became apparent. Big mistake.

'Kevin really is very good,' Orla said, her perfectly shaped nostrils flaring, 'all things considered – he's still very good.'

'Right,' I said. 'OK – well, nice to see you, Orla. I'd better not delay you any longer.'

Orla smiled her even-toothed smile, fluttered her fingers and was gone. By the time I was back inside my house with the front door closed I was seething with rage. What the hell was going on in that house? What was wrong with Kevin? Had he no self-respect? I didn't buy that shit about him using her – she was a total bitch and was using him as a convenient shag whenever there was nothing better on offer.

I stomped up the stairs and into the shower, trying

to calm down. But as the water cascaded over my head I remembered Avril. Poor, pretty, stupid, Kevin-besotted Avril – Jesus, he was a bastard having sex with Orla when he was supposed to be going out with Avril. What a scumbag.

I felt like going out there and then, banging on the door and confronting him. Luckily, I managed to talk myself out of it and went to bed instead. However, as soon as I opened my eyes next morning my first thought was of Orla and Kevin. It was a Saturday and I had no work, so I was determined to have it out with him.

I fed and dressed myself and Paddy, and took off for Kevin's before I could change my mind. After all, I had introduced him to Avril – I felt a sort of responsibility towards her.

It was a muggy, rainy morning and I had to run the short distance to his house, with Paddy splashing in the puddles as he ran by my side. As soon as I rang the bell Kevin and Mikey arrived at the door. Kevin was barefoot in track pants and T-shirt and had a big sleepy head. If he'd had hair it'd have been tousled. 'Ruth. Come in. I'm just making coffee.'

Paddy and Mikey took off into the sitting room where the *Scooby Doo* theme was playing. I followed Kevin into the kitchen where he poured us two cups of espresso. He downed his in one. 'That's the stuff,' he said, with a shudder. 'That'll put hair on your chest.'

'Thanks,' I said, sipping mine.

Kevin poured himself more. 'Sit down, Ruth,' he

said, motioning to the square breakfast island in the centre of the kitchen. I pulled a high leather and steel stool from under the counter and climbed on to it.

Kevin made some toast and joined me.

'Now I'm awake,' he said, 'how are things with you?'

'Not bad. You?'

'Frustrated. I've been on the phone for an hour trying to get a copy of the environmental-impact report for Ballymoran. Can you believe that? A full hour listening to how much the department appreciates my call interspersed with long blasts of Whitney Houston.'

'They have to have copies,' I said, temporarily distracted from the purpose of my visit. 'Freedom of Information Act and all that.'

'I went to their offices and checked the files. Everything's there except the report.'

'That's weird.'

'I know. Shipping receipts for transporting the asbestos, other minor impact reports, transcripts from the court case referring to the report, but no report. I'm waiting for them to call me back. I've told them there's a piece on their careless attitude ready to roll for the *Tribune* tomorrow.'

'That might light a fire under them. Did you try using Gary's name?'

Kevin smiled. 'As chairman, Ruth, he's directly responsible. I'll be using his name in the *Tribune*.' He rubbed his shaved head. 'I've a bloody headache from it all at this stage.' He yawned loudly. 'Slept badly.'

'You look tired. Late night?'

Kevin nodded.

'With Orla?'

Kevin swallowed a mouthful of toast. 'Yes, as it happens – how did you know?'

'I met her last night as she was going home.' I finished my coffee and played with the cup. 'What about Avril?' I said eventually.

The cut along his hairline had healed to a long, red scar that looked as if it had been drawn on with a pen. 'What about her?' he said.

I tried to contain my temper. 'Jesus, Kevin, have you no moral compass at all? Avril is mad about you and I have a pain in my head from listening to how great you are, and there you are shagging Orla behind her back.'

'How do you know it's behind her back?' he said.

'Well, isn't it?'

Kevin climbed off his stool, went to the coffee machine and refilled his cup. 'I don't see how my sex life is any of your business.'

I wanted to slap his face. 'You're going out with my friend. She's besotted with you and you're cheating behind her back. Definitely my business.'

Kevin folded his arms across his chest. 'Go on, Ruth, continue dispensing your truth. I'm all ears.'

'I'm just telling it as it is, Kevin. It's not fair on Avril. That's all.'

'It might have escaped your attention, Ruth, but

Avril is a full-grown woman, well able to make decisions for herself. I know none of us is perfect, like you, but we do the best we can.'

'What's that supposed to mean? Perfect like me?' I flashed.

'Just telling it as it is, Ruth. Surely you understand that. Perfect ex-wife, perfect friend, perfect mum, perfect birth-child, perfect relationship with the perfect Ferdia. Welcome to Walton's Mountain.'

Anger seethed inside me and I tried to hold on to it.

'Go on, Ruth, let it out for once. In all its ugliness. Tell it like it is – I dare you.'

'You know nothing about my life,' I said quietly.

'And you, Ruth, know nothing about mine, so you don't have the high moral ground. In your perfect little world everything is black and white. Well, I've news for you. My world is grey.'

I looked out of the window but I could feel his eyes on me. I wanted to defend myself. I wanted to tell him just how grey my life had been after Gibraltar, how hard it was to go on after that kind of humiliation and rejection. How all I'd ever wanted was to belong. A proper family. Blood relations. What was so Walton's Mountain about that? Kevin came up behind me and laid a hand on my shoulder. 'Look . . .'

His clear blue eyes were full of concern.

'I didn't mean to—' He was interrupted by the phone. He picked it up but kept looking at me. 'Hello?'

He listened for a few seconds, then put the phone on speaker and mouthed, 'Deep Throat,' at me.

'You're hot. Stay with it,' said a voice that sounded distorted and far away.

'Hang on, man, give me a bit more than that. What do you know about the report? Why isn't it on record?' said Kevin.

'You're hot. Don't take no for an answer,' the weird voice said. Then the line went dead.

'Fucking hell. That's not much help,' said Kevin, throwing the phone down on the worktop.

'It was so odd,' I said.

'It's really annoying me. I start work on other stories and half-way through I realise all I'm thinking about is this bloody thing.'

I was still smarting from his earlier words. 'I'd better go, Kevin. I'm meeting India later in town.'

'I'm sorry if I hurt your feelings, Ruth. I didn't mean to.'

I didn't answer for a few seconds. 'I know. Is that what you really think of me?'

'No. You're great. I was just angry with you for what you said.'

'I didn't mean to barge in and tell you how to run your life. But I can't help thinking Orla's using you, Kev. I wouldn't be your friend if I didn't say it out.'

Kevin touched my face with his fingers. I put my arms round him and he did the same and we stayed locked together until Mikey and Paddy ran into the kitchen looking for Smarties. We jumped apart and

Kevin went in search of sweets. Then Kevin's phone rang again and Paddy and I left. As we splashed home through the puddles I thought about what had just happened and how complicated life was. I wondered if I could run away to South America.

31

Even though Kevin and I had settled our differences I couldn't shake off his words. Was that how people saw me? If only they knew what it was like to be me. But I couldn't take it on – I had enough on my plate.

'I'd like you and Ferdia to meet him,' I said to Kathleen, a few days later, as I shook out sheets before I hung them on the line. It was a gorgeous autumnal day, with clear blue skies and a soft breeze. Kathleen handed me a peg.

'I'd like him to meet the important people in my life,' I continued.

'Are you sure?'

I stopped what I was doing. 'I am. I mean, I don't expect you to be friends or anything but . . .'

'Then I'll meet him.' She handed me another peg.

'Kathleen, if you don't want to it's no big deal.'

'I'll do it, Ruth, no problem. And if I don't like him I'll put a spell on him. How's that?' she said.

'Grand by me,' I said.

But the nerves set in straight away, once I'd rung Gary and organised a time and place – Monday, after work, at Drury's. We could sit in the bar: it'd be quiet at that time. I'd arranged for Ferdia to come half-way through. That way, if things were going badly, he could ease the tension. Deep down, though, no matter how nervous I was, I was glad this was going to happen. There was something nice and symmetrical about sitting down with both your parents, your flesh and blood, the people who created you.

Monday afternoon was wet and miserable. By one o'clock I'd finished for the day and was sitting in the bar with Kathleen waiting for Gary to arrive. She was relaxed as she sipped her water. Her blonde hair was newly streaked and her makeup flawless. Ferdia was hovering around like a chicken about to lay an egg.

I knew Gary had arrived from the exuberant sounds Ferdia was making as he ushered him into the bar. We both stood up as they approached.

'Ruth! Kathleen!' said Gary, and kissed us both. He smelt of expensive aftershave. Ferdia went to the bar to order drinks and we sat down at our table.

'So, isn't this wonderful?' said Gary, smiling broadly.

I nodded. Kathleen said nothing.

'What an awful day out there. The forecast was for sunshine. Not reliable, those forecasts,' he said.

I nodded again. Still Kathleen did not speak.

Ferdia returned with the drinks and put them on the table. 'Please excuse me, folks, gotta go back to work. This place won't manage itself, you know! I'll see you in a little while.' With a wave he was gone.

'Kathleen, you look terrific. You haven't aged at all,' said Gary, picking up his glass of fizzy water.

Kathleen smiled. 'Yes, I have, Gary, and so have you. The last time we met you were barely shaving.'

'So, Ruth, how are you? How's the wonderful Paddy?' He had evidently decided that Kathleen wasn't a good bet for the small-talk.

'Great, and Paddy's great too,' I said.

'Ferdia's a grand fella – we had a good chat in the foyer. Knows his politics, that guy,' he said.

'Yes, he does. He's great,' I said, mentally noting not to say 'great' again. Kathleen was eyeing Gary as if he was a whore at a christening.

'So, Gary, are you busy?' I asked, to keep the conversation flowing.

'Up to my eyes. There's always something else to do, isn't there? I have a clinic in Bruff in an hour, then a prize-giving in Ballydun.'

'Sounds hectic. Can I ask you a question?' I said.

He nodded.

'Didn't you tell me that you're the chairman of the Environmental Commission?'

'Yes. Why?'

'Well, my friend Kevin – I told you about him, the journalist – he's looking for a copy of a report about Ballymoran and he's having trouble locating one.'

Gary took out a pen and small notebook and made a note. 'I'll check it out. Leave it with me.'

Then there was a silence, which lengthened. I was all out of conversation topics and even poor Gary was stuck.

Then Kathleen spoke: 'Did you get my letter?' she asked him.

'Letter?' he said.

'Yes. The letter I sent you.'

'I didn't get any letter. Did you send it to my constituency office? They're desperate for misplacing things. Hang on, I'll just check.'

Gary reached for his mobile phone but Kathleen put up her hand like a Guard stopping traffic.

'Put the phone away, Gary. You know what I mean.'

He stretched out his arms helplessly. 'I don't know anything about a letter – I—'

'Oh, please. I found out I was pregnant. I gave a letter to my cousin, care of Blackrock College. I heard no more from you.' Kathleen folded her hands on her lap and looked expectantly at him.

'I never got that letter. On my word, I never got it.'

'On the word of a politician?' she asked.

Gary glanced at me uncomfortably. And then Ferdia was at the table, chattering. I excused myself and bolted to the ladies'.

Drury's ladies' toilet was well known among the staff for its exceptional mobile-phone reception. Every girl spent hours on her phone in there to her love interest or best friend. I'd never had need to take advantage of it before but that day was a godsend.

I found Kevin's name in my phone book and pressed call. As the number rang in my ear I wondered why I was so desperate to talk to him.

I just knew he would understand while I'd have to try to explain things to Ferdia and he'd want to understand but . . .

'Hello?'

'Kevin?'

'Ruth? Hey! How are you?'

'Grand. Not grand. Awful.'

'Where are you? What's up?'

'Remember I told you Gary and Kathleen were meeting up today?'

'Right. It's not going well, I take it?'

I sighed. 'Well, it certainly isn't Walton's Mountain. Apparently Kathleen wrote to Gary in Blackrock College and he claims he never got the letter and—'

'Kathleen announced this at the meeting?'

'Yeah. And I think she hates him. Why was I so dumb, Kev? I've really had my head in the sand . . . I mean, I thought it's all in the past and let's get on with life, for Paddy's sake at least . . .'

'Can I just say one thing, Ruth?'

'Of course.'

'You managed fine without either of them in your life for a long time.'

I closed the toilet and sat on the cold plastic lid. 'What do you mean? That I shouldn't have bothered contacting them?'

'No. You did the right thing, and if things work out that's a bonus. Just don't bank on it,' Kevin said.

I knew what he meant and he was right. You can't miss what you never had.

Easier said than done.

'Anyway, I'd better go back – I just wanted to talk to someone normal for a few minutes.'

'First time I've been called normal,' Kevin said. 'Are you OK?'

'Yes, really, I'm fine. I feel better now.'

'Good. Anyway, just remember that they're the lucky ones, having you as a daughter.'

'That's what Tracy said.'

'She told me and I agree.'

'Thanks, Kev – for everything.'

'My pleasure. Talk to you later.'

I hung up. Kevin might be a fool as far as his ex-wife was concerned and he might have the dress sense of a seventeen-year-old but he was a good friend. I felt much more grounded now. I flushed the toilet to pretend I'd been making legitimate use of the facilities, then washed my hands and checked my makeup.

Kathleen pounced on me as soon as I arrived back into the bar. 'Are you all right, Ruth? Where were you?' she whispered.

Ferdia and Gary were deep in conversation – something about stocks and markets.

'I'm grand,' I said, and saw suddenly how vulnerable she was in this whole scenario. In her anxious face I caught a glimpse of the sixteen-year-old girl who'd been left holding the baby. I kissed her cheek. She looked surprised and delighted.

'Don't worry your head about me,' I said. 'I just popped into the loo.'

'I think we'll go now,' she murmured. 'Gary.' She

stood up as she said his name and I followed her lead.

'Yes?'

'Ruth and I are going to take off now. It's been great, but it's time to leave,' Kathleen said. There was a wide, bright smile on her face, but I heard a slight edge in her voice.

Gary seemed not to notice. 'The pleasure was all mine,' he said, and kissed us both. He stepped back and ran a hand through neatly trimmed hair. 'We'll have to meet up again soon, Ruth. I'd like to see Paddy.'

'Why don't you come over for dinner some night?' The words were out of my mouth before I knew it. 'You can meet my friends and see Paddy and, well . . .'

Gary's eyes twinkled. 'That'll be terrific. I'd like it very much.'

'Great,' I said. 'Terrific. Talk to you soon.'

We walked outside to find it was almost dark and pouring rain. We stood in the shade of the hotel porch as Kathleen searched in her handbag. After a few minutes she produced a black polka-dot umbrella that miraculously transformed into the real thing. 'Where did you park?' she asked, stepping into the rain under the shade of her magic umbrella.

'At the back,' I said.

'I'll walk as far as your car with you – no point in getting wet.'

We set off, winding our way across the glistening

black Tarmac through silver and red, blue and green, black, white and gold cars and vans. The rain pelted down with a grey vengeance.

I had unlocked my car door and sat in before Kathleen spoke. She leaned down to me. 'I should have said something to you about the letter.'

I stared at the steering-wheel.

'I thought it didn't matter that he hadn't bothered to answer it, but when I saw the smug face of him in there . . .' She put a hand on my shoulder. 'It's always better to say these things out. I said it. Got it off my chest. I hope you weren't upset.'

'No, just surprised. That's all.'

'I know, and I should have said it right from the start.'

'It doesn't matter. It's all in the past. Can you call round tomorrow if you're not busy?' I said.

The rain bounced off her umbrella like small pellets. 'I'd like that. Maybe in the afternoon some time?'

'Whenever suits you – we won't be going anywhere.'

I closed the car door, turned on the engine and opened the window. Kathleen was still watching me. She looked so small suddenly, standing in the rain under the umbrella, water splashes up the legs of her white maternity pants.

'Thanks,' I said.

She shook her head.

'See you tomorrow.' I released the handbrake. With a wave I drove off, trying not to notice that she was still watching. She looked so forlorn standing in the rain that I wished I could have made everything all right for her. But there was nothing I could do. Especially as I wasn't much more than an emotional splatter myself, these days.

32

I invited Gary round for dinner exactly a week later. Tracy was driving me insane wanting to meet him, and I thought it mightn't be as excruciating as the other times we'd met if I was surrounded by a gaggle of people. I invited Kathleen but I knew she wouldn't want to come, and indeed she cried off, saying she needed an early night. I rang India, only to discover that Alyssa was sick: she had a horrible tummy bug that had almost landed her in hospital, and although she was on the mend they were all exhausted and in no humour to attend a dinner party. So I invited Ferdia – who was delighted to accept – and half of Gresham Terrace as well.

'I'd love to come to dinner and get a look at Gary Kennedy up close,' Tracy said, obligatory cigarette in her mouth as she slouched at my kitchen table beside Kevin. She flicked idly through *Hello!* magazine. 'Are you asking Derek as well?'

'Of course,' I said. 'Bring anyone you like – the kids, your sisters, your mother, Bock the Robber, I don't care.'

Tracy inhaled and gave a loud moan. 'Thanks, but I'll leave that lot at home. Derek and I could do with a night away from them. I'll ask my mother to babysit. Who knows? We might go for a bit of a *drive* afterwards, if you get my drift.'

'More information than I want, Trace, thanks,' I said. 'And you, Kevin? Will you come?'

'Can I bring Mikey?' Kevin asked.

'Sure,' I said, wondering how I could stop Mikey destroying my house while simultaneously cooking and acting as hostess. Still, it'd be worth it and, anyway, tearaway and all as he was, you couldn't help loving Mikey. Once he gave you that toothy smile you'd need a heart of stone not to be smitten. Kevin grinned, and for the first time I noticed it was an adult version of Mikey's smile.

'I'm joking. Orla's taking him for the weekend – she's picking him up at lunchtime on Friday.'

'So you'll come?'

'Free food?'

I nodded.

'Definitely. Can I bring Avril?'

I nodded again.

'It's a date.'

And so it was set up.

By Friday night I was at least three octaves above high doh. Kevin ended up doing a lot of the cooking. He offered to make a lamb korma and all I had to do was throw together some salad, boil rice and buy the trimmings.

At six o'clock on Friday Kevin arrived at my door with a stainless-steel pot of fragrant curry. Mikey, with his freshly washed face and neatly combed hair, was standing beside his father holding the Claw, who seemed to be begging me to take him back into my house.

'Orla cancelled,' Kevin said, with a wry twist to his mouth.

'These things happen.'

'I suppose.'

'Hey, Mikey Magoo,' I said. 'Paddy's on the swing. Take the cat out into the garden with you.'

Mikey ran off through the kitchen and out of the back door with the fat stripy Claw clutched to his chest. Kevin plonked the pot on the stove. I opened the lid and peeped in at the creamy contents. 'I could kiss you, Kevin Regan,' I said.

Kevin smiled and opened his arms. 'Go with your feelings, girlfriend,' he said, in a bad American accent.

I laughed and walked past him. 'Too much daytime TV. What time is it?'

'Six. When's the guest of honour arriving?'

'Seven – everybody's coming at seven and I still have to get ready.'

Kevin surveyed me. 'You look fine to me.'

'Mmm,' I said. 'Sweatpants and a sleeveless vest – very attractive.'

Kevin let his eyes linger on me. 'Exactly,' he said.

My skin did a funny tingling thing and I walked to the window in the pretence of checking on the children. 'Oh, they're fine – look! Just playing in the sandbox. Aren't they cute?'

He came to stand beside me and the hairs on my bare arms stood up. 'I'll stay and keep an eye on Paddy while you get showered,' he said. 'Mikey and I are ready – or as ready as we're ever going to get.'

The air around us had taken on a sudden electricity and my head was buzzing. 'Thanks,' I said, appalled that my voice had developed a wobble. 'I won't be long, I promise. Have whatever you'd like. What about Avril? Do you have to pick her up?'

'No, she's getting a cab. Take your time – there's no hurry.'

But there was, and it wasn't so much the hurry to get ready for the dinner party as the hurry to get away from Kevin. Why was he suddenly having this effect on me? It had to be sexual frustration. Please God Ferdia had found the Book, I thought, as I showered. He hadn't mentioned it but maybe he'd read it and was going to surprise me with his newly acquired knowledge. I hoped that was the case. Things were bad when I was lamping Kevin.

By the time I was dressed and ready it was ten to seven. I cantered down the stairs and found Tracy putting small pink rosebuds on each place I'd set at the long mahogany table. It was the centrepiece in the small room off the kitchen, which Emerson had always wanted to claim as a studio and I'd always wanted as a formal dining room. At least that was one battle I'd won – even if it was a Pyrrhic victory.

'Oh, my God, they look lovely,' I said, as she pinned a salmon-coloured rose to a white linen napkin.

'I saw it on *Queer Eye for the Straight Guy,*' she

said. 'You get brilliant tips on that programme, I only wish Derek'd pay some attention to it. Do you think we could get Kevin to watch it? He might discover that combats aren't the only trousers in the world. You look nice. Are you nervous?'

'Not too bad,' I said, taken aback by Tracy's jitters. Maybe I should be more nervous than I was. The doorbell rang and I hurried out to answer it.

'Hey, love, thanks for the invite,' Derek said, kissing me.

'Thanks for coming,' I said, stepping back to let him in.

Kevin appeared in the hallway. 'Will I turn on the oven?' he said.

I nodded.

'Where will I put the wine?' Derek asked.

'In the dining room, please.'

Derek went into the kitchen past Kevin, who was standing in the doorway. 'You look lovely,' he said.

'I thought I already looked lovely,' I said, because I couldn't resist.

'Well, you did and now you do as well – it's a bit of a mystery. I'm sure it all means something very important.'

'Like you're mad?' I said.

'I thought you said I was normal?'

'That was only because *I* was mad at the time,' I said.

The doorbell rang again. I swivelled round and opened it. Avril and Ferdia. Avril squealed with delight when she saw Kevin and ran towards him, her spindly high heels clacking like knitting needles on my hall floor. She stopped in front of him and kissed him full on the mouth. Kevin gave her a hug and stepped back into the kitchen.

Ferdia winked at me and put his arm round me. 'Bit of passion going on there,' he whispered into my ear. 'Come along now, people, come along, get a room as they say.'

I couldn't help tutting and Ferdia laughed as if it was all a big joke. I thought I might throw up, and then the doorbell rang again.

Ferdia did the honours this time. It was Gary. The two men greeted each other like long-lost friends, then Gary hugged me. 'Ruth! How are you? Great to see you again. Look at your lovely home.'

'Hello, Gary, please come in,' I said, returning his hug.

I was grateful when Ferdia took up the hosting. 'Step right this way, Gary,' he said, leading my father through the narrow hallway into the kitchen.

'Ferdia? I wonder would you mind introducing Gary to everybody while I get Paddy?'

'Of course,' Ferdia said, with his wide, generous smile.

Mikey and Paddy were squealing as they poured buckets of sand over each other.

'Sorry to break up the party, boys,' I said, hauling them out of the tortoise-shaped sandpit and dusting them off as best I could. Back in the kitchen, Ferdia was handing out drinks and all the guests were chatting and laughing. I flashed him a grateful smile.

I held Paddy's hand and pointed at Gary. 'Say hi to Gary, Pad. Do you remember we met him in the park and we fed the ducks?' I said.

Paddy smiled shyly at Gary, then buried his face in my leg. Gary bent down in front of him and rubbed the top of his curly head.

'How's the best young man?' he said.

'I'm starving, Mum,' Paddy said.

'Two seconds, sweetie,' I said. 'Why don't you all take your drinks into the dining room and sit at the table?'

'Good idea,' Ferdia said, leading the way.

Within seconds I was alone in the kitchen. I pulled my white crackle-glazed Japanese bowls and serving dishes out of the press and lined them up on the worktop. They looked lovely. Kevin's curry was simmering away on the stove and I was certain it was all going to be delicious.

Everything was under control. I'd already put the drinks, salads, dressings, yoghurt-and-cucumber and chutneys on the sideboard. All I had to do now was put the food into the serving dishes and we were ready to go. I began to relax for the first time that day. It was all going really well. As long as I could stop Mikey dreaming up some wild mischief for himself and Paddy we'd be all right.

I ladled Kevin's delicious-smelling korma into a large white bowl and arranged the poppadums and naan bread along a narrow white dish. No doubt the rectangular platter had been designed for sushi but it looked just as well with the breads. All I had to do now was drain the rice and bring it all into the dining room. I selected a delicate Japanese bowl that I figured would hold it and opened the lid of the rice pan. If I'd felt sick earlier when Avril was eating the face off Kevin in my hallway it was nothing compared to how I felt as I looked at the cold, wet, hard, uncooked grains of rice clumped in the bottom of the stainless-steel pan. I stood there, lid in hand, staring into it for what felt like hours.

'What's wrong?' Kevin's voice said.

'I forgot to cook the rice,' I said. 'I rinsed it and had it ready but I forgot to cook it.'

Kevin suppressed a grin. 'It's OK,' he said, 'it won't take long. Everybody'll just have to wait a few minutes.'

'I knew I'd make a mess of it,' I said. I wanted to sit down right there on the kitchen floor and have a long, loud bawl.

'You haven't made a mess of anything,' Kevin said. 'Everything else is lovely.'

'You cooked everything else, Kevin,' I said.

Tracy appeared in the doorway. 'What are you two doing?' she demanded. 'Everyone's starving and you two are in here making sheep's eyes at each other.'

'I forgot to cook the rice, Trace.'

She came over, looked into the pan and burst out laughing. 'Shit.'

'It's not funny,' I said, but Kevin and I were laughing too.

'Will I go down to the Kashmir Kavern and get some?' Kevin asked.

Tracy shook her head. 'I have about forty packets of microwavable Uncle Ben's at home – I'll get it and heat it up.'

'But, Trace—' I began.

'Ruth, throw that food into the oven to keep it warm, then you and Kevin go in and keep them amused and we'll be eating your delicious curry before you know it.'

'It's Kevin's delicious curry,' I said. 'He cooked it.'

'Remind me not to let my uncle Sammy employ you in his restaurant. Now, go!'

Kevin and I shoved my Japanese porcelain into the oven and hurried into the dining room. Gary was holding forth as we walked in.

'. . . and then Naughton said, "Well, Kelly can just go hop for votes so".' And Derek and Ferdia roared with laughter.

Kevin and I glanced at each other and he handed me a glass of wine. I thanked him and sat down beside Gary. Kevin sat beside Avril who leaned up close to him and made a noise like a mewing kitten. She was getting on my nerves. How the hell had I ever fixed them up?

'Ruth,' Gary said, and took my hand. I smiled.

'Oh, my God, love, Gary was just telling us the funniest story,' Ferdia said, wiping his eyes.

'That's great,' I said. 'Dinner won't be a minute. Tracy has . . . Tracy said—'

'Tracy's insisted on doing her special rice,' Kevin interrupted.

'That's right,' I agreed. 'Her special rice.'

'Her special rice?' Derek asked.

Kevin eyeballed him. 'She won't even let us help – told us to come in and talk to you while she prepared it.'

'Family secret,' I half shouted, avoiding eye-contact with Kevin. 'The recipe's a family secret.'

Kevin coughed loudly and Derek muttered something that sounded very much like 'Best-kept secret I ever heard of.' I jumped up, grabbed the wine bottles and offered refills.

'So, Gary, tell me, how's the old Environmental Commission doing?' Kevin said.

Good old Kev, I thought, changing the subject. That's what friends are for.

Gary sat back into the mahogany carver and looked into mid-air. 'Doing its job, Kevin,' he said sagely.

Kevin sipped his wine. 'Which is?'

'What's the Environmental Commision, Kevin?' Avril said, in a six-year-old's voice that made me want to clip her around the ear.

'It's this government panel that's set up to examine claims of pollution,' I said, before Kevin could answer.

'That sounds great,' Avril said to Kevin.

He sat up in his chair so that she had to sit forward too. 'Yep. If the commission produces a proper report of the area being examined and that report is freely available for any member of the public to see.'

Avril fixed her gaze on him as if he'd spoken some

deep and meaningful truth. Jesus, why did men like that simpering behaviour?

'And the report was available, Kevin. And it was used in the PAP versus Boru court case. You know the rest.' Gary said, leaning his elbows on the table and resting his chin on his fingers.

'PAP?' said Avril.

'So if all the correct procedures have been adhered to and no pollutants have been found in the Ballymoran area and it was all there for everyone to see during the court case, what is your problem?' said Gary.

Kevin blew out breath angrily. 'How does a company that was closed down for illegally dumping chemical waste end up with government contracts for disposing of asbestos?'

'I wonder where Tracy is with the rice,' Derek said. 'I'm starving.'

'Indeed,' Ferdia said.

Kevin didn't seem to hear. He was staring at Gary, who smiled. 'I read your piece on that. And your piece on the so-called missing report. It must be the silly season – all you journalists are reduced to rehashing old news.'

'There are four children in one school in Ballymoran, all with cancer,' Kevin said in a quiet voice, 'and I don't believe in coincidence.'

'I hear you, Kevin,' Gary said, 'and my heart goes out to those children and their families, but the commission has looked at Ballymoran through a microscope and it's as clean as a whistle.'

'I'd still like a copy of the report,' Kevin said.

Every eye in the room was on them – even Mikey and Paddy were taking a momentary break from crumbling a breadstick to watch the show.

'I'll check it out for you. This kind of thing happens all the time. The commission has moved offices seven times since its inception—'

'Oh, please! No hard copies, no back-up files?' Kevin laughed derisively.

'As I said, these things happen.'

'So, can the commission conduct a new study, since it has so carelessly misplaced the findings of the last one?'

'What? And waste tax-payers' hard-earned money all over again? The report is old news, Kevin. I suggest you find yourself another cause. This one has run itself into ground.'

Suddenly the double doors from the kitchen opened and Tracy appeared with a tray of food.

'Da-da!' she sang, and went to the sideboard.

'Your secret-recipe rice, love?' Derek said.

'That's right – who told you?' Tracy said, one hand on her hip. Derek winked at her and she winked back.

'Oh, my God, that looks wonderful!' I said, jumping up. 'Thanks a million, Tracy. Now, come on, everyone – let's eat.'

I paused then and looked at Kevin. He stood up too and Avril almost fell to the floor: she'd been leaning against him and hadn't expected him to move so suddenly. 'Here – let me help with the serving,' he said, and grasped the bowl of conjured-up rice. 'The guest of honour first,' he said.

My father returned his smile and the knot in my stomach loosened as Kevin piled rice on to his plate. I'd been afraid of a fight. Once Kevin got the bit between his teeth I knew he was reluctant to let go and the dinner-table wasn't the right place. At least, not my dinner-table. But the tension between them dissipated when we began to eat.

The rest of the evening went like clockwork. The food was delicious. Everybody was relaxed. Gary was charming and funny, better than a cabaret show.

By the time everyone went home Tracy and Derek adored Gary. Ferdia was already a devoted fan, of course, and Avril – when she wasn't all over Kevin – was his latest disciple. Kevin wasn't mad about him, but they were natural sparring partners, weren't they? Cat and mouse. Journalist and politician. Anyway, they were charming to each other for the rest of the evening. Even the children behaved themselves, although Mikey and Paddy fed their dinner to the Claw.

Finally everybody had gone home except Ferdia. I had a feeling he was in the mood for more than a quick peck on the cheek and when he followed me into the living room and practically pushed me on to the sofa my suspicions were confirmed. 'I couldn't wait to touch you all night,' he said, and kissed me. His hands travelled up and down my back. I was exhausted and couldn't face a bout of sexual frustration: I kissed him back, then pulled away. 'Ferdia . . . I'm – It's—'

'I read the Book.'

'The Book?' Jesus, how was I going to manage this?

'The Book. *I Come, You Come, We All Come Together*. I learned so much, Ruth, and I want to thank you for sharing it with me.'

He nuzzled my neck and licked my ear. I wondered was *that* in it. 'That's good. I'm glad you liked it,' I said.

'I loved it and it makes me happy to know that we can share our deepest thoughts and feelings.' He began kissing me again and my body started to respond. This was good. He'd read it and wasn't offended. He unzipped my trousers and I pulled off my jumper, then struggled with his pants. We lay on the couch in a tangle of half-on half-off clothes and he embarked on a routine I figured he'd memorised from the Book.

First I was glad, but then as the mechanical logistics became obvious – four tweaks on the right nipple, five on the left and so on – a wave of boredom smothered any spark of desire. To make matters worse, he kept interrupting the Routine to enquire how I was doing. I hadn't the heart to tell him the truth. Soon after he entered me I felt his shudders and knew that although he might have learned the theory, its application had escaped him.

He rolled off me. 'Was that a little too fast?'

I was speechless.

'Good. Next time, I think I know how to avoid that pitfall.'

How many men would have had the guts to take

on the Book? I admired him for that. And maybe his application would improve. 'It's grand, Ferdia. Rome wasn't built in a day,' I said I got up and pulled on some clothes.

We kissed at the front door, and as soon as he was gone I rooted for cigarettes. I found some in a coat pocket and stood at the back door smoking. What I really felt like doing was screaming. Frustration was tipping me into insanity.

After my smoke I went upstairs and got ready for bed. The telephone rang.

'Hello? Is that the Burkes'?' a snotty woman's voice said.

'Yes?'

'I have Mr Burke's luggage here.'

'I beg your pardon?'

'I said I have Mr Burke's luggage here.'

'Mr Burke?'

'Mr Emerson Burke, twenty-seven Gresham Terrace, Limerick, Ireland.'

I took a deep breath. 'There must be some mistake.'

'No, this is the Aer Lingus Lost Luggage Department at Shannon airport. I'm reading the name and address as I speak.'

'Check it again,' I said. 'There must be a mistake – Mr Burke doesn't live here any more.' I slammed down the phone. Bastard! How the hell had that happened? I got into bed and lay down but my body was as taut as a violin string. I sat up and fished my book from the bedside locker. The words on the page danced as rage surged inside me. Who did he think he was leaving my address on his luggage? And why the hell was he home again? He hadn't bothered to let me know he was visiting. What was going on?

Eventually I settled down enough to read. I felt vulnerable and hated it. I wanted not to care about Emerson or where he was or who he was with. But it wasn't as easy as I'd have liked. I didn't know that it was going to get even harder.

33

'What do you mean "back"?' I screamed at Emerson down the phone next morning.

'Look, calm down, Ruth. I finished shooting the movie and there was no point in staying in Gibraltar. I can do the editing here and I wanted to be near Paddy.'

I gulped air and tried to calm down but it was no use. 'You never even spoke to me about it,' I said.

'You don't invite discussion when I try to talk to you on the phone, Ruth.'

Bile rose into my mouth. 'Am I supposed to apologise to you now, Emerson, because I don't make things easy for you when you ring?'

'That's not what I meant.'

'It's what you said,' I retorted triumphantly. Bastard. Bastard. Bastard.

'All I meant was I thought we could speak better face to face. There are a lot of issues to discuss.'

'You can sing that, Buster.'

'Especially now that I'll be living in Limerick again.'

'The least you could have done was consult me before you moved back.'

'You're not the boss of the country, Ruth.'

I tapped my foot. Unfortunately that was true. 'Take my address off your luggage.'

'I'm sorry about that – it was one of those permanent address tags. The temporary ones tore off *en route*.'

Emerson's stupid baggage tags had outlived his marriage. 'Take it off immediately,' I said.

'I will – but I don't plan to travel for a while so it won't make any difference. Anyway, Ruth, how about it?'

'How about what?'

'Can we meet up and talk about Paddy? I'd really like to spend some time with him. I mean, I can arrange my work around you and him – you know, whatever suits and all that.'

I felt like crying. Wasn't my life complicated enough without having to look into Emerson's face all the time? I knew he was right to want to be with Paddy. I'd just have to get civilised and talk to him. After all, I'd promised God; hadn't I?

'Where are you staying?' I asked.

'In the Hutton, out the Ennis Road.'

'I'll meet you in the bar there at half two today and we can come up with some kind of an arrangement. Is that OK?'

'That'd be great. Absolutely great.'

'OK.'

'I'll look forward to it – two thirty?'

'Sure. Goodbye, Emerson.'

I hung up as the doorbell rang. Paddy was at the

kitchen table finishing his Weetabix and singing to himself. Tracy was on the doorstep in a red rugby jersey, her black hair interwoven with red wool, her face painted red with navy and white trim. She was waving a small flag with the three-castle Munster emblem.

'Am I lovely?' she said. 'Will I be the best-looking supporter at the match in Paris?'

'If you think I'm going to Paris with you in that get-up you've another think coming.'

'I think I look good,' she said, squinting at her reflection in the side of the kettle, 'but don't worry, I won't do the whole thing – I'll just wear the jersey. I can't get a ticket for Ferdia, by the way. Derek's tried all his contacts and no luck.'

'It doesn't matter,' I said. 'I don't think he's all that interested. Anyway, there's a big Drury's management thing on that weekend.'

I could see Tracy wanted to say something sarcastic but she was controlling herself. 'There's a Celtic League match on this afternoon in Thomond Park,' she said eventually. 'I have spare tickets – do you want to go?'

I shook my head. 'Can't – I have to meet Emerson.'

'What?'

I looked at Paddy, who was playing with the remnants of his breakfast.

'Pad? *Sponge Bob Square Pants*,' I said, pointing to the living room.

'Yes!' Paddy ran in and switched on the TV.

'Emerson has moved back to Limerick,' I said.

'You must be joking! Is Selma the Slapper with him?'

'Jesus! I don't think so – don't even say that.'

'Well, it's a logical question,' Tracy said.

I looked at her. 'It is, isn't it?'

'That bastard deserves to have to marry her and suffer for the rest of his life.'

I shrugged. 'I don't care what he does with his life.'

'I don't believe that,' Tracy said quietly.

'I know, but I'm working on it.'

Tracy was rifling through her cigarette packet.

'Give me one of those,' I said. She did so. I lit it and inhaled. I was finding less and less comfort in these bouts of smoking but I couldn't think what else to do.

'At least we have Paris to look forward to,' Tracy said.

I nodded, though it wasn't cheering me up all that much.

Tracy began to laugh. 'I have a great idea,' she said.

'What?'

'Well, if Balloon Balls wants to come back here to live the least he can do is make your life easier.'

'What do you mean?'

'That you have a babysitter for when we go to Paris – you didn't get anyone else, did you?'

'Good point,' I said. 'I'll let that bastard know that if he wants to be involved it'll be on my terms

– and Paddy's, of course. He can't waltz back in here and expect everything to go his way.'

Tracy nodded. 'That's better,' she said. 'I love it when you talk like a knacker. It gives me hope.'

After Tracy left I rang India. I knew she'd tell me I was doing the right thing and I needed all the encouragement I could get.

'Hi, Ruth. You heard, I take it?'

'He rang. He wants to talk.'

'OK. What are you going to do?'

I could hear Alyssa singing in the background. 'I'm meeting him. I'm taking your advice. Otherwise I'm just putting off the inevitable. I think he's going to be home for a while.'

'Selma's not with him,' India said.

I said nothing.

'It's over,' she added.

'That's Emerson's business, India.'

'Yes, but it's better to go to a meeting armed with all the facts.'

'Ever the solicitor, Ind.'

'It'll be fine, once you've ironed out all the details. And Paddy'll be thrilled.'

'I know. And thanks for everything, India.'

'For nothing, Ruth. Good luck today.'

34

By two thirty that afternoon I was so full of adrenaline that I could have lifted a car. I wore a tight black top with a boat neck, a long, denim skirt that fitted me like a glove and a new pair of knee-length black boots. It was Tracy who talked me into topping off the outfit with my almost full-length black leather coat.

'I'll look like Keanu Reeves in *The Matrix*,' I complained.

'Oh, if only that was true,' Tracy said, doing a mock-swoon, 'I'd ride you in a minute if you looked like him.'

'Get lost,' I said, laughing. 'Stay focused here, Tracy. I have to look drop-dead gorgeous if I'm meeting Emerson.'

'You do look drop-dead gorgeous,' she said. 'Just leave off your sunglasses and you won't look like Keanu.'

'Very funny,' I said, and checked my watch. 'Shit! I'd better get going. Are you sure you don't mind having Paddy for an hour?'

'I don't mind at all,' Tracy said, with a grin. 'I'm going to town. Derek has them all and he won't care.'

'Sure?'

'Positive – Paddy will keep Chloe company, which means Derek'll have some peace.'

'Thanks – and tell Derek thanks.'

'No problem – and, Ruth?'

'What?'

'Give him hell.'

I grinned. 'I'll do my best.'

The bar of the Hutton was fashionably cavernous and I doubt that I'd have seen Emerson except that he was sitting under a stained-glass window. He spotted me as soon as I walked through the doors and stood up. 'Ruth!' he called, with a wave.

Jesus! He looked fabulous. When had he shaved off all his hair? I wouldn't have thought it but now he could definitely have given David Beckham a run for his money in the looks department. I strode towards him, glad I was dressed up, tall and confident in my new boots. The closer I got to Emerson the better looking he became, and if I hadn't hated the bastard's guts I would have considered a quick roll in the hay.

'Ruth,' Emerson said again, as I stopped in front of him. He leaned forward as though to kiss me, but I stepped back and put out my hand. He looked surprised. We shook hands.

'You look terrific,' he said, as we sat down.

'Thanks,' I said.

'Can I get you a drink?'

'Coffee, please.'

Emerson beckoned to a hovering waiter and ordered two espressos.

'Well?' he said, as soon as the waiter departed. 'How are you?'

'I'm fine. Never better.'

The waiter reappeared and placed two white porcelain demitasses on the table in front of us. Emerson thanked him and I filled the vacant space in my small cup with milk. My heart was already racing so I needed to dilute the almost solid caffeine.

'How's Paddy?' Emerson asked.

'Great. He's with Tracy and Derek.'

'And Kathleen?'

'I'd be lost without her. Paddy loves her and she babysits lots. She says she wants to keep it up after the baby comes but I'm not sure. It might be too much for her.'

'The baby?' Emerson echoed.

'The baby,' I repeated.

'You're not . . .' His voice trailed off.

'Don't be stupid,' I said. 'Kathleen's pregnant – she's due at Christmas.'

'My God! That's a bit of a surprise.'

'Kathleen is a reasonably young woman—'

'I know,' Emerson interrupted. 'I'm just surprised, that's all. Who's the lucky father?'

'Well, that's the million-dollar question, isn't it?' I said, before I could help myself.

'You don't know?'

'She's keeping that bit of information to herself.'

Emerson sipped his coffee and I found myself relaxing into our familiar routine of being together. No way could I afford to do that.

'So?' I said, a little more sharply than I'd intended. 'What do you want to talk about?'

'Just wanted to touch base – I wondered if you'd mind me seeing a bit of Paddy. I'm a bit worried that he'll forget me – it's why I came home.'

'Paddy loves you,' I said. 'You can see him as much as you want. I'd prefer if it was regular, though, so I can make arrangements around it.'

I looked up and Emerson was staring at me. For a few seconds he didn't answer, then he blinked his long eyelashes and glanced away. 'I hope he hasn't forgotten me – I mean—'

'I can't listen to this, Emerson. If you have a problem you need to find someone else to discuss it with. I'm only interested in discussing what will affect Paddy, nothing else.'

'I understand.'

'How about you see him Mondays, Wednesdays and Fridays?' I asked, in a businesslike voice.

'Whatever suits you. What about weekends?'

I shook my head. 'I want my weekends with Paddy – except at the end of October – two weeks' time – when I'm going away.'

'That'd be great,' Emerson said. 'I'd be delighted to have him – and any other time that suits you.'

'OK,' I said. 'I'm going to ask Kathleen to stay over in the house – he's used to her, but if you could take him out and stuff it'd give her a break.'

'I'd be more than delighted,' Emerson said. 'And the other days?'

I shrugged. 'I'll have to work it out properly, times and that.'

Emerson nodded eagerly. 'Whatever you think is good.'

'Good for Paddy,' I said. I stood up.

'You're leaving?'

'I promised I'd be back in an hour.'

Emerson stood up and held out his hand. I studied his fingers – the same long, brown fingers that had touched me so often in the past. Weird. We shook hands again.

'Come at about three on Monday next week,' I said.

'Whatever you think is best.'

'Monday? Three?'

'OK.'

'One other thing,' I said. 'It's probably good that you're here now – saves me writing to you. I'm filing for divorce. I'll be going to my solicitor and I suggest you do the same.'

Emerson looked as if I'd slapped him and I fought the impulse to apologise.

'He's my solicitor as well,' he said eventually.

'Too bad – get another. See you Monday.'

I left, stumbling over a handbag some idiot had left in the middle of the floor. The adrenaline was still pumping through me as I drove away. I punched in Ferdia's number.

'Are you driving?' he asked, after I said hello.

'Yes, but listen for a minute, Ferdia.'

'Really, Ruth, it's dangerous to drive and speak on the phone – not to mention illegal. Pull in if you—'

'Ferdia! Shut up!'

He did.

'Emerson has moved home,' I said. 'I just spent the last hour with him.'

'Oh,' he said, and there was a long pause. 'I hope he's well.'

'For God's sake, Ferdia! He's fine. He wants to see Paddy, that's all.'

'Oh, really?' Ferdia said, and his voice was lighter, 'That'll be nice for Paddy, won't it? It's important for a boy to have as much contact with his father as possible. I was reading a study in *The Times* just last week—'

'I told him I was filing for divorce.'

Ferdia gasped. 'That's great,' he said. 'Really, Ruth! That's the best news I've heard in a long time.'

'Yeah,' I said. 'I'm glad it's out of the way. Anyway, I have to go here – I'm about to overtake four cars on a bend and I'll need both hands.'

'Ruth!'

I hung up, laughing, as I pulled up outside my house. Ferdia was a total idiot when it came to being teased. But at least he wouldn't be running off with a set designer, that was for sure. He wasn't the type.

When you're young, looks, excitement and fun are everything, but they don't count for as much as you get older. It was definitely a sign of maturity in

me, I decided as I went into the Walshes' to collect
Paddy. The older I got the more I could appreciate
the qualities Ferdia was strong in. Definitely a good
thing.

35

Although I'd known about the Paris trip well in advance, it still came upon me suddenly. All along I'd felt as if I had loads and loads of time to get ready and then – whoosh – Paris was ten days away.

'It happens to me all the time,' Tracy said. 'It's because you don't want to do the hard stuff – babysitters, leave Paddy, pack your clothes.'

It was the first time I'd ever been away from Paddy and it had seemed like a great idea in theory. But now when I imagined being away from my baby for four full days my eyes filled with tears. Tracy said it was natural. 'You'll be grand once we're there,' she said, 'and Paddy'll be fine with Kathleen and his dad. And don't worry – I can personally guarantee you a great time.'

By the middle of October our beautiful summer was a distant memory. The days were shorter and darker and everything seemed harder and more work than it did when the skies were blue. Paris was an attractive prospect.

Mind you, if I'd known exactly how good a time I was going to have – and how it would complicate my life – I'd probably have been happy to stay home and do some housework.

The weekend before we went away Tracy and I were shooting the shit as usual in my kitchen. I was low despite Paris. Tracy knew – even though I wasn't saying anything about how I felt.

'You need to come to town with me this afternoon,' she said. 'We have to buy clothes for Paris.'

'You go, Tracy. I'm wrecked. Mine will have to do.'

'There's twenty per cent off in Brown Thomas,' she coaxed.

The doorbell rang.

'Hi, Ruth! Hi, Tracy! Jeez, what a horrible day. Kevin and I were going to bring Mikey out but look at the weather – Jeez, you couldn't go out in that, could you?' Avril said, as she filled the kitchen with her energy. She made me feel tired just looking at her.

'Can we borrow Paddy and Chloe?' Kevin said. 'Mikey will drive me bonkers locked up all afternoon in the rain. I thought I might take them to Playworld.'

'Be my guest,' Tracy said. 'You wouldn't like to take a few of my other children as well?'

'Paddy'd love it,' I said. 'Thanks, Kevin. When were you thinking of going?'

Kevin frowned briefly before he answered and I knew he had heard the flat note in my voice. 'Well, we thought we might go now, then bring them for something to eat. We'll probably be gone the whole afternoon. Is that OK?'

'Now you can come to town with me, Ruth,' Tracy said triumphantly. 'There's nothing stopping you – Paddy'll be with Kevin.'

I shrugged.

'Come on,' Tracy persisted, 'it'll cheer you up.'

'Is something wrong?' Kevin asked.

'No. Everything's fine.'

'Come on, Ruth! We'll go to town and spend some money on glad-rags for Paris,' Tracy said.

'Clothes-shopping always cheers me up,' Avril said.

I threw my hands into the air. 'OK, OK! I'll go.'

'Great stuff!' Tracy clapped.

'I'll take the kids right now,' Kevin said, concern still on his face. 'You have a nice afternoon in town. The break will do you good and don't worry what time you come back. If I'm here before you, I'll take Paddy home with me.'

'Thanks, Kev,' I said, with the best smile I could muster.

He went to get the children into their coats and hats and Avril followed to help. From the noise and confusion that ensued I was pretty certain he was sorry she'd offered. Eventually the three small people were suitably clad for a wintry afternoon and they all set off.

Soon afterwards Tracy and I left for town and spent the afternoon trying on clothes. Tracy bought two pairs of trousers, a blouse, two jumpers and a load of sexy underwear. I couldn't even find a pair of shoes I liked, which showed how down I was feeling.

As I traipsed through the shops behind Tracy I couldn't pretend that my depression was unconnected to Emerson's return. But why that should bother me I couldn't figure out. After all, what difference did it make? Although Tracy did her best to distract me I couldn't pull myself out of my black mood.

By the time we got home it was almost six and a cold, sleety rain was hammering the streets. I let myself into my dark house, threw a couple of pizzas into the oven, then went next door to collect Paddy. As I opened Kevin's garden gate I heard my name and turned to see Orla hurrying towards me.

'Hi, Ruth! How are you?' she said, in an upbeat, breezy tone.

'I feel like shite,' was the answer I wanted to give. 'Great,' was what I said. 'Are you coming for a visit?'

'No – Kevin was called away, some big story he just *had* to cover. I said I'd take Mikey.'

'Oh,' I said. 'When did this happen?'

'Ages ago. I was tied up at a conference but Kevin said it was all right, his girlfriend –' Orla laughed '– would look after Mikey until I arrived.'

'Good old Avril,' I said, hackles rising. 'She's a lovely person – have you met her?'

Orla took out a key and opened Kevin's front door. 'Not yet,' she said, with mock-enthusiasm. 'I can't wait!'

Avril appeared in the hallway. 'Hello?' she said warily, as she took in Orla's lissom form clothed in an almost floor-length black cashmere coat.

'Hi, Avril!' I said quickly. 'You poor thing – you

got landed with the kids. This is Orla, Kevin's – Mikey's mum.'

Avril and Orla shook hands and I could see from Avril's face that she'd have liked a couple of hours' notice before meeting Orla.

'So? Where are the Terrible Three?' I asked.

'Upstairs, playing in Mikey's room,' Avril said. 'Kevin had to leave ages ago so I brought them to town and we picked up some stuff. Oh, my God! It's so much fun doing things with those guys. They look so cute in their new clothes and all.'

'You're very good,' I said.

'I'll just pop upstairs and throw a few bits and pieces into a bag for Mikey,' Orla announced.

Avril and I went into the kitchen as she trotted up the stairs.

'Where did Kevin go?' I asked Avril.

'You won't believe what happened, Ruth.' She spun to face me. 'Do you remember that guy with the red hair you bumped into and then he jumped off the tax office?'

'Sure I remember – what about him?'

'And you know Kevin's been trying to find that report about Ballymoran where those poor sick kids live?'

I nodded, concentration ebbing.

'Well, he had a call today from the head of the company who did the report – he was in America. He talked to Kevin all about it and it turns out that the dead guy was the engineer! Oh, my God! What about that?'

I looked at her uncomprehendingly. 'The dead guy was the engineer?' I repeated.

'What about that?' she repeated.

'The same engineer? The tax-office man did the Ballymoran report?'

Avril nodded, delighted.

'So where is Kevin?'

'Gone to see the boss guy – he thinks they might have a copy of the report in their offices.'

'That's good news, anyway.'

Avril switched on the kettle. 'She's beautiful.' She pointed towards the ceiling.

'So are you,' I said.

'Not like her I'm not – how can Kevin even look at anyone else when he was married to a woman like her?'

I was just about to launch into a looks-aren't-everything speech when a blood-curdling screech ripped the air. I ran towards it, taking the stairs two at a time, with Avril at my heels. Orla was standing in the bathroom doorway, holding her chest as if she'd had a heart-attack.

'What is it? What's wrong? What happened?' I said.

She stepped aside. In the centre of the brightly lit white-tiled bathroom stood Chloe, Paddy and Mikey. Half of Chloe's fringe was missing and the hair behind it had been shaved off. Mikey's right eyebrow had vanished, with a narrow band of his hair over his ear, and Paddy had a broad bald stripe down one side of his curly head.

'Jesus!' I said.

'Oh, my God!' Avril groaned.

'What did you do, guys?' I said.

Orla held out Kevin's razor.

'We were shaving like Daddy,' Mikey said brightly.

'Shit,' I said.

'Shit,' the three toddlers said in unison.

'Fuck,' Paddy said.

'Paddy! Is anybody cut?' I asked.

'But . . . but . . . there's . . . When did that . . . I never said that he could . . .' Orla babbled.

'What are you talking about, Orla?'

Orla went to Mikey and pointed at his left ear. A tiny gold stud earring glinted in the bathroom light.

'What the . . .' Then I saw that Paddy had one – and Chloe had two. I looked at Avril. 'They *can't* be pierced!'

Avril smiled broadly. 'Aren't they cute?'

'But they're not really pierced, are they? Paddy'd never sit still – I can hardly cut his toenails.'

'No, they're real,' Avril said proudly. 'Oh, my God! It's a new system, completely painless – brilliant! I couldn't resist and they look *soooooo* cute with earrings in their little ears.'

I looked at Paddy's pierced ear and shaved head and thought that at least Emerson was the type of person who was more likely to be amused than upset by the day's disasters. Unfortunately the same couldn't be said about Orla. She put Kevin's razor on top of the medicine cabinet, then picked up Mikey. 'We'll be off so,' she said, through tight white lips.

'Great,' I said. 'I'll drop Chloe home and bring Paddy in and put him to bed. Thanks a million, Avril.'

Avril smiled, oblivious to Orla's fury, and I wanted to laugh for the first time that day. As soon as Orla had left I told Avril I'd look after Mikey till Kevin reappeared and she went home. Then Paddy, Chloe and I ran through the rain to the Walshes'. Derek opened the front door and burst out laughing when he saw his shorn daughter. 'Who cut your hair, baby?' he asked her, and kissed her cheek.

'Paddy,' Chloe squeaked.

'Sorry,' I said.

Derek walked into the sitting room where Tracy and the other girls were curled on the sofa watching TV. 'Trace, look! This one wins the prize for the youngest shave and haircut.'

'Is she cut?' Tracy asked.

I shook my head.

Derek handed over Chloe, who snuggled up to her mother as her sisters examined her hair.

Tracy looked at Paddy. 'Who cut your hair, Pad?' she asked.

'Chloe,' Paddy said.

'And Mikey?' Tracy asked me.

I nodded.

Tracy chortled. 'Orla won't be delighted when she finds out.'

'To say the least,' I said. 'She already knows – she found them. But, Trace – look a bit closer. There's another bit of a surprise . . .'

'Oh, my God!' Jade squealed. 'Chloe has earrings!'

'What?' Derek and Tracy said together.

'And Mikey and Paddy,' I said. 'Some new painless system and they look *soooooo* cute, according to Avril.'

Derek guffawed. 'I don't believe it. It's a wonder she didn't get them a couple of tattoos while she was at it.'

'That young one means well but . . .' Tracy was lost for words.

'I know,' I said, laughing. 'You can take them out – the holes will close over in a couple of days.'

Tracy lay back on the couch. 'You're a bit brighter.'

'Nothing like seeing Orla freaking out to cheer you up.'

'I always miss the good stuff,' Tracy grumbled.

'Anyway, lads, I'd better get going – I have a couple of pizzas in the oven and they must be cremated by now.'

36

Boarding the plane to Paris was like braving the crowds on the first day of the sales. Kevin battled his way through the other passengers and got there first. When he reached the top of the steps he turned and gave us a regal wave.

'Keep us some seats,' Tracy yelled, as we followed him.

'The plane's a bit battered – do you think it's safe?' I said, as I tottered into the cabin on my favourite black stilettos.

Derek laughed. 'Ruth, it reminds me of an ancient Cortina without an MOT.'

A smiling cabin steward greeted us. She wore beautiful pearl-stud earrings and far too much makeup.

Kevin stood half-way down the aisle, waving frantically at us. We struggled past other passengers and plonked into the seats he had valiantly defended. Derek put our hand luggage into the overhead bins.

I sat next to Kevin, and Tracy and Derek were across the aisle. Kevin took out a newspaper and began to read the sport. My phone signalled a text message. 'Have a brilliant time. I love you. Ferdia.'

He was so sweet. I was sorry he wasn't with me. We'd had a lovely time last night. He had booked a French restaurant, Le Petit Matelot, in honour of my trip to France, and Gary had joined us for dinner. I was amazed all over again by how well they got on with each other. They were like father and son as they discussed rugby and politics – and I didn't care what Kevin thought: I loved having these new men in my life and Paddy's. Anyway, Kevin was such a cynic about everything – particularly politicians.

I stole a glance at him as he read his paper in the confined space. He must have felt me looking because his head turned and he grinned, eyes crinkling at the corners. 'You OK?' he said.

I nodded and had a mad urge to hug him to me but I resisted it. 'I'm grand. Did you get Mikey sorted?'

'Orla's staying in my place. It was the easy thing to do,' he said, as the plane taxied down the runway in preparation for take-off.

My stomach knotted and I suddenly felt sick. Kevin gripped my hand. 'It'll be fine, Ruth. I didn't know you were scared of flying.'

I wasn't, actually. It was the memories of the last time I'd flown. They came at me out of the blue in a whirlwind of fast images, smells and sounds. Paddy giggling as the plane descended to land. The weird runway through the town of Gibraltar. The smell of heat and sun as we climbed into a taxi. The shimmering sea, the clear sky. Emerson's naked body, sweaty from sex, and Paddy's voice:

Daddy, Daddy. Selma Rodriguez' black hair on white sheets.

'It's OK now – we're airborne,' Kevin said, still holding my hand.

To hell with Emerson, I thought. This is my weekend and I won't let him spoil it.

As if the cabin steward had read my mind, she arrived selling drinks.

'Let the party begin,' said Tracy, as she downed a gin and tonic almost in one.

'Come on, Munster,' shouted Kevin, and the whole plane erupted into loud clapping.

By the time we arrived at our hotel we were all in party mood. It was called Le Chat Bleu and was just round the corner from the Arc de Triomphe. The foyer was tiny and we crowded in, bags and all.

Tracy spoke in pidgin French to the concierge, her voice increasingly animated.

'Problem?' said Kevin.

'Depends,' Tracy said. 'I booked two single rooms for you and he says I booked a double. I know I booked three altogether.'

'Can we change it?' I asked.

Tracy shook her head, but there was a glint in her eye. I'd kill her stone dead for this. 'Full up.'

'A double room, twin beds, right?' I said.

'Nope. Double bed.'

'So, what'll we do?' Kevin asked, with an irrepressible grin.

'It's not funny,' I said.

Tracy nodded, but she was laughing. 'It's not funny.'

'I'll sleep on the couch,' said Kevin.

'No couch. I asked,' said Tracy.

'I have a great idea. The guys can sleep in one room and we'll have the other,' I said.

'If you think I came all the way to Paris to sleep with you, you're mistaken,' Tracy said, as she picked up the room keys. 'Ye'll just have to get over yourselves and sort something out. Come on.'

We trudged up the narrow stairs to the third floor. 'Nearly there,' Tracy huffed, as we reached the top.

'Nobody told me we were staying on the Eiffel Tower,' said Kevin, as he took a key from Tracy's outstretched hand.

'I should have let you book it all, Kevin Regan. And if I had, we'd have swum over here and be sleeping in the Métro.'

Kevin opened the door of our room and we walked in. The room was decorated in mock-Louis Quatorze style, with faded wallpaper. It wouldn't have been out of place in a brothel. Kevin sat on the bed and I checked out the adjoining bathroom, which sported 1960s pink tiles but was spotlessly clean. However, the bedroom window opened on to a tiny wrought-iron balcony that was really quite lovely. I opened it and looked down on to the narrow street. 'It's beautiful,' I said, over my shoulder, to Kevin.

'I've sorted us out,' he said.

He'd made a barrier down the centre of the bed with an old-fashioned bolster. It looked like a body. 'Brilliant,' I said. 'If you're about six inches wide.'

He lay down on one side. 'Try it first before you dismiss it.'

I lay on the other side and looked over at him, the bolster like no man's land between us. We laughed.

'It'll be grand, Ruth. I don't want to make a fuss – Tracy will feel bad.'

Kevin was right. We'd have to put up with it. And, anyway, we were two mature adults who also happened to be great friends. We could manage this, no problem.

'You're right,' I said, and jumped up. 'I bags the bathroom first.' I opened my suitcase and took out my washbag. He stayed on the bed, hands behind his head, a little smile playing on his lips. 'Why are you smirking?'

'I'm smiling, Ruth.'

'Smirking. That's a smirk, Regan, I've seen it many times before.' I walked into the bathroom.

'If Ferdia rings I'll tell him you're in the shower while I'm keeping the bed warm. How's that?' he called, as I undressed.

'Bastard. Say that and it'll be death in Paris, I swear.' But I was laughing too.

Kevin made us walk the whole length of the Champs-Élysées, right down to the Louvre. It was around six in the evening so the museum was closed, but the building was magnificent. 'How do you know this place so well?' I asked, as we sat on a low fountain wall, the Louvre behind us and the Tuileries gardens ahead. Paris was magic. I could see Derek and Tracy in the distance, holding hands and kissing like lovestruck teenagers. I was reminded of Emerson and me on our first trip to Paris.

'I once had a French girlfriend,' he said, scuffing the ground with his toe. He wore his usual green combats and a Munster jersey.

'No way. What happened to her?'

'She got sense, like all the women in my life.'

'Oh, poor Kevin. Nobody loves him. Now answer the question. What happened to the French one?'

'I met Orla and was besotted for the first time in my life.'

'The only time?'

'I'm not sure.'

Curiosity was getting the better of me. Was Kevin besotted with Avril? Ferdia and I were getting more serious so why couldn't it be happening to them as well? And if Avril was to be believed, Kevin was hot in the sack. 'So,' I said. 'Spill. Who else?'

Kevin looked into my eyes and smiled at me. 'You know,' he said.

'No, I don't.'

'Yes, you do.'

'Avril?'

'The Munster rugby team.' He stood up and stretched out a hand to me. 'Come on, we've some partying to do tonight.'

'Can't walk. You'll have to carry me. Stilettos.'

'I give in. We'll get the Métro home.'

That night we ate in a shabby little restaurant in Châtelet. The clientele were mostly French and the décor was downmarket, but Kevin had insisted that the food was incredible – and was he right! We had lentils as a starter, cooked the traditional French way, and by the time my delicious dessert of tarte Tatin and cream arrived I was on the point of orgasm, which – let's face it – was a distant memory now.

We finished our dinner with strong espresso, then walked round the corner to the Galway Bay, an Irish pub on the banks of the Seine. Tracy and I sat at a window seat, which offered a fabulous view of the Pont Neuf, while Derek and Kevin went to the bar.

'Isn't this heaven?' I said, as I watched the Parisian night go by.

Tracy crossed her legs. 'Who're you telling? I never bonked so much in my life!'

I laughed. 'You look fabulous, Tracy. It suits you.' She did look terrific in a low-cut clingy black top that gave her great cleavage. 'The tits are good. Are they new?' I asked.

'Cool, aren't they? I bought them on eBay. The Americans are way ahead of us in the chicken-fillet department.'

'Excellent.'

'I nearly lost one yesterday, though. Lauren decided to wash the windows and there she was, with a bowl of soapy water and my very expensive chicken fillet, giving the front window a once-over.'

I giggled, and searched the room for the men. They were still standing at the crowded bar, talking to each other.

'Where are those two eejits with the drinks?' Tracy moaned. 'I'll be as sober as a judge going home.'

'I'm not walking home, Tracy. If Kevin says anything about walking please say no,' I said. My feet were in serious pain now and I vowed to run down to the Champs-Élysées in the morning to buy a pair of flats. I'd have just enough time before the match.

'He said in the restaurant that we could walk home by the Eiffel Tower and see it all lit up,' she said.

'We'll do a drive-by in a taxi. How's that?'

'Good idea. You don't want to be too tired later. You never know your luck, Ruth, you might get a ride in Paris yet.'

'I don't ride my friends.'

'I wouldn't rule anything out,' said Tracy.

'Bitch,' I said, as the men came with the drinks.

We returned to the hotel late and I thought I'd have to be carried up the three flights of stairs to our rooms. But I made it eventually, barefoot and bleeding, with Kevin carrying the offending stilettos.

We said goodnight to Derek and Tracy, but they barely answered as they unlocked their door in a mad rush to get inside. My friends were sex mani-acs, I decided, as I cleaned off my makeup in the bathroom. I was trying to decide what to wear going into bed. I considered my jeans and a polo-neck jumper but I'd roast. All I'd brought was my cream silk pyjamas. I hadn't known when I was packing that I'd be sleeping with Kevin. I brushed my teeth and decided on the pyjamas.

Kevin was sitting on the edge of the bed in a pair of bright red boxer shorts and nothing else. He was holding his washbag.

'You're not wearing just those going to bed, are you?' I asked.

Kevin stood up and shrugged. 'It's what I always wear. Why? Had you something else in mind? Do you think I'll be too warm?'

'How about jeans and a sweatshirt?'

'I trust you, Ruth. I know you won't take advantage of me in the middle of the night.' He went into the bathroom and closed the door. 'But if you want to take advantage of me, please feel free. You have my consent,' he shouted.

'Bastard.' I changed hurriedly into my pyjamas, then jumped into my side of the bed.

When he came out I was tucked in, the covers up to my chin, pretending to read *The Rough Guide to Paris* while he climbed in beside me. The bolster running down the middle of the bed had all the room. Kevin picked up his book and began to read. Just then my phone rang.

'Hi, sweetheart. I just couldn't go to sleep without hearing your voice.'

'Hi, Ferdia,' I said. I considered going into the

bathroom with the phone but decided it was more awkward to get out of bed than to stay in it.

'How are you? Are you enjoying yourself? I bet it's fabulous there. How's the hotel?'

'Great.'

'Are you OK, Ruth? Am I interrupting you? I thought you'd all be in bed.'

'We are. I'm really tired, that's all.' I could feel Kevin laughing silently and glared at him.

'Sorry, darling, I shouldn't have bothered you. I just . . . I really miss you.'

'Me too.'

'I'll ring tomorrow after the match. I love you, Ruth.'

'Me too,' I said, and hung up.

'You should have sent him a picture,' Kevin said.

'Shut up, you,' I said, and picked up my book. I tried to concentrate on the words but I could hear soft moans from Tracy and Derek's room, which got louder and louder. 'Jesus, those two. They're like bloody rabbits,' I said.

'I'm jealous,' said Kevin, jumping out of bed and switching on the small TV. He fiddled with the knobs until he found MTV. Britney Spears' voice replaced the moaning. 'Sounds the same,' he said, as he got back into the bed.

I laughed, then wondered how I'd ever get to sleep. But I must have dropped off because when I woke in the early morning I suddenly remembered that Kevin was in bed beside me. I leaned over the bolster and watched him while he slept. Gradually my eyes grew accustomed to the darkness in the room and I could see him clearly. In sleep he had a beautiful face – the face of an angel, just as Tracy said.

Without thinking I outlined his facial features lightly with my fingers. His eyebrows, his planed cheekbones, his mouth. He stirred and I snapped my hand away. My God! What was I thinking? I checked my watch. Seven o'clock. I decided to get up and have a shower. A cold one.

37

The match was brilliant. I wasn't the greatest rugby fan in the world but my friends were converting me. Munster won in a really tight nerve-wrecker against Stade Français. The French team came out on the pitch looking like models for a L'Oréal ad – all damp locks, hair gel and tight Lycra jerseys. They even wore white socks – a complete no-no, according to Tracy. She said a rugby player in white socks was just not meant to be. Kevin maintained that they even shaved their legs. I thought they looked great and got murderous looks from my friends when I said so. The Munster lads would never star in shampoo ads but there was something comforting and reassuring about their big raw Irish heads.

The atmosphere was electric as we screamed support for our team. Tracy, Derek and Kevin were ecstatic and I could have sworn I saw tears in Kevin's eyes as the referee blew the final whistle. It was a perfect afternoon.

And the perfect *karma* continued. We ate that night in a café near the Île de la Cité, overlooking the Seine. After dessert and about ten large *pichets* of wine Tracy and Derek broke into a rousing rendition of 'Stand Up And Fight,' with Tracy urging the amused French clientele to join in. She'd thought everybody in the world would know the words of the Munster rugby anthem. The whole café applauded and called for more. A small dapper Frenchman opened a well-worn piano and an impromptu sing-song started up.

Of course, the Irish took over the show. Tracy and I did a duet of 'Mamma Mia' and Derek sang 'Blue Suede Shoes'. But the hit of the night was Kevin: he sang 'Ring Of Fire' and dedicated it to the woman he'd slept with last night.

It was almost midnight by the time we got back to the hotel, giggling as we climbed the steep stairs. We said goodnight to Tracy and Derek and went into our room. Kevin headed straight for the bathroom and I sat on the bed, shoes off, legs crossed, waiting my turn. It'd been a fantastic day, I thought, as I listened to Kevin washing his face.

We'd got on so well – even the bed-sharing wasn't a problem. That really was a sign of true friendship. I mightn't have had a lot of luck where marriage was concerned but I had some wonderful friends. Kevin came out and began to strip so I went to the bathroom to wash, remembering to bring my pyjamas with me.

Then we got into bed with the bolster between us.

'They're quiet tonight,' Kevin said.

'Pissed, I'd say,' I answered.

'Never stopped them before. Never stopped me either,' he said.

My phone beeped. A message. 'Goodnight, sweet-heart.'

'I bet that's Ferdia – here, give me the phone and we'll ring him.' Kevin grabbed it from me.

I screamed, leaned over no man's land and thumped his arm.

'Give it back.'

Kevin held it in the air and I tried to grab it, but he moved it further away so I pummelled his chest. 'Is that the best you can do?' he gasped.

I pinched him.

'You're such a girl!' He caught up the bolster and threw it out of the bed, then pinned my arms behind my head.

'I declare war,' he said, his face inches from mine. 'Beg for mercy and promise to walk everywhere tomorrow – no métros – and I'll consider leniency.'

'Piss off!'

'I mean it. This is war. One signal from me and it'll be off with your head!'

'Off your head, more like! Give me my phone!'

He held me like that for a few seconds, our faces so close I could smell toothpaste and garlic. Then he released my hands, but stayed leaning over me.

'My phone,' I said.

'What phone?' he whispered, and kissed me lightly on the mouth. He pulled away immediately. 'Jesus, Ruth, I'm—'

Before he could finish I'd pulled his face back to mine and begun to kiss him long and hard. My body screamed with delight and accelerated from nought to sixty on the sex speedometer. I stroked his head and he fumbled with my buttons. I sat up and whipped off my top, then wiggled out of the bottoms while he kissed me lower and lower.

I was in an agony of anticipation but he took his time and teased and cajoled my every cell into a frenzy. By the time he entered me I was practically singing. Then I exploded, with such intensity I was sure it must be illegal.

We fell away from each other, breathing as ragged as if we'd just climbed the three flights of stairs outside our door five times in a row. I fell asleep and slept the sleep of the happy sinner.

I woke as dawn broke. The sky was turning from black to grey and Kevin's breathing was deep and regular beside me. As I watched him, I was filled, strangely enough, with want, not guilt. Then Kevin opened his eyes and looked straight into mine. He traced my lips with his fingers. 'OK?' he whispered. I leaned down and kissed him slowly. I couldn't resist. I straddled him and off we went again. The next time we woke it was nine thirty. We jumped out of bed, and dressed quickly, not wanting to miss breakfast.

Derek and Tracy were sitting at a table by the window in the small dining room. I poured coffee and sat down opposite Tracy. Kevin sat beside me and began another rehash of yesterday's match with a more than willing Derek. Tracy watched me as I picked up a knife and cut into a flaky croissant. She kicked me under the table. I kept my eyes on the croissant.

'Well, the dead arose and appeared to many,' she said.

'Good morning, Tracy,' I responded.

'Sleep all right?' she asked.

'Great,' I said, and bit into the pastry.

'I didn't sleep a wink,' she said.

'Why?' I asked, knowing I shouldn't have said anything.

'The noise from the room next door,' she said.

'Those Germans are a noisy bunch,' I said, and Kevin grinned.

Tracy looked at me and then at Kevin. 'Tell me, are ye finding that double bed comfortable?'

Kevin laughed. 'I've got the day planned. We have to check out of here but I asked them last night if we could leave our bags in the luggage room.'

I smiled at him gratefully for deflecting the conversation away from the night before.

'What time is the flight home?' said Derek, who had been getting uncomfortable with his wife's line of enquiry.

'Eight o'clock, so we have the whole day. I was thinking Sacré Coeur, Musée d'Orsay and maybe the Eiffel Tower, if you really want to go there . . .' Kevin said.

'I'm tired already, just thinking about it. Maybe we should all go back to bed for a little rest,' said Tracy.

'All together? Great idea, Trace,' Kevin replied, and everybody laughed.

Just then the dining-room door opened and someone came in, face obscured by a massive bunch of blood-red roses. I nearly dropped dead. Ferdia stood in the middle of the room, holding the flowers and searching the tables for us. For me. His face lit up when he saw me and he walked to our table. Tracy looked as if she was watching the climax in an *EastEnders*' story line.

He reached our table, laid the flowers in front of me and kissed me. 'Surprise!' he said to all of us. 'I'm glad I caught you before you went off sightseeing.'

Kevin stood up. 'Take this chair, Ferdia.'

'Are you sure?' said Ferdia.

Kevin nodded and walked out of the dining room. I wanted to follow him but I didn't know what to say.

Ferdia sat down next to me, and took my hand. Derek coughed, and Tracy threw her eyes to heaven.

'You look great, Ruth. Paris agrees with you,' he said, examining my face. He was devastatingly handsome.

'Certainly does,' said Tracy, eyeing me. 'She slept like a log last night, didn't you, Ruth?'

I gave her a murderous look. Derek coughed again.

'I can't believe you're here, Ferdia.'

'Neither can I. I wriggled out of the last day of the course . . . I've got a little surprise for you – I'll tell you later. What's the plan for the day?' said Ferdia.

'The Eiffel Tower and other stuff, museums and things,' I said.

Tracy stood up, her chair scraping on the wooden floor. 'I'm going to pack. Come on, Derek,' she said, as she walked away.

As soon as they'd gone, Ferdia held my face in his hands and kissed me lightly. My body responded automatically. How could someone be such a good kisser and so lousy in the sack?

'Let's go upstairs – I'll help you pack,' he said. He tilted his head to one side in a really sexy way.

I couldn't let him upstairs, no way. 'What's the surprise?' I asked.

'Later,' he said cryptically. 'Now, let's do some packing.' He nibbled the back of my ear. The dining room was deserted except for a young girl, who was cleaning the tables. I called her over and gave her the roses. Her face lit up and she thanked me profusely. 'We can't be lugging them around with us all day,' I said.

'I know. I thought of that but they were so lovely. So you. Let's go pack.'

'Wait here, Ferdia, and I'll pack myself. I won't be a minute.'

He stood up, pulling me with him. 'Come on.'

I led the way up the stairs and by the time we stood outside the bedroom door my heart was pounding. Where the fuck was Kevin? I opened the door and went into the room, Ferdia following. He pushed me gently on to the bed, kicked the door closed and started to kiss me. I opened one eye and tried to peek around the room. I hoped Kevin wasn't in the bathroom. Then I saw that his bag was gone

from the top of the wardrobe. Ferdia was un-
buttoning my shirt, his breathing quickening. I didn't
want sex – not in this room, but I also didn't want
Ferdia to suspect what happened with Kevin. In
fact I didn't know what the hell I wanted any more.
God must have heard me as, just then, there was a
loud rap on the door.

'*Excusez-moi, s'il vous plaît. Lavage,*' a maid said,
as she opened the door. We sat up and smiled at
her.

'*Un moment,*' Ferdia said. She retreated and closed
the door. He did up my shirt buttons. 'I can wait,
but just barely.'

I got up and packed my bags. As we struggled
down the narrow stairs, I wondered again where
Kevin was.

Tracy and Derek were waiting for us in the foyer.
'The luggage room is over there,' she said, pointing to
a door to the left of the reception desk.

'We don't need a luggage room,' Ferdia said.

'But I—'

'Ruth, we're staying another night. It's all arranged,'
he said, putting his arms round me.

'But I can't. My flight is booked and there's Paddy
and work . . .'

'All taken care of. Kathleen is staying over again
with Paddy. They're going to Foto Island for the
day.'

Just then Kevin came into the foyer, a newspaper
under his arm. I smiled at him but he looked away.

'So,' said Ferdia, 'we're staying another night.'

'Ye shouldn't have bothered clearing out of the room so,' said Tracy.

'I've booked us into the Ritz,' said Ferdia, eyes shining.

'The Ritz?' I said.

'We're off,' said Tracy. 'Are you coming, Kev?'

We all walked out together.

'I'll get us a cab and we can head over to the hotel first. We'll meet up with you guys later,' said Ferdia. He stacked the bags on the pavement and walked to the corner.

Kevin stood a little apart from us, engrossed in the price display outside the hotel.

'See you later so,' said Tracy.

'No swearing in the Ritz, Ruth – and no spitting from the balcony either,' said Derek. 'We'll see you later. Ring us.'

'No chance we'll be getting a cab. I think we're walking again,' Tracy said.

'Goodbye,' Kevin said, then walked up the street flanked by Tracy and Derek.

'See you later, Kevin,' I said to his back. As I watched them go, a big part of me wanted to run after them.

38

The Ritz was everything it was supposed to be and then some. Our suite was incredible: the *en-suite* bathroom was huge with a double shower and a gigantic bathtub – the whole Munster rugby team could have used it as a changing room. There was ice-cold champagne in a bucket: Ferdia popped out the cork and poured us two frothy glasses. We sipped, kissed and cuddled on the sofa.

Then Ferdia stood up and led me to the king-size bed in the centre of the room. We stripped off and climbed in. I closed my eyes as Ferdia's kisses became more urgent and Kevin's face appeared. His kisses became Kevin's teasing ones and my body went into overdrive as I recalled the night before. I cried out as I climaxed and caught the delighted look on Ferdia's face. I lay back on the silky sheets and held him as his body rippled in post-coital shudders. No wonder they called it the city of lovers – the sex in Paris was great, no doubt about it.

'That was incredible, the best ever,' he said. 'I can't believe how good that book is – we'll have to write to the author. I love you,' he said.

'You're such a romantic, Ferdia Ryan.' Apart from the Book I thought. 'Paris, the Ritz, flowers.'

'Are you complaining?'

'Absolutely not! It's something I love about you.'

'Is that it?'

'What?'

'Is that all you love about me?'

I laughed and mock-punched him. 'Let's go and meet the others. We can have lunch with them if we hurry.' I jumped out of bed and rooted around the jumble of clothes on the floor for mine. Ferdia lay on the cream silk sheets, his body a tribute to Greek gods. He might have been sculpted from honey-coloured stone. I was so lucky to have a wonderful man like him.

And especially now when the sex was working out. Kevin's face popped into my head yet again and I banished it to the corner of my mind where Emerson permanently hung out. Last night with Kevin should never have happened. It was just the buzz of the match and the wine. If I'd been in bed with anyone else the same thing would probably have happened. A simple one-night stand – except that we were friends. I'd talk to Kevin later on.

'I have a better idea. Let's spend the day on our own – just you and me,' said Ferdia.

I was balancing on one leg, trying to put on my knickers. 'We told the others that—'

'Give me your phone.'

I slipped on my knickers, went to the sofa and rooted in my bag for it. 'Catch,' I said, and threw it to Ferdia, who caught it deftly in mid-air. He spoke briefly to Tracy as I finished dressing.

'There,' he said. 'All done. I told them we were delayed. That's OK, isn't it, Ruth? I mean, you do want to spend the day with me, don't you?'

'What do you think?'

We had lunch in a four-star restaurant in Châtelet and took taxis to all the sights, but everywhere we went I found myself searching the crowds of tourists for Tracy and the lads. By the time we reached the Louvre I wanted to go home. I was done with Paris.

But Ferdia had organised the Louvre visit like a military operation. He had maps of the inside, lists of must-see paintings and the fastest route through the place. I headed straight for the coffee shop.

'We can't have coffee, Ruth, we haven't time. We'll miss the *Mona Lisa* if we stop.'

I kept walking in the coffee direction. 'Why? Is she going somewhere? If it's a choice between a double espresso and the *Mona Lisa* there's no competition.'

Ferdia ran after me. 'I just wanted it all to be perfect,' he said, reaching for my hand.

I pulled him into the coffee shop and sat him at a free table in the middle of the crowded room. A waiter came immediately and took our order. Ferdia had put all his maps and paraphernalia on the small beech table. I scooped up the lot and rolled it into a ball. 'Forget these. It'll be perfect without all this stuff.

Let's just stroll around – if we miss some paintings it won't kill anyone.'

Ferdia reached out for my hand again. Jesus, Paris was really getting to him. 'As usual, Ruth, you're absolutely right and that's why I love you so much.' He put his hand into his jacket pocket and stood up. I knew what was going to happen next and froze in my seat. He went down on one knee in front of me, a small black velvet box in his hand. I could feel everybody's eyes on us. The waiter had come back with our coffee and stood at the table, watching the scenario unfold.

'Ruth, I planned to do this tonight, at sunset, on top of the Eiffel Tower, but I can't wait. Will you marry me?'

I took a deep breath, and it felt like everyone else in the room did too. Ferdia's eyes were earnest. 'I – I—' I stuttered.

'I know your experience of marriage is not good but, Ruth, I promise you, with me it'll be for ever. And I know this is very soon but you're the one.'

'Ferdia—'

'I know for certain that I want to spend the rest of my life with you. And I'll wait, Ruth. There's your divorce and all of that. I'll wait for ever if I have to.'

'I will.' I was surprised at how definite I sounded.

'What?'

'I will,' I repeated.

Suddenly the whole room burst into applause. Ferdia pulled my face to his and kissed me. Then he opened the box and took out an exquisite diamond solitaire ring and put it on my finger. It was a perfect fit. 'I'm the happiest man in the world, Ruth,' he said, as he sat down.

We stirred milk and sugar into our coffee. Where was Tracy with the fags when I needed her? 'Me too,' I said.

'I can't wait to tell everyone. I feel like taking a full-page ad in the *Indo*—'

'That's not a good idea,' I interjected.

'A joke. I'll ring my mum when we get back to the hotel. And I'll ring Fachtna, my brother. And there's George Holman at work . . .'

'Let's not tell anyone.'

Ferdia had his cup half-way to his lips and held it there. 'What?'

'Let's keep it a secret.'

Hurt passed over his face. He put the cup down. 'Why?' he asked, his voice quiet, staring at the cup as if it would answer his question.

'I mean for now. Let's keep it a secret until we get home tomorrow night and then we'll tell just a few people. I'd prefer it that way, Ferdia. I mean, I've just started divorce proceedings and I know I'll get all the rebound lectures.'

'Rebound?'

'You know, marrying on the rebound after one relationship crashes.'

'But that's not true, Ruth.'

'I know that and you know that, but it's what they'll say.'

Relief flooded his face. 'Ruth, you had me worried

there. I thought you had cold feet already. But you're right. I mean, it's more complicated for you with Emerson and the divorce. No, you're absolutely right.'

I smiled at him, conscious of the new ring on my finger, exactly where Emerson's used to be. My head was reeling with all the events of the past twenty-four hours and I needed to be on my own to do some serious thinking.

We had dinner in the Ritz and both of us were so tired that we went straight to our room afterwards. I rang Kathleen and we chatted for a while. When I ended the call Ferdia was asleep. My tiredness had deserted me. I considered cleaning the room, but I didn't think the maids would appreciate my doing them out of their jobs. I couldn't face French TV. I'd received a text earlier from Tracy, which read 'What happened last night?' I considered replying but decided against it because I didn't know the answer. Out of the corner of my eye I spotted some headed notepaper on a little console table. Maybe if I wrote everything down it would make sense. It was worth a try and, anyway, I was bored.

I got a sheaf of the embossed paper and sat on the sofa, legs tucked under me. I stared at the blank page for a full five minutes. I'd make a list, I decided finally. Lists were good and they always cut to the chase, didn't they?

I wrote Ferdia's name at the top of the page and Kevin's beside it.

FERDIA		**KEVIN**	
PROS	*CONS*	*PROS*	*CONS*
Stable	sex (improving)?	Great sex	Three women on the go
Reliable		Funny	Arty (= unstable)
Wants commitment		Best friend	Unfocused
Consistent			Mad
Gorgeous			Too easy going
Considerate			Cynical
In love with me			Smart ass
Focused			All over the shop
No baggage			Baggage (Orla)

I chewed the top of the pen. When I saw it there in black and white there was no denying who was the winner. I mean, Kevin's cons were as long as Ferdia's pros. And I was confident now that Ferdia and I could work out the sex thing. But there was one other spanner in the works.

EMERSON	
PROS	*CONS*
Paddy's dad	At least two women on the go (Selma and me)
Handsome	Arty (= unstable)
Kind	Unfocused
Generous	Unfaithful
Great sex	Untrustworthy
	Lied about loving me
	Cheat
	Wrecked everything

The only huge pro that Emerson had over the other two was that he was Paddy's father. End of story. But when I looked back at my relationship with him I could see that I'd allowed my heart to rule my life. And I'd learned a tough lesson. To base a relationship on such a flimsy foundation was stupid. This time I should listen to my head. If I'd learned anything in Paris it was that. I stretched out my hand and looked at the diamond on my finger.

39

When I arrived home from Paris I was determined that a new chapter in my life had opened. Which meant that the previous chapter – the one filled with grief – had ended. The end of a marriage is like a death. First you're in shock, then denial, then mourning. People don't know what to say to you so they avoid you. And you think you'll never get over it. That you'll never again trust life enough to take a chance. But now I believed Ferdia had changed that in me. I felt that he was the best chance I had and I was going to grab it with both hands. As for Kevin, I couldn't begin to think about him but I was sure it'd be all right: we were great friends.

When I arrived home on Monday night Kathleen was waiting up for me. I peeped in on a sleeping Paddy, then joined her in the kitchen for tea and a sandwich. She was staying the night and wore a turquoise silk dressing-gown over matching pyjamas.

'You look great, Kathleen,' I said, as I bit into an egg-salad sandwich she'd prepared. It was delicious.

'I feel wonderful,' she said, sipping her herbal tea.

'Anyway, how was Paddy for the weekend? Did Emerson take him for you?'

'We had a great time.'

I stirred my tea. 'And Foto Island?'

'Lovely. Emerson brought a picnic and we fed the—'

'Emerson?'

'Yes. He wanted to come and it all worked out rather well because he drove. You don't mind that I let him, do you?'

I thought about it. I didn't mind, but what was he playing at, hanging out for a whole day with his practically ex-mother-in-law? 'No. It sounds like you'd a lovely day,' I said.

'I told Paddy that when the baby is born I'd bring both of them down there again. I don't think he quite understands but it says in the baby books that you should prepare them for a new arrival.' She patted her stomach.

'Did anybody ring while I was away?' I asked, as I finished my sandwich.

Kathleen put her cup on the table and fiddled with a tiny stud earring. 'Ruth, you did it again.'

'What?'

'Just there. You did it again and we need to talk about it.'

I decided to let her explain herself.

'Every time I mention the baby you change the subject or ignore it.'

'I don't know what you're talking about.'

'I know you're having a hard time – I mean, there's Emerson and Gary Kennedy and Ferdia—'

'Ferdia?'

Kathleen sipped some tea. 'I see things some-times, Ruth, that others don't. Ferdia and you are not . . . well . . . not clicking in certain departments.'

Colour flooded my face. 'Enlighten me about Ferdia because we just got engaged so if there are any spirits who want to object I suggest they do it now.'

'Congratulations.'

'Thank you.'

'Are you sure?'

'That I'm engaged? Positive.'

'Are you sure he's the one?'

'No, but I was sure Emerson was and look where that got me.'

We were silent then and, despite my best efforts, tears welled in my eyes. I tried to blink them away but Kathleen came over and put her arms round me. 'It'll be fine, all of it. You'll see.'

I stood up and smiled at her. The tears had vanished. 'I know it will. Once this divorce is sorted I'll be grand. Ferdia and I can move on with our lives.'

Kathleen held on to my arm. 'Isn't it a bit . . . soon? You hardly know each other, really, and it's so sudden. Maybe you should slow down a bit.'

I walked over to the sink and began to clean it with the pot brush. 'We've known each other almost six months but thanks for your advice. I've survived all this time without it so I'll go it alone on this.'

'It's your life, Ruth, I accept that, but I love you and I want what's best for you. I know it's too little too late but it's what I can offer you now. Goodnight.'

She walked out of the kitchen and I remained where I was, furiously scrubbing an already spotless sink. There was nothing wrong with Ferdia and me. Obviously her psychic powers were a couple of episodes behind and Paris hadn't been revealed to her yet. And I was dead right about her and her advice. It was way too late for that. At least Gary never tried that on. It's fine telling people you love them when they don't need you. Where was she when I was tiny, like Paddy? And I wouldn't and couldn't play happy families about her pregnancy. Fuck that, I thought, as I scrubbed the shiny stainless steel.

Kathleen came back in for a glass of water. 'I get thirsty, so I have to bring a glass of water to bed.'

'Goodnight, Kathleen, and thanks for everything,' I said, without turning to her.

'No problem. Goodnight, Ruth.' She walked out of the kitchen and I thought she was gone until I turned and saw her standing in the doorframe, looking at me.

'You managed it again,' she said. 'You steered the conversation away from the baby.' Then she left me alone.

Deep down I knew she was right. I never thought about her baby if I could help it and certainly not in relation to myself. And it was a terrible thing to say but I dreaded the birth and how it might make me feel. I wondered if Kathleen wanted to hear that.

She was good at dispensing home truths but could she accept them? As I prepared for bed I wished I was back in Paris.

The next day I was in better form as I headed off to the hotel. My morning's work went well and the only thing bothering me was Kevin. I felt bad about what had happened. I had to talk to him and the sooner the better. Ferdia was like somebody who'd won the Lotto and beamed his way through the day. I knew he was busting to tell everyone but I was adamant that we keep it quiet. There was no need for *everyone* to know yet. I'd sent Tracy a text and told her to call in after I finished work. I had to tell her, even though I knew how she would react.

Avril didn't show up for work until nearly eleven. The minute I saw her face I knew something was wrong. Her makeup was flawless as usual but her eyes were red-rimmed. 'Are you OK?' I asked, as she came behind the desk.

'Oh, Ruth, what will I do?' she said, and burst into tears.

'What is it, Avril? It can't be that bad – tell me.' I pulled her into my arms and stroked her long red hair. 'Come into the back office and tell me.'

I sat her down and handed her a tissue, then perched beside her and watched as she carefully wiped her perfectly made-up eyes.

'Oh, Ruth, you'll never guess,' she said, and began a fresh bout of crying.

'Probably not,' I said, 'so you'll just have to tell me.'

She sniffed loudly. 'Kevin . . .' she said, and began to wail.

My heart thudded at the mention of his name and

steamy images of us flooded my mind. I composed myself. 'What about him?' I asked.

'He . . . Do you know what he did?'

'No idea.'

'He finished with me last night. Completely out of the blue. Can you believe it, Ruth?' The bawling started all over again.

My mind was racing. Why did he do that?

'He said he really liked me but I wasn't the woman for him.' She dabbed her eyes with the tissue. 'I don't understand it, Ruth. We had a brilliant time the night before he went to Paris and the sex was—'

'I know, I know,' I said, not wanting to hear about Kevin's prowess. I knew it first hand now, anyway.

'The sex was spectacular. That has to mean something, hasn't it?'

I patted Avril's shoulder.

'Hasn't it? I mean, we were making love, Ruth. It wasn't just sex. You'd have to love somebody to have sex like that – I know in my heart that's true.'

I realised then how young and naïve Avril was. I'd had terrific sex with the subject of her unhappiness. Some people were good at organisation, like Ferdia, or public relations, like Gary, or sex, like Kevin. But I didn't think she would be able for my head-versus-heart theory. She was far too young. 'Cheer up, love. It's not as bad as it seems,' I said.

'Can I ask you something, Ruth?'

'Sure.'

'You were in Paris with Kevin, right?'

'Right.'

'Did anything happen?'

I tried to sound casual. 'Like what?'

'Did he meet someone? I bet he met some bloody Munster supporter and went off with her. Did he?'

'No. Not a Munster supporter, anyway. Look, maybe he doesn't want to get into anything serious right now.'

'You're right, Ruth. Things are moving too quickly for him, that's all it is,' she said. She patted her eyes, then stood up and straightened her skirt. 'Thanks,' she said.

'Any time.' We went out to the reception desk.

My mobile rang and India's name flashed on the screen.

'Hi, Ind, I was going to give you a call later. Paris was—' I stopped mid-sentence. 'India? India, what's wrong?'

'I . . . Oh, Ruth, I'm sick of it all . . . all the juggling and . . .' She was sobbing.

'India? Where are you?'

'I'm . . . Look out the hotel doors.'

I did so and saw her huddled against the glass doors, her phone pressed to her ear. She waved tentatively at me.

'Avril, can you hold the fort for a few minutes?' I was already dashing out from behind the desk.

I went out into the damp autumn morning. India was huddled against the wall, her normally sleek bob sticking out at all angles. Tears streaked her face and she looked like she used to when we were at primary school. 'Oh, Ruth,' she said, and fell into my arms.

'What's wrong, India? Come on, tell me.'

'I ran away.'

'From Tim?'

She shook her head. 'From court.' Her eyes filled with tears.

'Hey, that's OK. Look, we'll go across to the Tavern for coffee. We can talk there.'

'What about your work?'

I smiled at her. 'It helps when your boyfriend's the manager.'

I steered her across the road and into the pub. We sat down in an alcove just inside the door. I ordered the coffee.

India looked wanly at me. 'I'm sorry.'

'Nothing to be sorry about. Now, tell me what happened.'

'I had this big case that was going to court today and I worked really hard and then—' She stopped as tears took over.

'Go on, Ind, it can't be that bad.'

'I got into court, with my files and my records and all my homework done. I looked around me, at my client, my colleagues, the judge, the packed gallery and, well . . . I just ran away.'

'Just ran?'

'Like the hammers of hell.'

'What's so bad about that?'

'Well, normally the solicitor hangs around until the case is over.'

I laughed and she gave me a watery smile. 'It's just . . . It's everything, really. It's trying to keep all the balls in the air and it only takes one little thing – like Alyssa's illness a couple of weeks ago – and it all comes crashing down and – I don't know. What's it all for?'

I looked at my distraught friend, sitting there in the dim light. She seemed like another person. This wasn't the India of old: this was a new, unpredictable, vulnerable India. A mother torn between career and child.

'It was the washing-machine this morning and Alyssa was cross and I got cross with her.'

'It happens to all of us, Ind.'

'No. I got cross with her because I didn't have time to drop a ball. I didn't have time for my baby to be out of sorts.'

'Give it up.'

'What?'

'Walk out, Ind. Just give it up altogether.'

'But the partnership and the practice! What would my clients do?'

'They'd find another solicitor and life would go on. Honestly, that's exactly what would happen.'

Something like realisation passed across her face. 'Give it up?' she repeated.

I nodded.

'You know, even saying those words makes it all seem trivial. Not as important.'

I smiled. 'India Burke, I never took you for a bolter but you ran away!'

'Well, finally my friends' bad habits are wearing

off on me. I recall your famous date last June. That was a good bolt.'

'All I'm saying is that sometimes things can really get on top of you and the most extreme option of all can put it into perspective.'

'So, think about giving up my job, then work backwards?'

I sipped my coffee. 'When will you have to decide about this partnership thing?'

'Beginning of December.'

'What does Tim say?'

India shrugged. 'He says make the decision that's right for me. Easier said than done.'

'You have a month. Take your time. Right now I think you should get Alyssa and go home. Have a rest. Go to the park. Doss.'

'Thanks, Ruth. That's exactly what I'll do.' We stood up and went out. 'Hey, tell me about Paris! Was it fabulous?' she asked, as we neared Drury's.

'Yes.' I hadn't the heart to go into my shit now, with India so fragile and upset. We hugged each other and I went back to work.

It was almost one thirty when Paddy and I got home. He went straight to the living room and switched on the TV. The doorbell rang and I thought it was Tracy. I was wrong. It was Emerson. 'Good weekend?' he asked, smiling.

'Brilliant.'

He dropped his gaze and scuffed his sneakers off the step. Then he looked up and smiled again, his head tilted to one side. A few months ago, that smile would have melted my insides.

'So?' I said. 'Did you want something in particular? A bowl of sugar, maybe?'

'I was wondering if I could take Paddy out to Ogonnolloe. We're having a birthday party for Mum.'

'Why didn't you ring me?'

Emerson said nothing.

'We have access arrangements and we should stick to them.'

He met my eyes. 'Sometimes arrangements can be flexible. Life can't always accommodate rigid plans.'

Just then Paddy came running down the hall.

'Daddy, Daddy, Daddy!' he shouted, and hurled himself at his father's legs. Emerson caught him and lifted him high into the air. Two pairs of identical aqua eyes looked at me.

'Well?' Emerson said.

I could see Tracy coming up the garden path. 'OK,' I said, 'but in future ring me first. I'll get his things.'

Tracy came in, planting a quick kiss on Paddy's cheek. 'Emerson,' she said, as she sidled past him.

'How are you, Tracy?' Emerson asked.

'I heard baldy-heads are all the go in Hollywood. Is it true?' said Tracy.

Emerson knew better than to rise to Tracy's bait. 'I wouldn't know anything about Hollywood,' he said.

I went and got Paddy's stuff and handed it to Emerson.

'I'll be back around eight. Is that OK?'

'Fine,' I said, and kissed Paddy before they headed off.

'Why is he here again?' Tracy said, as she took out her fags. 'Here, have one. Are you on or off them? I can't remember at this stage.'

'Neither can I, so I might as well have one.'

'So, tell me everything, you sneaky old bitch,' she said, as she sat at the kitchen table. I played for time and filled up the coffee machine. I was surprised it wasn't worn out – I was practically living on coffee.

'I'm waiting, Ruth. Don't mind the coffee. I don't want it – I want scandal.'

I sat down opposite my friend and lit my cigarette.

'What's that on your finger?' she asked.

I held out my hand and smiled.

'Is that an engagement ring?' she said. 'Who's the lucky fella?'

'Who do you think?'

'Well, it could be the one you slept with last Saturday night or the one you slept with on Sunday,' she said, dark eyes narrowed.

'It wasn't like that,' I said, and pulled hard on my cigarette. God, nicotine tasted so good.

'Engaged? Seriously?'

'Yes – well, sort of, and before you say anything I know what I'm doing and it's not on the rebound and I've thought long and hard. Ferdia is the man for me.'

'Ferdia?'

I nodded.

'When? In Paris?'

I nodded again.

'You're engaged?' she repeated.

'We're sort of engaged but waiting a while.'

'How can you be sort of engaged? Oh, I know, you're engaged to be engaged. Nice one, Ruth. Now tell me what happened.'

'We went to the Louvre and he just sprang it on—'

'Not that, you fool. You and Kevin.'

I stubbed out my cigarette on a nearby saucer and immediately wanted another. 'Nothing to tell.'

'Didn't sound like that to me on Saturday night. I thought ye were making a porn movie with all the moaning that was going on. So, spill.' Tracy cocked her head to one side.

'It was the wine and the match, the whole Paris thing, Tracy. It shouldn't have happened. I'm sure Kevin feels the same now.'

'You're a fool, Ruth Burke.'

'I know. I shouldn't have let it happen.'

'That's not what I mean. You and Kevin have something going on. Don't ignore it.'

'Kevin is great and he's a really good friend and that's about the size of it,' I said, and took another cigarette from the packet on the table.

'Bet the sex was great.' Tracy eyed me and shook out a fag for herself. She reached for the lighter – a souvenir flashing-Eiffel-Tower job – and lit our cigarettes.

'Avril was right. He's not bad,' I said, and we burst out laughing.

'Are you really engaged?' Tracy said, her face suddenly serious again.

'We're keeping it quiet, Tracy, so don't tell people.'

'A long quiet time of being engaged to be engaged? So, when is the big day? I hear fifty is a good age to marry.'

'Shut up, Tracy. I want the ink dry on the divorce papers first.'

'That'd be a good idea.'

'I've thought about it. I want someone I can trust to give me stability. And that's Ferdia.'

Tracy drew hard on her fag. 'Sometimes you have to go with the flow, Ruth. You can't control the world.'

'My relationship with Emerson was all about going with the flow and I've had enough of that crap.'

'Whatever you say. Did you meet Kevin since you came home?'

'No, but do you know what he did? He called it off with Avril.'

'You're not serious! That must be something to do with Paris.'

'Don't be stupid.'

Tracy arched an eyebrow. 'What did Avril say he said?'

'Something like "You're very nice but you're not the woman for me."'

Tracy laughed. 'Told you, Ruth.'

'You're wrong. It doesn't have anything to do with me.'

'Whatever you say. Anyway, what was the Ritz like?'

'Incredible. Ferdia's such a romantic.'

Tracy rolled her eyes. 'Spare me. What's *he* like in the sack? Tell me one thing. Did you make as much noise in the Ritz as you made in the Chat Bleu?'

I felt colour rise in my face. 'I had a brilliant time,' I said, stood up and went to the fridge. 'I really need to go food shopping.'

'Are you going to call over to Kevin?'

I twisted the ring on my finger. I noticed it was a bit tight – I'd have to bring it to a jeweller. 'I will.'

'Good. That's the least you owe him. I'd better go. I've a party tonight in Brookdale.'

Tracy left, closing the front door behind her. I stood in the silent kitchen, glad to be alone. She was right. I did owe Kevin an explanation, but I didn't feel ready to meet him yet. Not until I'd worked out exactly what had happened in Paris.

40

But I didn't get to dot the Is and cross the Ts as I would have liked. About an hour after Tracy left, Kevin arrived.

'Hi, Kev!' I said, way too brightly. There was something about him that made me feel bad. 'Tea? Coffee?' I said.

He shook his head and sat at the kitchen table. I tidied off the draining-board all the while chattering nonsensically about work, the Louvre and the match in Paris. Kevin didn't say a word. Eventually my inane chatter dried up and I just stood by the fridge.

'Tracy told me your good news,' he said.

Why had she done that? She should have let me tell him.

'I was going to call in to you in a little while,' I said.

He nodded, but I knew he didn't believe me. I wasn't sure I believed myself. 'Nice ring,' he said.

'Thanks.'

Silence.

'Ferdia is a good man,' I said then.

'I know.'

'I really like him and I think he's what I need in my life right now.'

'And I'm not?'

My breath stuck in my throat as he said it and his eyes gazed deep into mine. 'You're in my life already,' I said.

'What about what happened in Paris? Doesn't that change anything?' he asked.

I couldn't answer at first because, well, it was a good question – didn't it change everything? Hadn't our relationship moved into a new place? Being with Kevin was like being in exactly the right place. Everything – even the sex – felt right. But that was at a feelings level. Once I moved into my head I knew he and I would be a disaster together.

He didn't know what he wanted any more than I did, no matter what he thought. He was still all fucked up after Orla – he was definitely on the rebound. I had enough of my own baggage without having to deal with his as well. But, most of all, I'd been down the it-feels-so-right road before and it had been a disaster.

'Paris happened because we were drunk, Kevin. You're an attractive man and I like to think, you know, that I'm not a total dog . . .' I paused. 'Anyway, we were lonely and drunk and in the same bed and, well, these things happen.'

His eyes seemed to grow as I spoke and the hurt in them was so apparent that I looked away. I knew I was doing the right thing. He'd thank me for it eventually – just not right now.

'So you're saying it was just sex?' he said eventually, not much louder than a whisper.

'That's exactly what I'm saying. But, Kevin, we can get past it – you're my friend and I love you and I can't bear the thought of us not being friends . . .' I stole a quick glance at him.

He stood up, scraping the chair legs on the tiles. 'I need to go,' he said. 'I've work that has to be finished.'

We gazed at each other for a few seconds, then he raised a hand and left. I stayed in the kitchen. The front door closed and he was gone. Just like that. I'd told him the truth. Ferdia was what I needed in my life. Our future together would be secure, bright and good. Our marriage was the right step for everybody – for Ferdia, for Paddy, for me, even for Kevin. I wasn't right for him any more than he was right for me. It made no sense. I knew I'd done the right thing. Even so, once Kevin had left I sat at the kitchen table and cried and cried and cried.

I didn't run into Kevin for almost a week after that, and when I did see him it was on a TV screen. Ferdia had decided we needed to look at houses. His theory was that prices were going through the roof, particularly for large family homes – as he put it – and we should start looking now, even if the wedding was a couple of years off.

I knew this made sense, but eight viewings later I was happily resigned to staying in my own house for ever, regardless of its size.

All of this house-hunting was interspersed with Avril bawling her way through work. I didn't know anyone who could cry as much – except maybe my friend Ellen in Australia.

Then on Saturday night Ferdia stayed over for the first time. Bright and early on Sunday morning he opened the front door, wearing a dressing-gown, Paddy in his arms. Emerson was on the doorstep. Ferdia invited him in, which was a big mistake. In Johnny Cash's words Emerson had a face like a little whipped pup – and all of this before I'd had my first cup of coffee.

As if that wasn't bad enough, the sex the night before had been terrible. The worst ever. Lying in bed afterwards listening to Ferdia's contented snores, I tried to justify it. It was the first time in my bed in my house with Paddy in the room next door. So much for the Book. I seriously considered borrowing a Randy Rabbit from Tracy.

But nothing that happened that weekend could beat Kevin's TV appearance.

It was Monday evening. I was in Tracy's house with Paddy. Derek was working and she'd invited us down for home-cooked Chinese. Gary had rung me earlier and told me to watch the *Six O'Clock News*. Apparently there was going to be some big announcement concerning him, and as I was his family it concerned me. He wouldn't say what it was, only that it was good and that I was to watch.

Ferdia rang too, giving me more or less the same news as the press conference was on in Drury's. He was in a tizzy preparing for the event. I tried to calm him and had half succeeded by the time he hung up.

At six on the dot I switched on the TV in Tracy's kitchen. The kids were in the playroom watching a movie.

'What's this about?' asked Tracy.

'I've no idea, some political thing,' I said, as the news headlines were read.

Then the screen showed a close-up picture of Gary and the voiceover said, 'Gary Kennedy throws down the gauntlet for leadership of the People's Party.'

Tracy turned up the volume as the conference room in Drury's filled the screen. Gary sat at the top of a long table, flanked by members of the party faithful. Journalists and camera people jostled for position in front of him as he stood up and smiled. He really was a very charismatic man. That gene had skipped my generation but maybe Paddy had inherited it.

Gary addressed the crowd, stating his intention to run for party leader, which would be decided at the party's annual conference in four weeks' time. He said that another fine candidate was in the running but that he felt he was the right man for the job. There was a huge round of applause from supporters, and journalists began rapid-fire questioning. Gary handled it all beautifully, and it was almost over when I recognised a familiar voice.

'Gary, one question.' The camera panned to Kevin in green combats and grey sweatshirt, with a biro over one ear.

'Yes, Kevin,' said Gary, smiling broadly at him.

'The Ballymoran report can't be located. You were chairman of the commission responsible for that study. Any idea where it disappeared to?'

'Those studies and findings are available. Some can even be accessed online. You should try a little harder to gather your information. In fact, can I make a suggestion? Why don't you contact the engineer who conducted the study?' he said, and some of his cronies giggled.

Kevin smiled. 'Actually, the environmental engineer who signed off on the report died a couple of months ago. Surely you were aware of that, Gary?'

'No, I wasn't. As I said many times before, the Ballymoran case is done and dusted. The commission has moved on. We are presently conducting a major impact study into landfill sites and the damage they've caused over many years in this country.'

A small thin woman with a sharp jaw interjected: 'On the question of landfill sites, do you think that there can ever be justification for the use of incinerators?'

Tracy turned down the sound. 'Kevin never gives up, sure he doesn't.'

'No. But I think he's barking up the wrong tree this time, Trace.'

'I don't know. That Deep Throat fella thinks something fishy's going on.'

'Deep Throat is leading Kevin a merry dance. He's probably some bored civil servant with a voice-distortion machine – you can get one of those anywhere. Even Dunnes sell them.'

'Who would be mad enough to go to all that trouble?

'The world is full of mad people.'

Just as I was leaving for work Gary turned up at my house. 'Ruth, just passing, thought I'd call in, see if you'd like a lift to work,' he said, got out of his sleek black Merc and opened the passenger door.

'It's only down the road,' I said, as I sat into the leather-upholstered seat.

'We can talk on the way. I just had a quick coffee with Ferdia – such a great guy. You're lucky to have him,' he said, as he pulled into traffic on O'Connell Street. He didn't speak for a few minutes and neither did I. Eventually he said, 'I might have found something for you and Ferdia.' His hands on the steering-wheel were in better shape than mine and his nails had been recently manicured.

'Oh?' I said. 'Were we looking for something?'

'A fabulous piece of land. I might be able to help with the planning permission – if you're interested.'

'Oh.'

'Ferdia's really keen – he has a great eye for business,' said Gary. 'So, I take it you saw the news last night?'

'Yes. Congratulations, Gary. You'll be even busier if you get the party leadership.'

'I thrive on busy. It keeps me young.' He smiled at me, and I noticed that he had perfectly even white teeth. American teeth.

'Anyway, I wanted to let you know about that

piece of land. We'll have to make a decision on it pronto. Ferdia's all gung-ho. I left him the maps and the name of my surveyor.'

'Thanks,' I said. We'd reached the entrance to the hotel. Gary stopped the car, reached into his pocket and switched on his phone. New messages signalled their arrival one after another, then almost immediately it rang. He spoke into it and I opened the car door.

'Ruth, I'll be in touch – I'll ring you later. I want Ferdia and yourself to come to the Mayor's ball next week.' The phone was still glued to his ear. 'If you'd want to – you don't have to come. I know it's boring hanging out with your old man.'

'I'd love to.'

'I've convinced the Mayor to donate the proceeds to PAP. Look, I'll drop in some tickets – Kathleen might like to go too, and you can bring friends, if you like.'

'Great,' I said, knowing Tracy would love to go, especially as it was in aid of her current favourite charity.

'Your boring old man is honoured,' he said, and smiled.

I laughed, waved and closed the door. Gary was a lot of things as a father – mostly absent – but he certainly wasn't boring. Anything but, I thought, as I pushed open the shiny plate-glass doors of the hotel.

Ferdia greeted me with a barrage of questions about Gary and the site. I fobbed him off and headed into the back office to make a cup of disgusting instant coffee. I passed Avril on the way. She was at the desk, looking like she'd just witnessed the slow torture and death of her favourite puppy. I made my coffee, came back in and sat on the swivel chair next to her.

'How are things?' I said. Although everybody in Limerick knew how things were with Avril.

'I rang him last night and left four messages but he didn't reply. Ruth, I haven't seen him for a full week. I can't bear it.'

I felt like saying she should have checked out the news last night – she'd have seen both Kevin and her place of work. But I didn't want to encourage the tears and the allusions to great sex. 'Avril, all men are bastards. Forget him.'

Fat tears spilled down Avril's beautifully made-up cheeks. 'You don't understand. I'm in love with him, Ruth. He's just the coolest person in the world and the sex—'

'Oh, look! Four coachloads of Americans. Wipe your eyes, Avril, we'll need to be on our toes to get this lot sorted.' I put on my best smile for the invasion.

41

It was lunchtime when we'd finished allocating rooms and sorting out all the new guests and I sighed with relief as I finished the last registration on the computer.

I felt someone's eyes on me and looked up. Kevin. 'Can I have a word?' he said, his voice businesslike. He wore yesterday's clothes and was unshaven. I could hear Avril hyperventilating.

He smiled at her. 'Avril, hi,' he said. She paled, then ran into the back office. 'I need to talk to you.'

I stopped typing. 'OK.'

'In private. Can we go into the bar for five minutes?'

I could tell from his tone that he wasn't about to take no for an answer.

'She'll be back in five minutes, Avril,' he shouted cheerfully.

I didn't need to look at her to conjure up the stricken expression that had come over her face.

I sat into a booth in a quiet corner and Kevin went to the bar. He returned with two steaming mugs of coffee. We sat in silence for a few seconds and then he coughed loudly. 'There's no good way to say this,' he said. 'This morning, when I was making breakfast for myself and Mikey I saw these.'

He put his hand into his pocket, pulled out an envelope and tipped a stack of photographs on to the table. Then spread them out. They were black-and-white images of Mikey: Mikey on the swing, Mikey climbing the willow tree in their front garden, Mikey running from his playschool, Mikey in the supermarket. My stomach squeezed with fear and flipped completely when I saw that Paddy was in some of them. I picked up a picture of Mikey standing on our front wall with Paddy beside him.

'What are they?' I whispered.

Kevin's face was drawn and pale. 'I'm not sure. A threat, I think. They were pinned to my noticeboard in the kitchen.'

I picked up a photograph of Paddy and Mikey in the sandpit in Tracy's back garden. Chloe was there too, running towards them, her hands full of ice lollies.

'Jesus!' I muttered. 'Who took them? And, Kevin – oh, my God! If they were on your noticeboard somebody must have come into your house last night while you guys were asleep.'

Kevin didn't answer.

'But why?' I said.

'Ballymoran,' he answered. 'I know a threat when I see one and somebody wants me to know that they can get to me any time they like.'

'What are you going to do?'

'I'll tell the police but there won't be much they

can do about it. Mikey is at Orla's so, hopefully, he'll be OK. I don't want you to worry too much – these guys are just flexing their muscles. I don't think there's any threat to Paddy or Chloe. It's incidental that they're in the pictures. But I thought I should tell you.'

'Thanks,' I said, my heart still fluttering. 'Did you tell Tracy?'

'That's why I'm here – she made me come and tell you. Even though I truly feel there's no danger to Paddy and Chloe.'

'She was right.'

Kevin smiled weakly. 'I need to get going. I have to be in Dublin by four.'

I watched as he scooped the photographs back into the envelope and put it into his pocket. 'Did you show them to Orla?'

He nodded.

'Did she go mad?'

'She wants me to drop the story.'

'Well, I understand how she feels. What are you going to do?'

'If somebody feels the need to threaten me, it means I'm getting close to something they don't want me to know.'

'I suppose. But what about Mikey?'

He sighed. 'I can't even think about it. On the one hand, if I stop what I'm doing, God only knows what'll happen to the children who live in Ballymoran. On the other hand, if I keep going maybe my own child will be in danger.'

'A rock and a hard place,' I said, and laid my hand on his arm. Suddenly he grabbed me and hugged me hard. 'Better be off, so.' He released me. 'I'll see you when I get back.'

I stood in the empty bar and watched as he walked away, heart pounding with a surge of emotions. Suddenly Avril appeared in the doorway and beckoned me. 'Germans!' she half shouted.

I didn't feel capable of dealing with them but I didn't have any choice.

A knot of middle-aged men and women was forming in front of the reception desk. I plunged straight in but all the while I could see those black-and-white pictures. There was something so sinister about using those snapshots of innocence as a threat – I could hardly believe anybody would do something like that.

I'd almost come to the end of my good-natured German tourists when a small dark woman pushed her way through the crowd and tapped the desk with a long nail. 'Excuse me, please,' she said, in heavily accented English. I smiled at her, and then my face froze. I glanced at Avril in the hope that she might save me but she was talking to a tall man with a flamboyant grey handlebar moustache.

'What do you want?' I said.

'My name is Selma Rodriguez. I have booked a room since last night on the Internet,' she said. Her eyes were darting around as if she was looking for somebody's friendly husband to help her.

'Full up. Not a room to be had. Goodbye,' I said.

Avril's man was walking away across the foyer. She turned to Selma and me. 'Maybe I can help,' she said. 'I deal with Internet bookings.'

Selma glared at me and moved to Avril's side of the desk. I kicked Avril's ankle. She looked at me curiously and smiled at Selma.

'I said already that we're full up. It's November – the height of the tourist season in Ireland, isn't that right, Avril?' I said.

Selma stood there with her brazen Spanish face, hand on her skinny little hip.

'I will see ze manager if my room is gone away,' she said to Avril.

'You're in room sixty-nine, Ms Rodriguez,' said Avril.

'Apt,' I said, and kicked Avril again. She ignored me and handed Selma the room key. 'Have a nice visit to Limerick,' she said.

'I will have a wonderful visit with your city,' Selma said. Then she marched off, pulling her red Samsonite suitcase.

'Why were you kicking me?' Avril asked, as Selma disappeared into a lift.

'I don't like her,' I said.

'Do you know her?'

'No,' I lied.

'So, if you don't like the look of someone they don't get a room?'

I began typing again.

'What did Kevin want? Did he say anything about me?' she asked.

'No,' I said, eyes on the computer screen.

'So, what did he want?'

'He wanted me to feed the cat. He's away for a few days.'

Ferdia arrived into the lobby then with a small cluster of camera-bedecked Japanese men. He went to the display case near the front entrance and dispensed maps of the city to them. I stopped typing to admire my future husband.

'Maybe he called to see me,' said Avril.

Christ, would she ever shut up about Kevin? She hadn't a clue.

'Maybe,' I said, as Ferdia approached the desk. Avril sniffed.

'Ruth, I've organised four viewings for this afternoon and we'll see the site Gary told us about too. What do you think?'

I thought it sounded exhausting and that I'd much rather bring Paddy to the park. 'Great,' I said.

'When's Kevin coming back? Did he say?' asked Avril.

I wanted to scream. Instead I smiled. A big, bright, really pissed-off smile. 'Will you look at the time?' I said. 'Doesn't it fly when you're having fun?' I went and got my bag, came out and stood next to Ferdia. 'Ring me about the viewings,' I said.

Avril had disappeared into the back office again. That girl would seriously want to get a grip. Either that or a Randy Rabbit, I thought, as I walked out of the hotel straight into the arms of my estranged husband.

42

Selma was everywhere. In the foyer, in the dining room, in the hotel conservatory, in the coffee shop. But the funny thing was that, after the first day, there was no sign of Emerson. When I'd walked into him the day she came, I'd forced a smile, apologised as I would have to a stranger and walked off up the road.

I didn't care about any of them. All I could think about were those black-and-white photographs of Mikey and the others.

'He showed you,' Tracy said, as soon as she opened the door.

'I'm scared.'

Her face had taken on a determined set. 'It's meant to scare Kevin – I think he's right – but I don't think they intended any harm to Paddy and Chloe.'

'I know that,' I said, as I followed her inside, 'but I'm still scared to think of somebody watching us, and I'm terrified for Mikey.'

Tracy went to her kitchen window. 'The bollocks who took those pictures of my back garden must have climbed Mrs Dillon's horse-chestnut.'

I looked at where she was pointing and we shivered.

'What will Kevin do?' I said, as she made tea.

Tracy shrugged. 'I don't know, but he won't let those bastards intimidate him, that's for sure.'

I paced round the kitchen. 'Who are they, though, Trace? Who's threatening him? Who wants him to back off?'

'I don't know – if we knew that we'd know everything, wouldn't we? But he must be close to something.'

'That's what he says.'

'Anyway, I don't think there's anything to worry about,' she said.

'I hope you're right.'

'I'm always right.'

It appeared that she *was* right about the photographs. Kevin came back from Dublin and there were no new developments, and we all began to forget that we were being watched.

I developed a new problem, which started to take up my attention. Emerson. Not that he hadn't been a problem before, it was just that if I felt anybody was following me and watching me it was him.

And although I never saw him near Drury's again, he increased his surprise visits to me. I now had at least two a day and it was going to get worse: he was looking for a house in the area.

He told me this one Sunday morning when he came to collect Paddy. I hated to admit it but he looked great. When he caught me staring at him his eyes went all soft and smouldery – I knew that look.

'He has the runs so don't stray too far from a toilet,' I said, and scrubbed at Paddy's cornflake-encrusted mouth with a baby wipe.

Emerson laughed. He was standing in the middle of the kitchen. I had made a point from the start of never offering him a seat, smiles, coffee or small-talk. 'I've put in an offer on an apartment near here,' he said.

'Oh, that'll be lovely for you and Selma,' I said, 'although she does seem rather fond of the hotel.' I smiled sweetly.

'It's in Holland Place, right on O'Connell Avenue,' he said.

'Nice,' I said. 'Now, are we all set, Paddy?'

He beamed up at me. 'Where are we going, Dad? Can we go to McDonald's again?'

'Wherever you want, Pad.'

He ran off to get his coat.

'If I'm living nearby, it'll be great for Paddy and I can help out with the babysitting,' he went on.

'Don't do me any favours,' I said, my voice as tight as a drum.

'He's my son too, Ruth, and I'm only trying to help.'

'You didn't help in Gibraltar.' It was out before I could stop it.

'Did you ever make a mistake, Ruth?'

'Oh, for God's sake! That's why she's ensconced in Drury's, is it? A pretty long mistake.' I tried to control my voice and my temper. I couldn't believe the cheek of the man.

Emerson ran a hand over his head. His hair was growing back and it looked like blonde suede. 'I didn't ask her to come. In fact, I told her—'

'Enough. You're way off the ball now. I don't want to hear about your lovers and I'm sure you don't want to hear about mine, but maybe it's time you knew a few relevant facts. Here goes. Number one, I'm engaged to Ferdia Ryan. Number two, we're currently looking for a house, so I wouldn't go running off buying places around here to be near Paddy. Actually, we've seen a site we're interested in. We'll be moving soon.'

I stopped my barrage and gazed at Emerson's crestfallen face. And the horrible part was that I was delighted. I remembered, guiltily, all the promises I'd made to God about not being mean any more if Paddy and Chloe didn't die in the runaway car. But in that moment I felt that even God was on my side.

'Engaged? To be married?'

'Yep.'

'But you're . . . we're still married and . . .'

I didn't answer him, just folded my arms and smiled. I couldn't help it – I was really enjoying this. It'd never compensate for the hurt of Gibraltar but it helped.

'I'm sorry.'

'Sorry that I'm engaged? Don't be, Emerson. I've never been happier.' He flinched.

'I'm sorry about everything, Ruth. I'll get Paddy,' he said, and walked out of the kitchen.

*

After Emerson had brought Paddy home, I called in to see Tracy. Ferdia was coming over later with a bottle of wine and a movie. We had planned a quiet romantic night in and the signs were favourable for some good sex. Hell, I didn't expect good sex: average would be grand.

It was a beautiful mild November day, with blue skies and a watery sun. Tracy opened the door and bent to kiss Paddy. 'Paddy Burke, we'll have to buy you a new hat. Look at the state of that! Your buddies are in the garden, shovelling leaves. Do you want to help them?' she said, and led him to the back door.

'You're minding Mikey?' I said.

'Kevin had to go to Ballymoran. He said he won't be long. So tell me all the sca – I can't believe that Selma one's still here.'

I filled her in on all the latest happenings, including Emerson and his house-hunting.

'Speaking of house-hunting, how's yours going?'

'It's not,' I said, lighting a fag. 'If I have to go and view another bloody house I'll die. I've a personal relationship with all the auctioneers now. And Ferdia has me looking at fields as well.'

'Fields?'

'House sites. But they're just fields to me.'

'There must have been one house you liked,' Tracy said, as she put out her cigarette. 'What about that gorgeous one in Merrion Avenue?'

'Too dark.'

'And the one I love on O'Connell Avenue, the three-storey one with the cool balcony?'

'Too big. I swear, Tracy, the living room was the size of Thomond Park. You'd have to ring someone to talk to them if you were sitting at opposite ends.'

Tracy laughed. 'What about the sites?'

'Gary found a site for us that's supposed to be a gem. It's just a field with cows in it out towards Ballysheedy.'

'Do you get to keep the cows?'

'I hope not. Anyway, Ferdia loves it and wants to build a house now.'

'That could be the answer. You can draw up your own plans and get the exact house you want.'

'It's a lot of hassle and I don't like new houses.'

Tracy cocked her head to one side.

'What's the look for?' I said.

'You tell me,' she replied.

A sudden crash from the garden brought us to our feet and out of the back door. We ran down to the children and Derek's ever-growing water feature. Mikey and Paddy were in the middle of the pond, holding a brick each. The water feature had been levelled. The windmill was lying on its side in the murky shallow water. The turrets that had surrounded it were bashed to pieces and the peeing cherub, which Derek had added the weekend before, had no head and no penis.

'Oh, my God, Tracy, I'm so sorry,' I said, as I shooed the boys out of the water. 'Derek will have a fit!'

'They were playing bombs, Mummy. You had to drop the brick on the city but it broke,' said Lauren, earnest and scared.

'It's OK. The water feature was getting a bit over-crowded anyway,' said Tracy. We caught each other's eye and began to laugh, the children joining in. We brought them in and Tracy offered to give Paddy a change of clothes, but it was time for us to go anyway.

Just as I was leaving I remembered the Mayor's ball.

'Tracy, I can't remember if I asked you on the phone but Gary has a table at the Mayor's ball next Friday and he wants us all to go. He's persuaded the Mayor to give the proceeds to PAP. Are you on?' I asked.

'Brilliant! What the hell will I wear?'

Dusk was falling as Paddy and I walked next door to my house. He squelched along in his wet shoes, enjoying the sensation. I was just going in my gate when I noticed a strange car parked across the road. The driver – a woman in a blood-red headscarf and dark sunglasses – turned away. There was something in the set of her that was familiar. I stood there for a minute with Paddy, while the car revved, then pulled off really fast. Who the hell was it? Selma? The bastard who took the pictures of Mikey? Maybe I was just paranoid, but I decided to tell Kevin anyway. Better safe than sorry.

43

I awoke on the morning of the Mayor's ball, having had the most pornographic dream of my life. It involved Jude Law in a variety of sexual positions and I was mortified by its explicit content and intensity. I was glad that nobody could know what you dreamed but a tiny irrational part of me worried that maybe your psychic mother could. I reddened at the thought.

When I arrived at work Avril seemed a little happier so I risked asking her how things were going. Her eyes filled. I babbled on about the ball and what I was wearing while she dripped tears on to her keyboard. I didn't know how her computer was surviving all the drenchings. Ferdia came over just before eleven and asked me to meet him in the conservatory for coffee.

When I arrived he'd ordered and I sat next to him on a squishy sofa. He bent down to pick something up from the floor. 'I've got a little surprise for you,' he said, as he opened a large tube of rolled-up paper. He smoothed it out on the coffee-table. 'What do you think? Can't you just imagine this house on that site in Ballysheedy? Isn't it gorgeous?'

'Hmm,' I said, and sipped my coffee.

'Don't you like it? We can change it. I was stupid to go ahead and not consult you, but I felt I'd an idea at this stage of what you liked and I wanted it to be a surprise.' His shoulders sagged.

'It's lovely, Ferdia.'

He beamed at me. 'Really?'

I nodded. 'Really.'

'Oh, Ruth,' he said, and grabbed my hand. I hoped he wouldn't notice that I'd left the engagement ring at home again. He pointed at the plans. 'Look at this. The stairs are in the middle of the hallway and branch out two ways at the top,' he said. I could picture Paddy and Mikey swinging out of a staircase like that but I didn't say anything. 'Gary says we need to put in an offer immediately if we want the site.'

'Oh,' I said.

'So, what will we do?'

'It might be a bargain but it's still a hell of a lot of money.'

'There's a queue of people interested in it and only for Gary we wouldn't be in the loop at all.'

'I suppose we should put in an offer so.'

Ferdia's face broke into a huge grin. 'That's brilliant, Ruth.'

As soon as I got back to my desk Selma Rodriguez put in her first appearance of the day. As she approached I smiled at her. 'Can I help you?' I said sweetly.

She flashed her dark eyes at me and stopped in

front of Avril. At that moment a group of Canadian tourists arrived and I began to book them in. When I'd finished I saw that Avril and Selma were sitting on a sofa in the foyer, both clutching bunches of tissues. Selma was crying the loudest and Avril patted her shoulder now and again. I smiled and waved to them. Selma whispered to Avril and I wondered if she'd told her the source of her misery. That'd be a nice little shock to Avril.

I was delighted when India unexpectedly dropped in. 'Can we go for coffee when you finish?' she asked, 'I've got some great news.'

'Tell me now, Ind. I need cheering up,' I said, and glanced at the couch.

India turned round and Selma recognised her. Fresh tears flowed. India turned back and checked her watch. 'You finish in ten minutes, Ruth. I'll wait for you in the Coffee Dock, that little place around the corner. I don't want to draw Selma on me – I'm not able for her,' she said and left.

I finished my paperwork and Avril came back. Selma had disappeared.

'Poor girl,' she said, as she checked her makeup in her compact mirror. It was holding up pretty well, considering all the crying.

I said nothing, just worked away on my computer.

'There's always somebody worse off than you, isn't there?' said Avril.

I kept working. I knew now that Selma hadn't told Avril that Emerson was the source of her tears.

'I feel so sorry for her. She met this guy in Spain

and they fell in love and then out of the blue he said it was over and that he was coming back to Limerick. Imagine that,' said Avril, her eyes shiny with concern. Selma's woes seemed to have given her a lift. 'She's decided to stay, and I think she's right. You have to fight for love, that's what I told her. You have to fight your corner.'

'She's moving here? To Limerick?' Avril finally had my undivided attention.

She nodded.

'She's mad,' I said, as I closed down my computer and picked up my handbag to leave.

'No, she's not. I'd do the same if I was pregnant with his baby. Wouldn't you?'

Avril's words resounded in my ears as I walked to the local pub to meet India. Selma pregnant? I couldn't believe it. And if she was, Emerson was an even bigger ratfink than I'd thought. And what about Paddy? If Selma was pregnant, that baby would be Paddy's brother or sister.

I decided not to say anything to India. I stood outside the pub and composed myself. Maybe it wasn't true. Maybe Selma was lying to get Emerson back. I went inside. India was sitting in a window seat. I ordered a glass of wine at the bar, then joined her.

'Tell me your news,' I said.

'Yours first. Any developments since I last spoke to you? No surprise weddings?'

This was a reference to my engagement, which she'd thought was a huge joke when I told her. She said it was classic rebound reaction and that all I needed was a good holiday. I wasn't mad at her. I'd already had that fight with Kathleen and Tracy so by the time I got to India I'd known how the conversation would pan out. 'Nothing like that. But remember the site I asked you to enquire about on Monday?'

'Ballysheedy. Planning permission pending,' she said.

'We're putting in an offer.'

'Good for you, but I think you're mad. Slow down, Ruth. What's the rush?'

'I'm not getting married for ages, India.'

'A joint mortgage is worse than any marriage.'

I ignored her. 'Your news, India, or else I'll scream my head off and everyone will think you're with a deranged person.'

India smiled. 'They'll know, you mean. OK. You remember what I was saying to you the other day when I bolted?'

I recalled the conversation quite clearly.

'I've handed in my notice.'

I almost dropped my coffee cup. This was India, career woman *extraordinaire*: she'd never give up her job just like that. '*What?*' I said.

She nodded, her dark bob swinging. 'I handed in my notice.'

'My God.'

India's eyes shone with excitement. 'And we're going to Australia for Christmas.'

'Over to Ellen? You lucky things.'

'Wait. It gets better. Then we're going to travel

round the world, the three of us. Tim's taken six months' leave so it's now or never.'

'That's brilliant news, India. You look happier already.'

'It was the right decision. I wasn't enjoying the work any more. I wanted to be with my baby. And, luckily, we can afford to do this.'

'I envy you. What'll you do when you come back?'

India shrugged. 'I don't know. But suddenly my career isn't the most important thing in the world.'

I put Selma's alleged pregnancy out of my mind as I got ready for the Mayor's ball. It was no concern of mine and if Emerson chose to go around impregnating Spanish set designers then that was his business.

I dressed carefully in a new emerald green silk cocktail dress and strappy black stilettos. Although I must have possessed ten pairs already I'd used the excuse of the Mayor's ball to buy yet another. As I admired them I remembered how Emerson used to tease me about my shoe-buying. I came downstairs, walked into the kitchen and there he was.

'I was just passing and I just . . . You look unbelievable,' he said, blatantly assessing me. 'Incredible.'

'Thanks,' I said.

The doorbell rang. I hoped it wasn't more visitors. Kathleen, my babysitter, answered it. I could hear Tracy's voice in the hallway. Emerson touched my arm. My whole body tensed and my skin felt as if it had been burned. A picture of Selma's naked body on white sheets flashed before my eyes and I glared at him.

'I'm sorry,' he whispered. 'You'll never know how much.' Then he scooped Paddy up, kissed his belly and carried him into the sitting room.

Kathleen came in. 'They're waiting in a taxi – go on, off you go,' she said, and bundled me out of the door. I climbed into the taxi and it was only when we pulled off that I realised I was next to Kevin Regan.

44

'Why didn't you tell me he was coming with us?' I asked Tracy. I'd dragged her into the loo as soon as we reached the hotel.

'He's hardly with us, Ruth. He's with the Orla one and his newspaper has a table. What's the big deal?' She applied another coat of lipstick.

'You could have warned me.'

Tracy looked magnificent in a russet dress that showed off her Oriental features. 'Why? It's just Kevin, our pal. Why should I warn you?'

I fiddled with the clasp on my bag.

'Come on, let's get back. I don't want to miss anything,' she said.

Ferdia and Gary were deep in conversation when we arrived into the beautifully decorated dining room. A swing band played on the stage and a huge Christmas tree with hundreds of tiny lights twinkled in a corner. Tracy's eyes shone as she sat next to Derek at our table.

'What are they on about? The match tomorrow?' she asked Derek, nodding towards Ferdia and Gary as she sipped champagne from a long slim flute.

Derek shook his head. 'Nope. Insurance policies and pensions.'

'Fuck's sake.'

I scanned the room, pretending I wasn't looking for anyone in particular. And accidentally made eye-contact with Kevin. After a few minutes I chanced another glance in his direction. Orla was sitting next to him, her arm draped carelessly over his shoulders. She wore a simple long black dress that accentuated her lustrous blonde hair.

After dessert and speeches, the tables were cleared and the music began. Gary took my hand for the first dance of the evening and for a few minutes we were the only couple on the floor. He was a graceful dancer and made me look much better than I was. Flashbulbs popped as we whirled around. When we finished I noticed that Kevin and Orla had joined us at the table. I threw a murderous look at Tracy, which she ignored. She threw me a sly smile as she dragged Derek on to the dance floor.

As I stood watching the band, I became aware that Kevin was beside me. 'How's it going?' he said. Like all the men at the function, he wore the customary tuxedo, but instead of champagne he clutched a pint of Guinness. 'I thought it co-ordinated better with my suit. What do you think?' he said.

'You look fine, and that's the best excuse I've ever heard for having a pint,' I said.

He smiled, and a shiver ran through me. 'You'll be famous, tomorrow,' he said, pulling at his stiff white shirt collar. 'Fuck it, how do people wear shirts all day?'

'Why?' I asked.

'Front-page photo, Ruth. Gary and you dancing – handsome politician dad and beautiful daughter. Trust good old Gary not to miss a photo op.'

'He didn't ask the photographers to take the picture, Kevin,' I said, an edge to my voice. 'And speaking of photographs, no more horrible snaps of children, I hope?'

'No. Everything's quiet at the moment.'

'That's good,' I said, and pictured the Parisian bed as clearly as if it were right in front of me.

'So, tell me, how's the engagement going?' He narrowed his eyes.

'Fine. Great. How are you?'

'Grand, but wondering when the big day is. Should I hold on to the tux?' His tone was flat and mean.

'Why not? We can have a double wedding – you and Orla for the second time, me and Ferdia.'

'That, my dear, will never happen.'

I decided to change the subject. 'How's work?'

'Same old same old. You must be busy, though – I haven't seen much of you lately.'

I ignored the gibe. 'It's a busy time of year.'

'Yeah, what with engagements, divorces, house plans . . . You name it, Ruth Burke is doing it.' He smiled, as if this was meant to be a joke.

I surveyed the room. I could smell his aftershave, which brought back Paris in a wave of sexy images.

But I'd no intention of revisiting any of that. 'There's Tracy,' I said, too loudly.

He finished his pint as Tracy and Derek joined us. We sat down at our table. Ferdia was dancing with Orla and Gary had gathered an entourage.

Tracy poured herself a huge glass of champagne. 'Is there any alcohol in this stuff? I think it's just gassy lemonade.'

The music stopped so Ferdia and Orla joined us. Gary was still surrounded. God, he was like a superstar. I'd never known politicians could be so popular. Ferdia was sitting on one side of me, while Orla had squeezed between Kevin and me on the other.

'I know I've told you a hundred times but you look great tonight,' said Ferdia. 'I can't wait to take you home.'

I was too frustrated for bad sex tonight. I was liable to stab him if he did his usual three-minute how-was-that-for-you routine. I wished now that he'd never read the Book.

'By the way, great news. Our offer was accepted.'

I had decided in the last ten seconds that I hated the site and I hated the house.

'We could be signing contracts as early as next week. It'd be great if it was all done and dusted before Christmas.'

I desperately wanted one of Tracy's fags. Instead I slugged back my drink.

'We'll sort out a joint mortgage soon. I've a couple of builders lined up already,' he said. His face was like Paddy's when he'd done something good.

'Great,' I said. A new band was coming on to the stage.

'I figure we could be putting down foundations in the New Year, weather permitting. The planning permission will be granted in the first week of January so—'

'What if it's refused?' I watched the musicians tuning their instruments.

'That's where Gary comes in. He checked it all out this morning. No problem. I can hardly believe it because the site next door was refused.'

'Is he sure?'

'A hundred and fifty per cent. Isn't he terrific?'

I rooted in my tiny bag for my mobile. There were no messages so all was well at home. The last band member walked on carrying a saxophone. He had his back to his audience but I could see that he was tall and athletic. Christ, what was wrong with me? I was sitting here talking with my fiancé about our dream home and checking out the talent on-stage. Sad.

But I persisted with the ogling while Ferdia talked about underfloor heating systems and reclaimed red bricks.

'What are you staring at?' Tracy interjected, following my gaze to the stage. 'Bet I know which one. It's the fit one, isn't it? Cropped dark hair, sallow skin, tight arse?' she said, nudging me. Mr Gorgeous launched into a sax solo. He'd taken off his jacket and the muscles on his neck stood out.

I looked round and caught Kevin staring at me.

Orla glanced at me, then at Kevin, and began to kiss him. Tracy and I watched them instead of the stage. Eventually Kevin pulled away and I heard him ask her to stop.

Tracy rolled her eyes. 'See that one? She's an awful slapper, her. I heard that about doctors and nurses. Mad for it, the whole lot of them.'

Kevin got up and walked away, and Orla drank a full glass of champagne, gave us a disdainful look, then followed him to the bar where she began swinging out of him again.

'Who needs a wife when you can have an ex-wife like that?' I said to Tracy, as we resumed admiring the sax player.

'Kevin doesn't want her,' Tracy said.

'What do you mean?'

'Nothing. Forget it. Here, be brazen and we'll go out for a fag before Dryballs comes back.'

'Dryballs?' I said, taking the offered cigarette.

'I'm sorry. I didn't mean to call Ferdia names. I'm a bit pissed – the lemonade's finally kicking in.'

By the time we were all in a taxi, heading home, Tracy was on her ear. But she was funny and had us all laughing, including the driver. I'd talked Ferdia out of staying over at my place with the classic headache excuse. We'd left Kevin and Orla outside the hotel, waiting for another taxi.

At my garden gate Tracy told me she loved me nine times until Derek managed to cajole her in home. I was about to walk up the path when something caught

my eye. A car was parked directly across the road from
Kevin's house. I could make out the silhouette of the
driver and knew immediately that it was my stalker
friend. Fuck this for a lark, I thought, as I crept up
behind it. A curious bravado, composed of champagne
and sexual frustration, filled me as I prowled round
to the driver's door. I flung it open. 'Well, Selma,
Emerson doesn't live here,' I said. 'If you're going to
go stalking people the least you could do is find out
where they live.'

She took off her glasses and looked at me. 'Hi,
Ruth.'

'Avril!'

She removed her scarf.

'Jesus, Avril!'

She started to cry. I walked round to the passenger
side and climbed in.

'Avril, you really need to get a grip. This is just
the pits.'

Her sobs grew louder.

'Avril, there are other guys. I know you don't want
to hear this but it's true.'

'I just wanted a look at her. Just one look,' she
said, through her tears.

'At who?' I asked.

She rooted in her bag for a tissue, blew her nose
and patted her eyes dry. 'I rang him again on
Wednesday. I just wanted to hear his voice and I
cried and then he said it . . .' She stopped and wiped
her nose.

'What did he say?' I asked.

'That there's someone else.'

Yes, there was – his bloody ex-wife, that's who – but would Avril be able to take that information?

'Rubbish! Now, go home to bed and get a good night's sleep. It'll be grand in the morning.'

Avril looked at me as if I was an alien and then the car flooded with light as another vehicle came round the corner. 'Duck,' I said, and pulled her down. I knew it was Kevin.

The car pulled up and I could hear a giggly girl's voice as somebody paid the driver. Then it pulled off and I heard Kevin. 'Come on, Orla, we're nearly there.'

'Just one kiss.'

There was silence and I peeped out of the window. Avril was doing the same behind me. They were standing half-way up Kevin's footpath, bathed in silver moonlight. Orla had her arms round him and was trying to kiss him. He pushed her away gently. 'Bed, love. Sleep it off and you'll be grand tomorrow,' he said, extricating himself.

She caught him by the waist and pulled him towards her. 'Did I ever tell you that you've got a great ass?' she said, swinging her blonde head and kissing the back of his neck.

I could hear Kevin laughing softly. 'Many times. Now, let's get you to bed.'

'That's exactly what I had in mind too,' said Orla, as Kevin opened the front door and they disappeared.

'Fuck's sake,' I said.

'His ex-wife.' Avril burst into tears.

I put an arm round her, although I wasn't the best person in the world to console her. I was too busy trying to deal with the rage and jealousy that had erupted inside me.

45

I left Avril and dashed home, barely saying goodbye to her. I climbed into bed and cried into my pillow as all the faces of the people in my life flashed in my head like unwanted Internet pop-ups.

I slept badly and woke at five. The house was still and silent, and the ticking of the clock seemed deafeningly loud. I stared at the ceiling, trying to figure out what had woken me. It was something to do with Ferdia, I knew that.

I spent the weekend cleaning the house – the best scrubbing it had ever had – which helped me, in some strange way, to make sense of my life. Who needed therapists when you had Brillo pads and bleach?

I spent Monday morning engulfed in work. Gary rang at midday to cancel a dinner date. The annual convention was next week so he was really busy. On my coffee break I rang India. She was going to Australia on Saturday and I wanted to see her before she left. We made tentative plans to meet on Friday for lunch.

Then, on a whim, I brought up Selma's account

on my screen and was surprised to see that she'd checked out that morning. Good riddance, I thought, as Ferdia sidled up to Reception, grinning. 'Guess what, Ruth? We're signing at two!'

'So fast?'

'Brilliant, isn't it? Look, we can drop by the solicitor when you finish work, then go into the bank. I've the joint mortgage set up so we just need to sign on the dotted line.'

'Oh, right.'

'Ruth, you still want to do this?'

'Sure.'

'OK. See you in a little while,' he said, and went off, whistling to himself.

I sat and stared at my screen. India's voice echoed in my head: 'A joint mortgage is worse than marriage.' I rang Kathleen.

'Hi, Kathleen, did I wake you?'

'Oh, Ruth, is that you? No, I'm lying down, that's all.'

'Are you feeling OK?'

'A little tired, but fine otherwise.'

'Do you want me to call later?'

'I don't want to put you out.'

'I'll come over, Kathleen. It's no trouble. Paddy'll be delighted to see you.'

'All right, if you're sure.'

'See you then,' I said, and hung up.

Ferdia drove us to the solicitor's just before two o'clock. He found a parking space outside the office and we sat in the minimalist waiting room with the other clients. I picked up an old copy of *Hello!* from the table in front of me and Ferdia chose *National Geographic*. I tried to concentrate on the glossy photos of famous people but I felt like a small child sitting in the dentist's waiting room. The receptionist finally called our names and we followed her directions to our solicitor's office. Her name was Anne Franklin and I watched her shuffle papers efficiently. 'Here we are,' she said, putting a bundle of forms in front of us. 'This will only take a minute.'

'That's exactly what the dentist used to say,' I said, without realising I'd spoken aloud. Ferdia patted my arm, as if I really was a small child. And then it came back to me. The thing that had woken me a few nights before that I couldn't remember. It burst open in my head like a ripe watermelon, and suddenly it all became crystal clear. I watched Ferdia as he signed the papers, then turned to hand me the pen. I took it, then shook my head.

'No,' I said, in a low voice.

Anne Franklin and Ferdia gawped at me.

I stood up and dropped the pen on top of the papers. I pushed back the chair. 'I can't do this – I can't do it. I just can't,' I said. I picked up my bag and ran out of the office.

I stumbled out into the street and ran blindly down the road, vaguely aware of people jumping aside as I hurtled along. Finally I crashed into a group of surprised carol singers outside Brown Thomas and leaned against the plate-glass window to catch my breath. They launched into a vigorous rendition of 'Jingle Bells' and I walked down towards the river and sat on a low wall, watching the grey water as it rushed by.

The thing that I'd forgotten was so simple it was almost a joke. I was only with Ferdia because I was afraid. I didn't need him. Not Ferdia, not Kevin, not Emerson. I was a grown-up woman, the mother of a small boy, and I was well able to negotiate the world alone.

It seemed now as if a weight had lifted from my shoulders, and even though I felt bad about Ferdia, I was the happiest I'd been since Gibraltar. I opened my handbag, took out my phone and punched in a number.

'Ferdia? We need to talk.'

Ferdia picked me up at seven. Tracy agreed to babysit. We drove to Killaloe and he parked by the lake. It was dark and cold and clear, which was good because that suited how I felt. 'Ferdia,' I began.

He looked at the steering-wheel.

'I'm sorry,' I said.

He glanced at me and I recognised a glimmer of hope in his eyes. 'We can reschedule, Ruth. Or, better still, we can slow things down.'

I shook my head. 'I'm sorry about today, about the way it all happened, but we're—'

'It's over, isn't it?' he whispered.

I nodded.

The moonlight threw a glow like a spotlight round him. 'I've known since Paris.'

'How?' I asked.

He put his hand in to his pocket and pulled out a crumpled piece of paper.

'I saw it lying in a ball on the floor in the Ritz and I picked it up . . .'

He held it out and I recognised the pros and cons list. 'I'm sorry, Ferdia.'

'I shouldn't have read it but I did. And all the time I hoped you'd love me like I love you.'

'Oh, Ferdia . . .'

'It's OK, Ruth, honestly it is. I wanted you at any cost so I hurried our plans and today it all came undone.'

I put an arm round him and hugged him. 'You're a lovely person,' I said, into his shoulder.

He pulled away. 'It's him, Ruth, isn't it? It's Kevin.'

'No.'

Ferdia laughed softly. 'Do you know the three pros you'd written for him? Do you remember them?'

I shook my head.

'"Great sex, funny, best friend"? That's exactly what I feel for you.'

'There's no one else, Ferdia. I need to be on my own for a while and that's what I realised today in that office.'

He started the engine. 'I'd like to go now, Ruth.' He didn't look at me.

We drove home in silence. I felt bad for him but I also felt like someone who'd just been released from prison. I was free now – not from Ferdia but from fear. I wanted to go it alone, just Paddy and I.

The phone rang, making me jump, as I got ready for bed.

'Hello?'

'Ruth Burke?'

'Yes?'

'This is the Regional Maternity Hospital. We have a Kathleen Brennan here who has just been admitted. You're named in her file as next-of-kin.'

'Jesus Christ.'

46

Derek came to sit with Paddy and I drove to the hospital in record time. I parked the car illegally, dashed in and announced myself at Reception. They sent me upstairs where I accosted a young man in a white coat. 'I'm Dr Carr,' he said, as we shook hands. 'Are you related to Ms Brennan?'

'I'm her daughter. How is she?' I asked.

'Kathleen is fine. Her blood pressure was a little high but we've managed to stabilise it and the baby seems fine too. Would you like to see her?'

I followed him down the corridor and into a private ward. Kathleen was propped up on a pile of pillows. Her colour was poor and I was surprised by how young and scared she seemed.

'Kathleen, are you OK?' I sat on the chair next to her.

She nodded. 'I'm fine. I'm sorry I dragged you all the way over here.'

'I'm sorry I didn't call earlier, like I said I would. What happened?'

'I felt really unwell around six o'clock so I rang the doctor and he sent me in.'

'I should have checked on you.'

'Not at all. I can manage fine on my own. And the baby's OK.'

'Are they keeping you in for long?'

'They want to stabilise my blood pressure and they're telling me I'm anaemic.' Kathleen's eyes drooped and I knew she needed to sleep.

'Do you want me to ring anyone else?' I asked, wondering if the mystery father might make an appearance now.

She opened her eyes. 'Just Aila Harris. She can tell the others in the Psychic Circle. Her number is in the book.'

Next morning I rang the hospital as soon as I got up to check on Kathleen. A nurse with a thick Tipperary accent assured me that she was fine. Before I left for work Kevin called. 'Hi, Ruth.'

'Kevin.' I was surprised to hear his voice.

'Look, I'm sorry to disturb you but I wonder if you could do me a favour?'

'Of course.'

'I've had a bit of a break in the Ballymoran story.'

'What happened?'

'I rang the engineering firm who did the original environmental study and fluked out. The guy who answered the phone remembered seeing the report – do you know what he asked me?'

'No, of course I don't!'

'He asked me if they ever found the source of the pollution.'

'Holy shit! I thought the report said there was no evidence of pollution.'

'The report presented to the court said that.'

'Deep Throat is right so.'

'Seems like it. I'm meeting that guy – his name is Fred Foley – and I'm afraid I won't be finished in time to pick up Mikey. I asked Tracy but—'

'Absolutely no problem,' I interrupted – I knew an olive branch when I saw one. 'Good luck with your meeting.'

'Thanks a million – talk to you later.'

Mikey went to a different school from Paddy and Chloe so I rang Tracy and asked her if she'd pick up Paddy with Chloe. She told me she would but her voice was odd. I suspected she'd had a hand in the olive branch but I didn't ask. I was happy not to be fighting with Kevin.

I headed off to work where my day was uneventful. On the way home I drove into town to Mikey's Montessori school. I pulled up outside ten minutes early, closed my eyes and settled down for a short relax. Ferdia's forlorn face popped into my head but, sorry as I was for having hurt him, I knew that I wouldn't be doing him any favours by marrying him. I didn't love him and he deserved better.

I must have dozed off then because the next thing I knew there was loud kid-whooping going on outside my car. Twenty or so children were pouring into the small car-park in front of Mikey's school. I stepped out of the car and scanned the throng for Mikey but I couldn't see him anywhere.

A kind-faced middle-aged woman was standing at the school doorway, chatting to a man in a green parka, who was holding a struggling toddler.

'Hello,' I said. 'I'm Ruth Burke. I'm here to collect Mikey Regan. Is he inside?'

The woman smiled. 'No, dear. Mikey's aunt just collected him. See. There they are.'

I turned in the direction she had indicated. Mikey and a tall woman wearing a red jacket and an ankle-length black skirt were walking along the footpath across the road. I hurried after them, a slide show of black-and-white photographs running inside my head.

'Mikey!' I shouted, but he didn't hear me. '*Mikey!*' I broke into a run. This time he stopped walking and turned, saw me and waved. I crossed the road. The woman said something to him and pulled at his arm. I could see he wasn't too happy. 'Mikey!' I shouted again. '*Mikey! Come here!*'

He struggled as the woman bent down and whispered something, all the time pulling him towards a green car.

'Mikey!' I called.

He looked up at the woman, then kicked her hard in the leg. She shouted in pain, let him go and he was off, running towards me. The woman stood there for a second, watching him, then sat into the green car, which drove away immediately. I could see a man at the wheel and that it was a Toyota Corolla, but I didn't get the registration number because I was running towards Mikey, who was looking a bit the worse for wear.

'Is Paddy here?' he said, as he reached me.

'No, love.' I hugged him hard.

He hugged me back. 'Stupid làdy,' he said, and his bottom lip was trembling. 'She hurt me.' He showed me his wrist: a red weal stood out against the white skin.

We walked in silence towards my car. Mikey's hand stole into mine. 'She said we could rent a PlayStation game. She said she was taking me home – that Daddy said she was to get me.'

'I know she did.'

We continued our walk in silence until we reached my car.

'I kicked her,' he said, as I opened the back door to let him get in.

'I know,' I said. 'That's OK.'

Mikey gave me an astonished look.

'She hurt you. When people hurt you it's OK to hurt them back.'

'Even if they hurt your feelings when they take your football in the middle of a game?'

I grinned at him. This was the boy I knew. 'Probably not then, Mikey Magoo, but it was fine that you kicked that lady.'

I smiled reassuringly at Mikey as I buckled his seatbelt. I sat into the front seat and started the engine, my head spinning with what-ifs. I wanted to go and thump the teacher, but she hadn't known what was happening. She'd just believed that the woman in the red jacket was Mikey's aunt.

By the time I got there Kevin was in Tracy's. We

dispatched the kids to the garden with a picnic, and then I told them what had happened. Kevin's face drained of colour. By the time I'd finished Tracy's hands were clamped over her mouth and Kevin's eyes were almost black with anger.

'Call the police,' Tracy said, as the shock subsided. Kevin took out his phone, dialled a number and waited. Eventually he was put through to the person he wanted and began to tell them the story.

In the garden Chloe was laughing like a hyena and when I looked outside I saw that Mikey had put a plastic bucket on his head to the great amusement of his friends. Jesus – who were those people and what had they wanted with Mikey?

'Will you make a statement?' Kevin said, as he finished speaking.

'Of course – but I didn't get the registration number.' I could see that he was struggling with his emotions.

'You got Mikey and that's all that matters. Thanks, Ruth.'

'What are you going to do?' Tracy said.

'Send Mikey to stay with his mother for a while,' Kevin told her.

'She won't like it,' Tracy said.

'I don't care. I can't give up on Ballymoran – I know this is connected and I know the bloody Ring brothers are involved. I just have to get proof.'

'Easier said than done,' Tracy said.

'At least if Mikey's away it'll be one less thing for me to worry about.'

'Wouldn't you think that Deep Throat fella would just ring you up and tell you where to find the bloody proof?' Tracy said.

'I'm losing patience with him,' he said.

'He's all you have, though, isn't he?' I said.

'Unfortunately. Maybe your father would like to divulge some of the information I know that he has – the bastard,' Kevin said.

I didn't answer. He was upset, understandably so. He stalked out of the kitchen into the garden and I watched him hug and kiss a protesting Mikey. Then he came back in. 'Sorry,' he said. 'I didn't mean to sound cross with you.'

'I know. Don't worry about it. Maybe the Guards will be able to find out something.'

'I doubt it. But it's worth a shot, I suppose.'

'How did your meeting go?' I said.

'Your man never showed and when I rang their head office they said he was gone to Saudi on an emergency job.'

'That's weird,' Tracy said.

Kevin nodded. 'Who are you telling? Anyway, Tracy, could I leave Mikey here for half an hour? I need to go see Orla and break this news to her in person.'

'No problem. I'll guard him like he was the King of England.'

'Thanks, Trace,' he said. 'And thanks again, Ruth, I really owe you.'

We waved him goodbye and then we talked about all sorts of things in a bid to forget what had happened because it was too scary.

A Guard called to my house later that evening and took my statement, but Kevin had been right: there wasn't much they could do. Kevin told Orla what had happened and when she calmed down she took Mikey up the country to stay with some friends. But a pall hung over us and none of us spoke about what might have happened. The only thing I can say about the episode is that at least it took my mind off Ferdia.

By Friday everybody in work knew about our break-up. It was difficult but survivable, and I wasn't surprised to hear he'd put in for a transfer. We didn't talk to each other.

I met India in a trendy new bistro called Danny's and we splashed out on a bottle of champagne to celebrate her imminent departure. We ordered pasta and salad and caught up with each other's lives as we waited for our food to arrive.

'I'm glad,' India said. She was referring to the Ferdia news.

'That seems to be the general consensus. Tracy did a celebratory dance when she heard,' I said.

'How's Kathleen?'

'Still in hospital. I've a feeling they'll keep her in now until the baby's born.'

Our meals arrived and we began to eat. 'When is she due?'

'Christmas Day,' I said. 'The second coming.'

India laughed. 'You're terrible, Ruth.'

'Have you seen anything of Selma?' I asked, suddenly remembering her pregnancy.

'Don't ask.'

'OK, I won't,' I said, and speared a piece of cannelloni.

'You're not going to believe the latest developments.'

'I'd believe anything now.'

'She called Emerson and declared she was pregnant. Can you believe that?'

I took a long sip of champagne, feigning disinterest.

'Emerson told her she couldn't be, there was no way, and she went crazy.'

'How?'

'Roared the place down, swore in Spanish and a few other languages.' India waved a hand. 'She's gone home to Spain for Christmas, promising she'll be back. Poor Emerson.'

I dropped my fork and glared at her. 'Pity about him.'

'True. Anyway, Ruthie, I'm going to miss you so much. You will email, won't you?'

'Of course. I'll phone too. Are you excited?'

'I can't wait. I'll miss everyone here but I'm so looking forward to it. I've been working since I left college and this is such a change for me.'

We chatted through the rest of our lunch, savouring each other's company and I was sad that it would be a long time before we'd have lunch together again. But I was glad for India. She'd made the right decision.

Gary was elected leader of the People's Party five days before Christmas. I heard it on the news as I drove home from the hospital on Monday afternoon. I rang to congratulate him as soon as I'd collected Paddy. I got his answering-machine and left a message.

That night, just after I'd put Paddy to bed, Tracy called with a huge box in her arms. 'Any wine in the fridge?' she asked, as she plonked it on the table.

I opened a bottle, found two glasses and an ashtray and sat down with her.

'Help me,' she said, as she downed her wine in one.

'Jesus, Tracy, slow down. You'll be on your ear.'

'Will you make the chocolate willies?' she said, throwing stuff at me from the box.

'Oh, I get it,' I said, 'Christmas comes to Mary Winters.'

Tracy lit a fag and picked up a blood-red vibrator. 'Fuck's sake, Ruth. Do you know what this one's called? Santa's Little Helper! Limited edition. I've a huge Christmas party tomorrow night and I'm pulling out all the stops. Here, melt the chocolate, pour it into the willy moulds and throw it in the fridge,' she said, as she tied gold tinsel round the vibrator.

I found a pan and broke the chocolate into squares.

'Were you talking to Kevin?' She reached in for another, a black one this time.

'No? Why?'

'So he hasn't called in? Talked to you?'

Evidently she knew something I didn't. I waited for her to come out with it.

'Just wondering, that's all. I told him about Ferdia, seeing as you didn't bother.'

I poured the melted chocolate into the moulds.

'Hey, what plans do you have for Christmas Day?' she enquired.

'I'm going to hang out with Paddy. Kathleen was to come here but now it's just Paddy and me. We'll go to see her. Then Emerson's going to take Paddy to his grandparents.'

'Why don't you come to us for dinner? We'd love it – the more the merrier.'

I smiled at her. 'Thanks for the offer, but I'd rather stay here. I'm looking forward to it.'

'Well, the offer's there if you change your mind.'

'I know, and I appreciate it.'

'Did you hear from Gary since he got the big job?'

'No, I'd say he's busy at the moment but I'm sure he'll call for Christmas. Speaking of Christmas, Trace, I've no shopping done. What about you?'

'I've the kids well sorted and I'm giving Derek the snip.'

'Pardon?'

'The snip. A vasectomy. I'm giving him a voucher for the family-planning clinic.'

'Tracy Walsh! Forever the romantic, aren't you?'

'I am, really. Sex without the terror of pregnancy is a *very* romantic thing to give someone.'

47

'Mum. Wake up. Somebody wants you.'

I opened my eyes. Paddy stood beside my bed, holding my phone. I took it from him.

'Hello?'

'This is the Regional Maternity Hospital. Kathleen Brennan asked us to ring you. She went into labour during the night.'

I sat bolt upright. 'Is everything all right?'

'Everything's fine. She gave birth to a baby girl at six fifteen this morning.'

'Alone? Why didn't you ring me?'

'Because she asked us not to. She didn't want to disturb you.'

'I'll be right over,' I said, and hung up. I jumped out of bed and dressed while Paddy watched me from a cocoon of bedclothes.

Who could I get to babysit on Christmas Eve? I wondered, as I dressed Paddy and gave him breakfast. I rang Emerson while I waited for the coffee to brew. He agreed to come over straight away and had arrived by the time I was ready to go. I left father and son in the living room, playing Batman, and drove off.

I parked the car, then dashed into the hospital shop. I bought flowers and a pale pink teddy, then checked Kathleen's room number at Reception.

I made my way down the polished hallway, stood outside the door for a minute, then walked slowly into the room. Kathleen was asleep, her face peaceful. At the far side of the bed stood a metal cot. I sat down on a chair near Kathleen and stared at the cot. I could hear the traffic passing outside and the faint cries of newborn babies.

'Kathleen,' I whispered, and her eyes fluttered open.

She smiled faintly at me. 'Did you see her? Isn't she beautiful?'

I nodded. 'You should have rung. I'd have stayed with you.'

'It was the middle of the night. She's lovely, isn't she?'

'Was the birth hard?'

Kathleen rolled her eyes.

'I'll put these in water,' I said, and walked towards the *en-suite* bathroom. I stopped at the cot and looked in. She was wrapped in a lime green blanket. Her hair was the strangest colour – red, with hints of gold and brown – and her eyes were shut tight, in that scrunched newborn way. A thumb was lodged firmly in her mouth, which reminded me of Paddy when he was a tiny baby. She was beautiful but I didn't feel anything. This little red-haired child was my sister, but I felt no connection with her. She could have been any newborn. I put the pink teddy in the cot and stuck the flowers in a basin of water in the bathroom.

Kathleen had dozed off again, so I picked up my handbag and tiptoed towards the door.

'Ruth?' Kathleen said, as I opened it. 'Are you going?'

'I'll stay if you want me to but I thought you needed some rest.'

'I'm exhausted.'

'I'll come back later. Do you need anything?'

'I don't know where the red hair came from. It's strange that she's got it.'

'She's lovely,' I said.

'Aisling,' she said, her eyes closed. 'Her name is Aisling.'

I left the hospital and, on the spur of the moment, decided to go Christmas shopping. I rang Emerson, who said he'd be delighted to stay with Paddy, and headed off into the already crowded city. My gift-buying was inspired to say the least and I congratulated myself on leaving it all until the last minute: desperation makes you less fussy, I thought, as I bought a garden book on water features for Derek and a collection of girly bits and bobs for the Walsh children. I got Tracy a pair of boots that I knew she'd love and a silver pendant for Kathleen that was some Celtic symbol. I bought the baby five outfits and a giant Winnie the Pooh. I bought Paddy the 'big-boy' bike that he had his heart set on. And also a selection of books, Lego and play dough that he loved so much.

I stopped for a quick sandwich in the afternoon, happy so far with my shopping spree. I'd everyone catered for now except Kevin. I'd decided not to buy a present for Emerson.

Kevin proved the most difficult. Finally I settled on a boxed set of *Sopranos* DVDs – his favourite TV series. I was tired when I reached my car, arms aching from the assortment of bags and packages that I was struggling to carry. I paid another quick visit to Kathleen, then headed home.

That night, just as I sat down after an over-excited Paddy had finally fallen asleep, the doorbell rang. I opened the door to Kevin, who stood there with his arms full of gifts.

'Hi,' he said, and gave me a lovely open grin.

'Come in,' I said. 'Glass of wine? I'm just about to have one.'

'A beer'd be great,' he said. I told him to go into the living room and went to get the drinks.

When I returned he was sitting on the sofa, admiring my tree. 'Jesus, Ruth, that's a work of art. You could display it in Tate Modern.'

'Emerson did it with Paddy this afternoon. It's cool, isn't it?' I handed him a bottle of Budweiser. 'Oh, I forgot! Kathleen had her baby. A little red-haired girl,' I said.

'Red hair? Now, there's a clue.'

I laughed. 'Even she seemed a bit baffled by it so I doubt it's any help.'

'It all went OK, the birth?'

'Great. She had her in the middle of the night and didn't ring me until this morning.'

Kevin jerked a thumb at the gifts he'd dropped

on the couch. 'Presents,' he said.

'Go away,' I said, in mock-surprise.

'Ruth, I want to talk to you. I want to ask you something,' he said, his voice serious.

'Fire away.'

He peeled some of the label off his bottle. 'I heard about Ferdia.'

'I need to move on with my life. Ferdia is a great person but I have to be alone. I know that now.'

'Being alone is not all it's cracked up to be,' he said.

'I know, but it's better than being with somebody so you won't be alone.'

He finished his beer and stood up. 'Happy Christmas, Ruth.' He walked out and I stayed on the couch. I picked up one of the gifts he'd left. My name was scrawled on the wrapping paper. I opened it. It contained some expensive Java coffee and a new Johnny Cash CD. It was funny Kevin calling in like that and only staying for a minute. But at least we were friends again and that was good.

I went over to the golden tree and picked up one of the beautifully wrapped presents that Emerson had left. I checked the label and saw my name written in gold script. I unwrapped it carefully. Inside was a video. Curiosity got the better of me and I loaded it into the machine, poured myself another glass of wine, sat on the couch and watched as the TV screen flickered to life. I couldn't believe what I saw.

Emerson had made a movie of Paddy and me

since the day he was born. There was this fabulous soundtrack and a montage of images beautifully put together and interspersed with dialogue. Paddy's first word. A day out in the woods. Paddy on his first film set. Last Christmas. The images washed over me, but they didn't make me sad. There was a joyousness about the film. Like you knew that whoever had made it had put his heart and soul into it. I was struck by how talented Emerson was and wondered how he could have been such a bastard.

On Christmas morning Paddy and I went to the hospital. Paddy gave his new aunt a cursory glance, then sat on the floor and played with his Ninja Turtles van that Santa had brought.

After that we visited Tracy and Derek's madhouse, and then we had a quiet lunch. Emerson came for dessert and asked if Paddy could stay overnight at Ogonnolloe. I agreed. We never mentioned the video but I had succumbed to convention. I felt guilty that morning that I had no present for him so I rewrapped some chocolates that Avril had given me. I felt even more guilty when Emerson declared them his favourites and that it was good of me to remember.

I sat down in front of the TV by myself and decided to call into Kevin after the Christmas special of *Only Fools and Horses*. I didn't care if Orla was there: he was my friend and I wanted him to remain that way. I remembered vividly how cool we had been with each other after Paris – I'd missed his friendship so much. Anyway, I had to give him his present.

It was drizzling as I knocked on Kevin's door. He answered and seemed surprised to see me.

'Hi,' I said, and dumped the present into his hands.

'Come in,' he said, and I followed him into the cosily lit hallway. 'Drink?' he asked, as we headed for the kitchen.

'Why not?' I said. 'Paddy's gone with his dad so . . .'

'For the night?' said Kevin, and we caught each other's eye.

'It's starting to rain,' I said, as he poured two glasses of wine. 'Where's Mikey?'

'He's just gone to bed. Orla was to have him but she was called in to the hospital – some emergency.' He looked me up and down in that disconcerting way he had.

'What's wrong, Kevin? Don't you like my clothes?'

He laughed. 'I like them very much.' He picked up the present that lay on the kitchen table. 'For me?'

I nodded.

He opened it. 'You've made my day. Jesus, I think I'll start watching them now – you on?'

Before I could answer he'd walked into the sitting room. I followed and did a double-take when I saw the state of the room. Toys were strewn everywhere and the Christmas tree was tilted at an unbelievable angle.

'Mikey was busy,' I said to Kevin's back, as he fiddled with the DVD player.

'He didn't stop until his head hit the pillow,' he replied.

The theme tune from *The Sopranos* began. 'This is the coolest present I got,' he said, and flopped on to the sofa. He patted the seat beside him. 'Come on, let's pig out on *The Sopranos*.'

Three hours later I woke with a start. Orla stood above me with a face like a slapped arse.

'Cosy night in?' she asked, and flashed me a cold smile. I realised I'd fallen asleep on Kevin's shoulder. I sat up and rubbed my eyes.

'You're standing in front of the telly, Orla, and I'm on the last episode,' said Kevin.

'I'm off. Goodnight, Orla,' I said. As I passed her I felt her body bristling. Kevin paused the DVD and followed me. He opened the door for me.

'Goodnight,' I said.

He bent down and brushed my cheek with his lips. 'Goodnight, buddy.'

It was meant to be an innocent gesture but it felt incredibly sexy. As I walked home, with my cheek on fire, I chanted silently: We're just good friends, just good friends.

48

New Year came and went, and left an awful empty
stretch of time ahead. That time when summer
seems light years away and darkness rules. Kathleen
and Aisling started their new life together and that
child was so little trouble that I told Tracy I
suspected Kathleen had put some kind of good-baby
spell on her. I cleaned Kathleen's house for the
home-coming and Kevin cooked five different meals.
I bought Kathleen a state-of-the-art baby car seat –
the super-duper deluxe model – and loads of tiny
pink baby clothes. Tracy had come armed with
everything a new baby could possibly want. She said
that Derek was soon to cash in his Christmas present from his wife.

Kathleen and her baby settled straight into a cosy
routine. The weather in January turned nasty and
we even had snow, to Paddy and the other children's
delight. Kevin and Derek organised a snowball fight,
and the whole street joined in. Two hours and three
broken windows later – Mikey – it ended. But it was
one of those special times that you remember for
ever. The next day Paddy and Mikey threw a huge
tantrum because the snow was gone.

Work was the same old same old. Avril had stopped crying and had even started dating again. Ferdia was managing a hotel in Letterkenny. Our new manager was an efficient woman called Janet Moran, a nice, ordinary woman who was easy to work for.

Emerson and I were getting along really well, considering we were divorcing each other. He and Paddy had grown even closer and I vowed – no matter what happened – that I'd never come between them. It was just too precious a thing.

My father had fallen off the face of the planet shortly before Christmas. Kevin liked to pinpoint his disappearance a little more specifically than that: to the day on which he was elected leader of his party. But I just put it down to Gary being busy with his demanding new role. His personal assistant had returned my phone calls and said as much. It wasn't a big deal.

So, my life in the New Year trundled on – no excitement, no adrenaline rushes, no surprises. I was almost bored by its evenness – but then it all changed.

It started on a Friday morning half-way through January. I should have known something was wrong because for the first time ever I had to wake Paddy up. He was out of sorts at breakfast and I rang work to tell them I wouldn't be in that day. I made a bed for him on the sofa and he fell asleep instantly.

Tracy called in at lunch-time and we were just sitting down when Paddy woke, screaming his head off. We ran to the living room where he was standing up, his face bright red.

I lifted him into my arms, shocked at the fierce heat his body exuded. 'Tracy, he's burning up,' I said, as I sat on the sofa with him in my arms.

Tracy felt his forehead. 'Jesus, Ruth! Have you a thermometer?'

'There's one in the first-aid box in the kitchen,' I said, my heart constricting as Paddy moaned in my arms.

She came back and expertly took his temperature. 'A hundred and four – where's your doctor's number?'

'On the message board above the phone.' I was watching Paddy's face. His eyes were closing again.

Tracy came back with a bowl of water and a sponge. 'He says he's passing this way and he'll be here in ten minutes.'

I put Paddy down on his Winnie the Pooh quilt. Tracy stripped off his pyjamas and began to sponge him. Paddy protested but she was undeterred. She looked up at me and I could see in her eyes what both of us were afraid to say: meningitis.

I was never so glad to see Dr Power's kind face and I practically pushed him into the living room. He opened his bag and examined Paddy while Tracy and I stood guard.

'What is it, Doctor? Should I bring him to the hospital?' I asked.

'Let me finish, Ruth, and we'll decide then what to do,' he said. Paddy moaned softly.

Eventually Dr Power laid Paddy down and ushered us into the kitchen.

'What is it?' I asked.

'I'm not sure – probably a virus. We shouldn't overreact but we must be vigilant for the next couple of days. He'll be fine here.'

'Will he be all right?' I said.

'I'm sure he will, but at the moment he's a very sick little boy.'

'Wouldn't hospital be safer?' I asked.

'He'll be better off at home – trust me. You need to keep him hydrated and his temperature down. That's all anyone can do.'

'Calpol, and 7-Up,' said Tracy. 'You'll have to ring Emerson to help, Ruth. It's going to be a long weekend.'

The doctor nodded at us and walked to the door. 'I'll come back this evening on my way home, Ruth.'

I closed the front door and went back into the living room. Paddy was asleep. He seemed a little better, I thought, when I touched his forehead.

Tracy came into the room with a tray. 'I made you a sandwich, Ruth, and some coffee,' she said, as she put it on the floor beside me.

'Thanks.'

She felt Paddy's forehead. 'It's dropped a little. If it climbs again, sponge him straight away. Now eat something.'

I picked up a sandwich. I took a bite but couldn't taste anything.

'I rang Emerson – he's on his way. And Kathleen.

She wanted to come over but I told her not to bring Aisling. Just to be on the safe side,' Tracy went on.

'Oh, Tracy, what will I do if anything happens to him?' I said, finally voicing my worst fear.

Tracy knelt beside me and put her arms round me. 'Paddy will be grand. Small children run high temperatures all the time.'

Tears ran down my face and I wiped my eyes on my sleeve. The doorbell rang and Tracy went to answer it.

I fell to pieces when Emerson walked into the room. I ran to him and he enveloped me in his arms.

'What did the doctor say? How is he?' Emerson asked Tracy, as he stroked my hair. Tracy told him and handed me a box of tissues. I dried my eyes and sat close to him on the sofa. He kissed Paddy's forehead, then took my face in his hands. 'I promise you I'll be here every minute,' he said. He stroked Paddy's face and only then did I notice that Tracy had gone.

We spent the rest of the day at Paddy's side, taking turns to have a break. The doctor called again and was satisfied that Paddy's condition, while not improving, was not deteriorating. But later that night his temperature climbed again and we were back to sponging almost continuously.

Emerson and I spent that night and the next day pacing the house with Paddy. It was the only thing that comforted him. The doctor called again late on Saturday evening and said that if the temperature hadn't dropped by the next day we might have to bring him to the hospital.

Paddy was the crossest I'd ever seen him and sometimes only Emerson could comfort him. He'd walk with him and sing to him, endlessly patient with his boy. I looked at them at one stage during that long night and remembered why I'd fallen in love with Emerson.

When the fever finally broke it took both of us by surprise. Paddy had been dozing in Emerson's arms and suddenly opened his eyes. 'I'm hungry,' he said to his father.

I got the fever scan and checked his temperature. 'Ninety-eight point five,' I said excitedly.

'Yippee!' said Emerson. 'He's very damp, Ruth – here, feel him.'

'Tracy said he'd sweat like a pig when the fever broke. Hi, Baby, are you all better?'

'I'm *starving*,' Paddy said.

We fed him toast, and then I put him in clean pyjamas and laid him on the sofa. 'Read me a story, Daddy.'

'You're well on the mend now, Paddy Burke,' Emerson said, as he opened *The Owl and the Pussy Cat*.

I went into the kitchen and felt myself relax for the first time in two days. It had been the nightmare from Hell and I felt as if someone had just sprung me from the worst prison in the world.

I didn't hear Emerson come in until he was standing beside me at the sink. He put his hand tentatively on my shoulder, then took it away swiftly. 'He's asleep. He looks so much better, Ruth.'

'You look exhausted,' I said. He was unshaven and had one of Paddy's buttery handprints right in the middle of his pale blue sweatshirt. I reached out and traced it with my finger.

Emerson bent his head so that our lips were inches apart. Before I knew what was happening I'd put my arms round his neck and we were kissing with all the urgency of new lovers. We tore at each other's clothes and, semi-naked, standing up, reconsummated our dead marriage.

49

'Please go,' I said, as I picked up my clothes from the kitchen floor. 'Please go now.'

Emerson struggled into his jeans, his boxers still on the floor next to my red thong. 'Ruth . . .'

I stopped dressing, my body still tingling from the rediscovered pleasure of sex with him. 'Just go,' I said.

'Ruth . . .'

'Please go. I'm exhausted and I can't think straight.'

'Can we talk tomorrow?'

I just wanted him gone so that I could take in what had happened.

'I'll lift Paddy up to his bed,' he said.

'Put him in mine.'

Emerson left the room. He was back a minute later and smiled shyly at me. 'Goodnight, Ruth.'

'Night,' I said, as he left.

But despite my exhaustion I couldn't fall asleep. I listened to Paddy's regular breathing – such a change from the panting – and closed my eyes, but sleep wouldn't come. I relived the past hour in slow motion in my head but none of it made sense. I mean, the last thing on my mind at that moment in the kitchen was sex, and look what had happened. And the thing that disturbed me the most was its quality. The closeness and familiarity. Emerson's nearness. I didn't want him near me, not like that. I'd shut him out of my heart and I needed him to stay that way.

We never talked about what happened that night. Emerson tried to bring it up but knew me well enough to realise when he was being cut off at the pass. I kept our encounters short, sweet and ultra-polite. Being badly hurt can make you strong – provided you survive it.

One Saturday in early February I invited Kevin, Derek, Tracy and the kids to dinner in my house. I'd had numerous invites to theirs and it was my turn to do the catering. After I'd rooted in the presses and flicked through some recipe books I rang Fortune City and placed an order for that evening around seven.

I spent the afternoon getting ready for the dinner party. It felt like ages since I'd put on the glad-rags so I made an effort, despite Paddy's boisterous presence. Tracy, Derek and her brood were the first to arrive, followed almost immediately by Kevin and Mikey. Derek set up a video for the kids in the playroom while Tracy sorted out drinks. Kevin ran his eyes up and down my body as I poured wine into glasses.

'Stop that,' I said, and Tracy laughed.

Kevin continued and I thumped his arm, but he still stared, unfazed. 'You look great,' he said eventually.

'We'd never have guessed you thought that, Kev,' said Tracy.

'It's great to have Mikey home,' I said, as a posse of small people ran by.

Kevin nodded. 'I missed him.'

'So? Any developments on the other stuff?'

'Ballymoran? Not really.'

'And Orla?'

'She's going mad but I promised her I'd watch Mikey like a hawk and I do. I also had an alarm installed in my house – did I tell you that?'

I shook my head. 'Good idea, though.'

'I thought so.'

'You won't back away from the story?'

'I wish I could but I just can't – I wouldn't be able to live with myself.'

'Very brave.'

'Or foolish.'

'Or both?' I said.

The doorbell rang and I went to answer it. It was the Chinese feast.

'Cheat,' said Kevin, as we opened the fragrant cartons.

'No, just clever,' I said.

I lit the candles on the already laid kitchen table and dimmed the lights to a soft glow. I put Johnny Cash on the stereo and we all sat down to eat and chat. Half-way through the meal I surveyed the table, my friends' faces animated with laughter and conversation, and decided that this was a really nice place to be. I got up to open more wine and the doorbell rang. Derek, who had been checking on the children, called from the hallway that he'd get it.

Johnny was just launching into his version of 'Bridge Over Troubled Water' when the kitchen door crashed open. 'I love him!' Selma shouted, hand on her hip, eyes challenging me to a duel.

'You can have him,' I said, and continued to pour the wine.

Derek stood helplessly behind her. 'She just barged in,' he said.

She walked up to the table, eyes flashing at all of us, like a heat-seeking missile deciding which target to hit.

'I will have him, but you – you sneak him away again, you steal him from ze woman he love!' she screamed.

All the children had gathered at the kitchen door. Mikey was laughing but all the others were scared and Chloe was crying.

'Keep your voice down in front of the small children,' said Tracy, in a low, tight voice. She stood up and lifted Chloe into her arms.

Selma confronted her, like a lioness waiting to pounce. 'You shut your mouth, you stupid person. I will fight for my man, he's mine – mine, you hear?' she shouted, jabbing a finger menacingly at Tracy's face.

Kevin had grasped that she was in dangerous

territory. 'Come on now, Selma, let's go,' he said, took her by the elbow and tried to lead her out of the room. She turned on him, hand raised as if to hit him, and suddenly her face and hair were covered with Special Chow Mein. Mikey had thrown a carton of food at her. He was the best marksman on our street and we all had the freshly puttied windows to prove it.

'Get away from my dad,' he said. 'Get away or I'll kick you.'

'It's OK, Mikey,' Kevin said, but it was too late: Paddy had decided to join in the fun and flung a carton of Singapore Noodles. His shot landed on her chest and we all watched, fascinated, as noodles dripped off her. A king prawn was stuck to her forehead.

She walked over to me. 'You want him back. You stole my man,' she hissed.

Kevin's eyes swivelled to me. I was aware that Derek was on the phone behind me and I heard Emerson's name. Suddenly Kevin grabbed Selma, marched her along the hallway, opened the door and shoved her out on to the path. He came back into the kitchen and wiped his brow in an exaggerated way. 'Jesus, Ruth, you should have warned us about the entertainment,' he said, and everybody laughed.

Then the screaming started, a high-pitched incessant shriek of the kind you hear in scary B movies.

'Go and get your pellet gun, Derek. That'll shut her up,' said Tracy, and went to peep out through the side-lights of the front door. 'Jesus, lads, she's standing in the middle of the street.'

I went into the sitting room and peered out through the slatted wooden blinds. Kevin had gone out again to try to calm her and the neighbours were at their gates, watching the spectacle. I followed the others into the garden.

The screaming went on, and she wouldn't stop even when Emerson showed up and pleaded with her. Finally he stood behind her, wrapped both arms round her tiny waist, hoisted her up and carried her under his arm to his car. He drove away and the crowd dispersed.

We returned to the kitchen, and got out the pudding, a lovely French pastry.

Half an hour later I was in the downstairs loo when the doorbell rang again. Selma, the Return? I thought.

Kevin answered the door. 'Hi – what are you doing here?' I heard him say.

'I finished early at the hospital and I was wondering if I could see Mikey,' Orla's voice replied.

'How did you know we were here?' Kevin asked.

'You never seem to be too far away from this house,' said Orla.

'Mikey's with his pals and it's late.'

'I could wait for you next door, Kevin. You won't be long, will you?' she said.

'Please go, Orla,' Kevin said.

There was silence for a minute and I held my breath.

'I'd like to see Mikey, Kevin.'

'We have arrangements, Orla, and I think it's time we stuck to them. You should have picked him up this afternoon, like you promised. You can see Mikey tomorrow as we agreed.'

'Oh, but it was all right for me to take two weeks' holidays and have him when it suited you, Kevin.'

'For God's sake, Orla, somebody tried to kidnap the child.'

'And whose fault was that?'

I heard Kevin sigh. 'You can see him tomorrow.'

'Fine. Be like that so,' said Orla. I heard the click of her heels as she marched away, then the soft clunk of the door closing. I waited another minute before I came out of the loo.

'That was Orla at the door, Ruth. This is like the Night of the Long Exes. Derek, you don't have a secret ex about to call too, do you?' said Tracy, as she forked a piece of pear tart into her mouth.

Kevin stood up. 'I think I'll bring Mikey home, Ruth. He's tired and, well . . .'

'That's OK, Kevin. I understand,' I said. 'Here, I'll get him for you.' I went to the playroom and bribed Mikey to go home with a bright yellow lollipop, then watched Kevin and his son walk down my garden path. They looked kind of lonely in the dark, wintry night. But a tiny part of me believed that his ex-wife was sitting in that house, waiting for her boys to come home.

50

The next morning hailstones the size of golfballs slammed against my bedroom window. I focused on the bedside clock – six thirty. What day was it? Sunday? Yes, – great. I had no intention of getting up until I had no choice. Paddy was beside me. I couldn't remember him coming into my bed during the night but there he was. I snuggled down under the duvet, cuddled his warm body and dozed off again.

We were asleep for another two hours, then eased ourselves into the day, with breakfast – scrambled eggs and pancakes – in front of the TV in our pyjamas. I'd had just about enough of cartoons and was considering getting dressed when the doorbell rang. Kathleen and Aisling were positioned at a hail-avoiding angle in my porch.

'Good morning!' Kathleen sang. We kissed and I glanced at Aisling, who was fast asleep in her car seat. A cherry-coloured woollen hat was pulled down to the bridge of her tiny nose and a soft white blanket pulled up to her chin.

Paddy ran out and Kathleen made a fuss of him with chocolate buttons. He poked his baby aunt gently with his stubby fingers. 'Does Aisling have any legs?' he asked.

'Under the blanket,' Kathleen said, with an indulgent smile.

'Can I see them?' One fat hand was already yanking it off.

'Later, Paddy, when she wakes up,' Kathleen said, and rearranged it.

Apparently satisfied, he headed back to the TV.

'He's such an intelligent boy,' Kathleen said, following me to the kitchen. 'He's right, you know. He's hardly ever seen her legs because she's always wrapped up in a blanket.'

'Will you have some?' I asked, pouring coffee,

'I'm still afraid to risk it,' she said, settling at the table. 'Any chamomile tea?'

'Sure,' I said, rummaging in the press for the canister of herbal teabags. 'Here we go. How can you drink this stuff?'

Kathleen smiled. 'It's very calming, and great for Aisling while I'm breastfeeding. I don't want to do anything to upset her tummy.'

'Right,' I said, and put a cup of the pale green brew in front of her. She pulled off the baby's hat. Aisling's scant red hair stood on end but she didn't wake. Kathleen gazed at her as though she was the most fascinating sight on earth.

I prepared a mental grocery list. Eggs, coffee, milk, bread, cereal, honey, fruit and vegetables – did they still have asparagus on special offer?

'Ruth?'

I realised Kathleen was talking to me. 'Sorry?'

'You were dreaming.'

'What were you saying?'

She savoured the grassy smell of her tea and took a sip. Her blonde-streaked hair had grown a little since the baby was born and framed her face. She looked at me over the rim of her cup and I could see something hard to define in her bright blue eyes.

'I heard on the news as I was driving over that a general election has been called for the end of April,' she said.

'Mmm.'

'Gary'll be busy.'

I returned to my mental shopping list. 'Probably.'

'Are you all right, love?' she said.

'I'm fine. Why do you ask?'

'I was wondering, that's all.'

I drank some coffee and sat up straight. 'Really, I'm fine, Kathleen. How are you?'

'Well, that's the thing, I suppose,' Kathleen said, and her face was suddenly serious. 'I think I've never been better. Everything in my life is working out for me – I have everything I've ever wanted.'

'Really?'

'Yes, and your life is so difficult at the moment and I want to know if there's anything I can do.'

'No. Thank you.'

Kathleen put her cup on the table and glanced down at Aisling, who was making small baby snores. 'Look, Ruth, I know you don't want to talk about this and the last time I tried we argued and I don't want that . . .' She drank the chamomile tea as if it was a shot of whiskey. 'The situation with Aisling is difficult for you . . .'

'I don't know what you mean,' I said, and stood up suddenly. My chair squeaked on the tiled floor, making Aisling jump. I walked to the coffee-maker, refilled my cup and stood by the sink, with my back to Kathleen, staring out of the window at the dismal day. 'I'm delighted for you that you have Aisling and she's a lovely baby. Paddy is mad about her.'

'But not you, Ruth.'

'I said she was lovely.'

'I know,' Kathleen said, with a sigh. 'But you ignored my pregnancy and you've pretty much ignored her since she was born too. I'm not complaining but . . .'

'That's unfair,' I said, eyes fixed on the budding sycamore tree that was waving in the wind. 'I've bought loads of stuff for her – the car seat for a start. That's hardly ignoring her.'

'It's not that, Ruth. I know this is difficult for you – it has to be. By its nature it'd have to be difficult . . .'

'Look.' I swung around to face her, a big aching smile plastered across my face. 'I don't know what you want from me. I've done my best to be nice to Aisling – and I truly feel nothing but happiness for you that you have your dream baby at last. That's a great name for her, actually. Aisling – the dream. Perfect. But I have a life as well. I'm sorry if I'm not paying enough attention to you and yours but

I'm in top gear at the moment trying to sort out the shit in my own.'

'That's exactly what I meant. I want to know if I can help.'

'I'll manage.'

'Well, I know you have Emerson but still . . .'

Something broke inside me. 'Well, you could have Aisling's dad around if you wanted, I'm sure,' I said, leaning back against the worktop. 'Come on, Kathleen, how about an end to the mystery? You've kept us all guessing long enough. Who the hell is Aisling's dad?' I knew she was upset but I couldn't stop myself. 'Is it someone we know? Someone famous? He obviously has red hair, but who is he? Mick Hucknall? Brendan Gleeson? Chris Evans? They have red hair.'

Kathleen cleared her throat. 'I'd prefer not to say.'

'Jesus, Kathleen – you have the strangest attitude to the fathers of your children. First me, and all those years of not knowing the identity of my father, and now Aisling. Will she be getting a surprise father when she's almost thirty?'

'Ruth—'

I was past caring. 'Look, I'm fond of you and I'm fond of Aisling, but I feel as if you want something from me that I don't have to give. Do you want me to say I understand why you gave me away? Is that it?'

I paused but Kathleen didn't speak – just looked at me.

'Well, I do. You were sixteen – what else could

you do? Or maybe you want me to say I'm happy for you that you have a baby to look after at long last?'

'I'm not trying to make you say anything.'

'Doesn't feel like that. I try not to think about it too much – especially as it makes me feel disloyal to Mum and Dad, who, Kathleen, were the best parents in the whole world.'

'I know they were.'

'I'm OK about all of it, really. Sure I'd have liked it if everybody was delighted by my arrival. Like they were about Paddy. Or Aisling. But that's life.'

Kathleen stood up and took a step towards me. I shook my head, so she stayed where she was in the centre of the kitchen, her hands clasped in front of her stomach.

'I've had a good life so I've no reason to be mad at Aisling.'

Kathleen took a deep breath. 'I think you are.'

'Don't be ridiculous! I'm too mature to resent a small baby – it's hardly her fault all this happened to me.'

'It's only natural.'

'Believe what you like, but I don't go around taking my stuff out on small babies.'

'I know that, Ruth, and I know you'd never be anything other than kind to Aisling and you'd always do the right thing. But you are sisters and I'd like your heart to be in it.'

'I don't know what you mean.'

Kathleen took a step closer. 'I think you do.'

And she was right. I did.

'I gave you away, Ruth. It was the hardest day of my life and the biggest pain I've ever had to endure, but for all that it was worse for you.'

'No, it wasn't – my parents were terrific.'

'I know that, and every single night I say prayers for them because I'm so grateful to them for raising you to be the wonderful person you are.'

'So? It was fine for me.'

'But you'll always have to live with the fact that I gave you away, especially now I've got Aisling.'

'But the circumstances are different. I understand.'

'In your head.'

I couldn't speak.

'I was the one who named you "Ruth", did I ever tell you that?'

'No.'

'I was so pleased that your parents kept your name. When I was little I loved the story of Ruth, in the Bible, who left her people and went to live in a strange land with her mother-in-law who was like another mother to her.'

'I know the story,' I said.

Kathleen smiled. 'Then you'll understand why it seemed like the perfect name for you when I was in the mother-and-baby home.'

'I suppose.'

Neither of us spoke for what felt like ages.

'I don't know how to fix it for you, Ruth,' Kathleen said eventually.

'I'm not asking you to fix anything.'

'I thought maybe if I helped out – especially when Emerson did that stuff – I could make something up to you. But it's not enough, is it?'

'I don't know what you're talking about.'

Kathleen bent down and picked up the baby seat. It swung gently and Aisling slept on, oblivious to the drama going on around her. 'I can only tell you this. When I said a while ago that I had everything I ever wanted I didn't just mean Aisling, I meant you too. Most of my life I've wanted to be part of yours and now I am, and I can't tell you what that means to me. As for Aisling's name, well, she is a dream come true and I adore her. But if you'd asked I could have told you I called her after a friend I had in London. Aisling Henry, my first psychic guide. I called you "Ruth" because I knew you were going away but I could have called you "Aisling", if I'd thought of it at the time, because the real dream baby in my life was you, Ruth.'

And then she left. I stayed by the sink as emotion whirled inside me like a kaleidoscope of confusion. Loud cartoon music poured from the living room and the hailstones returned to pelt against my kitchen window. The telephone rang. I picked up the receiver.

'Ruth.'

'Kathleen?'

'Ruth, there's one thing I forgot to say. You wanted to know the name of Aisling's father. Have a look at www.nirvanahome.com and you'll find the answer.' She hung up.

I struggled to register what she'd just said. Nirvana?

But Kurt Cobain was dead, and even if he was like Elvis and not really dead, he didn't have red hair. Anyway, I didn't care who the hell had fathered Aisling. Tracy, on the other hand, was busting to know. As if she'd heard me thinking about her, the doorbell rang and she and Chloe arrived.

'Jesus, Mary and Joseph, am I glad you're home,' Tracy said, and almost ran into my hallway.

'Are you OK?' I said.

Her mouth was open as if she was about to speak but when she focused on my face she closed it. Then she said, 'What is it?'

I burst into tears.

51

When I had finished crying Tracy sat me at the table with her cigarettes while she fixed the children up with spaghetti and toast. I told her briefly what had happened with Kathleen. She listened and when I finished gave me a long, tight hug. 'Don't go anywhere,' she said. 'I'll be back in two seconds.'

I savoured my cigarette, promising myself that this really was going to be the last time I smoked. I kept turning over Kathleen's phone call. I decided that maybe I'd call up that website tomorrow at work. The front door slammed. Kevin and Tracy came into the kitchen. He smiled at me and the ache in my heart eased a little.

'Kevin brought his laptop,' Tracy announced. 'Go on, Kev, get going – I can't wait all day.'

'What are you doing?' I said.

'He's setting up his laptop,' Tracy answered.

'I can see that but why?'

'To put us out of our misery,' Tracy said, watching the screen as it sprang to life. 'OK, what was that website? Nirvanahome.com?'

'You want to find out who Aisling's father is,' I said. 'Jesus, you're one curious bitch.'

'What can I say? Well? Who is it, Kev? Is it somebody from Nirvana?'

Kevin stared at the screen. 'Well, unless it's a woman.'

He turned his computer to face me and 'Nirvana Home – Women Only – Women Always' jumped out at me in Gothic lettering. Tracy cursed. 'A bloody witches' site?' she muttered. 'That can't be right. Are you sure you have the right website?'

'Pretty sure,' I said, 'but I might have misheard. I'm not in the best shape today.'

Kevin came to sit beside me and rested his arm across my shoulders. I knew it was a mistake not to stop him but it was so comforting that I couldn't convince myself to object. We sat there side by side, looking at the colourful web page of celestial nymphs and goddesses. Suddenly he began to laugh.

'What?' I said.

'Well, I'm not saying it is, but see that link there? Maybe that's what Kathleen's talking about.'

Tracy ran to look at what Kevin was pointing to on the screen.

'Holy shit!' she said, as she read the tag line across the banner just below an ad for *chi*-enhancing crystals. 'It can't be.'

'"Mommy's Baby",' Kevin read aloud. '"Do you want a baby but don't want the complication of a man? Are you a Sister capable of doing it for herself? Then visit our site and see what nature has to offer you, courtesy of science."'

'Jesus, Kevin!' Tracy exploded. 'Come on, for fuck's sake! What are you waiting for?'

Kevin clicked on the link and we watched in fascination as a *Vogue*-style page opened in front of us. It was crammed with photographs of glamorous women in designer clothes holding beautiful babies, and everybody was stylish, laughing and happy. It might have been mistaken for a feature in any up-market women's glossy. The only difference was the subject matter.

The article sang the praises of man-free conception. For a fee, Mommy's Baby could supply you with good-quality (tested for a range of diseases and disorders) sperm and the apparatus to bring DIY to new levels.

'Christ!' Tracy said. 'That yoke looks like a turkey-baster.'

'Oh, my God,' I said.

'Maybe it's a mistake,' Kevin said.

I shook my head. 'I bet it isn't. No wonder she was so secretive about the whole thing.'

'Poor Kathleen,' Tracy said. Her pointy-chinned Oriental face was drawn and sad. 'I always imagined she had some bloke over in England – a rock star or a royal or someone like that – and there was only this . . .' Her voice petered out as she gestured towards the computer screen. 'Derek's a pain in the arse a lot of the time but I'd hate to have only that turkey-baster to talk to, wouldn't you?'

'Poor Aisling,' I said.

'Why?' Tracy said.

'Well, it was bad enough for me, so how do you think she'll feel when she finds out she doesn't *have* a father?'

'She does, though,' Kevin said.

'If you consider sperm from an anonymous donor a father,' I said.

Kevin shrugged. 'It's hardly ideal, but I can think of worse ways for a kid to come into the world. I can certainly think of worse people to raise one.'

'Definitely,' Tracy said. 'Kathleen is a great woman and a great mother. Look what she did with you, Ruth.'

'Gave me away?'

'No. Bust her arse to find you, then stayed with you through all the shit – even stayed around when you didn't want her and there was nothing in it for her. What else makes a good mother? Baking scones? Aisling's lucky.'

Tracy began to clear off the kitchen table while Kevin disconnected his computer and packed it back into its case. They were right. All along I'd been dogged by the fact that Kathleen had given me away, which had made me forget that she'd also come to find me. And not only come but stayed. For a second I put myself in her place, where the only way I could see a future for Paddy was to have someone else raise him. My heart reverberated to the imagined pain. 'You're right. Aisling *is* lucky. And so am I.'

Tracy and Kevin hugged me, then called their children and took off for home. I decided to visit

Kathleen. Just as Paddy and I were on our way out the telephone rang.

'Ruth?'

'Gary?'

'Ruth, darling, it's *sooo* lovely to hear your voice – I've missed you.'

'I believe congratulations are in order, Gary. Leader of the People's Party? How is the new job treating you?'

Gary chuckled softly. 'Manic – I must be mad! Why would I want a job that'd eat up my life this way? A job that'd keep me so busy I can't get a minute even to talk with my own daughter?'

'I don't know, Gary – why would you?'

I heard him take a deep breath. 'I know it sounds cheesy but I suppose I do it because I want to make a difference. Is that awful?'

'No, of course not.'

'I know it's not fashionable to say things like that but it's the truth and it's why I got into this game in the first place. The world is a difficult place but I'm plagued by the notion that any little thing I can do to make things better is worthwhile.'

I made a face. He was like the lead in a bad movie, but I believed he was sincere and that was all that mattered. 'Gary, sorry to hurry you but I'm in a bit of a rush. Do you need me for anything?'

'No, just wanted to touch base. Say hello to my beautiful daughter, find out how my grandson is doing.'

'Paddy's just fine, thanks, standing here with his coat on, raring to go.'

'I'll let you off, so. Give him a kiss for me.'

'I will. 'Bye, Gary.'

''Bye, Ruth, talk soon.'

I hung up and bundled Paddy through the sleet into the car, thinking of how it might have been to have only two parents and a 'normal' life. Calmer, maybe, I thought, as I started the engine, but a hell of a lot less interesting.

I drove to Kathleen's, full of plans for what I'd say, but as soon as she opened the door of her pretty red-brick terraced house I was tongue-tied. Luckily, she was her usual gracious self.

'Ruth! Paddy! How lovely of you to visit! Come on in out of that horrible weather – you'll get your death. You're not wet, are you?' She ushered us indoors. Paddy loved visiting Kathleen's house, and it struck me, as I sat on the yellow sofa in front of the fire, that I hardly ever bothered to visit her. It was symbolic, really, the way I left all the running around to her. There'd been a time when that was appropriate but not now.

We sat and chatted while Paddy played with the cars, bricks and crayons in the basket of toys that Kathleen kept for him. While we were chatting Aisling woke. Kathleen fed her, then I held her. That afternoon something changed between me and the baby. She gazed at me in her lop-sided two-month-old way, then gave me a wide gummy smile, and for the first time ever, I realised I loved her.

52

Next morning as I dropped Paddy to school I noticed the first daffodils of the year were opening. The sight cheered me.

Janet Moran, the hotel manager, was chatting to a deliveryman as I arrived and waved to me as I passed. Avril wasn't in. One of Janet's new initiatives was to rationalise staff hours so she'd reverted to the old practice of having only one receptionist on duty at a time. That was a relief. Although Avril had moved on in her Kevin-obsession she was still capable of bursting into tears at the thought of what might have been.

February was a time when people all around the world were planning their summer holidays, which explained the number of enquiries I had to answer from people interested in visiting the Irish mid-west. As I ploughed through emails I remembered the day before when Tracy had arrived at my house in the midst of my trauma. She'd had something on her mind. I'd forgotten about it at the time so I decided to give her a quick call between chatting to prospective tourists from Milwaukee.

She answered the phone on its first ring.

'Well, well! If Drury's receptionist was as efficient as you we'd have a lot more business,' I said.

'Hi, Ruth, how are you?'

'Good, actually. Thanks, by the way.'

'No problem. Is anything up?'

'No. I just remembered that when you arrived at my house yesterday you looked like you wanted to tell me something and then I started blubbing and that was that. So is everything OK?'

'Well, yes, I suppose it is – in fact it might be a little bit too OK.'

'What do you mean?'

'I'm pregnant.'

'What?'

'I'm pregnant. I had the wand with me and all to show you yesterday but you were upset.'

'Oh, Tracy, I'm so sorry. I'm such a bad friend at the moment, so self-centred. How do you feel about being pregnant?'

'Not great.'

'What does Derek say?'

'He's delighted.'

'I thought he was having a vasectomy?'

'Next Tuesday.'

We laughed.

'A bit late,' I said.

'Well, either he has it anyway or he'd better get used to the idea of celibacy once this baby's born,' Tracy said.

'It'll be fine – another lovely little Walsh for the world.'

'Exactly *and* I'll get big boobs – even if it's only temporary.'

'There you go. I'd better go and chat up some tourists – I'll call in on the way home. Do you need anything?'

'No, but thanks for calling. See you later.'

I hung up and became engrossed in matching requests with availability. I was so deeply involved with my work that I didn't hear anything until the first notes of 'Bewitched, Bothered And Bewildered' rang out. I looked up to see three men in evening suits and a pale, dark-haired woman in a green sequined dress sitting in front of me playing their instruments.

Janet Moran was a most innovative manager, I thought, as the cello, violin, double bass and viola filled the hotel with music. Ferdia might well have been a hotshot but he'd never have thought of anything as funky as a string quartet at twelve o'clock on a cold February Monday.

Just as they finished their first piece Janet appeared in the lobby. She joined in the rapturous applause generated by twelve German tourists in parkas. The performers took a bow and she approached the reception desk.

'Aren't they marvellous?' she said.

'Great idea, Janet! Mr Holtz and his group are loving it.' The Germans were clapping mittened hands to the opening bars of 'The Blue Danube'. 'Where did you get them?'

'I didn't – I was about to ask you if you knew who had.'

Were they sophisticated buskers, then? 'The Blue Danube' finished and they launched straight into 'When I Fall In Love (It Will Be Forever)'.

The automatic doors opened and a gigantic bunch of flowers walked towards us. As they got closer I recognised the long legs beneath them. With an almighty heave Emerson lifted the flower arrangement on to the counter, leaned over and kissed me on the mouth. I kissed him back. He tasted so familiar I wanted to cry.

'Happy Valentine's Day, Ruth,' he said, as the German tourists burst into applause that I was pretty certain was for us.

'Emerson . . .'

'Don't say anything. I fucked up and I'm not asking you to forgive me, but I want you to know that I love you and I always will. No strings, I swear, apart from these.' He waved his hand at the musicians behind him. 'I just wanted you to know. That's all.'

He kissed my forehead and left. The string quartet finished their set and took off with a trundle of collapsible seats, music stands and instrument cases.

I went back to my work, preoccupied with this new turn of events. I had loved Emerson – I'd thought we'd be together for ever and then he'd thrown it away in Gibraltar. I knew he was sorry – I'd have been sorry if I'd thrown everything away for a headcase like Selma – but that wasn't enough.

As I'd already said to him the night he'd called me, all drunk and tearful, missing me and Paddy, he should have thought of how much he loved us before, not afterwards. And the sex after Paddy's illness had been just that: sex. Nothing more.

The string-quartet thing was probably just a ploy to persuade me to let him come back into my life and my heart. But I wasn't sure I could do that, even if I wanted to. I didn't know what I felt for Emerson any more. But even if I still loved him could I ever trust him again after what he'd done?

How could you have a relationship without trust? I knew I needed to stay away from men for the time being, at least until I was confident that I was making a choice that wasn't based on fear.

Avril arrived for her shift full of questions about the string quartet.

'How did you know about it?' I asked, as I packed my stuff into a big straw holdall.

'Irene rang me about my wages and she told me. It's a beautiful thing to do.' Her eyes filled with tears. 'You're so lucky – if only Kevin would do something like that for me . . .'

Which made me smile. 'He isn't the type – and, anyway, Avril, I thought we'd talked about that. You're an independent woman and you don't need Kevin or any other man to make you complete.'

Avril's red hair shimmered. 'I know, I agree with that, but still . . .'

I grabbed my bag and left. As I walked home, I checked round every corner for Emerson, but there was no sign of him. I was impressed. Maybe he *had* just been apologising, and maybe he was telling the truth when he said there were no strings attached. I felt the first stirrings of respect for him that I'd experienced in almost a year. If he was sincere I knew we could have a wholesome, civilised relationship and that'd be best for Paddy.

53

Emerson maintained his respectful stance, calling for Paddy, being sweet, friendly and reliable. He never slipped into maudlin-regret mode so we began to get on quite well. When he received word that his movie, *Ferushi*, had been nominated for a Palme d'Or at the Cannes Film Festival, I was even pleased for him. That movie would always have bad associations for me but I was still delighted that his talent as a film-maker was being recognised. Very occasionally I remembered the trauma of walking into that hot trailer in Gibraltar. At those times I found it hard to be civil with him, but mostly I forgot what he'd done and we settled into an almost comfortable routine during February and March.

Gary was back in my life too. He called me on the telephone every day. Kevin and I never spoke about him – we didn't even talk about not talking about him – but I valued Kevin so it was a small sacrifice to make.

As I lay in bed at night I often thought of Kevin and sometimes had to admit that the feelings I had for him weren't strictly friendly, but I'd done the rebound thing with Ferdia. I wasn't taking any more orders from my head, but neither would I let my heart dictate. I needed to find the place between the two where I could balance – like the middle part of a seesaw. And I had to be alone to learn how to do it.

Almost overnight Tracy's pregnancy became obvious. Kevin teased her constantly about the size of her bump and called it the Twins – much to her annoyance. She was having her first scan at the end of March and was excited at the prospect.

'How are the Twins?' Kevin said, when he met her on her way to the hospital.

'Bastard,' she said.

'Lovely to see you too, Trace.' He was trying to stop Mikey climbing her wall. As I was on my way home from work I caught the whole show.

'If it's twins, Kevin Regan, I'll leave one on your doorstep, I swear,' Tracy said.

'You already have twins – it'll be fine,' I told her, in my best reassuring voice.

Tracy ignored me and fixed her eyes on Kevin. 'You and your slagging, Kevin Regan. Mocking is catching.'

'I've been blamed for a few things in my time, Tracy, but I think this time, for once, I'm completely innocent. Have a word with Derek.'

'Oh, I will, don't you worry,' Tracy said, and climbed into the car.

The next day after work I called to Tracy with the cutest little pair of baby shoes I'd ever seen. I'd spotted them in town and couldn't resist them.

Paddy carried them and banged excitedly on the door. Rhonda, her mother, answered.

'Ruth, she's in the sitting room,' she whispered, holding my arm tightly. 'She's taking it very bad.'

'What's up?' I asked, knowing already in my heart.

Rhonda shook her dark head. 'No heartbeat,' she said. 'Go in there and talk to her.'

I went into the living room. Tracy was hunched on the couch, a red throw round her knees. She looked up when she saw me and tears spilled down her face.

'I'm so sorry,' I said, sat on the couch and hugged her to me. After a few minutes she sat up and wiped her eyes with a bunched-up tissue. 'Oh, Tracy,' I said, 'it must have been awful for you.'

Her eyes were dry now, but with huge dark circles beneath them. 'We were joking, Derek and me, about Kevin and the slagging about twins and . . .'

I caught her hand and held it tightly. 'You don't have to talk about it if you don't want to, love.'

'The radiographer put the jelly on me and all of us looked at the screen and I knew straight away, Ruth.' She wiped fresh tears from her eyes. I realised then that I was crying too and reached for the tissue box on the coffee-table.

'It was the silence. Your woman was so silent . . . then Derek said, joking, "Well, tell us, is it twins?"'

'Oh, Tracy.'

'And I said, "My baby's dead." The woman didn't answer but she didn't have to. I knew.'

I pulled her small body into me, but she pushed

herself away. 'It's my fault,' she said, looking into the empty fireplace. 'The baby's dead over me.'

'Tracy, how can you say such a thing? You did everything by the book! You stopped drinking, smoking, you ate well—'

'I didn't want the baby. The night I found out I was pregnant I stayed awake all night willing it to go away.'

'Trace, everybody's like that at first with an unplanned pregnancy. It's the most normal thing in the world.'

Tracy looked at me with tired black eyes. 'I did everything by the book, all right, except the one thing that matters. I didn't love it at first. I didn't want it.' She blew her nose and resumed staring into the grate.

I took her face in both my hands and made her look at me. 'You're the best mother on the planet. You'd have loved that baby, and you can't go blaming yourself.'

'Do you know what the nurse said?'

'No.'

'"Sure aren't you young? You can always have another."' She laughed. An empty, hollow sound that I'd never heard her utter before.

'You poor baby,' I said.

Just then Chloe and Paddy burst into the room, followed by a protesting Rhonda.

'Come back out, you two,' said Rhonda, but Chloe had already launched herself into her mother's arms. Tracy buried her face in her daughter's shiny black hair.

'Tracy, open it! It's a surprise,' said Paddy, and handed her the beautifully wrapped gift before I could stop him.

She smiled wanly and opened the tiny parcel, took out the shoes and held them to her chest as tears streamed down her face. I could hear Rhonda sniffling in the background.

'Come on, Chloe,' I said, 'Let's find your sisters and go for takeaway. Would you like that?'

'Yippee,' she and Paddy shouted.

Tracy's sadness was painful to watch but at least I could repay her for all the love and support she'd shown me during those first horrible weeks after Gibraltar. I took the children to my house, cooked meals and made sure that people called to see her. Kevin practically lived up there and soon had her watching rugby videos with him.

'How's Tracy?' Emerson asked, a few days later, when he called to collect Paddy.

'Sad.'

'Only to be expected.' Emerson draped a long arm over the back of the adjoining chair. 'Can I ask you a question?'

I nodded.

'You know how I feel about you,' he said.

I didn't answer.

'And how I feel about what I did.'

I still didn't answer.

'And I know that I don't have the right to ask this, but I've thought about it for ages and I just

have to.' He fiddled with his wedding ring, which
he still wore. I was so still I could have been a statue.
'Ruth, do you think there's any way that you could
forgive me for what I did? I'll do anything you want.
Go anywhere you want. Be anyone you want.
Anything at all, if you'd even think about it.' He
stopped speaking but his eyes never moved from
mine.

'I don't know,' I said, because that was the truth.

'Will you think about it?'

'OK.'

'Thank you.'

Just at that point Paddy bounded in, full of excitement, and we were able to pretend to be normal as
they prepared to leave. Once they'd gone, though, I
was unable to think about anything – let alone a way
to salvage my marriage. I threw myself on to the
sofa and watched TV until I dozed off.

When I woke I lay there half watching *Seven Brides
For Seven Brothers* and tried to think it all out. Emerson
and I had once had something special – of that much
I was still convinced. We also had Paddy and he had
to be our priority. But how could I possibly forgive
what he did? I went outside into the garden.

It was slowly unfolding its secrets as the sun
became warmer and I remembered how happy I'd
been just a year earlier. Emerson was right – it was
worth having a go to see if we could recapture
what we'd lost. I felt scared but relieved.

Just after seven the doorbell rang. It was Emerson
carrying an exhausted but happy Paddy. 'We ate,'

he said. 'I brought him to Ogonnolloe and you know my mother – she just can't resist feeding people.'

I took Paddy from him and pulled off the Mickey Mouse hat. Paddy protested and jammed it back on.

'OK,' Emerson said, 'I'll be off. See you tomorrow?'

'Emerson?'

He turned back to me.

'I do want to try.'

His face dissolved into a wide smile. 'Oh, my God. Oh, my God. I don't know what to say, Ruth.'

'Don't say anything. I'm saying I want to try but I don't know if I can.'

His face became serious. 'I understand.'

'This isn't the time or place,' I said, indicating Paddy.

'Can we set a time and place?'

'How about tomorrow? You could stay for dinner and we could talk after Paddy goes to bed.'

'Perfect.'

I closed the door behind him. I wasn't sure if I was elated or terrified at what I'd done. All I knew was that I'd started a process. Though I wasn't sure where it was going to lead I knew that it might bring me to some kind of resolution of the events of the past year.

54

I didn't tell anyone about my decision. I couldn't. Anyway, if Emerson and I had a go at repairing our relationship it'd be soon enough then to tell people. So, next day I went about my business as normal. Talked to Kathleen on the phone about Aisling's inoculations. Helped Gary with his election mail-shot. Had coffee with Tracy and Kevin in the after-noon and avoided the subject of Emerson – even with myself.

I made lasagne and salad for dinner while Paddy was off with Emerson. I showered, changed into a pair of jeans and a low-cut pale blue T-shirt. I finished putting on some makeup just as the door-bell announced that my husband and son had returned. I hurried down the stairs, knees wobbly at the prospect of the evening together. On the doorstep Emerson, too, looked freshly showered and changed. He handed me a red rosebud.

'Thanks,' I said, and went to the kitchen, aware of the smell, the heat, the very presence of him. We had dinner and I enjoyed the normality of us all being together. By eight o'clock Paddy was grumpy so Emerson offered to put him to bed.

I settled into an old episode of *Quincy*. Half-way through – when Quincy was close to catching the murderer – Emerson came back. 'Everything OK?' I asked.

'Fast asleep,' he said. 'I read *The Cat in the Hat* three times and that seemed to do the trick.'

He sat down at the other end of the sofa and pretended to watch TV too, but I'd lost the thread of the plot. 'We should talk,' I said, but with my eyes fixed to the TV.

'OK.'

'I don't know what to say.'

Emerson didn't answer for a few seconds. 'Me neither,' he said eventually.

'I want to trust you,' I said, and this time I turned to him. Our eyes locked.

'I know.'

'But I don't know how, and if I don't trust you we can never make it work.'

Emerson nodded slowly. 'I have an idea.'

'OK.'

'What if I could do something that would prove how serious I am in wanting you back?'

'I believe you already.'

'I know, but what if I was to do something that might make it easier for you to trust me and would also show you how much I love you?'

'Like what?'

He smiled uncertainly. 'I could give up making films.'

'I couldn't ask you to do that.'

'You wouldn't be asking me – I'd be offering. I've had a lot of time to think in the past year and one thing I know is that film-making doesn't lend itself to family life.'

'But you love making movies.'

'Not as much as I love you and Paddy.'

'I don't know if it'd fix anything.'

Emerson edged closer to me, never once losing eye-contact. 'I know that but maybe it'd be a place to begin.' He laid his hand on the side of my face.

'It'd feel like I'd be punishing you,' I said, 'and that doesn't seem right.'

'You wouldn't be doing anything – it'd be my decision and it isn't a punishment.'

'What would you do if you weren't working in film?'

'Well, I'm thinking of setting up a TV production company and doing work for RTE and the English networks.'

I was humbled by the offer he was making, but still not certain that it would be enough to repair the damage.

'What do you think?' he asked. He was right beside me now and I could feel his breath on my cheek.

'Maybe if we move really slowly,' I whispered. 'Maybe if we start from scratch we'll see if things could work out.'

He kissed me gently on the lips and I kissed him back.

'We can go as fast or as slow as you like,' he

murmured into my hair, kissing my neck. 'I'll do anything for you.'

Then he kissed the base of my throat and I moaned just as the sitting-room door opened. I pulled away from him.

'Kevin! Jeez, how are you? How did you get in?'

'I think your bell's broken – I rang loads of times and the door was open so I let myself in. I'm out of milk and Mikey's asleep and I thought I'd see if you had a spare pint – sorry.'

I stood up. 'I have loads of milk – hold on a minute and I'll get some.'

'No, look, it's fine – I'll try Tracy.'

'Kevin, really – hold on. This is Emerson. You two have never met properly. Emerson – Kevin.'

Emerson stood up and they shook hands. I hurried out of the room into the kitchen and got some milk out of the fridge. When I returned they were facing each other like boxers in a ring.

'Here you go.'

Kevin thanked me formally but he was too busy staring at Emerson to look at me.

'Is that it, Kev? Need anything else? A cup of sugar, maybe?'

Kevin raised an eyebrow. 'There is one other thing, actually. I have to go to Ballymoran tomorrow with Brian Sheedy. He's the environmental engineer PAP are getting to do the new report. I'm worried in case I'm delayed.'

'Do you want me to pick up Mikey?'

'If you would.'

'No problem.'

'I'll call the teacher and tell her you're coming – I think she'll keep him in the classroom this time.'

'Great,' I said.

'Well,' he said, 'I won't keep you people from what you were doing. Nice to meet you, Emerson. I've heard a lot about you.'

Emerson nodded, his face as formal as Kevin's. 'You too. Take care.'

Kevin was gone before I could see him out. As the front door closed, Emerson sat back on the sofa. 'Seems like a nice guy,' he said.

'Kevin is a great friend,' I said, sitting on the arm of a chair.

We didn't speak for a few seconds and I hoped that Emerson didn't intend us to take up where we'd left off. I wasn't as sure about having sex with him as I had been ten minutes earlier. My heart sank: I could see there would be a lot more of this awkward carry-on in the future. I was too uncertain of how I felt to be embarking on mending my marriage.

'How about if we go to see a movie on Friday night?' Emerson said suddenly. 'I want to court you in the old-fashioned way. Wine and dine you. Bring you flowers and chocolates. Bring you to the movies – that sort of thing.' He stopped and looked into my eyes. 'I'm not in a hurry, I promise you.'

Suddenly my heart was light. 'Promise you won't become a bitter old man going on and on about how great you were when you were a hotshot film-maker.'

'I promise.'

'OK, then. Pick me up on Friday at eight – there's a movie I'd like to see.'

'Excellent. What is it?'

'*Girls Underground* – they say it's the chick flick of the decade.'

Emerson groaned.

'Ah, yes,' I said, examining my nails. 'Perhaps we might go clothes shopping on Saturday. And then? I don't know – but I'm sure there's another chick flick or two we can take in at the weekend.'

'How about if I hack off my leg instead?'

I grinned. 'Nothing like as much fun for me.'

The phone rang just after Emerson left.

'Ruth, sorry to rush but I'm a bit up the walls,' Gary said. 'I thought we might meet tomorrow – I'll be in Limerick. They're launching a new environmental-science project tomorrow at the university and I've been asked to open it.'

'Very nice,' I said.

'I was hoping you might come along.'

'Gee, Gary, thanks, but I can't – Kevin is going to Ballymoran and I have to pick Mikey up from school.'

'Oh, that's a shame. Maybe I'll give you a bell when I finish at UL?'

'That's fine,' I said. 'It'd be great to see you if you get a chance.'

'OK – better fly. Everything all right with you and Paddy?'

'Never better.'

'Hopefully we'll touch base tomorrow. Goodnight, dear.'

'Night, Gary.'

As I hung up it struck me again that Kevin was way off base with Gary. Little as I knew about the subject even I could see that he was well respected in environmental circles. Surely that meant something.

55

I told Tracy that I'd decided to give Emerson another chance. She didn't say anything for ages. Eventually the tension was too much for me. 'Well?' I asked.

She took a deep breath and gave me a lovely Tracy smile. 'He seems sincere.'

'I don't know that I can do it, but it's worth a try.'

She nodded slowly. 'Especially for Paddy's sake.'

'Exactly. It's definitely best for Paddy if we can sort out our differences. What do you think you'd do if you were me?'

'You mean after I'd castrated the bastard, murdered the woman and done time for my crime?'

'Whatever.'

'I don't know. When you have kids you have to keep them at the centre of your mind. I might give him a second chance but I don't know.'

I sighed. 'Me either, but time will tell. Meanwhile I'm making him come shopping and go to every chick flick that opens.'

'Good,' she said approvingly.

'Yeah, I just wish I knew if it was going to work out.'

Tracy sighed. 'If there's one thing I know about

life, Ruth, it's that there are no guarantees. You just have to learn to roll with the punches.'

I collected Mikey from school without incident and he and I called into the supermarket to pick up a few groceries. I had just pulled up outside my house when my phone rang. Mikey scrambled out of the car to join Chloe and Paddy in Tracy's front garden and I fished in my bag.

'Hello?'

'Ruth Burke?'

'Yes?'

'Hi – this is Brian Sheedy. Kevin Regan asked me to call you.'

'Oh, hello.'

'Um . . . there's been a bit of an incident – Kevin's been beaten up.'

'What?'

'He's fine, don't worry. We're here in A and E and they're checking him out at the minute. He asked me to give you a call to see if you'd look after his little boy.'

My head reeled. 'Of course I will,' I said. 'He's here with me anyway.'

'That's great. I'll tell Kevin. Nice to speak with you.'

'Hold on! What happened?'

'Kevin was beaten up,' Brian Sheedy said slowly, as if he was losing patience with me.

'I know, but how?'

'The usual way – a couple of big blokes gave him a hiding.'

Now *I* was losing patience. 'Yes, but why?'

'Well, we don't know the answer to that one.'

'Where were you? Did they beat you up as well?'

'No. I'd left before Kevin. I stopped at a garage five or six miles from Ballymoran and discovered I'd lost my wallet. I searched the car and then figured maybe it'd fallen out of my pocket. I tried calling Kevin but there was no answer so I drove back. Kevin's car was still parked on the road outside the last field we'd been in so I stopped. There was another car there as well – a green Toyota. I thought it was someone from PAP. I went in and there they were, these two huge blokes kicking the shit out of Kevin. I shouted and they ran away. That's it, really.'

'You were lucky they scarpered,' I said.

Brian Sheedy laughed. 'That's what my wife said. I didn't think about it at the time. Anyway, I brought Kevin here and that's about all there is to tell you at the moment.'

'Will he be OK, do you think?' My voice was shaking.

'He'll be fine – just needs to be cleaned up. I'll stay here and give you a call if there are any developments.'

'Thanks,' I said.

'Talk to you later.'

I stared at the phone for a few seconds after he'd hung up. Then abandoned the groceries, went in to Tracy and told her what had happened. She was in the middle of cleaning out her kitchen presses so her whole kitchen looked like an explosion had taken place.

'Fuck,' was all she said, as she knelt on the floor in front of the sink press. 'But he's OK?'

'I'm not sure. Your man says he is but they must have wanted to hurt him.'

Tracy stood up and peeled off her yellow rubber gloves. 'Somebody wants this whole thing covered up very badly.'

I nodded.

'Badly enough to try to put Kevin out of action.'

I felt a shiver of terror run up my spine.

She smiled. 'Which is a good thing, really.'

'What?'

She folded her gloves neatly and put them on the draining-board. 'It means he's nearly there.'

'Well, if he can stay alive long enough.'

Tracy grimaced. 'All he needs now is a break and then their goose will be cooked – the bastards.'

My phone rang and we looked at each other. With a shaking hand I pressed the pick-up button.

'Ruth?'

'Kevin! Oh, Jesus, Kev, are you OK?'

'I'm fine, really. Where's Mikey?'

'Here in Tracy's with me. Are you still in the hospital?'

'Yeah. They X-rayed me and I'm fine, except for three cracked ribs, a few cuts and a split lip – and they say I'll have two lovely shiners in the morning.'

'Who were they?'

'No idea – they had Dublin accents so I'd say they were hired muscle.'

'Jesus! What if Brian hadn't come along?'

'Yeah, but he did. The thing I can't figure out is how they knew I was in Ballymoran.'

'Maybe they followed you.'

'No,' he said, 'I don't think so – I've been looking out for that since they tried to take Mikey.'

'Who knew you were going to Ballymoran?'

'Brian, obviously. You. Oh, yeah, and your ex-husband – maybe he had me beaten up?'

'Very funny. Anybody else?'

'No. We weren't supposed to go until Wednesday, then Brian called me last night and changed to today. That was why I came in to ask you to collect Mikey.'

'Are you sure nobody else knew?'

'Positive.'

'Then maybe they're better at following you than you thought.'

'Maybe. Brian's going to drop me out to collect my car and then I'll be home. Will you hold on to Mikey until then?'

'Shall I go and get the car?'

'No, I'll be fine, as long as Mikey's safe. See you in a little while.'

I hung up. 'He's OK,' I told Tracy. 'Cracked ribs, cuts and bruises, but OK. He'll be here in a while.'

Tracy didn't answer.

'Tracy?'

'I have an idea.'

'What?'

'I think we should ask Kathleen. To have a bit of a session about Ballymoran.'

I laughed.

'Ruth, I'm serious. You told me yourself that the police often consult psychics and that she did a lot of that work in England.'

'That kind of stuff is sad – desperate.' I sniggered.

'Maybe,' Tracy said, 'but we're pretty desperate, aren't we? If she can't help us we're exactly where we are now, so what harm?'

'Kevin would never agree.'

'Who said anything about asking him?'

Which was how Tracy and I ended up sitting in Kathleen's darkened consultation room the next evening.

'Rider-Waite,' Kathleen said, when Tracy finished explaining what we wanted.

'What?'

'I have a lovely Rider-Waite tarot deck I like to use – very good for unravelling difficult problems.' She rummaged in the drawers of a mahogany sideboard. 'I know it's here somewhere,' she said, piling crystals, beads and tiny brown bottles on the dresser shelves. 'Aha! There we go.' She came to the table with a purple velvet-covered box in her hands. 'My very first deck,' she said. 'Never lets me down.'

Solemnly, she lifted the lid off the box and produced a deck of colourful tarot cards. Beside them in a separate compartment was a length of folded purple silk, which she opened out and spread on the table. Then she placed the cards face down on it.

'I wonder which of you should shuffle the deck,' she said softly.

Tracy stifled a giggle.

'Ruth, you should do it.'

I jumped at my name. 'Why?'

'I'm not sure but I feel strongly it should be you.'

I picked up the cards.

'Please shuffle them, concentrating on what you want to know,' Kathleen said.

The only question I could think of was, 'Why the hell are we doing this?' but I didn't say it so I shuffled and replaced the cards on the silk.

'Now. Using your right hand, cut the deck three times,' Kathleen hold me.

Again I did as she asked. She stared at the cards for a few seconds, then laid out twelve in a circle. I watched as the Victorian illustrations emerged, every minute expecting her to say something but she was focused on what she was doing. When she finished we gazed at the cards in front of us. She began to explain about swords and cups, pentacles and wands, then something called the major arcana.

'Things are going to resolve themselves,' she said. She pointed to a card that showed a young woman half clad in a length of violet silk, carrying two wands and surrounded by an oval garland of flowers. 'This card is called the World and it signifies integration and happiness.'

'Sorry?'

Kathleen smiled. 'Well, simply put, it means you'll find yourself and be happy.'

I smiled back. 'That's good news. Anything else?'

'Not really. See – here is the difficult time you've been through. Have a look at this card.'

I saw a man lying on the ground with ten swords stuck into him.

Suddenly Kathleen gave a loud moan. '*Ohhh-hhhhhhhh*,' Kathleen said, eyes closed, head thrown back. '*Ohhhhhhhh.*'

Tracy grabbed my thigh under the table. I hit her hand as her nails dug into me. 'Stop!' I hissed.

'What's wrong with her?' Tracy said, eyes wide with fear.

'Nothing. She'll be fine in a minute – it's just a trance.'

Kathleen sat upright and her eyes opened. She grabbed my hand. 'The answer is in your work,' she said.

'What answer?' I said.

'Search in your place of work and you'll find the new key,' she said, staring blankly at me.

I sat very still. Kathleen squeezed my hand. 'Search!' she shouted. 'Search! Seek and ye shall find, that's what he says – unsought goes un-detected.'

'OK, OK!' I said, untangling my hand. Kathleen slumped into her chair and her eyes closed again.

'Fuck,' Tracy whispered. 'What was that about?'

Kathleen's eyes opened. 'Whew!' she said. 'That was quite a blast from the other side.'

'Did they tell you anything about Ballymoran?' Tracy asked.

'No. Just that stuff about the key at Ruth's work, and that someone else knows.'

Tracy was frowning now. 'Maybe there's a key to a safety-deposit box or something at the hotel.'

I sighed impatiently.

'No, really, Ruth, maybe if we find the key we'll find something that'll help prove what's going on in Ballymoran. Do people in Limerick have safety-deposit boxes like in the movies?'

'I don't think so – except in banks maybe.'

'Are you sure we have to look for a key?' Tracy asked Kathleen.

Kathleen nodded. 'Positive. That's what he said.'

'Nothing else?' Tracy asked. 'No names or anything like that?'

I knew there would never be anything as useful as a name coming out of one of Kathleen's trances.

Kathleen was smiling at us as if she'd solved the Riddle of the Sphinx. 'Just that. The key is at Ruth's work and that somebody else knows.'

'Obviously somebody else knows. Is that it, so, Kathleen?'

Kathleen nodded. 'The cards don't tell me anything about Ballymoran – they're all about Ruth.'

I groaned.

'Go on, tell us,' Tracy said, sitting forward.

'No, we've taken enough of your time, Kathleen, we'll just go – see you later.'

'No way,' Tracy protested. 'What do they say, Kathleen?'

'They mostly show Ruth's journey and how she

has developed. There's just one card that I'm not sure of – this one.'

Kathleen waved her hand over a card that depicted a handsome knight on horseback, wearing a winged helmet and holding a golden cup in his right hand.

'What do you think it means?' Tracy asked.

'When I read the cards for a woman, this card often comes up in connection with love.'

'Oh. In a good way?'

'Very good usually – I could name at least five ex-clients who have married within six months of turning up the Knight of Cups.'

'But she's already married,' Tracy said.

'I know.'

'Could it mean a new start with Emerson?'

Kathleen fixed all her attention on the card. 'Could be. Not usual but possible. Usually it's a new and true love but maybe this reconciliation will bring you just that.'

I smiled and stood up. 'Hopefully. Come on, Trace, let's get going.'

I couldn't wait to get away so I kissed Kathleen and Aisling and said we needed to get home because Derek had to go to work and he was minding the children.

56

Tracy challenged me about my lie in the car. 'Derek isn't going to work. He's at home with Kevin and the kids watching a match.'

I pulled away from the kerb. 'I know.'

'They won't even want to go to the pub with Kevin in the state he's in.'

'I know.'

'So why did you lie to your mother?'

'That stuff gives me the creeps.'

'I don't know why if you don't believe it.'

'It just does.'

'I thought it was interesting. Can we go and have a quick look in Drury's for that key?'

'No!'

'For God's sake, Ruth, why not?'

'It's stupid, Tracy. Kevin's been searching for months for evidence to prove the pollution in Ballymoran and you think Kathleen can tell us just like that?'

'Well, if you have any better ideas for how we can help Kevin, I'm all ears.'

I glanced at her as I drove. Her mouth was set in an angry line. I couldn't believe I'd let her persuade me to ask Kathleen for a prediction and now she wanted me to act on some gobbledegook. The whole thing was insane. Tracy didn't say a word as I drove through the dark, evening streets. This had all been a big mistake. It was bad enough when Kathleen went into spontaneous trances and foisted her predictions on me but this time I couldn't even complain – I'd asked her to do it.

The neon sign advertising Drury's flashed over the rooftops.

'Oh, for God's sake!' I said, aloud, indicating right. 'If it'll shut you up, it'll be worth it.'

Tracy turned and grinned at me. 'Good girl.'

I parked the car and walked towards the front doors. Tracy followed me, chattering about keys and hiding-places and safety-deposit boxes. We went through the doors in the lobby. It was ten o'clock and the hotel was buzzing. I waved at Geraldine Farrell, one of the evening receptionists, and she waved back, then turned to a customer. 'Now,' I said, to Tracy, 'where would you like to look for the key?' I could see that her resolve was wavering.

'I have it!' she said suddenly. 'The keys to the hotel rooms! It must be one of those.'

'No such thing any more. We use electronic swipe cards.'

'Shit,' Tracy said, biting her lip. 'Are there any others?'

'Probably to the main doors of the hotel but I don't see how they could be significant.'

'Maybe one is new.'

'I just don't see how the keys to Drury's are going to solve this.'

'They're keys, aren't they? Where are they?'

'In the back office, usually – but they're just door keys, Trace, you're grasping at straws.'

Tracy ignored me. 'Can I see them?'

'Why?'

'Please.'

I led the way behind the reception counter, muttering an excuse to Geraldine about forgetting my purse as we passed. The office was in darkness so I switched on the lights, walked straight to the desk and opened the top drawer. Inside was a large bunch of Yale keys. Tracy picked them up.

'See?' I said. 'Just ordinary keys and they're not even new.'

Tracy scrutinised them while I tidied the top of the desk. Avril was a holy terror for leaving coffee cups around. Tracy dropped the keys back into the drawer.

'Can we go, so?' I said.

She nodded, scanning the office with her eyes. 'OK.'

'I'm sorry, Trace – I knew there wasn't anything here.'

I reached out my hand to switch off the light and jumped when Tracy screamed. Her face was animated and she was pointing. 'The safe!' she shouted. 'If I had important keys in an hotel I'd leave them in the safe.'

'There aren't any keys in that safe.'

'Are you sure?'

'Yes! I put stuff into it every day.'

'Maybe they're in an envelope or something.'

I shook my head.

'Are you a hundred per cent sure?' Tracy asked, grabbing my arm.

'Ninety-nine.'

'Humour me,' she said.

I stalked over, bent down in front of the safe and twisted the knob. The heavy door swung open to reveal a jewellery box and a small stack of envelopes. Tracy bent down beside me, removed everything and sat on the floor. I considered objecting but figured that if I just shut up she'd finish faster and we could go home.

She opened the jewellery box, had a look inside and replaced it in the safe. Then she turned over the envelopes, one by one, and shook them vigorously. She looked more disappointed with each non-rattly envelope. I said nothing. The second last was a large white one. When she shook it, it made the unmistakable shuffling noise of money. But no odd shapes along the sides and no clinking noises to indicate the presence of a key. Tracy handed it to me and I was just about to replace it in the safe when I saw the name scrawled on the front in Avril's handwriting: Mr G. O'Donoghue. My heart skipped a beat. It couldn't be. Not after all this time. Gingerly, I prised open the seal, pushing pictures of myself in the dole queue to the back of my head. If I was wrong I could be fired for opening a client's envelope without permission. When I tipped it forward a thick wad of money, secured with an elastic band, a bank deposit book and a wine-coloured passport plopped on to the floor.

Tracy picked up the money. 'Jesus, Ruth – whose is this? There must be at least a couple of thousand here.'

I opened the passport and flicked to the back page. There he was – Ger O'Donoghue – the distraught, suicidal drunk I'd picked up off the foyer floor less than twenty-four hours before he'd plunged to his death. Then I opened the deposit book and saw that he'd withdrawn 3,273 euro on 14 June.

'Who is he?'

'The engineer guy who killed himself off the tax office.'

'Jesus! Didn't he write that report for Ballymoran?'

'So Kevin said.'

'Spooky.'

'Coincidence.'

'I don't know about that,' Tracy said, replacing everything else in the safe. 'Will I lock it?'

I stood up, holding the passport. Tracy handed me the money and I replaced everything in the envelope.

'What will we do with it?' she said.

'Nothing.'

'But it might lead us to the key. Maybe his wife has a key to something?'

'For God's sake, Tracy!'

'Please – we'll bring it to his wife, how about that?'

'No way. Look, I'll call Janet and ask her what to do with it. She's the boss, though, so I have to do whatever she says – OK?'

Tracy waited impatiently as I dialled Janet's home number. When she answered I could hear movie music in the background.

'Hi, Janet – it's Ruth Burke. I'm in the office.'

'Hello, Ruth – are you OK?'

'Grand. I was just looking for something I thought I left behind today.' I glared at Tracy. 'My house keys – I thought I'd accidentally locked them in the safe this morning. Anyway, when I opened it I found this envelope and it was open and I don't know how to tell you this but – did you hear about the guy who jumped off the tax office a few months ago?'

'Yes.'

'Well, he was staying here at the hotel.'

'Oh, I thought he was local?'

'He was – I don't know why he was here.'

'What about him?'

'Well, this open envelope belonged to him.'

'Oh,' she said. 'That's odd. I wonder why it wasn't returned to his family after he died.'

'He'd checked out the day before so we weren't connected to the investigation, I suppose. It must have been overlooked.'

'OK – well, thanks for telling me, Ruth. I'll deal with it tomorrow.'

Tracy's face told me she was going to torment me, and before I could think better of it I heard myself say, 'Unless you'd like me to look up his home number now and see if I can contact his wife?'

Janet didn't answer for a moment and I was sure she suspected something.

'Well, if there's one thing I hate doing it's talking to people in awkward situations like this – would you mind, Ruth?'

'Not at all.'

'Make sure she signs for anything you give her.'

'Will do. See you in the morning.' I hung up and looked at Tracy. 'She says I can do it but to get his wife to sign for the envelope. What the hell do I do now?'

'Find his home number. Where would it be?'

'In the computer registration.' I reached past Tracy and switched on the computer. Less than a minute later we were looking at Ger O'Donoghue's registration last June. I copied down the home phone number, picked up the phone and dialled before I could change my mind. A quiet woman's voice answered after two or three rings.

'Hello – Mrs O'Donoghue?'

'Yes?'

'Um . . . um . . . this is Ruth Burke at Drury's Hotel . . . um . . . We were very sorry to hear of your husband's . . . death.'

'Thank you.'

'The thing is, we've just found an envelope in our hotel safe – your husband stayed here before he . . . Anyway, it was somehow overlooked. There's a quantity of money and a passport in the envelope and, well, it's yours now.'

'Oh.' Mrs O'Donoghue didn't say anything for a few seconds.

'Would you like to collect it?' I said.

She began to cry. I made a face at Tracy. Damn. Now what had we done?

'Look, Mrs O'Donoghue,' I said, after a little while, 'I'm really sorry. Is there anything I can do to help?'

She sniffed. 'I don't go out any more since Ger died . . . not much . . . well, not ever . . . I find it hard.'

I looked at the address on the computer screen and saw that it wasn't too far from my house. 'Do you still live at sixty-seven Young Street?'

'Yes.'

'Would it be a help if I dropped the envelope in to you?'

'Oh! That'd be great – if you wouldn't mind.'

'It'd be no problem – I'm afraid I'll have to get you to sign for it.'

'I'd be happy to do that.'

'OK. See you in about ten minutes.'

I hung up, grabbed a safe-deposit slip from the desk and walked out of the back office with Tracy at my heels, like an anxious terrier. We made straight for the car.

'Where are we going? To her house?' Tracy asked.

I didn't answer, just stuffed the envelope and the form into my handbag and started the car.

'Oh, my God!' Tracy said, hugging herself. 'I'll bet she has the key we've been looking for!'

'Oh, give it a rest! The poor woman has agoraphobia, by the sound of it. Don't start at her about keys. Maybe you should stay in the car while I go in and give her the envelope.'

Tracy laughed. 'No bloody way. I'm coming too.'

By that time we'd reached Young Street and I was struck by how odd it was that not only had Ger O'Donoghue stayed in a hotel in his own town, he'd chosen one just five minutes' drive from his house. Maybe they'd been fighting. I wouldn't have been too enamoured of a husband falling-down drunk like he was.

I pulled up outside the house. It was a tall redbrick terraced house with a neat garden and a stained-glass panel over the front door. The bell clanged and almost immediately a small, pointed face appeared round the door. The woman smiled and held it open for us. 'You must be from the hotel – please come in.'

Tracy and I followed her into a small, cosy sitting room. Somewhere else in the house a TV blared.

'Can I offer you some tea?' she said, motioning to us to sit down.

We perched on the edge of the sofa. 'No thank you, Mrs O'Donoghue,' I said, and held out the envelope towards her.

'Helen,' she said, taking it from me.

'I'm Ruth and this is Tracy, and we're very sorry to disturb you like this. If you want to check the envelope and sign the form we'll get out of your hair.'

She smiled distractedly as she opened the envelope. Her face quivered and she covered her mouth with a hand as she looked at her husband's photograph in the passport. The room was filled with an almost palpable sadness. What had been so bad that he could put his family through such suffering by killing himself? As if she'd heard my thoughts she looked at me. 'Ger didn't kill himself,' she said.

'Oh,' I said.

Her hands dropped to her sides. 'He didn't – I know he didn't. The police say they're sorry and all that but there was no sign of a struggle. No sign that anybody else was on the roof with him.'

She paused and two shiny tears ran down her cheeks. She wiped them with the back of the hand in which she was holding his passport.

'I'm so sorry for your loss,' Tracy said.

Helen O'Donoghue looked at her. 'Everything is wrong since he died. Everything. But I know something happened to him – even though nobody believes me and that's the worst part. That and sleeping alone.'

Tracy and I stood up. 'We'll be off, so,' I said gently. 'I wonder if you' mind . . .' I held out the hotel form to her. She picked up a pen from the mantelpiece and signed it.

'Thank you,' I said, folded the form and put it back into my bag.

★

Tracy and I hardly spoke two words in the car on the way home. I kept seeing those forlorn tears rolling down the woman's face and my heart ached. As I pulled up on our road, Tracy turned to me. 'I wonder if she'd talk to Kevin,' she said.

'Helen O'Donoghue?'

'Yeah. If she thinks somebody killed her husband and the Guards can't help, maybe he could. He's a journalist, after all.'

'Jesus, Tracy, who do you think he is? Clark Kent? He's already half dead from taking up the PAP cause – you'd hardly want him to be involved in yet another wild-goose chase.'

'I don't know,' she said. 'Ger O'Donoghue was the engineer who wrote that missing report, wasn't he?'

I nodded.

'She's his widow – you never know what information she might have that'd help Kevin.'

'I suppose.'

'I'll suggest it anyway,' she said, as we got out of the car. 'It might help that woman just to talk to somebody – tell them her story.'

'It can't hurt, I suppose,' I said. 'It's hard to come to terms with someone you love committing suicide.'

'I think I'll go straight to bed when I go in,' Tracy said.

'I'll just run in and collect Paddy, then we'll leave you alone.'

'Why don't you let him stay the night? He's surely asleep by now. You can come and collect him in the morning.'

I smiled. 'Thanks, Trace.'

We hugged briefly, then went our separate ways, each folded into a corner of the sadness we'd witnessed in Helen O'Donoghue.

57

The next day I went to work, then spent a lovely afternoon and evening with Paddy at Kathleen's. It was late when we got home and I had just put Paddy to bed when the doorbell rang.

'Hey,' Kevin said, grinning sheepishly as he clutched a bottle of sauvignon blanc. His face was a palette of red, black, yellow and blue, and I could see that the black eyes were coming in nicely. I stepped back and he followed me into the sitting room.

'What's the celebration?' I asked, fishing two wine glasses out of the sideboard.

Kevin grimaced. 'I'm not sure if celebration's the right word,' he said, as he uncorked the wine. 'I have something to tell you.'

'Oh,' I said, holding out my glass to be filled. He was getting back with Orla. That must be it, I thought, as the golden liquid filled the crystal glass. Well, I was trying to make things work with Emerson so why shouldn't he try for a reconciliation with her?

'Tracy told me about your adventures last night,' he said, sitting awkwardly on to the sofa. 'I went to see Helen O'Donoghue this morning.' He groaned as his ribs made contact with a cushion. 'She's one very traumatised woman.'

'What did she have to say?'

'She gave me a bag of files she found in their caravan in New Quay,' Kevin said. 'She's selling it and they were under one of the seats.'

'What was in them?'

'All sorts of things, but probably the most important is the original report about Ballymoran.'

'What?' I shouted. 'You're kidding me! What does it say?'

'It's pretty damning. Seems he found plenty of evidence of asbestos.'

'But I thought the report presented in the court case said there wasn't any,' I said.

'It did. But this report is a different kettle of fish. I can't know what was going on exactly for Ger O'Donoghue, and his wife said he never spoke to her about that sort of thing, but he was preoccupied and worried, she said, for a few months before he died and whenever she asked him what was wrong he'd say it was just work stuff and not to worry.'

'Maybe it had something to do with why he killed himself?'

'Maybe,' Kevin replied, 'and I said that to her, but she still swears he'd never have committed suicide.'

'But if he was worried . . .'

Kevin shrugged. 'She says she knew him better than anybody and she won't believe anything else.'

'So she thinks he was murdered?'

'Well, that's the only other explanation but there's no evidence to prove it.'

'Maybe we'll never know the truth,' I said. 'I must say, though, Kathleen's getting better at the old predictions.'

'What do you mean?'

'She kept telling us that the "new key" was at my work and in a way it was. The envelope with Ger O'Donoghue's stuff led us to his wife, which led you to her and she gave you the bag from the caravan in New Quay.'

Kevin laughed. 'Good old Kathleen.'

'I have to admit she was right – vague and cryptic, but right. I wonder what my chances are of getting the Lotto numbers.'

'Slim, but at least we know the truth about the Ring brothers and the asbestos.'

'Which is great,' I said. 'What'll happen now?'

'I've given the report to the police and there'll be a whole new investigation. They can get access to the Rings' bank accounts and other stuff I can't do.'

'So, the game is up,' I said, raising my glass. 'Congratulations.'

Kevin smiled weakly. 'It's not as simple as that – I'm afraid there's a a complication.'

I was puzzled.

'Gary,' he said. 'It appears he's into it up to his ears.'

'How do you know?'

'Ger must have been afraid because that bag is stuffed with photocopies of letters and reports, and even some taped telephone conversations with his boss and Gary. Tapes like that aren't admissible in court but even so . . .'

I didn't answer.

'One tape is particularly damning. Ger is telling Gary that he knows a false report was presented to the court with his name signed to it, and Gary is trying to calm him down and tell him there was probably a mistake, that he'll look into it and not to worry.'

'Did he look into it?'

'Well, Gary's line is that the Ballymoran report that was presented in court and is now missing was a perfectly good report. I've asked him plenty of questions about it and he denies all knowledge of any problem – a very different story from what can be heard on that tape.'

I shivered as the impact of what Kevin was saying came home to me. A horrible realisation dawned and I felt sick. Kevin was still talking, filling me in on the details, but I couldn't concentrate on what he was saying. Gary had used me to give him a family-man image in the press. He'd used me to get an in with PAP when all the time he'd been aiding and abetting the bastards who were dumping the asbestos that was killing the children. He'd probably used me in other ways I didn't know about.

And the worst thing was that I'd let him. I'd turned a blind eye to the false smiles and overly hearty hand-shakes. I'd told myself they were just tools of the trade. It was humiliating to think I'd been so desperate for recognition by my natural father that I'd willingly been duped. Then I had an even worse thought.

'Oh, my God!' I dropped my half-full glass.

'What? What's wrong, Ruth?'

I covered my face with my hands. 'I just realised something awful,' I said, through my fingers.

Kevin put his arms round me. 'Tell me. It can't be that bad.'

I dropped my hands. 'It is – it's worse. Do you remember how you were surprised that those thugs knew you and the new engineer were in Ballymoran? You said nobody knew? That the arrangement was changed at the last minute?'

He nodded.

'Gary knew,' I whispered. 'I told him,' I said. 'He rang and asked me to go to this launch and I said I couldn't. I told him I was picking up Mikey for you because you were going to Ballymoran with the engineer.'

I watched the pieces fall into place in Kevin's head. 'I'm sorry,' I said.

'You didn't do anything wrong.'

'They hurt you, Kevin! Jesus, except that your man came back for his wallet they might have killed you – or at least done you some terrible damage.' Kevin pulled me close and held me. Even though I felt guilty, ashamed and foolish, I also felt comforted, warm and safe. 'I'm sorry,' I said again, and pulled away. 'What will you do about it?'

'Tell the police, like I told them everything else.'

I began to pick up the pieces of broken glass and mopped at the spilled wine on the maple floor with a handful of tissues. Kevin helped me. When we'd

finished we stood looking at each other in the centre
of my living-room and I had a sudden flash of what
we must look like from the outside, which made me
laugh.

'What?' Kevin said.

'I don't know what we're like,' I said. 'Your eyes
are black and blue and mine are red – we must look
a sight.'

'Don't cry any more about Gary – he's just
another turkey-baster father.'

I sighed. 'I can't bear that I was so trusting in it,
though – pathetic! Wanting him to be everything I
needed him to be.'

'He's the bad guy, not you, Ruth. You just wanted
what everybody wants.'

'And what's that, Kev?'

'To be loved.'

'I suppose – and more fool me. Anyway, did you
write a piece for the paper?'

Kevin nodded. 'That's why I'm here – to warn
you. It'll be in the local papers and the *Independent*
tomorrow, then all over the press for a while yet, so
prepare yourself.'

'I'll be fine, but thanks for coming to tell me.'

Kevin brushed my lips with his, then turned
abruptly and left. I didn't follow him to the door
because somehow, as soon as he moved away from
me, the air around me felt cold and empty. I was
afraid I might ask him not to leave if I went after
him. And I knew that would be a mistake.

58

Once Helen O'Donoghue had given Kevin her dead husband's bag of files the whole Ballymoran débâcle unravelled like a badly knitted sweater. Kevin's articles were printed in the newspapers and all eyes were on Ballymoran. Everybody on the Environmental Commission resigned – all protesting innocence. The Ring brothers' operation was closed down pending an investigation by the Gardai. The government sent engineers, inspectors and specialists of every description to Ballymoran to mop up the mess. The PAP parents were reimbursed by the state and decided to use the money to fund treatments for the seriously ill children of the area. Kevin was a hero, and work showered in for him.

I was still smarting from the revelations about Gary but recovering slowly. He rang me three or four times but I refused to take his calls. However, it was almost impossible to avoid listening to him. His spin-doctors must have been working overtime because it seemed that every time I switched on the news, Gary was explaining how such a mistaken impression had been created about him. No, of course he wasn't involved in a cover-up over

Ballymoran, he said. How could anyone think such a thing? His record spoke for itself – twenty-five years as a candidate who upheld all moves to protect the environment. After all, who had led the government initiative in the Dáil to have asbestos removed from schools and hospitals in the first place? Gary. How could anybody think a man as concerned as he was about the environment and the health of the country's children could have been party to such criminal behaviour?

And it was working. Not on me – I was cured of my belief in Gary – but on the general population. At first there had been nothing but criticism of Gary but as the weeks passed the tide started to turn in his favour. Poor Gary, was the new line: he had been duped just like the rest of us. He settled down comfortably as leader of the People's Party, and those who had shouted for his resignation were accused of using this serious human tragedy as a political football. Until the shit really hit the fan.

One Monday morning, two weeks after the story had broken, we awoke to a major scandal. Nora Dundon, a secretary on the Environmental Commission, had gone to the *Irish Times* and spilled every single bean. They had all been involved in the dumping of asbestos in Ballymoran, she said. Nora had proof of backhanders, proof of bank deposits – off-shore as well as in Ireland – documents that showed everybody knew all along what was happening. Not only that, they were profiting nicely from the suffering of Ballymoran's children.

Nora could show that Boru Buildings had falsified the documents that they claimed proved they were exporting the asbestos to bona-fide treatment plants in Finland. It turned out they were exporting only a small percentage of the total waste as it was very expensive to have it processed, and the rest was being buried in the Ballymoran area.

I listened to the morning news, read the papers and Gary was as guilty as sin. Not only had he pressed for the reforms in the law to have the asbestos removed from public buildings, he'd been responsible for awarding the contracts and, coincidentally, Boru Buildings had been awarded almost half of them. Nora had documentation to back up every allegation and by lunchtime that day Gary had announced his resignation.

I wasn't surprised to learn the full extent of his dishonesty and corruption – by then I was well aware that he was a bastard. I didn't like it but I was getting over it. Worse things had happened to me. So what if I felt foolish? All I could do was live and learn, and try not to let my emotions run away with me. The bigger surprise was Nora Dundon, who turned out to be Deep Throat.

I could hardly believe it when Tracy told me. 'She rang Kevin this morning before it hit the papers.'

'Why did she come forward now? Why not earlier?'

'She was scared after Ger O'Donoghue died but she was also determined to expose it. Then when Kevin found the documents and all the information about Boru Buildings came out she knew she was on more solid ground.'

'It's like a movie.'

'I know. Anyway, that's it. All the mysteries are solved,' Tracy said.

'Yes, they are,' I said, nodding in agreement. But one of the biggest mysteries of all – how I was going to sort out my life – was still alive and thriving inside me.

59

Ever the consummate politician, Gary Kennedy checked himself into an addiction treatment centre.

'That fella's not an alcoholic,' Derek said, when I told him and Tracy.

'I know that, but he's trying to wriggle out of the shit that's going down about the Environmental Commission.'

'But won't it make him look bad if everybody thinks he's an alcoholic?'

Tracy laughed. 'It's the height of fashion, you fool.'

'Bastard,' Derek said.

'Bastard,' Tracy said.

'Bastard,' I echoed. 'Total bloody bastard. I'm well rid of him.'

Once he had gone into rehab Gary disappeared from the papers and I was glad. But almost as soon as he left the limelight another of the men in my life took his place. At least this time it was positive. Emerson's Cannes nomination was all over the papers.

I was glad for him, but when I read his interviews, his love of film-making was so obvious that I wondered could he ever really give it up. But I didn't dwell on it. Anyway, Trácy was so delighted with Emerson's new-found fame that I was carried along on the wave of her enthusiasm.

During all the hassle about Gary, Emerson had been a rock. He listened endlessly to my moans. He was always there when I needed him, and there were still no strings attached. I knew we couldn't go back to our pre-Gibraltar relationship but maybe we could build something new. So when he asked me, I was happy to accept his invitation to accompany him to Cannes.

'Brilliant!' he said, when I told him I'd love to go. His face lit up and I knew he was astounded that he hadn't had to spend days persuading me.

I sidled over to him and wound my arms round his waist. 'Why wouldn't I want to be present when my husband wins the Palme d'Or?'

Emerson bent down and kissed me. We hadn't had sex since our reconciliation, but I had a feeling that Cannes would change all that. As I prepared for the trip I selected sexy underwear to bring with me, and that was always a good sign. Maybe things were going to work out between us, after all.

It was spring and the weather had improved. Cherry blossom, new leaves and the tweeting of baby birds filled the world and I was cautiously optimistic. I saw little of Kevin for weeks after the Ballymoran scandal as he was always busy. Sometimes I found myself thinking about him and about that night when he'd told me what Gary had been up to and how I'd felt when he'd left. But I was committed to giving my marriage my best shot, so mostly I kept him out of my head.

One early May afternoon as I was arriving home from work, my head full of plans for Cannes, I found him waiting at my door. Emerson had collected Paddy from school and they had gone to Ogonnolloe so I was alone. So was Kevin. My heart gave a small jump when I saw him and I couldn't help but smile. He smiled back.

'Hey, stranger!' I said.

We walked together into my house and he followed me to the kitchen. As I chattered, filled the kettle and tidied away breakfast dishes, I was acutely aware of his presence. It was as though all my senses were amplified and that I could smell him, hear him, see him and feel him without touching him. I tried to think of something to talk about but nothing would come. He seemed to be the same as he trotted out half-sentences.

'Dublin was very busy . . .' he said.

'Oh,' I said, in front of the fridge with a litre of milk in my hand. 'Is that right?'

'Very busy,' he said.

'It was pretty busy here the last few days as well,' I said. 'Desperate traffic.'

'Oh.'

Eventually I'd put everything away and made tea. We sat on opposite sides of the kitchen table, looking at each other and looking away. My stomach was

sick and I didn't know why. Eventually Kevin gave
a long sigh.

'What?' I could see he was afraid of something.

'You can't go back with Emerson,' he said.

'What?'

'You heard me, Ruth. You can't go back with
Emerson. It's not the right thing to do.'

'Kevin, look . . .'

He held up his hand. 'Just hear me out. Why are
you doing it?'

'It's none of your business.'

He raised an eyebrow.

'OK. He asked me and I . . . There's Paddy – and
I know what he did was wrong but I can't just walk
away as if I was a kid.'

Kevin didn't say anything.

'What if it was you and Orla? Wouldn't you
think you should give it a shot? For Mikey's sake,
if nothing else?'

'I used to think I would but . . . now I know it'd
be a mistake if we got back together. You reckon you
had a good marriage before the stuff Emerson did
in Gibraltar, but have you asked yourself questions
about that? And even if it was good, a marriage is
like anything else. If you hit it hard enough you'll
destroy it.'

I didn't answer for a while. 'I don't know why
you're saying this, Kevin,' I said eventually.

He held my gaze. 'You're only doing it because
you think you should. Perfect Ruth has to do everything right all the time. And that's OK except how

do you know the right thing? Sometimes what looks like the right thing is wrong.'

He paused. I could hear my heart beat in my ears.

'All I'm saying is that you're making a mistake,' he said.

Anger was stirring inside me. 'Well, it won't be the first I've made.'

Kevin's lips tightened. 'What's that supposed to mean?'

'You know what it means, Kevin. Ever since Paris . . .' I stopped.

'Ever since Paris what?' he said.

'Paris ruined everything between us.'

'Is that what you think?'

I nodded. 'That's exactly what I think.'

'In that case I'd better go home.'

'Sounds like a plan.'

And then he was gone. This time, although I still felt the emptiness in the air after he'd left, I was too angry to be sad. So what if he thought I wanted to be perfect all the time? I didn't care what he thought of me. High-handed, pompous bastard! He could just fuck off and sort out his own shit and stop visiting it on me. I was sick of it. If Kevin couldn't get on with his life after his failed marriage that was too bad but it wasn't going to be true of me.

My friendship with Kevin was over – I'd struggled against admitting it for months but now it was clear: the sex had destroyed it. I put Kevin and everything to do with him out of my head to the point that I didn't even tell Tracy what had happened between us. Instead I focused on Emerson and my upcoming trip to Cannes.

Emerson left for the festival five days before I did. I'd decided a weekend in the South of France with the glitterati of the film world would be about all I could stick. Before he'd left, Emerson had arranged for Paddy to stay with his grandparents while I was away. There was great excitement in Ogonnolloe at the prospect of his arrival and any number of activities planned for his stay.

I arrived at Cannes airport on Friday morning to find Emerson waiting for me with a tiny bouquet of freesias. I knew by the look in his eye that he had high hopes for our first night in Cannes. But when we arrived at the Intercontinental Carlton – our luxurious hotel – I knew from the gnawing sensation in my abdomen that the only thing I'd be hugging that night was my stomach. My period had arrived a week early accompanied by a savage migraine. Luckily Emerson knew the drill and went to find a chemist. He came back half an hour later armed with strong painkillers, tampons and a hot-water bottle.

'You're a saint,' I said, snuggling under a pile of bedclothes as I watched him get dressed for a high-powered dinner with Directors Uncut, the avant-garde professional body of which he was president.

'I feel bad about leaving you alone,' he said, his tie half undone.

'I'll be grand. I'm drugged. And, anyway, the important thing is that I'll be better tomorrow – I wouldn't miss the award ceremony for the world.'

He kissed me and then he was gone. I watched ten minutes of bad French TV then fell asleep. I woke briefly at five a.m. and saw that he wasn't back but I was too sleepy to care.

The next time I woke it was seven and Emerson was sitting on the side of the bed, taking off his shoes. He was still in the clothes he'd worn to the dinner.

'Sorry, love. Did I wake you?'

'Emerson, it's seven in the morning.'

'I know, I know – that thing went on and on. Everybody was there.'

He undressed, lay down beside me and seemed to fall asleep as soon as his head hit the pillow. I, on the other hand, was wide awake and slipping into a morass of doubt and questions. I didn't want to go down that road again.

I jumped out of bed, showered, dressed and left my sleeping ex-husband in the darkened room. I felt like an impostor as I walked through the marble colonnade past the reception desk and down the white marble steps that led to the street. Across the road the Mediterranean spread like an azure carpet as far as the eye could see. The air was crisp and cool but the sky held the promise of a hot, sunny day. I needed coffee and walked rue de la Croisette in search of breakfast.

I found a tiny café that looked promising, sat at a table on the pavement and ordered coffee and a croissant. I watched the town come to life. Deliveries to shops, ordinary people going to work, revellers in evening clothes on their way home after a night on the tiles. They must have been at the same party as Emerson. A horrible knot of mistrust was forming in my gut and I didn't want to give it oxygen. I had no intention of living my life as one of those shrewish, jealous wives. That wasn't me. I had to trust him. He had been working all night, just as he'd said – end of story.

'Ruth?'

I jumped. 'Holy shit! Kevin! What the hell are you doing here?'

He stood on the pavement, folded newspaper in hand, dressed in cream combats and a khaki T-shirt. A pair of sunglasses was perched comically on his bald head. 'I'm covering the festival. Filling in for Laura Kelly at the paper.'

'I didn't know you were coming. You never said a thing.'

'Last minute. Is the coffee good?' he said, pulling up a chair.

I was still too surprised for ordinary conversation. Kevin beckoned the waitress and ordered in excellent French. She flirted shamelessly with him.

'Where are you staying?' he asked, pouring honey over a croissant.

'The Intercontinental Carlton.'

'Fuck off.'

'What?'

'Did you mortgage the house to pay for the room?'

'Seems Miramax are footing the bill.'

'Jesus! I wonder are there any bookies open – I'll put a few bob on Emerson's movie to win tonight.'

He wiped croissant crumbs off his chin with a linen napkin. Once I'd recovered from the surprise of seeing him I remembered our last meeting and I figured he was remembering too because we didn't seem to have anything to say to each other. We sipped our coffee and smiled awkwardly from time to time and my heart ached for what we'd lost. We'd been such good friends. I wished he'd go away and let me have my breakfast in peace. Suddenly he put his head into his hands.

'What's wrong?' I said, laying a hand on his arm before I could stop myself.

For a few seconds he didn't answer by which time I'd buried Mikey, had Kevin fired, sick, remarried to Orla and in debt to mobsters.

'Jesus, Kevin, you have to tell me what's wrong.'

He dropped his hands. 'I'm lying.'

'About what?'

'I made Laura give me the Cannes gig – she owed me. Then I had to persuade my editor – that was the hard part, but here I am.'

'Kevin, what the hell are you talking about?'

'I told you, Laura gave me—'

'Stop. How did you lie to me?'

'Would you like more coffee?'

'Answer my question.'

'I came here because of you. Last Chance Saloon.'

I wanted to say I didn't know what he meant but that would have been a lie.

'What happened in Paris—' he began.

'Don't,' I said. 'It was sex, Kevin.'

'It was more than that. When I came back I sorted myself out. I finished with Avril.'

I laughed but he didn't notice.

'More importantly, I finished with Orla.'

That surprised me.

'After Paris I saw my relationship with her for what it was.'

'And what was it?'

'I was afraid to let go. To be alone.'

'I know that feeling.'

'The only thing about it, Ruth, was that once I resolved that problem it left me with another.'

'Which was?'

I could almost see him brace himself to answer. 'You. When my head cleared I saw the beach at Fanore, Paris, our friendship – everything about us – in a different light. I've thought long and hard about this but with all my reservations I still couldn't convince myself. I tried to tell you and I couldn't. But even after that I knew I had no choice. I had to come clean. There's you and Emerson. There's Paddy. There's Mikey. But I still had to say it. I love you.'

I stared into my coffee cup. I didn't even look up when I heard the chair scrape and him walking away. I fiddled with the twenty euro he'd thrown on the table. My head whirled like a merry-go-round. I could no longer deny the truth that if there was one person on the planet with whom I'd made an immediate, close and real connection, it was Kevin Regan. But was it love?

60

I spent the rest of the day in a daze. When I got back to the hotel Emerson was up and showered, eager to show me round Cannes. And I was happy to comply – anything so that I wouldn't have to think. First we traipsed through the rows of national pavilions where the film folk from each country congregated to show their wares. Emerson seemed to know everybody in the Irish pavilion but he didn't engage with them.

When we'd finished that we had some lunch at a small café on rue de la Croisette. The long crescent-shaped street arched elegantly round the immense stretch of golden sandy beach. It was bright, glamorous and bustling with energy but it was lost on me. I felt so flat and depressed that nothing could lift my spirits. Every now and then Emerson asked if I was OK. I'd reassure him and make a supreme effort to chat.

After lunch he asked what I wanted to do and I suggested shopping. He led me into the commercial centre of Cannes and I spent all afternoon filling my head with clothing issues. Where could I find shoes to go with the trousers I'd bought in the Brown

Thomas sale? Or exactly the right shade of pink lipstick? What could I find to bring home to Paddy? Kathleen? Tracy? Derek? Avril?

Emerson never complained, just followed me from shop to shop carrying the bags. By the time I'd completed my purchases it was almost dinnertime. Emerson told me he'd reserved a table for us back at the hotel.

'I need to get to the Palais pretty early,' he said. 'Is that OK with you?'

'Fine,' I said, in the understatement of the century. The more I had to do to keep me distracted the better.

We made our way back to the hotel, deposited our bags, then set off for the chandelier-hung dining room. A solemn waiter met us at the door and we were shown to a table that was a masterpiece in linen, silver and crystal. We ordered a huge seafood platter between us, but I barely managed to swallow a couple of prawns. Emerson made up for my lack of appetite and I thought how wonderfully relaxed he was, considering the ceremony was almost upon us. I said as much to him.

'I might be a bit like my sister.'

I laughed for the first time all day. 'Which one?'

'India. There was a time when my career was everything to me – but unlike her I'd never have admitted it. Now I don't know. Sure I'd love to win, but there are things I want more than the Palme d'Or.'

We sipped our Sancerre and he looked into my

eyes. 'I need to say something to you. About last night. I should have come home to you.'

I didn't answer.

'It really was just work but, all things considered, it puts you in a difficult position. It has to be hard for you to trust me, Ruth – you mustn't think I don't appreciate that.'

'That's up to me.'

'No, it's up to me to reassure you and prove myself. I've already made enquiries about TV work.'

'Emerson, please! What's the point in you trying to be someone you're not just to make me happy? It won't work.'

'But I've told you, nothing means more to me than you and Paddy.'

'Either our relationship has what it takes to recover or it doesn't. Dramatic gestures won't fix anything if the fundamentals aren't there.'

'I love you, Ruth – that's as fundamental as you can get.'

I poured myself another glass of wine.

'Do you love me?' he said.

I took a deep breath. Did I love him? I used to. And I knew that in a way I always would – how do you evict people from your heart?

'Well?' He took my hand.

'I do love you,' I said. 'I'm just not sure if that's enough.'

'I don't expect guarantees. It's enough for me that you love me.'

I looked at his beautiful face, so like Paddy's.

'Come on, Em – it's time to go and get into our glad-rags. They're waiting down in the Palais d'Arts to give you that gong.'

By the time the limousine arrived to transport us to the Palme d'Or ceremony I was in the magnificent white silk sheath dress that Tracy had convinced me to buy before I left. It had cost a fortune but it was nothing compared to my shoes, whose price could have funded a medium-sized *coup d'état*. They were a triumph of art and engineering – six-inch steel spike of a heel, an arched instep lined with white leather and two barely there plaited gold straps across the front. I loved them, and had frequently taken them out of their box to admire them, so it cheered me up that their time had finally arrived. I didn't know then, of course, that it was also going to be their swan song.

61

I discovered a lot of things that night. For example, it's almost impossible to jump a wall in a full-length dress. John Malkovich in real life is no great shakes. And champagne and confusion are a lethal combination – but in the limo *en route* to the Palais d'Arts, the corporate-supplied champagne seemed just what the doctor ordered. Emerson barely wetted his lips while on the short journey I downed two full glasses and it didn't knock a stir out of me.

We pulled up in front of the Palais des Festivals et des Congrès and I heard Emerson's sharp intake of breath at the sight of the towering blue-carpeted steps leading to the auditorium. As soon as the driver opened the car door a sea of flashbulbs erupted. 'I never knew you were famous,' I said, as we reached the bottom of the steps and the throng of adoring fans screamed louder.

'Look behind you,' he said, with a grin, as he waved at the fans.

I turned round to see Tom Cruise in a knot of bodyguards. To his left a limo decanted Jude Law with a stunningly beautiful blonde woman. I remembered my recent erotic dream about him and blushed. We trotted up the steps and into the galleried foyer.

'Emerson!' a voice called, over the hum of the crowd. We turned as a burly, fiftyish man in a tuxedo made a beeline for us.

'Morty!' Emerson shouted, and stepped forward to hug him.

'We're gonna do it, son,' Morty said, mock-boxing him. I suppressed a laugh.

Emerson mock-boxed in return. 'Don't jinx it, Mort.'

Emerson and Morty were suddenly engulfed by a gaggle of glitzy people. I stepped aside and watched. Snatches of conversation about nominations and rivals floated by me. Emerson caught my eye and emerged from the throng. 'Come and meet everybody,' he said, and before I could answer he'd pulled me into his clique and was introducing me to one person after another.

I smiled and shook hands, then heard an unmistakable voice calling my husband's name.

'Emerson!'

The crowd parted like the Red Sea and Selma Rodriguez, resplendent in a scarlet dress cut to her navel, stood in front of me.

'Emerson! Darling! It is so very wonderful to see your face.' She glued herself to him and, standing on tiptoe, kissed him full on the mouth.

Emerson stepped back. 'Lovely to see you, Selma. Have you met my wife, Ruth?'

I knew from the silence that had suddenly

descended that everybody was aware of their affair and my stomach squeezed with humiliation. Emerson put his arm round me and struck up a conversation with Morty about distribution rights in America. A fat, middle-aged woman in a green sequined dress took Selma's arm and steered her into the crowd. I exhaled with relief. Fuck Selma – she was the past and I had to concentrate on the future.

We moved *en masse* into the Louis Lumière Auditorium. It was impressive: row after tiered row of red-velvet seats climbed from an enormous stage upwards into the high futuristic ceiling. The entire crew of Emerson's *Ferushi* was seated together in the same section. Selma, thank God, was as far away from me as she could have been.

As the awards ceremony got under way I tried to be interested in the proceedings but it was hard and I found myself dozing during the interminable speeches. Every now and again Emerson would squeeze my hand and I'd smile supportively. After an age I heard the familiar word *Ferushi* and sat up in my seat. I could feel the tension as the nominations were announced and clips were shown from each movie. Emerson stared straight ahead with a frightened smile. I clasped his hand as we watched.

'*Ferushi*'s the best,' I whispered, as a Tunisian nightclub scene faded.

He didn't answer. Slowly, Michael Moore opened the envelope and said something I didn't catch – but there was no mistaking the winner. Everybody in our two rows – except Emerson – leaped to their feet, screaming, hugging and kissing. He was still sitting in exactly the same position. 'You won, love,' I said, tugging at his arm.

He looked at me uncomprehendingly.

'*Ferushi* won,' I said.

A huge smile spread across his face and he stood up. 'I can't believe it.'

'Go up quick,' I said. Everybody around us applauded, and Michael Moore looked like a man about to lose patience as he waited for Emerson.

'You deserve it – you worked hard.'

'Thank you,' he said, as a lanky, blond man pulled him away from me towards the stage.

I realised I was crying then as I clapped with everybody else. Emerson looked so handsome as he thanked everyone and he was so at home on-stage.

The rest of the ceremony went by in a blur of speeches and obscure films. After the official awards were over we were whisked by Miramax to a huge celebration party, which, conveniently, was held in the Grand Salon of the Intercontinental Carlton.

As soon as we arrived into the party Emerson was surrounded three deep in congratulations and back-slapping. I grabbed a champagne flute from a passing waiter's tray, downed the contents in one and signalled to another waiter. He was distracted by a starlet, who batted her beautiful eyes and convinced him to take her coat to the cloakroom. He left his tray of drinks on a table beside me.

'That's convenient,' a woman with an Irish accent said. I turned towards the voice. A short, plump woman in a badly fitting black dress was standing beside me. 'Eleanor Fahy,' she continued, offering me her hand to shake. 'I was Best Boy on *Ferushi*.'

I shook her hand.

'Great that Emerson won, isn't it?' she said.

'Brilliant,' I said. 'He deserves it.'

She nodded. 'He's very talented.'

We were joined by Emerson and the rest of the *Ferushi* crowd, all talking and laughing and generally getting pissed. They were a friendly bunch, who did their best to include me, and I chatted away, but my heart wasn't in it. Luckily, however, the waiter appeared to have forgotten his tray of champagne so I helped myself. I knew I'd promised myself not to use alcohol as a crutch but at that point I needed a crutch or I was going to fall on my ass.

'Oh, my God, that's John Malkovich,' Morty said, in awestruck tones, as the tall, gaunt actor swung by, waving at us as if he knew us. Morty waved back. 'That man is a legend,' he said.

'The scrawniest-looking legend I ever saw – he could do with a feed of bacon and cabbage,' I heard myself say.

Everybody laughed. I perched on the small table beside the champagne tray and took another full glass. Selma walked by in a haze of cigarette smoke flanked by two doting young men in tuxedos. I drank another two glasses of champagne and burped, which made me laugh.

All of a sudden a pint of Guinness appeared in front of me.

'Don't mind that old sissy drink. Here, have one of these,' a familiar voice said.

I almost fell off my perch. Kevin was in a tuxedo and frilly shirt with his bow-tie half undone and pulled to the side. Right behind him stood Emerson and Morty.

'Jeez Louise! You'll never believe who I just met,' Morty said, his face as bright as a Las Vegas neon sign. 'Quentin Tarentino! Fucking Quentin Tarentino! This is the hand that shook the great man's hand. Tell 'em what happened, Emerson.'

'Morty met Quentin Tarentino,' Emerson said, with a grin.

'No, man – tell them the real news.'

'Ah, it's just talk at the moment,' Emerson said.

'No way! He wasn't bullshitting. He really wants you to make that movie. You lucky fucker! Six months in the Serengeti! No one in his right mind would turn that down.'

'Everything's up in the air at the minute – I'm not sure which direction I'm going,' Emerson said.

'You have to stick with making movies. You're gifted, man,' Morty said. 'I'd love to be a fly on the wall at that lunch tomorrow with you and Quentin.'

The word 'Serengeti' rattled around in my head. Where the hell was it, anyway? Wasn't it a desert or a plain or something in Africa? I took yet another flute of champagne from the tray. Kevin plonked his empty Guinness glass beside me on the table and helped himself to champagne.

'Six months is a long time to be away from home,'

Kevin said, swaying as he downed the champagne and took another.

Emerson smiled and sipped his pint.

'How do you feel about it, Ruth? Do you think Paddy'll like the playschools in the Serengeti?' Kevin said, looking directly at me.

I remembered that that morning he'd said he loved me. And now my husband was going to Africa. And I was sitting on a table pissed out of my head. It was all like a soap opera. I laughed.

Kevin looked angry. 'I'm amazed you find it funny, Ruth. Six months in Africa? With his track record?' he said.

'That's way out of order,' Emerson said, moving closer to him.

Kevin put down his glass and swivelled to face him. 'Some people never seem to learn their lesson,' he said.

Emerson put his pint on the table. 'You've had too much to drink, Kevin.'

'Fuck you. *In vino veritas.* You had your chance with her.'

'What's that supposed to mean?' Emerson said. He was losing his temper too.

'You know what it means.'

'Whatever happens between my wife and myself is our own affair.'

'Your affair? I'm glad you brought that up.'

'Kevin,' I said.

He turned to me, and I saw hurt in his eyes.

'Don't worry, Ruth – I'll deal with him,' Emerson

said. 'Now, come on, Kevin – don't say anything you'll regret in the morning.'

'Fuck off,' Kevin said.

'Go home and get some sleep.'

'You don't deserve her.'

Emerson bent down until their faces were only inches apart. 'And yet I have her. Now, go home to bed,' he said.

'You patronising wanker,' Kevin said, and punched Emerson square in the mouth.

Emerson staggered, wiped blood from his lip, and lunged at Kevin. They fell to the floor in a tangle of tuxedos and fists. Somebody screamed and Morty moved towards the mêlée, but before he could break it up I'd already reached the brawling cavemen.

'Fuck you,' I said, standing over them. They looked up at me. 'Fuck you both – rolling around on the floor like two kids fighting over marbles.' Kevin's nose was bleeding into his mouth and Emerson's top lip was split. I'd had enough.

I turned on my expensive heels and legged it through the over-dressed crowd into the colonnaded foyer and down the front steps of the hotel. Then I ran on to the road. A taxi blew its horn at me and the driver shouted abuse as I staggered on to the traffic island. Across from me was the sea and the long, lit-up promenade. I knew that if I could just think on the beach for a little while everything would calm down inside me.

'Ruth!'

I turned. Kevin was on the hotel steps.

'Ruth!'

Emerson was behind him.

Shit. I stepped out of my stilettos and picked them up, then crossed the road. When I looked back they were running down the steps. For a second I was frozen to the spot. Then I turned and ran like Flo Jo down the promenade – weaving between movie-sated revellers.

After a few minutes my lungs felt as though they might burst. I hiked up my skirt and I tried to climb on to the sea wall but the dress was too narrow. I took the hem in both hands and pulled until I heard a satisfying rip, then climbed up and jumped.

62

I landed on a shelf of rock, twisting my left ankle as I hit the ground. 'Ouch!' I roared, as I tried to stand up.

'You OK, man?' a voice said, from out of the darkness.

I whipped round, a stiletto in each hand to defend myself.

I heard a quiet laugh. 'You're lucky you didn't break your neck – that's at least a six-foot drop,' a deep American baritone said.

My eyes adjusted to the darkness and I saw an unkempt youngish man in jeans and a dark sweatshirt. He wore the hood up, his feet were bare and he had a beard. He was drinking something from a cup.

'Coffee?' he asked.

I considered my options. Coffee in the shelter of the sea wall with a total stranger who might be Son of Sam? Or I could go back up and face the chaos? Son of Sam won.

'Thanks,' I said, limping across to sit beside him. He picked up a stainless-steel flask, poured some coffee into a small matching cup and handed it to me. 'I'm a bit pissed so coffee's no harm at the moment.'

'You're Irish?'

'I am. You're American?'

He laughed. 'I am. You're hiding?'

'I am. Are you?'

'Sort of.'

We sipped our coffee in silence as we gazed at the sea.

'This is very good coffee,' I said. 'Java?'

'Right on.'

'Do you come here often?'

'Only when I get overwhelmed,' he said.

'Overwhelmed,' I echoed.

He refilled my cup. As he poured I caught a glimpse of something that looked suspiciously like a Rolex strapped to his wrist. I hoped he hadn't stolen it from his last victim, but I was past caring.

'John,' he said, holding out his hand.

'Ruth,' I answered, as we shook.

'How are you feeling now? How's the ankle?'

I wiggled my foot. 'Sore, but I don't care. A sprained ankle is the least of my worries.'

'I guessed that.'

I put my head into my hands. 'I can't believe what just happened. First Kevin punched Emerson's face in front of everyone.'

'Oops.'

'And then they rolled around the floor of the Grand Salon like two yobbos.'

'That sounds entertaining.'

'Not if they're fighting about you like you're some sort of a prize at a carnival.'

'Hence the escape?'

I nodded. 'They followed me.'

'Kevin and Emerson?'

'Who else? I mean Kevin told me this morning that he loved me – completely out of the blue. How am I supposed to feel about that?'

'I don't know. How do you feel about it?'

I saw that he had kind brown eyes and the most exquisitely defined cheekbones. At least if he was a psycho he was a nice-looking one. I didn't answer his question. 'Emerson is my husband and we have a baby – Paddy. Emerson had an affair last year.'

John didn't answer.

I took a breath and continued: 'He says he's sorry.'

'And is he?'

I thought for a moment. 'Yeah, he is.'

'But you can't forgive him?'

'No, it's not that. I can forgive but I don't know if I can trust him.'

'Do you think he'll be unfaithful again?'

That was a good question. Did I? The sea lapped the shore with a soft slapping noise. 'What I want is for none of it ever to have happened. We had a good marriage and he took a hammer to it. Maybe Kevin's right. Maybe the damage is irreparable.'

I began to cry and John put his arm round my shoulders. A huge full moon hung over the Bay of Cannes, reflected in the still water. When I had finished crying, I fished a tissue out of my bag and

blew my nose. My telephone rang. Without looking
at the screen I hit the power button and switched
it off.

'So how does the other guy fit in?' he asked.

'Kevin? He's lost the plot, going around declaring
love at eight o'clock in the morning – he's supposed
to be my friend, not another complication.'

'Mmm,' John said, lighting a cigarette. He held
the pack towards me and I accepted gratefully.

I inhaled deeply. 'What does "mmm" mean?'

'May I say something?'

'Go right ahead.'

'Well, Ruth, it strikes me that this Kevin guy
wouldn't be a complication unless he meant something to you. Love is a bitch for complicating stuff.'

'Love? Love my arse! Emerson loved me and he
ran off with Selma. My mother loved me and she
gave me away when I was five days old. My father
said he loved me when all he really wanted was a
photo opportunity to further his political career.
Now Kevin says he loves me. How long do you think
that'll last?'

John smiled. 'Can't say – and not just because I
don't know him. There are no guarantees where love
is concerned.'

'I don't believe in love.' I flicked my cigarette butt
on to the sand.

'And what about your baby? Don't you love him?'

'Kevin asked me that once.'

'And your answer?'

'Of course I love my baby.'

'Then you believe. What you need to do is learn to live without the happy-ever-after guarantee.'

'So, you're saying that no matter what I do there's no guarantee I'll be happy?'

John offered me another cigarette and we lit up. 'No. I think you can be happy and have lots of love but just don't put all your eggs in the man-basket.'

I laughed. 'That's a great phrase.'

'Glad you like it.'

'I don't know if I'd be any better with women, though.'

'My philosophy is that you can't rely on other people to make you happy.'

'Or rely on other people at all.'

'You don't mean that.'

'Yes, I do. Life is a lot harder than I ever thought – just when you think everything is going along fine, wham, shit happens.'

'Mmm,' John said. 'I can't deny that's true. But love happens too.' I looked at him. 'I figure it's probably the pay-off for the shit,' he said.

'There'd need to be some sort of a pay-off, considering all the pain and suffering when the shit happens.'

He nodded. 'Lucky it's there.'

I sighed. 'It's so complicated but you might be right. I do have loads of people in my life who I love and who love me.'

'Attagirl,' John said, fumbling in his pocket to find his ringing phone. 'Hey, V. No, I'm fine. I'll see you in a few minutes.'

He gave me a quick hug before he stood up. 'I gotta go,' he said.

'Thanks for the coffee.'

'Any time.'

I stood up as well. My ankle ached. John was picking his way across the rocks towards the steps that led up to the promenade. I called his name and he turned. 'Thanks,' I shouted.

He raised a hand and was gone.

I hobbled in the opposite direction, swinging my shoes as I made my way towards a long stone pier that projected into the sea. It took me ages to walk its full length but it was worth it. I was so far out that I felt as if I was standing in the middle of the water. Like an island. Like Venus in the painting.

It was only a little over a year since Gibraltar, yet my life had changed out of all recognition. I'd moved from a trusting innocent to being logic-driven and armour-clad. I couldn't control what life was going to throw at me – good or bad. John had been right: shit happens and so does love. If that was true I'd just have to learn how to roll with the punches. Tracy had been right too.

'Ruth?'

I turned. Kevin was standing behind me. Even in the dark I could see that his lip was swollen and that there was a huge bloodstain on the front of his white shirt.

'Jesus, Kevin, in less than a year you've slammed your head on a steering-wheel, had the shit kicked out of you and your ribs cracked, and now your nose looks suspiciously like it might be broken.'

He touched it gingerly. 'Nothing like this ever happened to me before I met you.'

'I keep telling you I'm bad for you.'

He took a step towards me and stopped. When I didn't move he took a step closer. Our faces were almost touching. Gently I stroked his cheek, then kissed his lips. He stood perfectly still.

'I'm afraid if I move you'll fly away,' he said.

He kissed me then and I heard the surf breaking all around us and the faraway sound of music. We wound our arms round each other and stood in silence for a few seconds.

'Guess what?' Kevin said, into my hair.

'What?'

'When I was coming down here to look for you I met this guy and I'd swear he was Johnny Depp.'

I pulled back and had a look into his face. 'No way! I got to see John Malkovich and you saw Johnny Depp – I knew there wasn't any justice.'

'It gets weirder,' he said. 'I stopped him and asked if he'd seen a woman in a white dress and he didn't answer me at first so I was going to walk away and then he said, "Are you Kevin?"'

'No way!'

'I swear.'

'And?'

'And I said, "Yeah, I'm Kevin," and he said, "She went thataway," and then he walked off.'

'So that's how you found me?'

Kevin nodded. 'Pretty much – but now I come to think of it, it was hardly Johnny Depp, was it? I mean, I saw him earlier at the Palais.'

'Hardly,' I said, with a grin. 'Excuse me one minute.'

I pulled away from Kevin and walked out to the edge of the pier. I lifted my shoes, kissed each in turn, then flung them into the sea with all my strength, laughing as I heard the faraway plop.